ONCE A PRINCESS

Veronica Sattler

ZEBRA BOOKS
Kensington Publishing Corp.
http://www.zebrabooks.com

To Gail Shaffer, with love

ZEBRA BOOKS are published by

Kensington Publishing Corp.
850 Third Avenue
New York, NY 10022

All Kensington titles, imprints, and distributed lines are available at special quantity discounts for bulk purchases for sales promotion, premiums, fund-raising, educational or institutional use.

Special book excerpts or customized printings can also be created to fit specific needs. For details, write or phone the office of the Kensington Special Sales Manager: Kensington Publishing Corp., 850 Third Avenue, New York, NY 10022, Attn. Special Sales Department. Phone: 1-800-221-2647.

First Printing: September 2001
10 9 8 7 6 5 4 3 2 1

Printed in the United States of America

Prologue

Kent, England
1792

"Inform the child I wish to see him."

The man receiving the curt instruction scanned the face of the woman behind the desk. He wondered what she'd look like if she smiled. He'd never once seen her smile. At present, the perfect features were tight and closed. She perused the sheet of foolscap he'd just handed her, much as if he no longer existed. Suppressing a sigh, he bowed and turned to go, but at the door he hesitated, and swung back to face her. "Ah, if I may make a suggestion, Your Grace?"

Regina, duchess of Hartswood, looked up from the paper and frowned at her son's tutor. "Well?" she asked irritably.

He tried not to squirm under the supercilious gaze. "Ah, as Your Grace knows, the current—and, indeed, *minor*—shortcoming aside, his lordship's performance has always been exemplary. And, ah, as you are about to meet with him, I was wondering . . ."

A perfectly plucked eyebrow rose in annoyance as the tutor's courage failed him. "I haven't all day, Mr. Snopes."

Snopes again resisted the urge to squirm. The blue eyes that pinned him to the carpet were stunning, but they were also the coldest he'd ever seen. "Your Grace, if I may be permitted to attend the interview—"

"You may not. Good day, sir."

As he left, the duchess's eyes narrowed on the tutor's retreating back. The man's credentials were excellent, yet Snopes might well have to be dismissed. His references not withstanding, Snopes, she suspected, was not up to her standards. He was too soft on the boy; and that would never do. Her son was heir to one of the foremost dukedoms in Britain. He must be prepared to wear the ducal coronet and perform its duties to perfection. Mollycoddling him now would only succeed in marring that perfection. "Yes, Barrows?"

"His lordship awaits without, Your Grace," her butler announced from the doorway.

"Send him in, and see that we're not disturbed."

The servant withdrew. Seconds later, a raven-haired boy entered the library. Though just turned ten, he was tall for his age, and astonishingly beautiful. His eyes, identical to those of the duchess, were an unusual blue, indigo tinged with violet, and fringed with thick, black lashes—lashes many women would kill for, his mother thought with smug satisfaction.

Her eyes traveled coolly over the child's face, noting his perfectly carved cheekbones, beneath which lurked her dimples—dimples that could charm any male between the ages of twelve and eighty, and had, when she chose to grace them with her perfect white smile. In fact, all of her son's perfectly chiseled features were a boyish version of her own. This, too, she noted with a satisfaction that never diminished, no matter how often she observed their likeness.

"Good afternoon, Your Grace," the child murmured. He'd been instructed, long ago, never to address her as *Mother,* much less *Mama,* as some lads called their mothers. Not that it mattered. He'd no wish to call her those words.

The dimples Her Grace was so proud of were not in evidence. She wasn't smiling, and neither was her son. She greeted the child with a curt nod, then gestured with the tutor's report she held aloft. "Do you know what this is, m'lord?"

The deep violet eyes stood out starkly in the sudden paleness of the boy's face. "I—I believe it is the latest report from Mr. Snopes, Your Grace."

"Indeed," said Her Grace, still unsmiling. "And do you know what his report contains?"

"N-no, Your Grace."

"No?" She smiled then, but the boy knew it wasn't a real smile. It was cold, and didn't reach her eyes. "Then I shall tell you," she added in a lilting voice he'd learned was deceptive in its mildness.

She left the heavily carved, ornate desk behind which she'd been standing and came toward him. "Mr. Snopes is aggrieved to report your recent performance in geography has been found *wanting.*" She was a tall woman, and used her height to her advantage, bending over the child with a look of supreme displeasure on her face. "What have you to say for yourself, m'lord?"

"I—I am sorry for it, Your Grace," the child stammered.

"Sorry? Sorry! What sort of reply is that?" She gestured toward the double windows, where an army of gardeners could be seen working on the grounds of the ducal estate. "Servants such as those may be sorry for a shrub untidily clipped or a bed unsatisfactorily prepared, and that is bad enough. But you—you, the heir to a dukedom, may *not* use it as an excuse for failure! For you, failure itself is unacceptable. And sorry is for the lesser creatures of this world, do you understand? It is not for their betters!"

"Y-yes, Your Grace."

"Then you will explain, m'lord—*without excuses*—how it happened that you were unable to identify all of the thirteen colonies of His Majesty's former government in America!"

The boy's gaze dropped, and he murmured, looking intently at his toes, "I missed only a part of one name, Your Grace."

"What was that? Speak up—and demonstrate the courtesy of looking at me when you do so!"

The boy swallowed around a lump that had lodged in his throat and dragged his gaze upward. "I m-missed but part of the n-name of one colony, Y-Your Grace. B-but I identified all thirteen successfully o-on the map."

"*Did* you?" she queried with a sharpness she wielded like a weapon. A sharpness honed to a razor's edge on the sarcastic whetstone anyone who'd displeased her would have instantly recognized. "And you missed a mere part of one little name?"

Again, the child swallowed. "I-I left out the *N-New* . . . in *New Jersey,* Your Grace . . . and n-named it merely *Jersey,"* he mumbled shamefacedly.

"*Mis*named it, you mean!"

"Y-yes."

"Yes—*what?"*

"Y-yes, Your G-Grace," the boy stammered, fighting tears under the relentless tongue-lashing.

"And to what do you attribute your error?"

"I . . ." The child's gaze dropped to the carpet in misery, but only for an instant. Recalling her prior admonishment, he hastily raised it, hoping she wouldn't notice he fastened it on a point just above her perfectly groomed head, and not on her face. "I . . . must have f-forgotten, Your Grace," he finally managed, blinking back tears.

"Forgotten! Is that all you can supply for a failure that resulted in confusing two significant geographical entities? *Jersey* is one of His Majesty's islands off the coast of England. It is *not* one of those former rebellious colonies you were required to identify!

"Now," she went on, in a singsong taunt that dripped with sarcasm, "can you imagine, *M'lord Brilliant,* what would happen if you were one day so to confuse the two—perhaps as you sat in the Lords and invoked one in a speech?"

The child didn't reply. He'd long ago learned when to hold his tongue during one of these diatribes. She'd supply her own response soon enough. He was not to be disappointed.

"You would become a laughingstock!" she snapped, her eyes narrowed with intimidating scorn. "A *laughingstock,* do you hear?"

His tears were running freely now. There was a childish attempt to dash them away with the heel of his hand before the boy choked out a reply. "Y-yes, Your—"

"What's this? *Tears?* I won't have it! You are a future duke, not some sniveling crofter's son! You will cease this mewling demonstration at once, or I shall have you *whipped,* is that clear? At once!"

While the boy made a manful effort at complying, the duchess gazed at him with cold displeasure for several agonizing seconds. "Very well," she said at last. "I shall be sending your tutor instructions on how you are to be disciplined for your failure. In the meantime, you are to see that it was your last, do you hear? I'll have your promise on it."

"I p-promise, Your Grace."

"Promise *what?*"

"Th-that I shall endeavor to d-do better, Your Grace." The child was shaking with his effort to will back the tears, but he staunchly kept his gaze riveted to that point above her head.

"Indeed, you *will* do better—or suffer the consequences!" His mother eyed him carefully for a long moment, as if to assess the impression she'd made on him. At last she gave a curt nod of dismissal. "You may go."

As the door closed behind him, the duchess crumpled the tutor's report in her fist, squeezing the sheet of foolscap until her knuckles went white. It was as if, in so doing, she could squeeze every drop of imperfection out of the boy himself, and remove from him all the imperfections he'd inherited from his sire.

His very *absent* sire, she thought bitterly, pitching the wad of foolscap to the floor with a vengeance. She'd no doubt the duke, her husband, was the source of anything found wanting in their son. Just as His Grace was the source of all she found wanting in their marriage—damn him!

It was an old grievance, but one the years had failed to assuage. As she brooded on it yet again, she crossed to a Chippendale wall mirror near the door, pausing to scrutinize her reflection for a length of time. Finally, with a grim smile, she turned and began to pace the rich Aubusson carpet underfoot.

She knew she was beautiful. She'd been the reigning beauty of her day. The dozen years that had transpired since hadn't whittled an iota of perfection from her exquisite face and form. Long-limbed and graceful, with the exact combination of wit and pleasing conversation a man would find irresistible—not so clever as to appear superior and not so dull as to bore—she'd charmed and dazzled the *ton* that Season as no one else in recent memory had.

She'd been the darling of Almack's. She'd received invitations to every fete and cotillion on the social calendar, more than she could possibly accept, and she'd had offers in the dozens from a host of eligible men, most of them titled, all nicely plump in the pocket—and eager! Yes, they'd all been eager to have her. Except one.

Was that why she'd accepted him? Was it some perverse element in her makeup that had made her accept the proposal of the least enthusiastic of her suitors? No, of course not! That would be tantamount to a flaw, and she had none—none! She was nothing if not a perfectionist by nature, and everything she'd done that Season had been *flawless.*

She might perhaps admit to being just a tad intrigued by William's slowness in coming up to scratch. Even so, there were still the overwhelming facts of his desirability. He was a duke! And not just any duke, but one well favored by the Crown. He was also rich as Croesus—and young and handsome in the bargain. In fact, the duke of Hartswood was universally acknowledged as the foremost catch of the marriage mart that Season.

Why shouldn't she, the belle of London's *haut ton,* have selected him as her rightful, perfect mate? It was only her due: the perfect mate for the perfect marriage.

And afterward, when the announcement appeared in the *Morning Post,* hadn't everyone hailed them as the perfect match? A love match, they'd called it.

The ignorant fools!

Regina's lips twisted bitterly, and she ceased her pacing

to stare up at a large double portrait over the mantel: The duke and duchess of Hartswood on the occasion of their wedding. The wedding of the decade, according to the papers, a perfect denouement to that celebrated love match.

The love match that wasn't.

William, duke of Hartswood, had never loved her, and never would. Because dear William, her so-called perfect husband, loved another, and always would.

She remembered every detail of the day she'd learned the truth. The day he finally confessed, but only after she'd badgered him about it. Badgered him, yes, when it became impossible to deny that he longed to be away from her. Her loving bridegroom, throwing himself into a military career that took him away from home—from *her*—as often as he could manage it. Damn his ungrateful hide!

Yes, ungrateful and unappreciative. How *dare* he avoid her? How dare he love another when he was married to the most desirable belle of that or any other Season? The most beautiful woman in all England, some said. She deserved *better.*

Turning from the portrait, Regina began to resume her pacing, then halted. Her gaze fell on the crumpled foolscap lying on the carpet, and her eyes narrowed. The heir was another matter. The duke might not love her, but he did profess to love their son—the son he was never home long enough to know, much less take a hand in shaping.

Well, she would have the last laugh. Let William love his son. The child was hers. Hers not only in his beauty, a mirror of her own perfection, but hers to shape as she wished. And shape him she would. He would be perfect. He would learn to love and appreciate only things that were absolutely perfect. He would be like *her.*

PART I

One

The Principality of Mirandeau
May, 1814

Prior to her nineteenth birthday, Princess Leonie of Mirandeau had never attended a funeral. Yet this was her second, she thought numbly, only half listening to the bishop intone the mass for the dead in the capital's ancient cathedral. Her second, and she'd yet to turn twenty.

Her mother's funeral. Her poor brain still hadn't taken in the enormity of it. Her father's—dear God, was it only a few short months ago?—had been her first. In the space of less than a year, she'd become an orphan.

She and Jamie both, she corrected, her gaze moving to the small, somber figure of her brother, Prince Jameson, in the pew beside her. Soon the requiem mass would be over, and they would proceed outside into the mocking sunshine of a perfect spring day. There, Jamie would follow immediately behind the open carriage bearing Leona of Mirandeau's flower-bedecked coffin. Leonie would ride sedately behind her brother in a closed carriage. Jamie was the heir, the new ruling prince . . . or would be after his coronation, so he took precedence in the cortege.

Odd . . . only the second funeral of your life, yet see how familiar you've become with the protocol. Oh, Mama, how shall I bear it? How shall I go on without you, Mama? How?

As if his thoughts were aligned with hers, she felt Jamie

tremble and stifle a sob. She reached out to squeeze his hand. Blinking away tears, he squeezed back, gave her a wan smile. Poor Jamie, she thought, both orphan and ruling prince within a few scant months.

Of course, Jamie wouldn't actually *rule* their tiny principality. Not even after the coronation, which had been postponed, time and again, over the course of their mother's lingering illness. Jamie was only nine years old, so Mirandeau would be in the hands of a regent.

Would be? It is already in those hands . . . God help us. Her eyes slid involuntarily to the end of the family pew, where her father's brother sat, flanked by his wife and their small son. Leonie's gaze no sooner touched on her uncle's saturnine face before it skittered away. The regent looked nothing like her father. Though younger than Prince Frederik by a few years, Archduke Roderik actually looked a deal older. Her father's face had been open, with clear gray eyes that always held a hint of laughter, even when he wasn't smiling. But he'd smiled often, and laughed, especially with her and Jamie.

Not so Roderik. The regent's face was harsh and uncompromising, with a disturbing slash of mouth, and dark, hooded eyes. The only animation Leonie could recall seeing in them came when the archduke had one of his famous tempers. *Infamous tempers,* she corrected with a shudder.

The unwilling recollection of her uncle's fits of rage had her eyes darting again to the end of the pew. Not to Roderik this time, but to Lady Emilie . . . and Sam. Both were frequent victims of those rages, according to Jamie. Not because they deserved them, she knew, but simply because they were nearest to hand.

Her uncle's wife was properly Lady Aulaire, but no one called her that. For reasons never made clear, she'd retained the missish Lady Emilie, except on official documents. Lady Emilie rarely appeared in public, poor thing, and Leonie barely knew her aunt. A pale, timid soul, rumored to be a scholar. "Quite the bluestocking," Mama had once remarked, though not in a cruel way. Mama was never cruel or hurtful. But as her daughter didn't attend social functions where the peerage gathered, Leona had sometimes filled Leonie in on the personalities and quirks of those who comprised Mirandeau's upper crust.

Not that Lady Emilie was given to attending the *ton's* gatherings. From what Leonie had been able to surmise, Roderik's wife was a nonentity in court circles. All Leonie herself had observed was a quiet, bespectacled creature who cringed in the shadow of her husband—no mystery there—but was devoted to her young son, *Sam.*

With an inner sigh, Leonie glanced at her cousin, then back at her brother. Lord Samuel, the regent's heir, was but a few months younger than Jamie, and could have been his twin. Dark-haired and gray-eyed, they favored their fathers' family, whereas Leonie resembled her English mother. But while Sam looked like the prince, he was otherwise nothing like him.

Sam was a shy and sensitive child with a poetic soul. Or so Leonie had once described him to her mother, and Leona had agreed. Yet Sam's very nature seemed, in the end, a curse. Roderik hated that softness in Sam, Jamie said. Fortunately, Jamie was fond of his gentle cousin and they were great friends, which seemed to appease Roderik. Leonie worried about Sam, and thanked heaven Jamie had befriended him. Without that, and perhaps Lady Emilie's love and devotion to temper Roderik's dislike, Leonie made no doubt Sam's sensitivity would long ago have been ground to dust under her uncle's powerful heel.

And what of you, my girl? How long will your fragile self survive, now there's no loving parent to protect you? Now you have only Jamie, and, despite his strengths, your brother's but a child. He can't be expected to stand between you and . . . the world.

Leonie and her brother were very close, despite the gap in their ages. But, much like Jamie and Sam, they were radically different in temperament. Mama even used to joke about it, saying if she didn't know better, she'd swear Leonie was Sam's sister, not Jamie's. "Sam's the perfect cousin for my children," she'd once remarked with a laugh. "He looks just like the one and behaves quite like the other."

Perhaps that was because no one behaved quite like Jamie. Or *was* quite like Jamie, Leonie thought with a fond glance at her brother. Jamie was every inch a prince—a born leader. He was clever and quick, with an abundance of self-confidence she'd give anything to possess, even in some small measure. A natural athlete, the prince was as daring and brave as he was handsome. Everyone said so. His outgoing personality had them all, from the lowliest stable hands to the highest lords and ladies, eating out of his hand.

Leonie knew she was none of those things. Well, perhaps, as her parents had insisted, she was every bit as bright as her brother, but there the resemblance ended. She knew she was awkward, withdrawn, and given to solitude, with no skills at getting on and about in Society. And that was because she did not *go* on and about. The world of the *ton* was alien to her. She did everything she could to avoid it. How could she not, when she found it so painful?

Unlike those things she did so enjoy: reading for hours, immersed in that wonderful world of books in the library, riding Raven over Mirandeau's green hills. Ah, her beloved Raven, so gentle it was hard to credit he was a stallion. But Mama had taken great pains to find one with a biddable nature, for she'd known her daughter had her heart set on a stallion. How surprised she'd been when Mama had given her Raven.

A sharp stab of grief nearly brought Leonie to her knees, for they were standing now, while the bishop pronounced a blessing. *Dear God, please . . . not* here. *Not where all can see me baring my—quick, think of something else! Something warm, and positive.*

Her eyes went at once to her brother. As if he understood her need, Jamie touched her hand and smiled at her before both dutifully dropped to their knees in prayer. Jamie's beautiful smile . . . so sweet, it could charm the proverbial birds out of the trees, as Father had often remarked.

Leonie knew she had none of Jamie's charm and none of his physical beauty. She was plain—worse than plain, she suspected. Which was why she hadn't looked into a mirror in . . . well, more years than she could recall. After all, what was the point? She rarely appeared in public. In court circles, she was regarded as unimportant—when she was even regarded at all.

In Mirandeau, only males could inherit the crown. Without that option, the only value a princess of the blood could claim was that of a marketable bride—Roderik's phrase, not hers, and she hated it. Hated the thought that her only currency of exchange, her only potential value even if she were perfect, was as a commodity. Not a person, but a *thing,* used to secure an advantageous political alliance.

Yet even that was beyond her. She'd never had a single suitor, royal or otherwise. Not one, though she was nineteen, in a Europe where royal houses arranged marriages for their offspring years in advance of the dates when the weddings would actually take place. No, not a single offer for her hand, not even a flicker of interest, for one overriding reason: No royal family of Europe, or elsewhere, wanted to wed its precious offspring to a princess who'd been born a cripple.

Kent, England
The same day

William, duke of Hartswood, thanked the footman who'd delivered the package. He made himself wait for the servant to leave, all the while staring at the small parcel, his heart hammering in his chest. The inscription indicating its place of origin was barely legible, yet he had no trouble recognizing a place that was never far from his thoughts: *Mirandeau. Dear God, after all this time . . .*

His hands trembled as he placed the parcel in his lap and began to unwrap it. The trembling made him clumsy, and he swore softly before a third attempt succeeded. A small jeweler's box tumbled into his hand. Achingly certain of its contents, he set it aside, his unsteady fingers reaching for a creased sheet of vellum lying amid the wrappings.

Smoothing the vellum over the knee of his good leg, he was taken aback by the spidery script scrawled across the sheet. But a glance at the signature confirmed the sender. His pulse racing, he began to read: *Dearest William . . .*

The duke's knuckles were white as he gripped the paper, his mind full of dread as it tried to absorb the words. He didn't hear the door open, didn't hear booted feet crossing the thick carpet toward the chair where he sat.

"Forgive me for barging in on you, Your Grace, but this won't wait. Barrows informs me there's a problem with the . . . Father? Father!"

Failing to get a response, Randall Darnley, marquis of Hawksrest, placed his hand on the duke's shoulder and peered at his face. "Good God, you're white as a ghost! What's wrong?"

It was as if William hadn't heard. "But this was written weeks ago," he murmured, staring numbly at a date scrawled at the bottom of the sheet.

"Father, look at me," Darnley insisted, using a quiet voice that nonetheless held command.

"My God, she could already be . . ." William's voice faltered. He raised his eyes and stared vacantly at the tall figure of his son.

"Father—damn it, talk to me!"

Blinking twice, the duke shook his head. "Rand . . . thank God you're here."

"What the devil's hap—you're shaking!" Darnley crossed to a small sideboard, grabbed a crystal decanter, and quickly poured out a measure of brandy. "Drink," he ordered, handing it to William.

The duke took a careful swallow, started to lower the glass. His glance took in the younger man, who scowled at him. Without a word, William downed the rest.

"Another?" Rand asked, taking the empty glass.

"Thanks, but no . . . I'm all right." William gestured for his son to take the chair opposite his.

Rand ran his gaze over his father, zeroing in on the rigid contours of William's right leg, which was thrust stiffly forward. He rarely thought of the wooden leg that had replaced the limb the duke lost on campaign; but there was so much pain on his father's face right now . . .

"The leg's fine, too," the duke assured him. "Now, do sit, and I'll explain about"—his eyes went to the things in his lap—"what isn't. That is, if you don't mind listening."

Smothering an oath, Rand asked, with a growl, when William had ever known him to mind listening—and sat. "The source of your . . . concern, I collect?" He indicated the items in William's lap.

With a sigh, the duke nodded and handed over the jeweler's box. "This just arrived from abroad. Have a look, and I'll explain."

Rand opened the small box, then gave a long, low whistle. Inside was a magnificent emerald ring—very old, judging by the setting, which was exquisitely worked gold filigree. The handsome gem at its center was large without being vulgar, and mounted to show off its gleaming facets to perfection.

"A gift?" he asked, glancing at the wrappings.

William sighed. "It was, yes, long ago. Given by me to the woman I . . . would have married. It was in this family for generations, and was to have sealed our betrothal. In the end, I gave it to her anyway . . . as a parting gift."

"You loved her." It wasn't hard for Rand to deduce. His father was a warm, caring man. Impossible not to picture him having loved a woman once—and deeply, he suspected. He also knew William had never loved his duchess, as he himself had not. His mother had not been a woman to inspire love.

"I loved her," the duke replied, "with all my soul. She's the only woman I have ever loved. I still do, with every fiber of my being, and it's been thirty-two years since I saw her last."

Rand felt no surprise, though he wondered why it had taken so many years for William to speak of it. After all, his wife had succumbed to the smallpox when Rand was eleven—or so the official version went. He knew the duke had wed out of duty, like so many of the nobility, strictly to get an heir, while his heart lay elsewhere. Yet unlike many of his peers, William had never taken a mistress. The surprise would lie in the identity of the woman who'd returned his father's gift, and her reasons for doing so.

"Leona and I were childhood sweethearts," William went on with a soft, reminiscent smile. "Innocent, yet certain in the love we declared long before the marriage we never once doubted would take place. She was an earl's daughter. I had my ducal patrimony to look forward to. Our families seemed agreeable. Her mother was delighted. Your grandfather approved, for Leona's dower lands marched with ours. Her ancient lineage was sufficient to satisfy even your grandmother—"

Rand rolled his eyes, producing a wry smile from William. Both knew the approval of William's mother constituted the ultimate test of suitability. Her Grace, the current dowager duchess of Hartswood, was a high stickler.

"In short," William summarized, "it appeared a certainty Lady Leona Fairchild would become my loved and cherished bride."

"What went wrong?" Rand asked carefully, aware of the deep regret in his father's voice.

"M'lord Fairchild had loftier ambitions for his daughter."

"Loftier than . . . that's absurd. She would have been a duchess."

William heaved a sigh. "The earl liked *princess* better."

"Princess!"

William nodded. "But not just any princess. He betrothed Leona to a prince who was a ruling head of state in his own right: Frederik of Mirandeau."

"Good God."

"My poor Leona was devastated . . . heartbroken . . . when her father gave her the news. We both were. Even his countess was taken aback, for the earl had conducted the negotiations without consulting anyone beyond his solicitors. Prince Frederik, it seemed, had seen Leona at the opera one night when he was a visitor, attending as King George's guest, and was instantly smitten. He begged an introduction, which His Majesty was happy to provide. Yet Leona could scarcely remember meeting him.

"Two months later," William continued with a deep sigh, "she learned she was betrothed to the man. She begged the earl not to force her into the marriage, but he was adamant. Neither Leona nor I, nor anyone in either family, could persuade him to change his mind. I have your grandmother to thank for the hour he grudgingly allowed Leona and me to say our final farewells."

"And that was when you gave her this?" Rand indicated the jeweler's box.

"I gave her the ring then, yes, and a solemn promise. I told her that if ever she had need of me, to send it . . . and I would come."

"I see," said Rand, glancing at the creamy vellum his father fingered absently while staring into space. Seeing in his mind's eye, Rand suspected, the face of a woman he hadn't laid eyes on in thirty-two years. Though Rand wondered what was in her message, he wouldn't ask. He respected William's privacy, just as he respected the man himself, the loving father he'd come to know only after his cold, unloving mother was dead. But Rand's reluctance to pry went deeper than that. Some things weren't meant to be shared.

Again, William surprised him. "She's dying, Rand," he said bleakly, his gaze on the spidery scrawl of Princess Leona's letter.

Rand felt a surge of compassion at the desolate look on his father's face. Wordlessly, he placed a hand on the older man's shoulder.

William looked at him then, and his lips tightened. "There's more—as if that weren't enough!" he said angrily, giving the letter a shake. "She says here . . . Rand, her words imply there's been foul play."

"Foul play? Are you certain?"

"Fairly. True, she was clearly ill when she wrote this. The barely legible hand . . . even her sentences aren't entirely coherent. Yet I believe she knew what she was—"

"Wait a moment," said Rand. "Her husband . . . didn't I see Frederik of Mirandeau's obituary in the paper a few months back? Is it *his* death she's referring to or—"

"Both. Her husband's *and* the end she sees coming for herself." William's lips twisted in anguish.

"Then, by sending you the ring . . ."

"She's asking for my help, yes," William said, "but not for herself. Leona has two children, a girl and a boy. Her fear for *their* safety drove her to send this."

"Christ!" Rand swept a hand through his hair. "But how can you be sure? I mean, given she lay ill when she penned that note . . . well, you yourself said it isn't entirely coher—"

"It's coherent enough for me," William cut in fiercely. "And even if there were a doubt, I'd no sooner hesitate on something like this than—"

"Agreed. Forgive me for bringing it up."

William nodded, but absently. He was eyeing his right leg. He got on quite well with the wooden replacement, and had for years, though a walking stick had become a necessary part of his ensemble. He'd even learned to ride with it, though not with the skill that had been second nature to him when he was a horse officer in a fighting regiment.

"God in heaven!" he cried suddenly, thumping the prosthesis with his fist. He met Rand's gaze with a look of helpless frustration. "I promised I'd come—swore it—but you know how this damned thing slows me down! I'm hardly up to traveling to Mirandeau with the sort of haste implicit in that message! She may not have much time, damn it, and here I sit—"

Rand was already on his feet. "I'll leave for Mirandeau at once," he said.

* * *

After his son left, William gazed for a long time at Leona's letter. Then he folded it neatly and tucked it inside the jeweler's box, empty now, for he'd insisted Rand take the ring. He'd need it if Leona was still alive. Dear God, the thought that she could already be gone—she'd been so vibrant, so full of life!

Blinking back tears he wasn't ready to shed, William forced his thoughts back to his son. If Rand found Leona alive, he'd need to show her the ring. If there was, indeed, skullduggery afoot, she'd need a reason to trust him, a complete stranger. The ring would confirm that Rand was his father's surrogate.

And even if Leona were gone by the time Rand reached Mirandeau, her children would need to trust him. Did they have any knowledge of the ring? They were quite young yet, especially the prince, for it had been years before the royal couple was blessed with a child, and then more years before there was an heir. William knew, for he'd quietly kept abreast of things in the tiny principality over the years. Even the young princess couldn't be more than . . . what? Nineteen, twenty?

Leona's children . . . children that should have been *his*. If they had been his, he'd never have left them and Leona alone for months on end as he so foolishly had Rand and *his* mother. But Regina had been . . . Regina. He'd simply been unable to live with all that cold arrogance, and, later, the bitterness. Yet why hadn't he seen what his absence did to Rand?

Rand. His son worried him greatly. He never came to know the lad until the loss of his leg forced him home from the wars. Only then did he realize how badly the boy needed him. Regina, who oddly enough died the day before he came home, had reared the child without love or affection. When William returned, it was nearly too late for him to make it up to the lad. In the end, however, he succeeded in winning the boy's love—and he thanked God for it.

Yet there were still times when it was hard to puzzle him out. When it was hard to know what moved Rand the man.

Ah, if only he'd been wiser and had taken a hand in shaping his son before Regina did her damage.

Take the matter of the fiancée's death. He knew Rand had suffered a heavy loss, but it was now two years since Lady Cynthia Shallcross perished in that sailing accident. True, the Shallcross heiress had been the sort men dream about . . . young and accomplished in all the womanly graces, exquisitely beautiful. And the accident's occurring only days before their wedding made the loss doubly shattering, to be sure. But . . . *two years!*

And Rand still refused to speak of it. Clearly, his grief ran deep. Not that anyone blamed him for grieving over a woman he'd loved and lost so suddenly. That only spoke well of his character. But Rand's grief didn't appear to be lessening with time. That was what was so disturbing.

Heaving a sigh, the duke stared at the jeweler's box that now contained Leona's letter. Time ran so quickly, he thought. Life was so damned short. Never had he had a greater sense of its brevity than when he'd seen that parcel and realized what it was. How the devil could thirty-two years have passed so—

"Ah, there you are, William!"

The leg didn't deter him from rising quickly as his mother entered the room. The dowager expected nothing less, and one didn't fall short of Her Grace's expectations if one could help it. "Good day, Mother," he said, planting a kiss on the papery cheek she offered.

"I hope it may be a good day," she said crossly, gesturing him to sit as she lowered herself into the chair Rand had vacated. "At the moment, I have my doubts."

William waited, knowing he'd learn why. He adored this diminutive woman who'd taken a firm hand in raising him, despite the habit of others of their class to leave the rearing of children to servants. She played the *grande dame* to the hilt, of course. Nonetheless, she had still managed to nurture her only son with an abundance of love and genuine affection. Emotions that, even as a small child, he'd had no

trouble detecting under the crusty e
robe of state.

Her Grace, Elizabeth Margaret
dowager duchess of Hartswood, may
stature, but few in her august presence e
her crown of snow white hair and a bac ramrod
straight, despite her advanced years she gave the impression of being far taller than she was. Yet this impression didn't come just from the physical. His mother was a formidable presence in any room she inhabited, and woe to those who failed to realize it. But William knew something else that made her a giant, though she'd never tolerate his saying so to her face: It was her large and generous heart.

"I shall begin," said Her Grace, "by asking why I found you so blue-deviled when I entered just now. Do not deny it. I know a case of the megrims when I see it!"

William sighed, hoping to satisfy her uncanny knack for unearthing information by giving her the most innocuous response he could think of. "It's about Rand, if you must know. He's still showing no signs of coming to terms with Cynthia Shallcross's death, and it worries me. She was an exquisite creature, I own. Still, I'd hopes he'd find someone else by now, and get on with his life."

The dowager had her own opinions of the late Lady Cynthia, but decided it was pointless to voice them now. "Speaking of my ever-vexing grandson," she said tartly, "I just observed from my window overlooking the drive our young Corinthian's departure in that wretched high-perch phaeton. Those high steppers were within an inch of taking to the treetops!

"I demand to know the reason," she continued in the irascible fashion that was as familiar to William as her snapping black eyes, "for such an indecent display of haste."

Seeing no help for it, the duke explained about the package from Mirandeau. His mother being his mother, she'd long ago ferreted out the reason the Hartswood betrothal ring had gone missing from the family vault, so this didn't take as long as it had with Rand. When he explained why her ed grandson had gone in his father's stead, William ught he saw a glint of approval in her eyes. Then again, with the dowager, one could never be certain.

"Hmph," she grumbled, "then let us hope this errand of mercy, concerned as it is with the needs of the living, will put the lad right. Overlong grieving is bad *ton,* William. Simply not the thing!"

Two

Rand watched the coast of England recede as he stood at the rail of a Royal Navy frigate bound for Calais. It felt odd to be sailing toward France so openly, after years of doing anything but. Just as it felt odd to be a civilian again when he'd spent years in the service, doing his part to bring Napoleon down. But Bonaparte was banished to Elba, and Major Randall Darnley was no more.

Now he was simply Hawksrest, not that it constituted much of a change. His fellow officers had called him that all along—those of sufficient rank, at any rate. But what also hadn't changed was that Hawksrest was still in service . . . after a fashion.

Rand heaved a sigh of resignation. Having sold out after the Corsican's defeat, he'd thought his clandestine work for the crown was behind him. The Foreign Office had other ideas.

"We understand your desire to return to private life now the war's over, Hawksrest," the Foreign Secretary told him the morning he'd been summoned to Whitehall. "Yet we're hoping you might be persuaded to remain in service for a while . . . in an unofficial capacity, that is."

As Castlereagh appreciated plain speaking, Rand's response had been blunt. "As a civilian spy, you mean."

"Precisely," his lordship had replied without batting an eyelash. "It's the fragile nature of the peace, do you see. While we've every intention of restoring order in Europe, and I'm attending the Congress of Vienna with that objective, some of us at Whitehall feel it's—shall we say *premature?*—to count Boney out."

Rand was aware of the rumors that Napoleon was far from finished—that he still commanded enormous loyalty and support, especially among those who'd fought under him, that it was only a matter of time until *l'emperor* was brought back to power to rule in triumph. Apparently these hadn't been mere rumors, not with Whitehall putting its stamp on them, unofficial or otherwise.

And because Rand agreed with Whitehall, he'd said yes to Castlereagh's proposal. By informal arrangement with the Foreign Office, he was now a secret observer for the crown while the Peace was being negotiated. Which was why he'd felt it necessary to stop briefly in London before traveling to Mirandeau. His connection with Whitehall not only made it possible to travel to the Continent more quickly, it demanded he inform his superiors where he was bound, even on personal business, in case they had need of him.

As it happened, they did. The supposedly friendly principality was suspected of having supplied arms to the French before Napoleon's defeat. Now, with fears Boney's supporters were secretly at work to undermine the Peace, Whitehall needed to know if someone in Mirandeau was involved in such designs—and, if so, what his game was.

So now he had a double mission. While he hadn't been asked the nature of his personal business, he'd told the secretary it might just as easily be accomplished while acting undercover. This was true: Leona needn't know Rand was William's son when he showed her the ring, merely that he'd been sent by the duke and entrusted to act on his behalf. Castlereagh had been gratified to learn he'd be going by only one name, and not his real one. Problems invariably arose when an agent's personal acquaintances—untrained civilians—were required to keep secrets.

Whitehall had supplied Rand with credentials which would enable him to pose as a palace guard. It was now less than twenty-four hours since he'd left Kent. With luck, he'd reach Rienna, Mirandeau's capital, in about a week. He only hoped Leona had that much time left.

Rand's hope was in vain. He reached Rienna a full week after Princess Leona's state funeral. Flags everywhere flew at half-staff. Swags of black crepe hung over the doorways of all public and most private buildings. And when Rand went to the palace to apply for the guard's post, which Whitehall's, spies had learned needed filling, every person he saw wore a black armband, if not an entire outfit of that color.

Going by the name of Hawk Randall, Rand entered the regent's service the day he arrived. Archduke Roderik had a prodigious fear of assassination, he'd overheard a veteran guardsman mutter to a pair of cohorts. The man beside him had grunted agreement. The other had added the regent was "right frantic" to see the palace guard brought back to its full complement of forty men. Rand barely had time to eat before he found himself in uniform.

"There ye be, Y'r Highness." The head groom, a man everyone called Oats, stepped away from Leonie's stirrup and gave Raven's withers a pat. "Davey 'n Jocko be y'r escorts, same as always." He canted his head toward a pair of mounted grooms waiting patiently across the stable yard. "Try not t' leave 'em too far behind, eh, lass?" he added with a wink. "Eatin' the black's dust makes 'em a mite dry in the gullet."

Leonie blushed, despite the familiarity of the old man's jest. Oats had been with the royal stables for ages, had even helped select her first pony, yet she still found herself warming under his gentle teasing. "I'll be careful, Oats," she promised. "But poor Raven's missed our rides"—she didn't add *since my mother died,* but knew they were both thinking it—"and he does so enjoy a good run, don't you, lad?"

The big horse appeared to agree, dipping his head and prancing restlessly, eager to be off. His mistress was just as eager. A slight pressure from her knee had the stallion moving across the yard at a brisk trot.

The trot became a canter when they left the paved yard, but only until they took the first fence. In open country now, the grooms following as best they could, Leonie bent over the stallion's withers and called for an all-out gallop.

"Aye, lad, that's the way of it!" she cried, her gurgle of laughter swallowed by the wind. Hearing herself, she felt a twinge of guilt, and hoped the grooms hadn't caught it. She was in deepest mourning, her riding habit an unadorned black. Laughter would appear so unseemly.

Yet in her heart she knew it wasn't. Mama wouldn't mind. Her mother would, in fact, have encouraged it. *Ride Raven for me, Leonie!* she'd urged, shortly after Papa's funeral. *Life must go on, child. And I've never seen you more alive than when you're giving that stallion his head. Go on. No one would understand better than your father. He loved seeing you ride as much as he adored hearing you laugh. Ride, darling—ride like the wind!*

And so Leonie rode. She cleared fences and hedges with room to spare. She grew giddy with the sheer power of Raven's strides eating up the ground. She laughed as they swept across the flats. *Freedom!* cried a voice inside her head. *Madness!* her sensible self countered. *Life!* the other voice insisted. *Don't be a fool!* sensible warned. *Does Jamie need another funeral?*

The last finally did it. Léonie slowed Raven to a discreet walk. She was nothing if not sensible, she reminded herself as the stallion fought the bit, clearly anxious to follow that other voice that urged her to ride out her grief.

A glance over her shoulder took in the pair of hapless grooms in the distance, racing frantically to catch up. She really shouldn't do that to Davey and Jocko. They were only trying to do their job. Bad enough their princess was on her horse only two days after burying her mother, racing madcap over the countryside. It must seem the outside of enough to the poor beleaguered servants.

Yet how else was she to deal with the grief that threatened

to tear her apart? Aside from her books, riding was the only remedy she had. It was her sole physical outlet, and it helped ease the pain, just as it had eased her over the pain of so many things in her life.

She'd always had her books, of course, but riding added another dimension to her narrow world. Between the two, she could forget the loneliness that came of having no companions her own age, among those who might jokingly be termed *her set.* Her crippled foot, she'd learned early on, made the gently bred young ladies of Mirandeau's *ton* uneasy. And even if it didn't, she was unable to partake of dancing lessons and games of tennis and croquet on the lawn. Reading and Raven helped assuage the boredom . . . and the grief.

They helped her forget, too, that she was ugly and misshapen, despite what her parents always said to the contrary. She wasn't blind. She saw the pitiful glances and shudders cast her way when people thought she wasn't looking. Nor was she deaf. People thought she never heard the whispered remarks as she passed, but she did.

Not that she was about to indulge in self-pity. She was merely being sensible. There it was again, her favorite word for herself. Yet it was accurate. Take the matter of getting on in the world. People's pity and discomfort were something she'd lived with for a long time. She'd long ago learned to view them dispassionately. Her only difficulty arose when meeting someone new. Newcomers were unable to keep aversion off their faces. So she avoided meeting people, and beautiful people in particular. In her experience, they were the most insensitive.

Fortunately, she'd nearly always managed to beg off going to court functions, the sort her brother attended with regularity. But Jamie didn't mind being on display. Then again, Jamie had great beauty and charm—and a body that was whole.

Raven grew restless, and as she bent forward to soothe him, her gaze dropped to the unique, closed stirrup Oats had adjusted for her. Her parents had ordered it, and its many predecessors, custom made for her, from the time Oats had set her on her first pony. Had ordered, too, the specially designed riding boot it accommodated, enabling their daughter to ride despite having a twisted foot.

She still remembered the pain she'd suffered in the beginning—excruciating pain until her twisted muscles grew accustomed to that first boot and stirrup. She remembered, too, the sense of triumph she'd felt when she mastered riding *and* the pain, without letting anyone suspect!

The only one who knew about it, even now, was Jamie. And that was only because she'd heard him groan when he'd gotten off *his* pony for the first time. He knew she'd heard him, though she'd said nothing. Then, all of five years old, her brother had gazed at her consideringly for several seconds. "It must have hurt you awfully in the beginning, Leonie," he'd said with a compassion that belied his years. And before she could think of dissembling, she'd nodded, then quickly sworn him to secrecy. And this had provided a fillip to Jamie's mastery of his own aches and pains. She'd not heard a groan out of him, not a complaint of any sort, since.

But Jamie was brave in ways she wasn't. He wasn't even cowed by their uncle. Remarkable, when many adults were terrified by Roderik.

Roderik. Just the name made her shiver. Truth was, she was absurdly afraid of him. After all, he'd never actually *done* anything to her. But with his sardonic looks and the fits of rage he unleashed at others, her uncle had always frightened her. Yet always before, Mama and Papa had been a steady bulwark against that fear. And now they were gone.

She realized she must approach her fears sensibly. Her best hope lay in the regent's habit of ignoring her. In the past, unless she was unfortunate enough to encounter him accidentally, he'd paid her no attention. She must contrive to avoid crossing paths with him, then. Which meant being clever enough to know where Roderik was at all times. Could she do that? Yes, she could. She was sensible, but she was also clever.

* * *

Given her determination to avoid strangers, Leonie felt more than a little discomfort when she and the grooms returned to the stables. There, being outfitted with a mount bearing the insignia of the palace guards on its saddle, was a newcomer. She knew this at once, for it was a small point of pride with her to know every palace servant and retainer on sight. She knew them all, their positions and their names, and she'd never seen this man.

Worse luck, he was the most beautiful adult male she'd ever laid eyes on.

Feeling twice as ungainly as she normally did, she quickly turned Raven's head, pretending to adjust her riding habit. A plausible ploy, for the habit fit her poorly, and it was an awkward affair, with its extended length of skirt designed to drape gracefully from a sidesaddle. *Gracefully—hah!* She rarely combined that word with opinions of herself in the same breath.

Still, she was hoping the newcomer wouldn't notice her—or, better yet, that he'd leave before she dismounted. She pretended, as well, not to have seen him. In her mind's eye, however, she saw every detail of his handsome face and physique.

He was very tall and broad-shouldered . . . athletic, she thought, with a lean waist and narrow hips, which the tunic of his guard's uniform showed off to perfection. When he'd moved, long, muscular thighs flexed beneath the uniform's breeches, which fit like a second skin.

And that face! Should an artist wish to depict Adonis, this man could pose for his likeness. He had hair as black as a raven's wing and features so perfect they beggared description: a broad brow beneath the tousled curls worn á la Titus; high, sculpted cheekbones offsetting a square, angular jaw; a straight nose, neither broad nor fleshy, but exactly proportioned for his face. Only his eyes refused to jell in her mind, for he hadn't been looking at her.

Unable to help herself, Leonie risked a second peek,

glancing at him over her shoulder. Gazing back at her was a pair of heavily lashed, deep-set eyes she could swear were . . . cobalt? No, *violet.*

Then realization hit. He was looking straight at her!

Blushing to the roots of her hair, Leonie couldn't move for an awful moment that seemed to stretch into forever. His violet eyes were intense, as well as beautiful. She wondered if this was how a deer felt when the hounds bayed at its heels.

"Y'r Highness?" Oats's tone was solicitous as he came to collect Raven, leaving her no choice but to dismount. "Is aught amiss, lass?"

"No! I—I mean, not at all," she stammered, somehow managing to slide off the stallion's back without falling on her face. "I—I was just remembering s-something I forgot to attend to," she mumbled, catching up the train of her habit as best she could.

Giving Raven a hasty pat on the neck, she surrendered him to Oats, turned, and gritted her teeth. *No help for it now. He'll see the limp, and whatever those eyes were meant to say before, it will change. It always changes . . . and pity for Princess Lame and Ugly wins the day again!*

Oats nodded and led Raven off to cool him down. This took him past the new guard. The newcomer wisely drew his mount aside. It never paid to underestimate a stallion in close proximity to other horses. Unfortunately for Leonie, this put him directly in her path. As his eyes had been on the stallion, the man clearly wasn't expecting this. His eyes widened. To keep from careening into him, she lurched to a stop mere inches from his boots.

"I beg your pardon," he said courteously as Leonie froze. And as she stood there, tongue-tied, this newcomer, this impossibly handsome stranger with the violet eyes, bowed gracefully, not a hint in his demeanor of anything untoward. Bowed like the courtiers she'd once imagined bowing at the dances she never attended. And when he straightened, he did nothing more than regard her with grave but steady eyes.

Still tongue-tied, Leonie swallowed thickly and managed

a nod. Commanding her legs to move, she scurried away as fast as her limp would allow. Her thoughts tumbled in confusion. He'd *seen* her in mid limp, looked directly at her, and there was nothing of pity in his eyes. Neither pity nor discomfort—*nothing* to indicate she was different in any way whatsoever.

Had the world suddenly gone mad . . . or had she?

"His name's Randall . . . Hawk Randall. Only he said I may call him *Hawk.*" Jamie's narrow chest expanded proudly as he recounted this for Sam and Leonie's benefit. He obviously felt he'd been granted man-to-man status by the new guard, whom he'd met just that morning. Like most boys his age, Jamie couldn't wait to grow up.

The three lay sprawled over the Axminster carpet in the comfortable sitting room off Leonie's bedchamber. This was a favorite gathering place for the royal pair and their cousin when the weather was foul and they couldn't go outdoors. And when there were no lessons or other obligations, of course. This afternoon, a spring rain pelted the palace's mullioned windows, and routine duties had been canceled for the week following the funeral.

"Randall . . ." Leonie mused with an insouciance she didn't feel. She'd been thinking almost constantly of yesterday's encounter with the man. Though she was determined to give nothing away, her heart was thumping so hard she feared the boys would hear it. "Isn't that an English name?"

Jamie shrugged. "English, Scottish . . . Uncle's no stickler for the country they come from. He only cares that they're up to snuff in the guarding department. Old Fossit says there's any number of foreign folk among the forty . . . more outlander guards than homegrown."

"Fossit should stick to being your tutor," Leonie told him with asperity. "He obviously knows next to nothing about the palace guard. Three Swiss plus a couple of Swedes—and now this Englishman, of course—hardly constitute a majority."

"Well," said her brother, "Uncle snatched up Randall in a prodigious hurry. Had him rigged out and sworn in, all of a single day! Didn't wish to give him a chance to change his mind, I'll wager."

"Why?" Leonie asked. She was more than curious about the process that had brought the stranger into their midst. The stranger who, despite his own arresting beauty, had treated her like something other than a freak. "Are proper candidates hard to come by?"

"He picks only big men," Sam put in quietly, "and they must know what they're about with the barking irons . . . and sabers, of course." Archduke Roderik had been in charge of the palace guard long before he became regent, so Sam knew a thing or two about their selection. "That would explain the Swiss and Swedes, I collect. Mama says those countries spawn giants. Is your Hawk Randall a giant, Jamie?"

"Oh, he's big, all right," Jamie replied with a grin, "but there's not a smidgen of fat on him!"

"Right." Sam nodded, as if this made sense. "He never picks the portly ones. Won't allow them to gain in girth, either, once they're taken on." His eyes darkened for a moment. "That would make him *furious* . . . and they'd be sacked!"

Leonie mused, not for the first time, about her cousin's habit of never mentioning his father by name, or even by his title. It was always *he* or *him* when Sam spoke of Roderik, and then only when the conversation drove him to it. She suspected if Sam could manage it, he'd never speak of his sire at all.

"Listen," said Jamie. "I think it's stopped raining." He sprang up and ran to the window. "It has! Let's go and see if we can find Randall, shall we? He might let you call him Hawk, too."

"Jamie," Leonie cautioned, "you know we're not supposed to be haring about, what with . . . well, we're in mourning, love."

"I know," he murmured, greatly subdued.

Leonie glimpsed the silver shimmer of tears in his eyes before he hung his head, and she wanted to kick herself. Jamie was all vital energy and life, the very essence of what Mama had always hoped her children would embrace. With the flexibility of youth, her brother was rebounding from their loss far better than she. She'd no right to rob him of that.

"Well . . . perhaps a quiet stroll about the grounds," she told him, smiling. "Mama wouldn't mind a quiet stroll."

"She wouldn't?" Jamie brightened.

"I know she wouldn't," she said stoutly.

"C'mon, Sam!" Once more a bundle of energy, Jamie grabbed his cousin's hand and pulled him to his feet. "With the rain letting up, there might be guards on the practice field. I'll wager Hawk's a nonesuch with the saber. It'll be famous, watching him!"

"Mind you don't get in anyone's way," Leonie cautioned as they reached the door, "and do return in time for tea." She threw Sam a wink. "Jamie's persuaded Cook to bake scones, I hear."

"I merely asked if there were any that happened to be, 'er, lying about." Jamie gave his sister an innocent look that fooled no one. Roderik had proclaimed an absence of treats for the week of high mourning. But the prince was Cook's favorite, and Jamie adored scones.

Jamie's brows suddenly arched, as if he were surprised to see his sister still on the floor. "Aren't you coming, Leonie?"

Parade her limp before all those guards? Before Hawk Randall? Easier to sprout wings and hare off to the moon! Randall may have seemed indifferent to her deformity yesterday, but perhaps he'd been too overset by their near collision to notice. Next time, she might not be so lucky.

"No, love," she told Jamie, rising from the floor with her usual lack of grace. She smoothed the dull black skirt of a mourning gown that was as uncomfortable as it was shapeless. The moths had gotten at her old ones—with Leona's illness, the maids had been allowed to grow careless—and this, like her ill-fitting riding habit yesterday, had been borrowed from a minister's wife. "I found a book I believe I shall like," she added with an apologetic smile. "I'll remain here and read."

Jamie and Sam exchanged a glance that said they ought to have expected as much. Leonie was never any fun when she had one of her books to occupy her.

"Shall we tell you all about it when we return, then?" Sam asked with his shy smile. "If we get to see anything famous, I mean."

"I certainly hope so," she replied, grinning. "I shan't eat a bite until I've heard every detail!"

With a laugh, Jamie clapped Sam on the shoulder and urged him out the door. When it shut behind them, Leonie heaved a wistful sigh. *Hawk . . . Hawk Randall. What color might those eyes appear in moonlight, I wonder.*

Abruptly, she gave her head a shake. "Do be sensible, Leonie," she scolded, and went in search of her book.

But somewhere in the recesses of her mind, a rebellious voice whispered, *Violet . . . just a deeper shade of violet.*

Three

Rand sat on his bunk in the guards' barracks, cleaning his musket rifle. Others who were off duty did the same, or polished their swords or just relaxed now supper was over. Talk ebbed and flowed around him, and Rand kept an ear open. He often picked up useful information from such casual conversation.

Still, he was an old hand at keeping an ear tuned while he bent his mind to other things, and foremost in his thoughts was the mission for his father. He'd already concluded, now he'd met them both, that his father's childhood sweetheart had left behind two interesting children.

The young prince was an engaging, delightful scamp, with leadership written all over him. Rand smiled to himself, recalling how the lad had approached him that morning while Rand was on duty outside the council chamber. Bold as you please, Prince Jameson had marched up to him, and introduced himself. *You must call me Jamie,* he'd insisted, and when he'd finally convinced Rand it wouldn't be improper—*all my friends call me that*—had added with a nonchalance Rand didn't believe for a minute: *And shall I call you Hawk, then?* The little sly boots!

Yes, this prince would do very well playing the part fate had determined should be his from birth. Winsome, confident, intelligent, and remarkably handsome to boot, Prince Jamie was a natural for the role.

Princess Leonie, on the other hand, was far more complicated—and a different kettle of fish entirely from her outgoing brother.

Of course, he hadn't known it was Leona's daughter he ran into yesterday—literally, almost—in the stable yard. There'd been no introduction—not that there should have been, given the gulf in status between a princess and a guard—so he'd learned who she was only by chance. After she left the yard, he'd heard someone order an extra ration of oats for *Her Highness's* mount, adding the stallion had earned it, as he'd had a *bit of a run.*

Bit of a run, indeed! Rand could hardly credit what he'd witnessed: that little slip of a girl mounted on a magnificent beast the likes of which most men wouldn't dare attempt. Not only mounted on the animal, but handling it expertly—a great brute of a stallion that would have given *him* pause. And then, to discover she was *lame.* Well, lame she might be, on the ground—but not on that black, by God!

How old could she be? Twelve? Thirteen at most, he decided. The duke hadn't said, but Rand could still see in his mind a small, heart-shaped face that was all eyes. A child's face, the eyes a deep mossy green. He remembered, too, a smattering of freckles across the bridge of a slightly retroussé nose. And a generous mouth, he thought, but whose exact shape he hadn't quite discerned. Just the rounded O of shock when he'd nearly knocked her off her feet.

He recalled, as well, the thick copper plait hanging halfway down her back. A child's simple braid, unadorned since she was in mourning, but he could imagine it at other times with a bright ribbon tied on the end. Yet what stuck in his mind most of all was her waiflike appearance, that slight, childish figure rigged out in an ugly black riding habit that looked as if she hadn't grown into it yet.

Were Mirandeau's coffers so bare its princess had to parade about in clothes that looked as if they'd been plucked from the parish alms heap? This didn't comport with what he'd seen elsewhere, however. Prince Jamie's garments appeared new, and complete to a shade. Even the guards' uniforms and servants' liveries were all in fine trim. Still, it wouldn't hurt to look into the state of Mirandeau's finances. The little princess narrowly missed resembling a street urchin, and no mistake.

But there was nothing beggarly about the girl's pluck. A blooded stallion, by God!

On the other hand, she'd had the look of a scared rabbit about her. True, he'd nearly run her down, a frightening experience for any child, he supposed. But he remembered, too, how she'd hared off immediately after, as if some bogeyman were after her. Was she just painfully shy, then? Or could her lameness be somehow connected to that frozen look in her eyes?

A few casually asked questions had elicited that Her Highness had been "born with a foot that wasn't right." Crippled from birth, then, and not through some injury sustained later on, as he'd imagined. Learning an equestrienne's skills couldn't have been easy for her. What an intrepid, doughty little thing she must be!

Pity about the foot, though.

Rand's eyes darkened with a distant memory, his hand stilling on the rifle's stock. There was a time, as he well knew, when he'd been unable even to look at such an imperfection of body. When things imperfect had disturbed him, and for reasons he hadn't cared to examine too closely. Fortunately, William's influence—and his courage—had cured him of that. The duke set about learning to walk, ride, even hunt, the moment he'd healed from the amputation. And Rand the child, unable in the beginning to consider that stump of a leg without breaking into a cold sweat, had gradually come to admire and respect him, no end. The father whose quiet courage had taught him so much about being a man.

He supposed Princess Leonie might possess the same kind of courage . . . or did she? Devil take it, he knew fear when he saw it, and the child had been riddled with it. It was not merely the wide-eyed fright owing to a near-miss collision, though that had been there, too. No, this was the fearful skittishness of someone who was always looking over her shoulder to see if an enemy followed . . . or lurked in the shadows.

Reminded his first reason for being in Mirandeau was to protect Leona's children, Rand told himself his next objective was to get to the bottom of her daughter's fears. Indeed, to the bottom of the mother's fears for both her children.

And then he must somehow remove the source.

"What do you mean Fossit's gone?" Leonie asked her brother. It was now a week since the funeral, and Jamie had come with this news immediately after breakfast, which he'd shared with Sam's family, at the regent's invitation. Leonie had not been invited—*summoned,* she thought, was a more accurate word. For this she'd been profoundly grateful and had happily breakfasted in her chambers.

"Old Fossit's been turned off, sacked," Jamie clarified. "We're to have a new tutor, someone Uncle's very keen on, I collect. Sent all the way to London for him."

Leonie nodded, for there was nothing unusual in an English tutor. Mirandeau's aristocratic families had engaged Englishmen to educate their offspring for ages. The country's original tongue had been French, just like Monaco's; in fact, the two principalities had much in common, including size. But hers suffered a rift with France during the Hundred Years War, when Mirandeau had sided with England.

At that juncture, Papa's forbear, one Prince Etienne, had decreed English to be Mirandeau's official language, even styling himself Prince Stephen thereafter. Of course, since most of his subjects had been bilingual and thus fluent in English to begin with, this had been accomplished without much fuss.

"When shall we meet him . . . the new tutor?" Leonie asked. She was never overly fond of Fossit, but her parents had allowed her to sit in on lessons with Jamie and Sam whenever she wished. Her old governess had been ill equipped to teach her anything of mathematics or Greek and

Latin, all of which fascinated her. "Let's hope he's better than Fossit with his geography," she added wryly.

Jamie suddenly looked uncomfortable. "Er . . . Leonie, there's been another change, as well, I'm afraid."

"Oh? Well, do stop being so mysterious, Jamie. Tell me."

"Uncle says you're . . . 'er, not to be included"—Jamie looked embarrassed, which didn't happen too often—"any longer. In our lessons, I mean."

Not included? She was dumbstruck and sat very still for a moment, while her brother gazed at her unhappily. "Did he say why?" she asked at last.

Jamie shook his head, clearly as mystified as she was. "Said the lessons were to be for me and Sam, exclus—ex-clu—"

"Exclusively?" she prompted. Her brother's vocabulary was quite extensive for a nine-year-old, but words were more her strong suit. Jamie's forte was history.

"Right," he said. "And when we asked, well, when *I* asked, 'cause Sam didn't say a word, Uncle said the why of it was none of our affair."

"None of your . . . well, if it's not *your* affair, I should like to know whose it is!" Her brief flare of indignation died as quickly as it had come, and Leonie heaved a sigh of resignation. It was a minor thing, really. She was long past school age. Still, she'd looked forward to those lessons on occasion. Her world was narrow enough, even when Mama and Papa were alive, and Fossit's instruction had widened it. Not to mention how she'd enjoyed sharing those sessions with the boys. Jamie and Sam were her only friends, after all, and some of their schoolroom discussions had been quite lively—and wonderful.

"Uh-oh, have to run," Jamie announced, glancing at the clock. "Seems I've been growing again, and I'm wanted for a fitting—a refitting, I mean—of my coronation robes. Then it's off to meet the new tutor. Petty . . . Petrie, I think his name is. Tell you all about him at tea," he called behind him as he scampered out the door.

Left to her own devices again, Leonie heaved a forlorn

sigh. She would miss sharing those lessons. A small thing, yes, but she suddenly felt bereft. More bereft than she'd felt since . . .

Your brother's but a child. He can't be expected to save you from the world. The thoughts that had pressed in on her at her mother's requiem mass echoed in her mind. Catching herself, she shook her head to clear it.

The regent's order severing her from the lessons was unimportant, she told herself practically. Hadn't she already resigned herself to the change? Which was the sensible thing to do, after all. Yet on the heels of her resignation, she felt a prickle of dread. *This is only the beginning,* the disturbing voice inside her said. *Roderik's in charge now. Never discount what your instincts have long told you, even if you had to discount those things poor Mama said. Never, never forget: Roderik is the* enemy.

Rand carefully re-rolled the map he'd been studying and placed it back among the others on the shelf. The palace's library was well supplied with maps, ancient and modern, and histories of the principality going back to the Middle Ages. When he began asking questions about the country's geography and terrain, the guards captain referred him to the library. It might be used, he'd explained, by the staff during certain designated hours. Rand had received permission to be here tonight between nine and ten.

A glance at the tall-case clock in the corner told him his hour was nearly up, which was just as well. He'd learned enough to augment the reconnaissance trips he'd made on horseback during his off-duty hours this week. His assessment of how things stood in the principality was beginning to come together.

Among the places he'd reconnoitered were several hidden coves and inlets, a fair number of which dotted Mirandeau's coastline, according to Whitehall. The maps had now verified their shapes and locations. Most of the coves boasted sandy beaches, and one he'd noted in particular was flanked by wooded terrain that stretched far into the interior, ideal for smuggling goods in or out of the country. Goods such as firearms? Or armed men, now he thought about it. He'd have to get word to Whitehall as soon as possible.

Then there was the political situation. The regent appeared to have lost no time in establishing himself. He already wielded enormous power, with a rule none dared question—it was said he had a violent temper when crossed. All of which told Rand the archduke had been building his base of power for some time. Such a thing didn't happen overnight.

Finally, he'd heard some disturbing rumors. True, they were only whispered *on-dits,* but as he'd learned at Whitehall, rumor sometimes turned up fact. And these rumors were ugly: Prince Frederik's fatal riding accident was deemed highly suspicious, and more than one person thought Princess Leona had shown signs of being poisoned. Bloody hell, if even half of this were true—

The tall-case clock began to chime the hour, prodding him from his thoughts. Better hurry, he thought, making for the door. In the hallway outside, an on-duty guard waited, likely to check he'd not stolen something. He was on duty himself in an hour, and he still had to change into his uniform. And shave again, he thought, rubbing a hand over his chin.

"Oh! I do beg your pardon!"

Dropping his hand and raising his eyes at the same instant, Rand halted just in time to avoid slamming into the source of that double exclamation. A heart-shaped face peered at him over a stack of books. The stack was half as tall as she was, and it was clear she'd trouble navigating with it. And what was a princess doing with such a ridiculously heavy load, anyway?

"Here, allow me, Your Highness," he said, deftly relieving her of it.

"Oh—it's *you,*" Leonie blurted out before she could think.

"If *you* is meant to signify a bumble-brained fellow clumsy enough to have run you down two times out of two," Rand said dryly, "I'm your man."

Leonie felt herself reddening and managed to keep from bolting, much as she'd have liked to. *Lord in heaven, Hawk Randall again, looking just as handsome out of uniform as in.* "Not—not at all, sir," she stammered. " 'Twas *I* nearly ran *you* down . . . 'er, this time."

Rand chuckled wryly. "Depends on one's perspective, I suppose, but I'm game for calling it even if you are. Now, where would you like these, Your Highness?" he asked, indicating the books with a dip of his chin.

"O-over there, please," she said, pointing to the table where Rand had been examining the maps.

"Are you certain?" he asked, noting her plain black gown fit her no better than the riding habit had, and was equally unattractive. Her eyes were lovely, though, huge as he remembered, and green as moss in the shade; but now, by candlelight shining from several sconces and a branch set on the table, he saw the green was flecked with chips of amber. "I could return them to the shelves, if you like," he added with a smile.

"That—that's awfully kind of you, but . . ." Leonie began, hating her stammer, yet grateful she could speak at all. His smile . . . this was the first she'd seen it, and it was doing all sorts of strange things to her insides. *Sweet heaven, he has—those deep grooves bracketing his mouth when he smiles are a male version of dimples.*

Aware he was waiting for her to finish, Leonie swallowed and made herself go on. "B-but, sir, it's really n-not necess—"

"Y'r hour's up, Randall." The guard, a man named Minton, poked his head in, eyeing Rand with a disapproving scowl. But after taking a quick step forward, he gave Leonie a deferential bow. "Er, beggin' y'r pardon, Y'r Highness, but the rules say the library's not fer staff, 'cept 'tween nine 'n ten t'night." The scowl was back as he motioned Rand out with a thrust of his chin.

Rand frowned, glancing at the tower of books on the table.

"It's all right, Mr. Randall," Leonie told him. "I'm quite accustomed to shelving my own books. And if the pile's large"—she shrugged—"serves me right for being so greedy.

But I thank you for the offer." *There! Not a single stammer. Mama's training's borne fruit, after all. Even if it's the library, and not some* tonnish *drawing room.*

" 'Tis Your Highness who is kind," Rand replied, wondering what was behind that hint of satisfaction on her face. It had banished the frightened child for a moment, and he found himself wondering how she might look with the self-confidence of her brother.

Ignoring Minton's glare, he murmured for her ears alone, "Surely, Princess, when its object is knowledge, greed is a virtue."

He made her a leg even more elegant than the courtesy she remembered from the stable yard, *winked at her,* and swept out the door.

Desperate to keep the guard from noticing her burning face, she said something so out of character for her she was to wonder at her cheek for days afterward. "Well, don't just stand there, Minton. Help me return these books to the shelves!"

In the days that followed, Rand grew increasingly troubled by things he observed in and about the palace, and in the streets of Rienna. Princess Leonie wasn't the only one with fear behind her eyes. Many of the palace servants had a frightened look. Merchants and shopkeepers in the capital grew tight-lipped and nervous when Rand tried to discuss anything having to do with the palace. Then he found himself dismayed one day to see fear—if not outright terror—in the demeanor of a lad he thought was Prince Jamie. *No,* he'd told himself, *not that bold little spirit! If this thing, whatever it is, has infected the prince . . .*

But it hadn't been Jamie, after all. A closer look had revealed the frightened child was left-handed—he'd been scribbling a note he then handed to a page, all with his left hand—and Rand distinctly recalled the prince was right-handed. After this, this other lad—Rand could have *sworn* he was Jamie—had hurried by him without so much as a nod of recognition. Rand also saw him dart fearful glances at the council chamber door, where Rand was again on duty.

At the first opportunity, Rand had questioned the page who took the lad's note and learned the look-alike was young Lord Samuel, cousin to the prince and princess, and Archduke Roderik's heir. This was doubly disturbing in light of something else he'd seen. He'd caught a glimpse of the regent's wife that morning. A pathetically cowed creature who'd jumped when her husband barked an instruction at her. Rand was immediately reminded of those rumors about the regent's nasty temper.

The regent was obviously the common denominator here, but was that so unusual? Rand had known men in England who ruled their families with an iron hand. Absolute in the power granted by church and state, they were petty tyrants whom no one in their own homes dared gainsay. Fact was, these domestic despots weren't always male, either.

Rand's eyes clouded with memories . . . ghosts of childhood pain he'd sworn to forget, but which still haunted him on occasion. *The past is gone. It has power over you only if you allow it,* he told himself severely, and shook his head quickly to clear it. *Concentrate on your mission.*

Archduke Roderik would bear careful watching, he decided. Whether a mere domestic tyrant or something far worse, the regent was at the center of things. An investigation would logically begin with him, in any event.

His decision bore results earlier than Rand had expected. A few nights later, he was forced to conclude that Archduke Roderik had to be the source of all the fear—not just the fear he'd witnessed within the regent's little family or among a few domestic servants, but a fear that seemed to permeate the very air of Mirandeau itself. On the night in question, Rand was witness to what Roderik was capable of, and it wasn't pretty.

He was sitting in a tavern with five other guards, enjoying a pint of ale. After a brutal, taxing session on the practice field earlier that day, they all felt they'd earned it. The common room was smoky and dark, filled with the usual tavern noises: an undercurrent of talk punctuated by occasional shouts of laughter, the clink of glasses, and in the corner, a singer accompanying himself on a lute. Rand was a few minutes into his second pint when the lyrics of the song began to penetrate:

Old England had its monsters,
One Richard I can name.
He killed the little princes, reaped everlasting shame.
And Will, the Bard of Avon, told cleverly and true,
How wicked Claudius did slay the father of the Dane.
But listen now, good people! To Mirandeau's regret,
An equal monster dire has done the greatest evil yet.
For Frederik went a-hunting, with brother at his side,
Yet one rode back, and one did not—by treachery beset.

"Arrest that man!" The enraged cry came from the back of the room, and all heads turned.

Pint of ale raised halfway to his mouth, Rand watched, incredulous, as the speaker suddenly came charging forward. He was dressed as an ordinary citizen, so none had marked him sitting in the shadows, but there was no doubting this was the regent. Roderik's familiar, high-pitched voice rose another notch as he pointed at the unfortunate singer. "That man's a traitor," he shrieked, spittle flying from his lips. "Arrest him, I say!"

The guards at Rand's table glanced warily at one another. Clearly they wondered, as he did, if the order was directed at them. As palace guards, they really had no jurisdiction here. But their looks said the enraged regent might not see it that way.

As it happened, the regent didn't. He meant them, all right. As they hesitated, the tavern grew deathly quiet, the singer frozen with terror. Roderik seized upon the guard nearest him, a burly veteran named Magnus. "Idiot!" he screamed, grabbing him by the sleeve so hard it tore. "What do I pay you for?" Next he backhanded him, a vicious blow across the face. Magnus, who could easily have broken him in two, did nothing.

"You will do your duty, and arrest this—this traitor!" The regent stabbed a finger wildly at the unfortunate singer, who Rand noticed was not a young man, for his hair and beard were liberally streaked with gray. Then Roderik honed in on their table, shouting at all six. "Arrest him, or I'll see you hanged along with him!"

Hanged? Rand thought in disbelief as they all rose with alacrity and formed a cordon around the hapless singer. Last he'd heard, Mirandeau had a court system modeled after England's, where the accused had a right to trial, where evidence was heard before a judge and submitted to a jury of one's peers. Yet the regent's words implied *he* was the sole judge and jury—and executioner, as well, evidence be damned.

And what evidence was there against the poor wretch? Rand asked himself as they led the old man away. A few verses that merely echoed what rumor already implied? Verses that, after all, had *named* no one behind the so-called treachery? Then again, there had been that phrase, *with brother at his side.* What the devil had he stumbled into here?

Four

Leonie emerged from the inky shadows behind the stables, deep in thought. The regent was keeping late hours these days, which was normal if he were in council. So had Papa, from time to time, when he and his ministers needed to settle some item which couldn't be put off till morning. But Uncle wasn't in the council chamber tonight. He was riding off into the dark, dressed as a yeoman farmer. It was past midnight, and the only reason she'd seen him do this—three nights running now—was owing to her resolve to avoid him, to know where he was at all times and contrive not to be there herself.

Not that she'd expected to be tracking him about in the dark this way. When she enlisted Jamie's help, all she'd anticipated was word saying, *Uncle's left his apartments now,* or *he's in council now* or *he's retiring now,* and she would do the rest. Jamie had cronies among the pages, kitchen help, and stable lads, and he'd assured her they could be trusted to pass such information and keep mum about it. After all, this wasn't about state secrets. They understood it was merely an innocuous means of keeping the princess out of her uncle's path each day, nothing more.

But no one had been more surprised than she by the message Jamie relayed when he slipped into her rooms three nights ago. A stable boy named Collie had alerted him with a pebble thrown at his window and reported that the regent had just ordered his horse saddled. That he'd ridden off in the middle of the night to God knew where!

That first night she'd not seen him leave, of course, but Leonie was curious. More than curious. So after the hard part, which was persuading Jamie not to tag along, she'd sneaked out and hidden behind the stables to await the regent's return. He was gone more than two hours, and the light cast by the lanterns outside the stables had revealed his mount's legs and flanks were coated with mud . . . river mud, if she were any judge. She'd ridden Raven along the Rienna countless times. She knew the river's unique black mud when she saw it.

Point was, Leonie asked herself now as she slipped back along the shadows to her rooms, what was Roderik up to? Why this skulking about in the middle of the night? Moreover, Uncle had a high opinion of himself and had always dressed more grandly than anyone, even Papa. He'd never don a common yeoman's garb unless it served a purpose.

Disguised, then, and haring off at a time when few were about. Collie had been frightened when he told Jamie what he'd seen and had begged him not to ask for that particular favor again. Apparently Roderik had warned Collie not to mention the comings and goings of his betters. And Jamie felt such a warning from Uncle was really a nasty threat. Of course, that could simply be a nine-year-old's imagination running wild. Or could it?

Roderik, she suspected, was fully capable of issuing threats . . . and a great deal more besides.

"It's all very peculiar," Jamie told his sister the following day. He glanced at Sam, who nodded in agreement. "I should be glad to be excluded if I were you, Leonie."

They'd gathered in the princess's chambers again and were discussing the boys' new tutor. Leonie had seen Mr. Petrie, but only from a distance, yet the Englishman was at once so distinct, so different in appearance from anyone she'd ever seen, she brought him firmly to mind with no trouble at all.

He was a lean shanks, and no mistake. An absurdly tall,

impossibly skinny individual with a shock of flaming hair. Jamie had already dubbed him The Scarecrow, while Sam favored Sir Stork. Even at a distance, Leonie had seen the boys weren't exaggerating about his looks, and she found either sobriquet apt. Bent forward from the waist as he'd hurried across the courtyard, his scholar's robes flapping about a pair of long stick legs, the tutor resembled nothing so much as a gangly black stork or a scarecrow whose head someone had dipped into a bucket of orange paint.

A break this afternoon in the prince's increasingly crowded schedule had afforded the first real opportunity for the boys to discuss Petrie at length, and they'd come to fill Leonie in on the particulars. Foremost was their assessment that the tutor was given to flagrantly broad gestures and peculiar, theatrical airs.

"He's forever flapping his arms about as he speaks." Jamie demonstrated by waving his own comically about, making her laugh.

"And he rolls his R's ever so much," added Sam, trying to imitate the tutor, then giving it up with a shrug and a glance at the prince.

"Indeed he does," said Jamie, picking up his cue. "He rrrolls his Rrr's everrr so much!"

His sister and Sam both laughed at the excellent imitation.

"Well, as you could plainly hear," said Sam, "I should have enormous difficulty doing that. That is, if Mr. Petrie were to ask us to, but he hasn't—has he, Jamie?"

"No, he hasn't," the prince agreed, "and that's what's so strange. He hasn't asked us to do anything *he* does. And he hasn't asked us to do anything Old Fossit wanted of us, either—right, Sam?"

His cousin nodded vigorously. "No sums, no maps or histories, none of the classics . . . though he does seem rather fond of quoting Shakespeare from time to time."

"But that's merely The Scarecrow's way of speaking," Jamie put in. "He doesn't require *us* to recite the lines."

"Well, what *does* he require of you?" Leonie asked.

The boys looked at each other blankly for a moment.

"Well, he makes Sam watch me," Jamie began.

"And I must then do whatever Jamie did," Sam finished.

"Whatever Jamie . . . *did?"* Leonie questioned uncertainly.

"I told you it was peculiar," said her brother. "The Scarecrow calls it lessons in deportment and manners, but *I* call it devilish queer."

"Let me see if I've got this right," said Leonie. "Your tutor requires nothing more of you than having you demonstrate manners and the like to each other?"

"Not to *each other,"* Jamie corrected. *"I'm* to do all the demonstrating, and *Sam's* job is to do all the copying—right Sam?"

"That's right. If Jamie walks a pace, then I must do it, too, but do it exactly like Jamie. Or I must observe how Jamie utters his words, then say them as if I were Jamie. Then there's the precise way Jamie sips his tea, which I must ever so carefully examine and—"

"And *ape* him?" Leonie cut in, incredulous.

"That's right," they both said at once.

"But . . . but what's the point? Did Petrie say?"

"Deportment and manners, is all," Jamie replied with a shrug.

"But it makes no sense!"

"That's what *I* said when I told Mama about it," Sam said. "Or, rather, I said it seemed a deal of nonsense. But Mama gave me a strange look, and I thought I heard her say, 'I'm not so certain about that.' But she said it ever so softly, so perhaps I didn't hear her right. Then she told me . . ."

"Go on," Leonie urged, seeing him hesitate. She was exceedingly curious, for she seldom heard anything of note regarding Lady Emilie. Sam spoke of his mother occasionally, but only in general terms.

Sam hesitated a moment longer, eyeing them both carefully, gauging how much he should say. He then took a deep breath and blurted out, "She told me not to let *him* hear me call it nonsense. You won't tell, will you?" he added anxiously, looking from one to the other.

"Of course not!" Jamie exclaimed. "What do you take us for, a pair of sapskulls?"

"Never in life, dear Sam," Leonie added, giving him a hug. *Lady Emilie knows something about this, I'll wager—or, more to the point, about the regent's hand in it.* "What's said here never goes beyond these walls."

Sam gave an abashed smile and nodded, knowing she was right. He was safe here. The princess's rooms were one of the safest places in the palace. Leonie didn't even hold with keeping a ladies' maid, not on a regular basis. He recalled her saying once she could do without some long-eared chit gadding about her rooms, disturbing her privacy. Splendid girl, his cousin. Not at all missish and hare-brained—or toplofty, like some of the lords' daughters he'd seen.

"Well," said Leonie, pondering, "it is all very peculiar. Your Mr. Petrie has some queer notions of what lessons are about. Still, I suppose whatever's behind them will make itself known eventually. Mama always said, if one is patient, things have a way of sorting themselves out. Perhaps this will, too."

But if Leonie thought the sorting out was to come anytime soon, she was mistaken. Petrie's lessons in "deportment and manners" continued just as the boys had described. Jamie was unfazed by this, and continued to make light of it in private, at the tutor's expense. Sam, on the other hand, seemed increasingly uncomfortable with the entire business. Not that he ever said so, but he no longer laughed when Jamie gave his cunning imitations of The Scarecrow. Leonie was simply at a loss as to what to make of it all. Then one day, about a week later, something even more puzzling happened.

She was just about to leave her rooms to go riding when she saw someone had slipped a folded sheet of foolscap under her door. Odd, she thought, bending to retrieve it. What she saw when she unfolded it was odder still. It was a hand-printed note *entirely in Greek.* Moreover, and very cleverly, for it gave nothing away to someone who had no Greek, at the bottom of the page was not a signature, but a designation: *Your cousin's mother.*

Lady Emilie, writing to her? She'd barely ever exchanged two words with the timid woman, much less, written correspondence. Quickly, she scanned the page, easily translating the simple Greek phrases:

> *Please meet me at dawn, tomorrow, behind the stables. I have an urgent message. Tell no one, I beg you, and burn this after you read it.*

"What on earth?" Leonie murmured, giving her head a perplexed shake. Scanning the note again, just to be sure she'd not mistranslated—she hadn't—she went at once to the banked fire in her sitting room and did as it instructed. Seconds later, the foolscap was a curl of blackened ash, and Leonie was pacing to and fro, deep in thought.

Something was afoot, but what? To say she was anxious over the matter was the grossest of understatements. She was terrified. Something so secret, it had to be transmitted in this manner boded ill. Lady Emilie had to be desperate to do it, and, as Leonie thought about it, she knew there were only two concerns that would drive her aunt to such an extremity: Sam or . . . the regent.

Her next thought was to approach the boys with this, for they might know something, but she discarded the idea at once. *Tell no one,* the note had said, and Lady Emilie must have had good reason for it. Even if the urgent message she planned to relay involved her son, it could well be something Sam wasn't meant to know.

Something dangerous immediately came to mind, and Leonie shivered. If that were the case, then it pointed inexorably toward that other possibility . . . Roderik. Was this somehow connected to his midnight excursions, or was it mere coincidence that the rendezvous was to be behind the stables, where Leonie herself had spied on him? Her uncle, she knew, would not have been able to read Lady Emilie's note. Papa had once remarked that his brother was not the scholar his wife was, for he had little Latin and no Greek.

Shaking off a feeling of dread, Leonie caught up the skirt of her riding habit and limped to the door. Nothing would come of leaping to conclusions, she told herself sensibly. Dawn would see this mystery solved soon enough. She would simply have to be patient. Meanwhile, there was nothing like a ride on Raven to steady her nerves.

But long before dawn, Leonie found her nerves anything but steady. She'd gone to bed early, having ridden Raven to the point of exhaustion, for one thing. For another, she needed the sleep if she were to rise before dawn. As a precaution, she'd left instructions with one of the chambermaids—the poor things began their days ungodly early—to awaken her a quarter hour before daybreak.

She knew she was having a nightmare. Roderik was galloping behind her in the darkness, chasing her with a vengeance, and screaming that she was a stupid cripple. She heard him curse his plodding mount and demand that she surrender Raven so he might catch her! She knew it was bizarre, knew it was just a dream, but that didn't stop the—

Someone was shaking her awake. Glad to be shut of the dream, she opened her eyes. *The rendezvous!* She sat up groggily, expecting to see the maid with a taper. But there was no light, and the voice she heard in the dark was no maid's.

"Leonie, you've got to wake up!" Jamie sounded more overset than she'd ever heard him. "Something dreadful's happened!"

"Jamie?" She rubbed sleep from her eyes, straining to see if dawn were breaking, but there wasn't a glimmer beyond the draperies. "What . . . what time is it?"

"Half-ten, maybe more," he said breathlessly, "but *listen.* Sam's in a bad way, Leonie!"

"Sam!" Alert now and wide awake, she struck a spark from the tinderbox she kept handy and lighted the lamp beside her bed. "What about Sam?"

"That's what I've been trying to tell you!" Jamie sounded

near tears, which was so unlike him it riveted her attention. His face looked pale and drawn, now she could see it. "Sam's been *whipped,* Leonie! Whipped awfully for not learning his lessons!"

She felt the blood drain from her face. *Not Sam! Not sweet, gentle Sam, who never caused anyone a bit of trouble.* "The tutor?" she asked in a horrified whisper. Yet she found herself unable to imagine even that oddball doing such a thing.

"Sam won't say," he told her grimly. "I only heard about it at supper. Monday's my day for fencing lessons, and I hadn't seen Sam all afternoon, but one of the lads got word to me in the dining hall."

Leonie didn't need to ask which lads. Jamie had friends all about the place. "Did you see Sam yourself?" she asked.

"No, he was locked in his bedchamber. But I convinced a maid to let me in their apartments while Uncle and Lady Emilie were still in the dining hall, and I spoke to him through his door. He wasn't crying, Leonie—at least not then—but . . . but he sounded so *scared.*"

"And he wouldn't tell you who did this?"

"No. Said it was better if I didn't know. But, Leonie, if it *was* The Scarecrow, he didn't do it while I was there. He wouldn't dare," Jamie added fiercely. "I should plant him a facer if he tried!"

She squeezed his hand, letting him know she applauded his loyalty and courage, while her mind raced. Could this have anything to do with their aunt's message? How she wished she were free to discuss it with Jamie! Her brother, with his network of friends among the help—his network of eyes and ears—might be able to find someone who could shed some light on this whole frightening business.

"Go back to bed, love," she told him gently. "No sense oversetting yourself about it any more than you already have. We'll see what's to be done about it in the morning, I promise. *Beginning at dawn. That is, if Lady Emilie hasn't been frightened off.*

* * *

Lady Emilie, as it turned out, was frightened, well enough. Yet she hadn't let this deter her from keeping the rendezvous. Leonie found her waiting in the shadows of an ancient oak behind the stables. She was wrapped, head to foot, in a black kerseymere cloak. Her face looked pinched and pale within the folds of the voluminous hood.

"Thank God you've come," she murmured, clasping Leonie's hands. Her own were ice-cold, and the pale blue eyes behind her spectacles were anxious and fearful as they met the princess's. They looked almost haunted, Leonie thought.

"You're certain you weren't followed?" she asked, darting a nervous glance beyond her niece's shoulder.

Leonie tried to smile, but feared it came out a grimace. "I'm an old hand at evading curious eyes, Aunt."

Emilie nodded knowingly. "I'm sure you are, my dear. And in that way, we're kindred spirits, you and I. No need to give them fodder for their little cruelties, *n'est-ce pas?* Not when it's just as easy to become invisible, as it were."

Leonie did smile now. "I call it blending into the woodwork, myself."

"Just so." Emilie smiled, too, giving her niece's hands a fond squeeze, and Leonie was at once struck by a sense of warmth and deep intelligence beneath the bland façade. How strange, she thought, to suddenly discover a real person behind this shadow of a woman, this aunt she'd hardly known all these years.

The smile vanished, and Emilie's face went grim. "I collect you're aware of what happened to Sam yesterday. I know His Highness spoke to him, if only briefly."

"Jamie . . . Jamie told me he'd been—been whipped," Leonie stammered, barely able to speak of it.

"He was beaten with a *riding crop,* Leonie. Until his poor back was—was a m-mass of *welts.*" Emilie's voice broke on a sob.

"Dear God!" Leonie bit her lip to keep it from trembling. She wanted to do more than sob; she wanted to howl her pain and outrage to the heavens. *Gentle little Sam, who's so mild and tenderhearted he weeps for a mouse caught by a cat!*

"Who did this thing?" she asked, her voice suddenly fierce.

Emilie had collected herself, and now she heaved a sigh—a sound so sad it seemed to Leonie the weight of the world was conveyed on that brief expulsion of air. "A lackey did it," she said, "but he did it *on my husband's orders.*"

Leonie swallowed thickly, and managed a nod. "I was afraid . . . so awfully afraid you'd say that. Oh, Aunt—"

"Listen to me, Leonie, for I haven't much time." Emilie was suddenly all business. "The regent's not in the palace this morning. He left an hour before dawn, something to do with a ship that came into port, which is why I could get away to meet you at this hour. But he's due back soon, so we must conclude this swiftly."

"Yes . . . yes, of course." Leonie cast a glance at the yard. The stable help began their day early, and she wouldn't want to have to explain this rendezvous to them, either.

"Then listen carefully, child. What I am about to tell you will be shocking. God knows, if I thought there were anyone else in a position to help, I'd not burden you with it, but—"

"I'm not certain I'm in any sort of position to help, Aunt Emilie. Still, if there's even a chance of aiding Sam . . . well, shocking or not, you must tell me."

"Even if I speak of *treason,* Leonie? Yes, well you might gape, for I did, too, when I began to learn the things I did!"

"G-go on," Leonie whispered.

"Very well, then." Emilie took a fortifying breath, and plunged ahead. "I've reason to suspect, Leonie, that—that my husband was behind your parents' untimely deaths. No—hear me out! That Roderik is mentally unbalanced is a fact I've lived with for a long time. He's a madman, pure and simple. Surely you're familiar with all the tales of his temper? Those hideous rages he finds impossible to control?"

Hesitantly, Leonie nodded. She was still reeling. *Dear God, she's saying that . . . that Mama and Papa were murdered by Roderik!*

"Those rages aren't normal," Emilie told her, "and the man who has them is . . . less than sane. Now, listen to me, I beg you. When your uncle brought your father's body back after the riding accident, an accident that happened when the two of them were *alone,* please recall, I was the first to see them returning. You see, I'd just purchased a spyglass—a telescope, it's called—to study the stars, a hobby of mine, and I happened to be trying it out that morning. And from my window, I saw Roderik's face long before others saw it. Leonie, it was *triumphant.*"

"B-but are you . . . are you certain?" She still couldn't take it all in. There *had* to be another explanation. "I—I mean, facial expressions are such nebulous things. They—"

"Nebulous? Perhaps, if we're speaking of strangers. But Roderik is no stranger. I've been married to him for twelve years, God help me. And I'm telling you, his face was triumphant, but only until he came within the courtyard, where others could see. Then it changed, and I saw it. It was as if he'd put on a mask of grieving."

"I . . . see," Leonie murmured unwillingly. The problem was, she *did* see. She had no trouble at all imagining her uncle doing exactly as her aunt had said. She shivered and wrapped her arms about herself for warmth, though the air was far from cold.

"What I saw that day," Emilie went on, "convinced me that Roderik found some way to kill Prince Frederik and make it appear an accident. But to my deep regret, it failed to prepare me for what followed, and it should have."

"For what followed?"

Emilie gave her a long, compassionate look. "For the slow poisoning of—"

"Never say it!" Leonie cried, covering her ears.

"Oh, my dear, how I wish I didn't need to," Emilie cried, taking Leonie in her arms. "And even more, I wish I'd realized it was a possibility when your mother first took ill."

She set Leonie gently apart from her and looked sadly into her eyes. "But, as you must know, I don't go about in society. And Her Highness kept to her rooms, save for visits from her physicians—and you and the prince, of course. By the time I overheard two chambermaids gossiping . . . a-about her symptoms, that is . . . well, it only then dawned on me that Princess Leona might be suffering from a . . . a gradual poisoning."

Leonie closed her eyes briefly against the pain that threatened to undo her, but said nothing.

"After that," Emilie continued, "I went to the library and read what I could find on the subject of poisons, and . . . well, the symptoms those two servants described all pointed toward belladonna. You may know it as deadly—"

"Deadly nightshade," Leonie whispered.

Emilie nodded grimly. "Also called belladonna because ladies used it in small doses to dilate the pupils of their eyes and give them a pallor, which was thought to enhance their beauty."

Leonie didn't want to think about it, but she couldn't help herself. *Those were exactly Mama's symptoms.* In the beginning, she *had* looked beautiful, astonishingly so, given she wasn't feeling at all well. But then, Mama had always been beautiful. It was only toward the end . . .

"Why are you telling me this now, Aunt?" she asked sharply. "Mama and Papa are gone . . . d-dead. What good could my knowing *how* they died possibly do, even if it was—"

She couldn't say it. *Murder* was such an ugly word, *treason* even uglier.

"Because he's not finished, Leonie! Because I've every reason to believe your brother will be next."

Five

"My *brother?* Wh-what do you mean?" Leonie asked, her heart thundering in her throat. *This can't possibly be happening. It's another nightmare; that's all. Any moment now, I'll awaken and find it's all a bad dream.*

But the feel of her aunt's hands clutching hers was very real. So were the words she spoke next. "The boys have told you about the new tutor's peculiar lessons, haven't they?"

"Tell me about Jamie, Aunt! What about *Jamie?"*

"Jamie's in danger, Leonie, grave danger, and it begins with those lessons that are being conducted on Roderik's orders for the sole purpose of teaching my son to mimic his royal cousin. The cousin he so resembles—and is meant to replace."

"Whaat?"

"Remember what I said, child. Roderik's mad, and in his madness, he's thought up this scheme. You see, my husband talks to himself sometimes . . . times when he forgets I'm there to hear him." She gave a helpless shrug. "I've long been invisible to him, anyway.

"Well," she went on when Leonie said nothing, "one of the things I overheard him saying is that the prince is a thorn in his side, that he has too much a mind of his own. Don't you see, Leonie? Roderik's greedy for power, power beyond that of regent. But to have that power, he needs a weak prince he can manipulate and mold to his will. Your brother is far too unmalleable for his purposes."

Try as she might to deny what her aunt was saying, Leonie

had to concede it all made a grim kind of sense. What other reason could there be for Petrie's so-called lessons? Sam *was* being taught to ape Jamie! And yesterday Sam was beaten—on Roderik's orders—for not learning his lessons. "S-so you believe Uncle's g-grooming Sam to—no. No. I'm sorry, Aunt. It—it's too incredible to believe. How? How can he possibly think he'll get away with such an insane ruse?"

The older woman's lips twisted in a bitter parody of a smile. "Insane, yes . . . to us who are sane.

"But think, Leonie. How could he possibly have believed he might get away with mur—with what came before?" she asked. "But he did. Trust me on this, child. I know what I saw that day through my glass. That was the beginning, and much as we may not wish it, all the rest fits."

"But . . . if you're mistaken?"

"Then I'm mistaken. But if I'm not . . . tell me, are you willing to risk your brother's future on it? On the possibility that poor Sam will be installed in his place—permanently?"

Leonie's head throbbed. She began to massage her temples, considering, one by one, the implications and possible consequences of all she'd heard. Then it dawned on her. "What do you want of me in all this, Aunt? What can I possibly do about any of it . . . even if it is true?"

"Someone must find a means of thwarting the regent's designs. I was hoping that person—with whatever help I'm able to give, of course—would be you."

"Me! You want *me* to do something about it?" Leonie asked, dumbfounded. She'd have found the suggestion laughable if the matter weren't so grave. Help thwart *Roderik?* She was the most helpless creature in all Mirandeau, and the most cowardly! "Look at me, Aunt," she demanded, taking a deliberate step on her twisted foot. "Only *look at me.*"

"What I'm asking for," Emile said patiently, "doesn't require physical strength or agility, child. What's wanted is courage, yes. Yet, even more, the situation requires someone with intelligence, which you possess—as do I, it's true. But what you also possess is the freedom to move about, and that I lack. Roderik may not pay me much attention, but he knows where I am at all times. This morning, you must know, is a rare exception."

"But Uncle scares me to death! And you want me to *thwart* him?" Leonie sucked in her breath, then gave a mirthless laugh. "Hasn't Sam told you about the lengths to which I've gone simply to avoid being in his path?"

Emilie heaved a weary sigh. "My dear, if I thought there were anyone else—"

"But don't you understand? I'm not at all brave like—like Jamie. I'm the world's greatest coward!"

"Please, my dear—"

"No!" Leonie cried, clapping her hands over her ears. Then, looking at the older woman in anguish, she lowered her hands, adding more quietly, "I'm powerless against him, Aunt Emilie, as we all are." She shook her head sadly. "I'm sorry, but I just can't do what you're asking. Please, please forgive me, but . . . I *can't.*"

Silently, Emilie looked at her, a world of sadness in her eyes. In the distance, a dog barked. Closer by, a faint sound could be heard from inside the stables. Finally, she nodded and patted Leonie's hand. "It's all right, child," she said quietly. "I understand."

Leonie watched her turn and walk away.

Swearing under his breath, Rand turned his mount around and headed back toward the palace. Tracking the regent was proving more difficult than he'd imagined. Tonight was the first he'd been free to follow the archduke on one of his midnight forays. To track him safely, however, he'd had to secure a mount that didn't come from the palace stables. No telling how many eyes and ears the regent had reporting to him.

But in the time it had taken Rand to reach the animal—he'd paid a small fortune to a band of gypsies for its use, and they'd left it waiting in a small copse behind the kitchen garden—Roderik had already ridden off. Rand tried to track him, but the sky was overcast, with neither moon nor stars to light the way, and he'd failed.

Heaving a disgusted sigh, he wisely let the gypsy horse pick its own way over the pitch-black field they'd crossed in vain, and ruminated on his assignment for the Foreign Office. The regent was undoubtedly involved in something highly suspicious with these clandestine forays, but what? Whitehall had its suspicions, and so did Rand. But as he'd been told two nights ago by the agent aboard the British navy frigate that had put into the cove where he'd left a prearranged signal, they needed solid evidence to back up those suspicions. And it was Rand's job to get it.

But how was he to do that when his own free time was so limited? And when the regent had everyone else tied up in terrified knots? The fate of that unfortunate singer they'd arrested had only served to increase the terror. The poor man had escaped the hangman's noose, but only because his heart gave out as they led him to the gallows, and he'd died on the spot.

Barbarous, that's what it was, and from what he'd been able to learn, no one had uttered a word of dissent against the regent's actions. Oh, there'd been whispered comments and mutterings, well enough, most accompanied by fearful looks and glances over the shoulder, but that was all. Not a soul—not the principality's ministers, not the members of the Privy Council, not the judges and barristers of the courts—had come to the hapless old man's defense.

And then there was that ugly business with the regent's son. The incident had been gossiped about everywhere in the palace, the barracks being no exception. It seemed the child was close to his cousin and through Prince Jamie, was known to almost everyone. When word of his being whipped had reached Rand's ears, he'd been sickened and furious.

Whippings of any kind, but especially of children, didn't sit well with him. Even now, days later, the mere thought of Lord Samuel's punishment set him brooding, painful memories of his own childhood beatings all too vivid in his mind.

The lad had supposedly earned the beating by failing at

his lessons. Rand's gut twisted with revulsion. *Earned* it! How, in God's name, could otherwise sane and rational adults possibly justify such brutality to helpless children? He felt a powerful kinship with young Sam. As with himself, a parent had ordered the punishment, and it certainly hadn't been the meek and mousy Lady Emilie. The regent had much to answer for, and Rand itched to bring that about.

Fact was, he couldn't wait.

Exhausted, yet unable to sleep, Leonie lay in her bed and stared at the embroidered canopy overhead. So it had been for several nights running. The reasons behind the sleeplessness were twofold: First, there was Sam's mother, whose suspicions had shocked and frightened her, and whose plea for help had left her guilt-ridden. Then, there'd been that nerve-racking ride to the river in the dark. A ride she'd dared, she realized now, only because of Emilie's frightening suspicions . . . and her own feelings of guilt.

Trouble was, while she'd denied Aunt's plea for help, she hadn't been able to clear her mind of the suspicions—of what they pointed to if they were true. And they well might be.

Though she'd been too overwrought to remember them, much less mention them to Emilie, Leonie had troubling memories of something that could conceivably give credence to her aunt's fears.

While she lay ill and dying, Mama had rambled on about some disturbing things. At the time, Leonie had attributed them to her being out of her head with fever. Now she wasn't so certain. In fact, she'd already accepted the central core of Mama's ramblings: *Stay away . . . away from him, Leonie! And Jamie . . . must keep Jamie away. Listen . . . begging you. Roderik . . . Roderik . . . the* enemy. *Roderik . . . evil . . . stay away!*

The late spring breeze stirring the draperies was warm and balmy, but recalling her mother's words made her shiver. Caught up in the shock and grief of Mama's dying, she'd mostly put aside those words and the circumstances under which they'd been uttered. Yet they came to her so clearly now.

Of course, the warning to stay away from Uncle had been a foregone conclusion, at least where she was concerned. The urging to keep Jamie away, however, was another matter. Perhaps because there was absolutely no means of keeping her brother away from the regent who represented him as prince, she'd put it out of her mind . . . until her talk with Lady Emilie.

Since then, she'd remembered it now, however, and other things, as well, bits and pieces of what she'd assumed were fevered ravings. Like those words about the ring. The emerald ring Leonie was to employ, somehow, if she and Jamie needed to . . . *escape.* Yes, that was the word Mama used.

Oddly enough, the ring was real. Long ago, her mother had shown it to her. She'd shown it to her in its hiding place, which she made Leonie swear not to reveal to anyone. A beautiful ring, Leonie remembered, with a handsome emerald at the center of an old-fashioned setting of gold filigree.

She remembered, too, that the jeweler's box containing the ring was wrapped in a sheet of yellowed foolscap. And on that sheet was written a nobleman's name and direction. Mama told her that if ever she and Jamie needed to leave Mirandeau, she was to go to that man . . . a duke, as she recalled. Leonie had thought this awfully strange at the time. Leave Mirandeau? Mirandeau was their home. Why on earth would they ever wish to leave it? And the man whose direction was on that sheet—he lived in England.

Finally, Leonie thought as she shifted on her mattress, hoping the change would induce sleep, there was that ride to the river. Foolish, but there it was. She'd been so shaken by Aunt's fears, she'd spied again on Uncle the very next night and followed him.

Foolish? She must have been addled! Sheer madness to follow Roderik in the dark to his own secret rendezvous, and yet she'd done it. All the way to the Rienna on a moonless night. None of which she'd have accomplished if it weren't for Raven, who knew the way from their many excursions to the river. Of course, she'd seen that mud on Uncle's horse, so she knew to point the stallion in the proper direction. Still, she'd never have dared it without Raven's ability to pick out the path in the dark.

And now, God help her, she had to deal with what she'd learned.

Uncle had met with a group of men—four or five, she thought, but in the dark it was hard to be certain. The rushing river had made hearing equally difficult, but she'd no trouble discerning they'd all spoken *French.* Yes, French, though Roderik was no linguist, and his command of the language, according to Papa, was only fair. Even more troubling, however, were the words she'd distinctly heard him utter—several times, in fact. *L'emperor.*

Deal with it? How could she *think* such a thing? Her knees had been shaking so, she'd barely been able to climb back on Raven and go home after the group broke apart. Even now, if she were standing as she recalled it all, she'd wager they'd be buckling under her. Bad enough she had Aunt's suspicions disturbing her sleep. Now she'd seen Uncle meeting strangers secretly in the woods at night, clearly up to something she didn't want to think about!

It was all too much of a burden for one cowardly girl, she thought, punching her pillow and trying to find sleep. Tomorrow, she'd share it with the least cowardly person she knew. It was time to have a talk with Jamie.

Sharing the burden with her brother did bring a sense of relief. Unfortunately, it also brought complications Leonie hadn't thought of. True, Jamie didn't have a cowardly bone in his body, and he was bright, clever, and resourceful, but he was still a child. A child quite used to having his way, even if it was through charm and a buoyant enthusiasm that was difficult to resist.

They met for breakfast in Leonie's chambers the next morning. Over tea and muffins, she informed him of the talk with Sam's mother. Jamie's first response was to ask her about Sam. And she told him what Emilie had said: that Roderik had ordered the whipping.

"The blackguard! A filthy blackguard, through and through!" Jamie cried, his small, capable hands clenched into fists. "We ought to—"

"Wait, there's more," Leonie hastily broke in, as much to cool his anger as to tell him the rest. She'd never seen Jamie like this—his eyes flashing dangerously, his normally cheerful face red with fury. "But I want you to listen calmly, Jamie . . . or at least, with a semblance of calm. Flying into the boughs won't help Sam . . . or us."

"Us?" he asked, taken aback. "What's it to do with us?"

"That's what I'm trying to explain—or relate, as it was explained to me by Lady Emilie. Now, will you listen?"

Jamie listened, his eyes growing wider by the minute as she took him through the shocking details of their aunt's story. To his credit, he didn't interrupt, didn't say a word until she finished. ". . . and that's why she believes Sam's being taught to ape you, Jamie. I know it all sounds too fantastic, and there isn't a shred of—of proof. Yet in a strangely horrible way, it—"

"It fits!" he cried, smacking a fist into his palm.

"Yes, but what if she's mistaken, and it's all just a jumble of coincidences?" she countered. "Without any evidence to support—"

"The stripes on Sam's back are evidence enough for me," he cut in, grim with anger.

"Yes, but don't you see? We know, from what Sam's told us over the years, how much his mother loves him. I expect she'd do anything for Sam, Jamie, including—"

"Well, so would I!" he cried. "And you . . . wouldn't you, Leonie?"

Leonie knew a moment of acute discomfort. The feelings of guilt she'd carried around for days had only grown stronger. But so had her fear, which had led to the guilt in the first place. And her habit of being cautious and sensible, she tried to tell herself. But it was mainly fear that had paralyzed her into refusing to help Aunt in whatever she might devise. But her brother, who knew nothing of fear, might not see it that way. Might not be able to see it that way.

"You know I adore Sam," she began cautiously, and he nodded. "But think a moment, Jamie. We're speaking about Uncle, here. About crossing him," she added with a shudder. "I d-don't even know where we'd begin."

"We could *escape*—and take Sam with us!" he exclaimed. "We'd leave at night, of course," he added, greatly excited now as he warmed to the idea. "The lads at the stables would help. They could have our horses ready and waiting in the forest, hidden until we came for them, without anyone being the wiser!"

"Jamie," she began, both impressed and dismayed by his bold but childish daring.

"Oh, I know it wants planning, Leonie, but we could *do* it. We'll—we'll use our jewelry for funds!" he said excitedly, displaying the gold signet ring Papa had given him on his last birthday.

Mama's emerald ring would fetch a deal more, flashed in Leonie's mind, and she immediately squelched it. "And go where?" she questioned, trying to sound sensible. A difficult endeavor, in any event, around Jamie. The prince's youthful enthusiasm and sense rarely occupied the same space.

Jamie pondered her question for a moment, deep in thought.

Just when Leonie was about to conclude she'd made her point, he exclaimed, "I have it! We know Mama had family in England, don't we?"

"But—"

"I know, I know, she rarely mentioned them. I collect she wasn't all that fond of her relatives. But they're our blood kin, Leonie. I can't imagine they wouldn't wish to help us. We'll go to England!"

"Jamie, stop it!" she cried, alarmed now by the leaps and bounds he was taking. Thank heaven she hadn't mentioned Roderik's clandestine meetings. If Jamie knew about them, no telling what sort of maggoty scheme he'd rig up next.

Jamie frowned at her. She reached for his hand and gave it a reassuring squeeze. "I know you mean well, sweetheart," she said, more calmly than she felt, "but I think perhaps . . . well, aren't you being a bit premature? I mean, how can we possibly steal away under Roderik's very nose?"

"His nose needs a bunch of my fives," he growled, making a fist to demonstrate.

"And even if we could," she went on, determined to ignore his bravado, "what if Lady Emilie's wrong? What if her entire story's a Banbury tale, concocted out of poor Aunt's lonely imagination?"

Jamie's face took on a stubborn look, a look rarely seen, but which his sister knew all too well. "Sam's welts were nobody's imagination," he said adamantly.

Sam again. Trouble was, she knew he was right to see Sam's welfare as their priority. Guilt flared through her. Doing her best to suppress it, she tried a different tack. "Jamie, promise me you'll take some time to think about this before you do anything, all right? I mean, even your notion of haring off to England needs reconsidering. We've no idea whether Mama's estranged family even exists any longer. They could all be dead by now. And if they aren't, once we arrive in England, how do we find them? We've no idea of their direction. Promise me you'll think on it," she finished hopefully.

Albeit with great reluctance, he did. With a breath of relief, Leonie watched him leave for yet another fitting of his coronation robes. But as the door closed behind him, her upstart brain spun another unwelcome thought. *While you've no idea how to locate Mama's family, you do have the direction of a certain English duke.*

There were times, Leonie thought irritably as she limped along a palace corridor, when it was dashed inconvenient to have a brother with a bulldog mentality. It was but two days since Jamie had promised to give his wild scheme some thought. Two days, and he'd already begun pestering her to subscribe to it. So what was she doing? Slinking along deserted corridors, hoping desperately not to be noticed by anyone, that's what. On her way to see Sam's mother, when all she wanted was to immerse herself in a good book and forget about the entire frightening affair!

Of course, to be honest, her conscience had been chafing her no end. Poor Sam had emerged from his rooms looking downcast and dreadfully unhappy. He'd hardly spoken at all the two times she'd seen him. And the look in his eyes . . . dear God, she thought she knew fear when she saw it, yet what she'd known was as nothing compared to the haunting terror in that child's eyes.

So, prodded by guilt, not to mention her tenacious brother, she'd carefully reexamined all the horrible things Lady Emilie had told her. Beginning with the assertion that Roderik was mad. She'd looked for errors in Aunt's logic. She'd searched for possible alternative explanations of the things she'd cited. In the end, she'd been forced to conclude that while her aunt's reasoning *seemed* logical, the conclusions Emilie had drawn were so absolutely fantastic, perhaps the poor dear herself was mad.

And yet . . . and yet . . . Aunt hadn't seemed the least bit unbalanced. She'd appeared rational and totally in command of her wits. In other words, sane as a bishop, whereas *Uncle* . . .

She wouldn't think about that right now, she told herself stoutly. She was here to see Lady Emilie. She would question her more carefully, now she herself was in a better frame of mind. Yes, that's what was wanted. She'd question Aunt more . . . sensibly, now the shock of that first blast had subsided. And this was an opportune time. The regent was currently occupied with the Swiss ambassador, according to Jamie's network of—*uh-oh!*

The slipper on Leonie's good foot slid on the marble floor, her twisted appendage bumping behind as she lurched to a sudden stop. The archducal apartments lay just ahead, at the end of this final corridor. And there, standing in front of the door, was a palace guard. What on earth was a guard doing outside the regent's apartments in the middle of the afternoon?

He hadn't seen her yet, so perhaps she'd just turn around and—good heavens, it was Hawk Randall! In the second it took to identify him, Leonie hesitated, and then it was suddenly too late to make her escape.

"Your Highness," he said, turning and acknowledging her appearance at the end of the corridor. He made the same elegant leg she remembered from before.

Drat! Nothing for it now but to carry on, I suppose. At least I shall discover why he's been posted outside Aunt's door. Lord, Hawk Randall, looking handsomer than ever. She limped toward him.

She did wish he weren't seeing her limping this badly, though. She rarely walked the distance she'd done this afternoon—the regent's apartments were at the opposite end of the palace from hers—and her entire left side ached terribly, her twisted foot throbbing with pain.

Still, she was accustomed to such pain. It came from pushing herself beyond her physical limits, which she often did, for she had to get on. But she'd become quite good at hiding the pain from others. He'd not see evidence of it on her face, at least. "Good afternoon, sir," she said, summoning a pleasant smile.

"Princess," he replied, nodding and smiling back at her.

Lord, those dimples again! It's practically indecent for a man to be that handsome—and then somehow treble the effect with a smile. "It's . . . Mr. Randall, isn't it?" she said, striving to recall the sort of exchanges her mother had termed small talk.

The smile became a grin—*treble? Make that quadruple!* Leonie thought as her heart skipped a beat—and then he chuckled. "Not by your brother's lights, I fear."

"I beg your pardon?"

"The prince, your brother, seems to have, uh, arranged to call me Hawk."

"Wait, don't tell me," she said, holding up her hand. "He insisted you call him Jamie, then used the familiarity to cozen you into allowing him a similar liberty, right?" *The little mischief!*

The grin again. "I see Your Highness is familiar with his, ah, methods?'

"His tactics, sir, pure and simple. Jamie should have made a brilliant career in the military, if not the Foreign Service."

Rand laughed. She was right on target. Fact was, strategists of all persuasions could take lessons from Prince Jamie!

"As for this tactic," Leonie continued, unamused—she was thoroughly annoyed with her sibling, and wished Randall to know this was no laughing matter—"I fear I'm quite familiar with his you-must-call-me-Jamie maneuver."

She was, in fact, scandalized. She recalled Jamie boasting the new guard had allowed him to call him Hawk. Why hadn't she realized he'd used one of his old tricks to bring that about? "The little jackanapes!" she huffed. "He normally reserves such mischief for his cronies. To employ it with an adult—the *idea!"*

"Before you decide to box his ears, I must tell you, I don't really mind," Rand replied, hiding a smile prompted by the charming display of incensed propriety. *What a pretty child she is! Much prettier than I thought. She ought to be vexed more often. All that lively animation becomes her.* "In fact," he added, "perhaps Your Highness might like to do the same?"

"What, call you by your Christian name, sir? I hope my parents raised me with better manners than that!"

"I'm sure they did," he said gravely, still hiding his enjoyment of the sparkle in her unusual eyes. "I was merely thinking of the—shall we say, awkwardness? I refer to His Highness addressing me in the familiar mode while his older sister . . ."

"Hmm," she murmured as he let his words trail off. Was he making sport of her? There'd been a certain twinkle in his eye, but what did she know of men's twinkles? "I'll think on it," she said prudently. Her mother had always used that. It allowed one to reply while giving nothing away, she just now realized. *Why, this small talk business isn't all that dif-*

ficult, after all. I shall have to bone up on it. Perhaps Miss Austen's novels will serve, if I take careful notes.

"Please do," Rand said courteously, now admiring the thoughtful intelligence behind those eyes. *Intelligence, wit, and no artifice at all . . . rather an intriguing little package, the princess. Quite charming, once you get past the shyness. Wonder what she'll be like when she grows up.* "And now, how may I help you, Princess?"

By not flashing those devastating dimples half so often. By not looking directly at me with those incredible violet eyes. By not being so beautiful and, at the same time, kind. "Help me?" she asked, quite helplessly lost in the depths of his gaze.

"Forgive me, Your Highness, but I must assume you've not come here to chat with a mere guard, delightful as the guard finds such a prospect. I was therefore inquiring if I might assist you in your actual objective." Another smile. "In coming here, that is."

"Oh." Hoping not to appear as flummoxed as she was—*delightful as the guard finds such a prospect*—Leonie drew herself up to her full height, such as it was, and raised her chin a notch, trying to appear dignified, if not regal. Regal, she knew, was quite beyond her. "Oh . . . yes. Yes, of course. I've come to speak with Lady Emilie. Is she at home?"

Rand suppressed a sigh. She obviously knew nothing of what had happened this morning, yet by teatime, he'd no doubt it would be the subject of every *on-dit* the *ton's* gossipmongers served up as scandal broth. "Lady Emilie is within her apartments, yes," he replied carefully, "but I, ah, regret to inform Your Highness that she is not . . . receiving visitors."

"Not receiving?" This was such an unexpected reply, Leonie didn't quite know what to make of it. Why, if she was within, wouldn't Aunt be receiving? There was something odd here. A palace guard posted outside the door—the *regent's* door. No, surely not. Perhaps Emilie wasn't feeling well. Yes, that had to be it. "Is Lady Emilie indisposed, then?" she asked. "I do hope she hasn't been taken ill!"

"As far as I am aware, her ladyship is well," Rand replied gravely.

"Well." *Thank goodness for that, at least.* "I am gratified to hear it, sir. But if my aunt is not ill or indisposed, may I ask—that is, do you know why she isn't receiving?"

Rand didn't like the reply he was about to give her, but he had no choice in the matter. He was, ostensibly, merely a servant with a duty to perform. "I regret to inform you that Lady Emilie has been confined to her chambers by order of the regent. I'm sorry, Princess Leonie, but she is not permitted visitors."

Six

That child knows something. Rand studied Leonie's slight frame as she retreated down the corridor. While the limp was more pronounced, her posture revealed a rigidity that hadn't been there when she arrived. Striving mightily not to cave in, he guessed, and, even more, not to show it. But her open, expressive face had already given her away and told him a deal more, besides.

She'd been shocked, of course. So had he been, on first learning of this odious assignment. The regent's wife was, for all intents and purposes, a prisoner in her own rooms, a turn of events so curious and unexpected he'd been pondering it ever since.

But the princess had been more than shocked. She'd been shaken to her very toes. And terrified . . . for her aunt? She'd come for the express purpose of seeing the woman, and when he'd explained why that was impossible, her eyes had flown to the door behind him. But something told him the fear went deeper than concern for a relative. Neither a blood relation nor one she'd ever been close to, from what he'd picked up. Yet the scuttlebutt had it that both royal children were attached to young Sam . . . and Sam had recently suffered that whipping. Was that the connection? He'd learned Lady Emilie doted on her son.

Which was more than could be said of her husband, if Rand was any judge—and he was. He'd seen the looks of cold disapproval the regent seemed to reserve especially for his son. They matched those of another in Rand's memory.

Looks of icy disdain he knew all too well on a face he'd gladly forget. But how could he, when he was reminded of it every time he shaved? Every time he looked in a mirror, and saw *her* eyes staring—*stop it!*

Tearing his thoughts back to the present, Rand considered what this confinement of the regent's wife could signify. When the guards' captain announced this assignment, he'd asked for a volunteer, not his habit unless the job carried high risk. Routine as it seemed, however, playing jailer to the innocuous Lady Emilie had proved distasteful to the men. Magnus, Rand recalled, had spit on the floor in disgust, and promptly left the barracks. Several others had followed, leaving the door open for Rand, who saw an ideal opportunity to spy on the regent's comings and goings. Already assigned elsewhere, he'd "reluctantly" offered to take this post if another would assume his. The captain had jumped at the offer, likely fearing a want of volunteers would force *him* to take it.

Having engineered this assignment, then, what was he to make of what was behind it? Lady Emilie's plight was puzzling. What threat could Roderik possibly see in the timid woman? Had she dared to cross him over poor Sam's punishment? Somehow, he couldn't picture it.

True, he could imagine another sort of female standing up to her husband to protect a child. His grandmother came immediately to mind, and Rand smiled. The dowager duchess of Hartswood could be a lioness when it suited her.

But Lady Emilie was no lioness. She was a cowed and frightened mouse. Yet even mice had ears. Had she overheard things of a political nature, information that could be damaging to her husband? This seemed more likely. He made no doubt the regent was playing some deep game. He still stole away from the palace from time to time, always late at night.

Rand ground out an oath. He was increasingly frustrated by the lack of opportunity to track the archduke. And Whitehall was growing impatient. His last communiqué from the frigate had suggested he quit the palace guards and assume a new identity, perhaps as a merchant traveler. This would allow him more freedom of movement, the message had said.

He'd scotched the idea. His first priority was the protection of the prince and princess, and there was no better venue for it than this. Whitehall, he knew, would view things differently, but Whitehall didn't need to know how he'd arranged his priorities.

Perhaps if they were still at war, he'd be compelled to give his intelligence work precedence. But it was no longer wartime, and he'd made William a promise. Not only did he regard that promise as sacred; he realized he'd begun to care for Leona's children. Jamie and Leonie were living, breathing human beings, not pawns in a game the Foreign Office sought only to win. In no way would he abandon them to an uncle who was a ravening wolf. A wolf in need of defanging, even if his midnight forays turned out to be innocuous. Not that Rand believed for a moment that they would. He'd remain in the palace.

Numb with shock, Leonie scurried back the way she'd come, desperate to reach her rooms. She felt suddenly vulnerable in these open corridors and would have given anything for the ability to run. But the pain from her bad foot was shooting up her side, aggravating her limp and making speed impossible. Clenching her jaws, she did her best to ignore it, just as she ignored the perspiration beading her brow, all too aware it came more from fear than physical exertion.

The taste of that fear was acrid on her tongue, and she cursed her clumsy, stumbling gait. *Lady Emilie has been confined to her chambers, by order of the regent.* Hawk Randall's words rang in her mind like a warning bell, and the trip-hammer beat of her heart drummed the refrain: *by order of the regent . . . by order of the regent . . . by order of the—*

"Well, well, if it isn't the little cripple!"

Roderik. Raw terror nailed Leonie to the floor. By dint of will alone, she made herself look at him. The cold smile on the saturnine face held a mixture of boredom and amused contempt. He wasn't a tall man, but she was small, even for a woman. Roderik loomed over her, a predator confident of his prey, his interest whetted by the fear he instilled. She willed herself, as well, not to cower under that bone-chilling gaze. But will took her only so far. She couldn't force a word past her lips.

"What's the matter, little bird?" A taunting singsong calculated to intimidate, Roderik's high-pitched voice echoed along the corridor. "Cat got your tongue?"

Whether anger at his smirk loosened that tongue, or mere desperation, Leonie didn't know. One thing was certain. Silence would only prolong the torment. "G-good afternoon, Uncle," she got out.

"Is it?" he asked mockingly, and cocked his head to one side. He sounded cunning . . . sly. And that cocking of his head . . . as if he listened for a voice only he could hear, Leonie realized with a shiver. He certainly didn't appear to be questioning *her.* He wasn't even looking at her. Then, in the next instant, he was—and worse. Roderik ran his eyes over her, his piercing gaze noting every detail, and she knew what the field mouse feels in the shadow of the hawk.

"Your taste in attire, my dear, is abominable," he sneered. The sneer was familiar, and she was able to disregard it, just as she ignored the substance of the remark. She was long past feeling hurt from Roderik's cruel barbs. It was the sudden change of subject she found unnerving.

"I've seen laundresses whose clothes fit better than yours," he added with snide disdain. Then, suspiciously, "Who is your ladies' maid?"

"I—I don't have one, Uncle," she stammered, further rattled by the abrupt question. Lady Emilie's words echoed in her mind: *a madman, pure and simple.*

"Don't have one? Don't *have* one! And just who is responsible for that oversight?" he demanded, so sharply Leonie flinched.

"I . . . I'm sure I d-don't know," she lied.

"Well, I won't have it, do you hear? You'll see the steward

at once and have him assign you one. I'll not have you parading about in those ugly—do you know where I've been?"

Dumbfounded again by the switch in mid sentence, she could only shake her head.

"Meeting with the Swiss ambassador, you ignorant chit! And I'll have you know Herr Mauer was splendidly turned out. Splendidly!"

He leaned toward her, and it was all Leonie could do not to back away. "What if he should observe a member of Mirandeau's royal family," he shrieked, "dressed like a ragpicker's daughter? You're a *disgrace.* Time you realized we have an image to uphold!"

Still dumbfounded—the regent had never taken the slightest interest in her appearance—she could merely produce a nod of assent. But it was wasted. The tirade over, it was as if Leonie no longer mattered. The regent strode brusquely past her without another word.

Thank you, God. Faint with relief, Leonie leaned against the wall for support. It was several minutes before she stopped shaking. When she resumed moving, she pushed herself to greater haste than she'd believed possible. Devil take the pain!

Back in her chambers, Leonie slumped on her bed, kneading the muscles she'd abused with her useless foray. To distract herself from the pain, she concentrated on the appalling results of that endeavor. Hawk Randall's news had been devastating, and she still trembled from the encounter with Roderik. She wanted to crawl under the coverlet, go to sleep, and pretend this afternoon had never happened.

Lady Emilie confined! Why, it was almost as if the regent had made her a—no, he *had* made her a prisoner. It was no different than house arrest, except no one had had to do any arresting. Poor Aunt had been there for the taking.

Until today, she'd felt there was still room for doubting Emilie's suspicions. Her uncle, she'd reasoned, might be unpleasant, but surely he couldn't be *that* evil. His wife's incarceration changed everything. Roderik's acting in such an ignominious fashion on the very heels of that rendezvous behind the stables couldn't be a coincidence. What had he learned? She mustn't be deceived by his behavior toward her in the corridor. That it hadn't indicated he knew of his niece's involvement could simply mean he'd been lulling her suspicions before he locked her in, too . . . or worse.

She felt torn, plagued with indecision and afraid to move, yet the situation screamed for action. If he was informed of the rendezvous, then he had to be aware his niece knew things she shouldn't. That she was still at large meant nothing. Knowing how weak she was, he could afford to bide his time like a big nasty cat toying with a helpless prey. Only a fool would sit still and wait for him to pounce.

Yet fear ate at her. She tried mightily to quell it. There were more important things at stake than her own safety: Jamie's . . . and Sam's, not to mention the future of Mirandeau itself. But what could she do? "I'm not like those heroes in the novels I've read," she whispered to the empty room. "I'm only a defenseless girl, and a lame one, at that."

The situation requires someone with intelligence, which you possess. Emilie's words again, and Leonie wanted to shout, "But so do you, Aunt. and look where you are now." Then she felt ashamed. Emilie was no hero out of books, either, yet she'd summoned the courage to—

A loud knocking at the outer door threw her pulse into double time. *Uncle! God in heaven, has he sent the guard?* She made her way cautiously into the sitting room. "Who—who is it?" she called, eyeing the door as if it were a portal to hell.

"Leonie, let us in—hurry!" Jamie's voice, and he sounded frantic.

Leonie's eyes widened in shock as she pulled the door ajar. Jamie stood there, holding Sam upright with a shoulder wedged under his cousin's arm. Sam slumped against the prince's small, sturdy body, his head hanging down. She thought he was unconscious until she heard him whimper.

Compounding her shock, behind them stood the redheaded tutor. "Jamie," she managed as her brother eased his burden forward, "what in God's name—"

"Fetch some linens and water, quickly! Sam's been beaten bloody!" Jamie's voice became a snarl of rage. "The blackguard did it himself this time!"

She gasped, then ran for the bedchamber to do his bidding. Behind her, she heard him urge Petrie to be careful as they helped Sam into the room. "Bring him in here and put him on the bed!" she called as she tore her coverlet aside and yanked at an embroidered sheet.

She grabbed the porcelain pitcher on her washstand and poured water into the matching bowl, then carried it to the bed. She set it on her bedstand as they carefully laid Sam on the mattress, face down. She was just reaching for the sheet when Jamie and the tutor stepped aside.

"Merciful God . . ." Leonie's face went as white as the sheet that slipped from her nerveless fingers. She stood frozen and sickened, her horrified gaze riveted to her cousin's small back . . . to the torn and bloody shirt that stuck to it in crimson shreds.

"We found him in the schoolroom, on the floor," Jamie said through bloodless lips. "He'd apparently been lying there for s-some time. He—he was c-curled up—" He broke into a sob and reached for his sister, burying his head in her shoulder.

With a shock of revulsion, Leonie realized the regent had to have already accomplished this when she'd run into him in the corridor. Yet all he'd spoken of was ladies' maids and fancy dress. Nothing of the heinous act he'd recently committed had shown on his face. *Only a monster could have done such a thing,* she thought as her arms wound tightly around her brother. *A monster and a madman, just as Aunt said.* With these thoughts, she felt something settle quietly into place inside her, and a new resolve was born. It was time to act.

* * *

They tended Sam's ravaged back as best they could, afraid to call for the court physician lest the regent hear of it and do God knew what. The tutor stood nervously by, letting the prince and princess do most of the work. It was a harrowing business, with poor Sam moaning in pain as they tended him.

In the end, however, Petrie proved perhaps the most helpful of all. He remembered a vial of laudanum in his room, kept for emergencies, and fetched it. They got some into Sam, and he soon fell into a deep slumber. Greatly relieved, Leonie was able to apply an unguent the tutor had also brought, and dress the child's wounds without causing greater pain.

They left Sam sleeping on her bed, and adjourned to the sitting room to discuss what was to be done next. Perched on a settee, a comforting arm around her brother, Leonie was just trying to gather her thoughts when the tutor began to pace—and to talk while he did so. What he said left his royal audience gaping.

"I must begin by informing Your Highnesses," he intoned in an important voice, "that I am not really a tutor at all. What's more, I never have been." Pausing to allow them to digest this, he then resumed his pacing, leaving Leonie with the impression that she and Jamie had just become an audience.

When the regent's man first contacted him in London, Petrie explained, he'd been an out-of-work stage actor—between engagements, was how he put it. Leonie felt Jamie's shoulders stiffen with the actor's next revelation. The archduke hired him expressly for the purpose of teaching Sam to mimic the prince.

"His Grace's man told me this was strictly for His Highness's protection, you understand," Petrie explained, sweeping his arm toward the prince in an elaborate gesture. "Said he required a substitute to masquerade as Prince Jameson when it was too dangerous for His Highness to appear in public himself."

Jamie blinked in astonishment. "If that was ever in the works, this is the first I've heard of it!"

"Indeed, Your Highness," Petrie told him. "You see, I was to, 'er, keep the information from you. His Grace said he didn't wish you alarmed by talk of . . . well, assassins. Said you'd enough on your plate, what with losing your dear parents so recently. And I was to keep mum about it with, 'er . . . well, he referred to Lord Samuel as 'the substitute' when we discussed it. How was I to know the unfortunate child was the regent's own son?

"That was my first clue that something wasn't on the up and up," he went on. "But where I really began to grow uneasy . . . well it happened a few days after I arrived."

Here he paused—for dramatic effect, Leonie suspected—and was rewarded when both she and Jamie leaned forward expectantly. "That," said Petrie, "was when I was told Lord Samuel would even be impersonating the prince at his forthcoming coronation.

"Well, I was just as shocked as you are," he added as the impact of this news registered on their faces. "I mean, coronations—at least those in my own country—involve oaths and anointings, don't they? Did the regent really mean to have another child take those oaths? I asked myself. Did he mean to have his son's head anointed by the bishop, and a prince's crown set upon it? A crown rightfully intended for his cousin?"

"Did you mention any of this to the regent?" Leonie questioned, and saw a look of alarm cross the actor's face.

"Er . . . actually, no," he replied, withdrawing a handkerchief and mopping his brow. "You see, I'd just been to that hanging . . . well, a near hanging, I suppose you might call it. The unfortunate fellow never made it to the gallows. Died en route—from fright, they say."

He mopped his brow again. "I had a fright of my own when I learned the details. The poor chap was a singer, a performer—like *me.* What they were saying about his being condemned to hang was that he'd angered the archduke with his last performance."

"And Uncle accused him of treason!" Jamie put in. "The kitchen lads told me." He glanced at his sister. "Um . . . sorry, Leonie. I didn't tell you 'cause we're not supposed to know about things like hangings, remember? Papa said so."

She nodded grimly. If there'd been any during her lifetime, she wasn't aware of them. She rather doubted there had been. Mirandeau was a peaceful country for the most part, with very little crime. At least, it had been . . . before Roderik became regent.

"I collect," she said to Petrie, "this singer's fate made you . . . er, nervous about approaching our uncle about his intentions regarding the coronation?"

"Nervous!" Petrie looked affronted. "I prefer to think of it as being discreet," he said with a sniff. "I mean, Shakespeare himself said, 'The better part of valor is discretion'!"

Leonie hid a smile. The Bard had put those words in the mouth of Falstaff, who took pride in being a devout coward, which wasn't the same as saying them himself. But if Petrie wanted to disguise his cowardice as valor, she'd be the last to assign blame. She'd been a devout coward herself. "So you, er, refrained from speaking to the regent, is that it?" she asked.

"Well," he reflected, resting his forefinger on his chin, "I was finally forced to speak to him, but that was about Lord Samuel and his lessons. He wasn't doing very well, you see."

"Do tell," Leonie said, her eyes narrowing ominously. The reminder that this strutting peacock had been the cause of Sam's first beating made her blood boil.

"Shh." Jamie placed a cautioning hand on her arm. "We might need him as an ally," he whispered.

"Then we *are* in desperate straits!" she hissed.

Oblivious to this exchange, Petrie was still pacing and gesticulating. "I told His Grace it simply wouldn't do. Lord Samuel has no talent for the theatre, and that's not *my* fault. After all," he sniffed, "I cannot be expected to work miracles!"

A low growl from Leonie had Jamie nudging her to be

quiet, none of which the actor noticed. He was really into his role now. "But would the man listen?" he asked with an arm flung wide. "He would not! Said failure was *not* an option, and ordered me to rehearse Lord Samuel in His Highness's coronation robes. I collect there'd been additional fittings in which the cousins' measurements were compared, and the robes altered to fit Lord Samuel."

"That explains all those extra fittings," Jamie said between his teeth.

"Now, I ask you," Petrie queried with a flamboyant sweep of both arms, "what if there are assassins lurking? The archduke's own son would be in harm's way. Monstrous! And now he's *beaten* the dear boy."

Pausing, the actor eyed the door for a moment. Then, throwing his narrow shoulders back, he gave his waistcoat a tug and cleared his throat. "I shall tell His Grace I simply cannot go on with this charade. I may be in need of an income, but I am an *artist*—not an insensitive lout!" He whirled dramatically and made for the door.

"Wait!" Leonie leapt from the settee and caught his arm. "Mr. Petrie, I beg of you, please don't go to the regent! Our lives could be in danger if you do."

"Eh?" He looked hesitant, but not really convinced.

"I mean it," she said. "Our lives could be forfeit if you speak to him"—noting his look, she had a sudden inspiration—"and so could *yours.*"

That got his attention. Jamie gave his sister's arm a squeeze to let her know he approved of her tactic. The actor froze and swallowed thickly. "I beg your pardon?" he said nervously.

Leonie motioned him to the chair opposite the settee. When he was seated, she took a deep breath, and set forth the plan that had slowly begun to take shape in her mind.

"Mr. Petrie, please believe me when I say the situation is dire. If you need to know how dire," she added, pointing to her bedchamber, "just take another look at that child's back."

Petrie's eyebrows shot to his hairline, and he quickly nodded.

"It is imperative," she continued calmly, despite her heart's thudding against her ribcage, "that His Highness and I, along with Lord Samuel, leave Mirandeau as soon as possible—in secret. And I assure you, sir, it is just as imperative that you do the same."

She paused and glanced at Jamie, who nodded encouragement. "My brother and I wish to take our cousin to England, Mr. Petrie. We have family there. And since that is where you come from, we're hoping you'll be able to help us."

The actor listened, wide-eyed and nervous, to what she had in mind. But it wasn't until Leonie offered to pay him handsomely that he actually agreed. After some discussion, they decided Sam should be able to travel within a day or two, but the sooner, the better. They agreed to meet again at midnight to check on his condition and solidify plans.

Then Petrie took his leave, as did Jamie, saying he had some preparing to do, which meant he'd be conferring with his network of cronies. When the door closed behind them, she was left alone with Sam . . . and her thoughts.

She was appalled at what she'd done. How could she have hatched such an insane scheme, or believe she might see it through? Yet she had no choice. If Roderik installed Sam in Jamie's place, it would hardly be for Jamie's protection. Jamie had no enemies. Everyone loved him. And if Sam were forced to be an imposter, the real Jamie would have to disappear . . . to *die,* she reasoned with a shudder.

She made no doubt of the possibility. What Roderik had done to Sam was the final proof of his insane ambition. Having twice committed murder, he'd remove anyone who stood in his way.

She must—and would—muster the courage to do this thing. Jamie would help, but she was the adult. She had no illusions about Petrie. With luck, he might steer them to England, but the man was clearly incapable of heroics. It was all up to her, and that began with an emerald ring wrapped in yellowed foolscap and hidden beneath a loose floorboard in Mama's dressing room.

Going in to check on Sam, Leonie found him resting quietly. She thanked heaven for Petrie's laudanum, if not for the man himself. Then she crossed to the inner door that connected her suite of rooms to her mother's. The door Leonie hadn't opened since that hellish morning she'd forced herself to enter and had personally selected the garments Mama was to wear in her coffin.

The bedchamber was dim. All the draperies had been drawn and would remain so for the year of formal mourning, as was the custom in Mirandeau. With a painful swallow, Leonie ignored the things that were so achingly familiar: the Georgian furniture Mama had favored and Papa had ordered specially for her from England's finest cabinetmakers, the collection of enameled Battersea boxes assembled and arranged with loving care on the mantel, the soft green and rose colors of the hand-painted scenes on the silk wall coverings imported from Paris. All painful reminders of her mother, but they wouldn't bring Mama back. Mama was alive in the hearts and minds of her children. These were only things.

She moved past them and strode directly into the dressing room. There she found the little silver chisel Mama kept hidden behind the bronze statue of a horse that a much younger Leonie used to pretend was Raven. Throwing back a corner of the Turkey carpet, she knelt and bent to her work. It was easy to pry up the loose floorboard, just as Mama had shown her. And there was the yellowed sheet of foolscap that bore the Englishman's address. But the emerald ring . . .

It was *gone.*

Seven

Rand knew something was afoot the moment Jamie rounded the corner. The lad was definitely not coming to see his uncle. The regent was in the dining hall, entertaining the Swiss ambassador, and Jamie had to know this. More likely he was taking advantage of Roderik's absence to snatch a visit with Sam. But Sam wasn't in—oddly enough, Rand hadn't seen him all day—and even if he were, all callers were barred. Surely the prince was aware of this by now. Then again, knowing Jamie . . .

Rand smiled to himself. It would be interesting to watch the little slyboots try his charm to gain what his sister hadn't.

"Why, it's Hawk Randall!" the prince exclaimed, with perhaps a shade too much surprise. "Fancy meeting you here."

"Prince Jamie," Rand said, bowing courteously.

"Now, Hawk," the boy admonished with a good-natured grin, "you know I'm just Jamie to my friends. Furthermore, I shall take it amiss if you go on bowing to me. You see, by this time of day, I'm unfailingly bowed out of all countenance. I depend upon my friends to grant me some relief."

"Do you, indeed?" Rand replied, hiding a smile.

"Quite. All day long, people have been bobbing at me, in the dozens"—Jamie leaned forward and whispered conspiratorially—"and *ad nauseum,* if you know what I mean!"

"As bad as all that?" Rand managed, still with a straight face.

"Oh, you've no idea!" With a huff of exasperation, Jamie

began ticking off on his fingers. "First to bow is the footman who announces the maid with my morning chocolate. Then *she* does it . . . well, she curtsies, which amounts to the same thing. Next, there's my valet, a good enough fellow for an upper servant—they're usually the worst snobs, you know—but this one bobs so much, it's like he's on springs! Then there's my secretary. A pompous twit who bows before he hands me my day's schedule, bows again once he's handed it over, and bows yet a third time when he—"

"Peace!" cried Rand, laughing and putting a hand up to halt this breathless recitation. "You've made your point. No more bows."

Jamie's brow arched skeptically. "Promise?"

"I do. Yet, of necessity, it must apply only to those situations in which we find ourselves alone, you understand."

The prince nodded, but rather absently. He was eyeing the regent's door with a speculative look that had Rand smothering another chuckle.

"May I be of some service?" he asked instead.

"Well, you see, Hawk . . ." The child hesitated, and appeared to be debating how to go on. This time his glance at the door seemed uneasy, and Rand finally took pity on him.

"Perhaps it will expedite matters if I told you your cousin is not in," he offered diplomatically.

He was totally unprepared for Jamie's response. The look the boy gave him seemed to belong to someone else. It was troubled, the bright young face so drained of confidence, he couldn't credit this was the same child.

"Hawk," he began, with an uncertainty that was equally alien to him. "Do you . . . do you suppose I might speak to Lady Emilie . . . just for a few minutes?"

Lady Emilie! Why the devil would he and his sister both want to see the aunt? Taken aback, Rand was silent for a moment. *Something serious is going on here. And if I'm to be of any use to William*—and *to Leona's children—I'd bloody well better learn what it is!* "Forgive me, Jamie," he replied while his mind searched for a means to accomplish this, "but my orders are to let no one in."

"Not even me?" the boy asked, clearly trying for a grin and failing.

"Orders are orders, I'm afraid, so—wait a moment. There might be something I can do. A very small thing, you understand."

"Yes?" At once, the child perked up, eager and hopeful in a heartbeat. Rand was so glad to see this, he had a flash of remorse for what he was about to do. He throttled it. This was for the lad's welfare . . . and his sister's.

"It is true," he said, "that I'm to allow no callers past this door. On the other hand, no one said a thing about, ah, communicating *through* the door. Can you make do with that?"

"What a splendid fellow you are, Hawk! I *knew* I could count you as a friend." Jamie cast an appraising glance at the heavy oak door. "Er . . . shall I knock, or will you?"

"Oh, it must be you," Rand assured him. "I ought to have as little"—he moved down the corridor as he spoke—"to do with it as possible. And you'll want privacy, so I'll simply take myself out of earshot . . . like this," he added with a wink.

Throwing him a grin, Jamie turned and knocked.

But Rand carefully kept himself within hearing range. As a result, he was privy to a conversation that raised the hairs on the back of his neck. A conversation conducted almost entirely in Latin, courtesy of the resourceful and clever Lady Emilie!

Fortunately, thanks to a childhood tutor named Snopes, Rand understood every word. By the time it was over, he itched to grab Jamie and his aunt, give them a shake and ask if they'd both lost their minds.

"Thank you, ever so much, Hawk," Jamie called over his shoulder as he left. "I won't forget this—and that's a promise!"

Rand ground out an oath as he watched him disappear around the corner. Devil take it, those children were planning to run away! Jamie, his sister, and their cousin—with the aunt's blessing. The little *fools.* Roderik would fry them up and eat them all for supper!

"Do the boots fit?" Jamie whispered into the dark. He knew Leonie was beside him only from the rustling sounds she made in the hay as she changed clothes. Lamps were never left burning inside the stables overnight for fear of fire, and the light from the lanterns hanging outside didn't penetrate the inky gloom of the loft.

"A deal better than Collie's shirt and breeches," Leonie muttered, fumbling with the laces of the boots Jamie had procured from the stable lad. "The shirt's huge, while these breeches . . . well, they're frightfully snug!"

"Best we could do," her brother offered apologetically. "The other lads are all mostly my size . . . and Sam's."

"Speaking of Sam," she said, and Jamie heard the worry in her voice, "do you really think he's fit to travel?" Though they'd planned to give Sam more time to heal, Lady Emilie had insisted they leave tonight. With the regent at a farewell ball for the Swiss ambassador, she'd pointed out, there'd be no better time. They needed all the advantage they could get.

The prince sighed. "Sam says he is, and we'll just have to take him at his word." Upon his return from that awkward exchange through an oak door, Jamie had found his cousin awake and anxious. He'd relayed Lady Emilie's advice, and while Leonie fretted that tonight was too soon, Sam wouldn't hear of waiting.

"I think he'd go even if he had to crawl out of here," Jamie whispered now. "He's . . . I think he's that frightened, Leonie, of being anywhere near his father. I've never seen him so scared—not that I blame him."

"Poor child," she murmured, "cursed with that monster for a father. Thank God, his mother loves him. Please don't say anything to Sam, but I heard him cry out for her while he was—Jamie, Aunt doesn't know, does she? What Roderik did to him, I mean?" They'd agreed not to tell Emilie about this beating. The poor woman was already worried sick about her son. They'd decided telling her would be pointless and cruel.

"I didn't say anything, if that's what you're asking," Jamie replied, indignant. "She asked where Sam was, though, and I told her he was with you and—well, I had to tell her the Scarecrow was in on it. That's when she sounded a bit . . . well, I think she suspects something, but that's all. She's awfully clever, you know. When I explained about Hawk allowing us to talk through the door, she switched to Latin. Good thing mine's up to snuff!"

"Which is more than can be said of your French," his sister muttered as she finished lacing the boots. "Now, where's that hat?"

"Here—and do hurry! They'll be wondering what's keeping us." They'd decided to leave in pairs to make detection harder and meet in the forest behind the stables. Jamie's cronies already had the horses waiting there. Sam, also in borrowed clothes, had gone off with Petrie half an hour earlier.

"I doubt it," she replied, stuffing her thick braid under a cap that smelled of hay and horses. "Sam wasn't able to move very fast, which is why—"

"Sst—someone's coming!"

Both dropped to the loft floor, and not a moment too soon. A murmur of indistinct voices became louder as the stable doors opened. *"Eh, bien,"* came to them very clearly, followed by a string of other words, all in French.

"What are they saying?" Jamie whispered, wishing he'd paid better attention to his French lessons. "Who the devil *are* th—"

Leonie gripped his arm, signaling silence. She knew these voices. The rough cadences and crude accents of their rapid French were all too familiar. These were the men Roderik had met in the woods. Lying absolutely still, she concentrated on what was being said, and got an earful.

Sweet merciful heaven, she thought several tense minutes later. Disgruntled over a message that Roderik couldn't see them tonight, the Frenchmen were finally leaving. *They're plotting to return Napoleon to power! And Uncle's in league with them. But Boney's on that island, and Mirandeau's allied with the powers that put him there. Which means that Roderik . . . this is* treason!

"Whew!" Jamie exclaimed when the doors closed behind the five strangers. "I was afraid they'd—Leonie, who *are* those men?"

She debated telling him, then decided against it. Such men were dangerous, and knowing about them could be equally dangerous. The less Jamie knew, the better.

But this also confirmed how dangerous the regent was. No wonder he wanted to rule without interference! He was a traitor to his country, and it was her duty to—no, she didn't have the luxury of pursuing this, even if she knew how, which she didn't. She had to concern herself entirely with their escape.

"They're thieves," she told her brother. *Not exactly a lie, since they're planning to steal a throne.* "I wish we could do something about it," she added, grabbing her saddle pack and moving down the ladder, "but we'll have to leave them to the palace guards. It's what they're hired for, after all."

"Hawk'll put an end to their mischief, I'll wager," Jamie muttered as he followed her down. He heaved a sigh. "A shame I shan't be here to see it. I'm truly going to miss him, Leonie. Wouldn't it be famous if Hawk came with us?"

Leonie felt her face warm. She, too, would miss the man. Hawk Randall had never once treated her like anything but a normal person. She'd even had a small hope . . . well, some things simply weren't meant to happen. Not to her, at any rate. "Do be sensible," she said to her brother. "Randall works for the regent. He'd be the *last* person to come with us."

"He'd come if he knew why we're escaping," Jamie replied with the stubborn faith of a nine year old. "He would!"

As it happened, he was not to be disappointed.

Leonie worried her lip with her teeth as she guided Raven away from the Rienna. Was it her imagination, or was the forest too quiet tonight? It was certainly darker than she remembered. Then again, she couldn't recall ever riding this deeply into it. Perhaps it was merely that clouds now hid the sliver of moon that had aided them earlier. A backward glance took in Sam, Petrie, and then Jamie, following her in single file. Beyond them, under a faint sprinkling of stars just visible through the trees, the river glistened here and there, but was largely discernible only by its sound.

A sound that was fading as they left the certainty of the river farther behind, she thought glumly. Shadows lay thick along the path, and nothing looked familiar. Was she right to have left the river where they had, to head west at that point? She wasn't certain. Perhaps she ought to have asked the others. But they were following her lead, with the assumption she knew what she was about. Asking might have worried the boys, and she hadn't wanted to risk that. If only she'd been able to determine how far upriver they'd ridden!

Before leaving the palace, she'd found a map of the area and shared it with Petrie. Then she'd committed it to memory, insisting he do the same. Yet now they were actually traveling the route, little seemed to correspond with what was in her head. Only the path of the river had been apparent. Not for the first time in the two or so hours they'd been riding, she felt a ripple of fear: What if they became lost?

They'd come away from the palace so easily, she'd been hopeful . . . elated, even. Now she realized their early success didn't mean they were free and safe. Petrie, it turned out, was more hindrance than help, a complete dolt who couldn't even stay on a horse! They'd had to stop four times so far to help him find the stirrups he'd slipped, or pick him off the ground and heave him back into the saddle. He'd confessed, as well, to having no woods lore . . . but then, neither did she or the boys.

At least the boys were competent riders, she thought, trying to put a positive face on things. Too, she could rely on Raven to pick his way safely over unfamiliar ground. And Sam, who'd been her biggest worry at the outset, was doing admirably, bless him.

If only Raven and the boys could assure her they were going the right way.

Rand ground out an oath as the moon slipped behind a drift of clouds. Without benefit of moonlight, discerning hoofprints even in the spongy ground along the riverbank became bloody damned difficult. Devil take it, he'd lost enough time as it was!

Every hellish thing had conspired to slow him down, he thought irritably as he dismounted to scour the ground for tracks. First, Magnus, whom he'd bribed to take over his watch, had shown up foxed. It had taken an hour to find a willing replacement—a Swede whose ignorance of palace politics kept him from objecting.

But by then, it was going on midnight. Aware the children were set to leave at that hour, he'd raced to the barracks to change, then on to those cursed gypsies, who'd tried to fob him off with an inferior horse. It had taken the better part of an hour—and a deal more coin—to convince them to sell him a decent mount. *Sell* him the beast, not hire it out! It didn't help his mood to know it had been his own fault. Why the devil had he let them see how badly he wanted a sound horse?

There—fresh prints! With a grunt of satisfaction, Rand swung back into the saddle. He urged his horse forward, trying not to think about the possible dangers facing that trio of innocents up ahead. Or the greatest danger of all: the one they fled, when he discovered they'd gone missing.

Leonie gazed helplessly at the unexpected fork in the path. She hadn't an inkling of which branch to take. There was no longer any doubt, she thought with dismay. They were lost.

"Leonie?" Jamie's voice sounded uncertain, trebling her own sense of doubt, and she steeled herself for what followed. "Are we meant to take the right . . . or the left?"

"I—I'm not exactly—"

"I *knew* it!" Petrie shrieked, dropping his reins and waving his arms frantically, which only served to agitate his mount. The gelding flattened its ears and sidestepped nervously. "We're lost, aren't we?" the actor shouted, looking straight at Leonie. "Hopelessly lost! We'll all *die* here—starved to death or eaten by ravening beasts. If that madman doesn't find us first! Oh, I knew I shouldn't have—"

"Mister Petrie!" Doubt and dismay took a back seat to anger, and Leonie sent him a scathing look. "You will cease such maudlin hysterics, sir." She glanced at Sam, saw the pale oval of his face frozen with fear, and glared at the actor. "You are alarming the boys needlessly, and I insist you—"

"Needlessly!" he huffed, but without the hysteria and at a lower volume, Leonie noticed with a small jolt of satisfaction.

"Needlessly," she repeated, encouraged by her success. Petrie might be a theatrical bag of wind, but he was years older than she. That she'd stood up to him—something she'd never dared with any adult, ever—bolstered her confidence.

Doubt and dismay remained in the back seat, and she gave a decisive nod. "We shall stop here for a respite, everyone, while we consider what's to be done. Jamie, what did you fetch from the kitchens?"

"All manner of excellent fare," he cried, catching her confident mood and expanding on it as they all dismounted. "Every morsel came straight from Cook's hand."

"Scones, I'll wager," Sam said dryly.

Leonie was relieved to note his fear had disappeared, at least for the moment. *Now, to find a means of keeping it away . . . and a means of finding the coast!*

"Ahem, Your Highness?"

"Yes, Mr. Petrie?" Leonie's confidence rose another notch as she noted his polite manner of address. The Scarecrow learned quickly, she'd give him that much.

"Er . . . shall I spread this blanket as one might for a picnic?"

"Why, that's an excellent idea, Mr. Petrie. But first, sir,

we must secure our mounts. Only my Raven is trained not to—*what was that?"*

Petrie froze. He'd heard it, too, and so had the horses. Their ears pricked, and Raven raised his elegant head, his nostrils quivering as he tested the air.

"S-someone's coming," Sam whispered.

Hearing his fear, Leonie placed a comforting hand on his shoulder. She tried to quell her own trembling while her eyes swept the pitch black of the surrounding woods. Nothing moved. It had grown eerily quiet.

Then she noted the horses. All four were intent on the darkness beyond the fork. She strained to see what had caught their attention—

As three men with pistols broke through the trees.

Rand puzzled over the prints that had led him westward since veering away from the river a good hour earlier. The reappearance of the moon allowed him to make better progress, but it also revealed something he hadn't noted before. There were four horses in the children's party, not three. And from the depth of one animal's prints, its rider was heavier than the others. An adult, then, which could be a good thing—*if* their companion knew what he was about.

Who the devil could it be? One of the guards? Doubtful, for while the men were fond of the children—Jamie, in particular—it was highly unlikely they'd chance the regent's wrath. Then perhaps a relative, some distant relation sufficiently removed from the palace to escape Roderik's influence. Yet given the extent of the regent's reach, this was equally unlikely. Moreover, no such individual had turned up in his investigations, and he'd been thorough, even by Whitehall's standards.

He tried to remember if Jamie or his aunt had mentioned an escort, but nothing came to mind. True, parts of their exchange had been inaudible murmurs, not that this had concerned him at the time. After all, what he *had* heard was sufficient to apprise him of what was afoot . . . and give him waking nightmares ever since. Now, however, discovering the children had been prudent enough to take an adult—an *armed* adult, he hoped—let him breathe a bit easier. For the first time since learning of their foolish enterprise—*bloody hell!*

Rand froze as pistol shots exploded up ahead. "So much for breathing easier," he growled and, with an added curse, spurred the gypsy mare forward. Crouched over her withers as she ate up the ground, he told himself it could have been the unknown adult firing to protect his charges.

The musket rifle he slid from the saddle said he didn't believe it for a minute.

"Best learn 'at nag some manners right quick, laddie." The largest of the men who'd come at them with pistols waved his at Raven. Leonie was the laddie he addressed. "Next time it'll be ol' Wally 'oo shoots," he snarled, "an' I won't be aimin' over 'is bleedin' 'ead!"

Leonie nodded fearfully at the brutish looking Wally. She took him to be the leader of these outlaws, though it was his cohorts who'd sent two balls whizzing over their heads a moment ago. *To put a proper scare into us,* she decided, *and they've certainly succeeded!*

She tried desperately to calm Raven, who'd just tried to take a chunk out of the man's arm. Bad enough these churls were about to steal the horses. She couldn't bear it if they felt her enraged stallion wasn't worth the trouble and shot him instead. They still might. Raven was not at all pleased with this bully-ruffian who'd tried to seize his reins from her. Her normally sweet-tempered mount was regarding Wally with blood in his eye.

"Nick"—Wally indicated the smaller of his companions, a blond man with a scar—"them ponies ain't a-tall puny. Oughta do ye real nice. Take the bay. Lem, you can 'ave t'other."

"I ain't ridin' no pint size nag!" cried Lem, a short, stocky man with black whiskers bristling across his face. "What about *'is* 'orse?" He jerked a thumb over his shoulder, indicating the quaking, ashen-faced Petrie.

Wally glanced at Petrie's gelding, then cast a shrewd eye over Raven, who pawed the ground and continued to regard him with blatant hostility. The brigand shook his head. "Wish I could oblige ye, Lem, but I fancies 'at un, meself. Ye'll ride yon pony or"—he dipped his chin at the snorting stallion—"the black. Take yer pick."

Growling an obscenity, Lem shoved his spent pistol into his belt and grabbed the pony's reins from Sam. The child backed away fearfully. This brought him next to Leonie, who put her arm around him, and motioned for her brother to join them. Jamie surrendered his pony, Jumper, to Nick with a glare, and moved to her side. Petrie, meanwhile, had dropped his gelding's reins and was inching away from the outlaws. He looked, Leonie thought with a mixture of pity and disgust, as if he were about to faint.

"What about the black devil?" Nick asked. The empty pistol he used to gesture at Raven was still smoking, and Leonie took heart. With only one loaded weapon among them, perhaps the brigands weren't planning to shoot everyone, as she'd feared. And since they weren't willing to risk their necks on Raven, she might even be spared the theft of her beloved stallion.

Wally's next words put paid to the latter. " 'E's a right 'andsome stud, 'e is. Oughta fetch a good price."

"I dunno, Wally." Nick scratched his head with his pistol barrel. "Flashy brute like 'at . . . somebody might rek-a-nize 'im, 'mongst the gentry, I mean." He eyed Leonie's party in their homely garments. "This lot likely stole the nags theirselves," he added with a snigger.

"An' 'at stud be a wild un," Lem put in peevishly. "Oo's gonna 'andle 'im—*you?*"

"We ain't takin' 'im t' no gentry," Wally replied smugly. "There's them gypsies we seen, an' gypsies knows their 'orseflesh. Won't ask no questions, neither."

"But gypsies ain't got none o' the ready," Lem protested. "Ain't worth—"

"Shut yer gob! If they ain't got the blunt, we'll take some o' their own nags in trade—nags what ain't so flashy. As fer 'oo'll 'andle the stud till 'e's sold"—Wally glanced at Raven, then at Raven's owner—"why, the laddie 'ere, will do."

Leonie swallowed thickly as the thief sent her a nasty grin. *Is he saying what I think he's saying?*

"We're takin' 'im with us," said Wally, confirming her fears.

"I think not," came an adamant male voice from the inky darkness beyond the clearing.

All heads swung in that direction. A tall figure separated itself from the shadows, moonlight glinting off the polished barrel of a musket rifle held at the ready.

"It's Hawk!" Jamie shouted with obvious delight.

Wally aimed and fired.

Eight

Leonie wrapped her arms around the boys and ducked as gunfire shattered the night. She kept her eyes squeezed shut, but this only enhanced her awareness of the nightmare exploding around them. Rough curses, shouts, and the shrill neighs of horses rang in her ears. The acrid smell of gunpowder stung her nose. Worse yet was the taste of fear on her tongue.

The assault to her senses was so overwhelming, several seconds passed before she realized it had grown oddly quiet. Only the restless movements and snorts of the horses broke the stillness. Was everyone else dead? Deciding that knowing the worst might be better than imagining it, she risked a peek—and gasped.

A body lay on the ground. Not Hawk Randall's, as she'd imagined, but Wally's. The brigand had taken a ball through the chest . . . a direct hit to the heart, she suspected. But . . . where were the others? A haze of sulfurous smoke hung in the air, making it hard to see through the gloom. Blinking to clear her eyes, she gazed dazedly about, only half aware of the pair of nine year olds squirming in her embrace.

"Leonie, do let go!"

At Jamie's protest, she loosened her death grip. He scampered away, but Sam clung to her side, even when her hold slackened. "The bad man's dead, Leonie," he whispered.

"Princess?" Rand was still dealing with the shock of learning who this was. He'd come upon the scene in a panic, dreading what he'd find. His dread had intensified when he stole close and saw neither Leonie nor the adult in her party, despite the presence of four mounts. And the presence of a third lad had mystified him.

Yet before he had time to puzzle it out, he'd been forced to act. Then came the shock: The laddie the dead outlaw had mentioned was Princess Leonie. Her brother and cousin had just confirmed it. "Are you all right?" he asked, running anxious eyes over the slight figure in boy's attire.

Leonie looked up, met his concerned gaze and . . . ridiculous to think of amethysts right now, but there it was: Hawk Randall's eyes, reminding her of amethysts. Eyes that were almost too beautiful for a man, she found herself thinking next. Thick lashed and luminous, in the faint moonlight they held just a hint of that violet shade she knew she'd never forget. "I—I'm fine, Mr. Randall," she murmured. Then, managing a shaky smile, "Owing to you, sir. Thank heaven you happened to—"

"Hawk!" Jamie shouted from across the clearing. "The other two got away!" He'd retrieved Jumper and Sam's pony, Puck, and was squinting into the darkness beyond the path.

Rand had just hunkered down to ask Sam how he was faring. It disturbed him that the child backed away. He was clearly terrified, his small face pinched and drawn. Was he in pain?

"Hawk?" Jamie sounded impatient. "Aren't we going after those villains?"

Rand glanced at him, then back at his sister. "I believe we may safely assume His Highness has survived the ordeal unscathed," he said wryly. "How shall I answer him?"

Amethysts washed by moonlight, and no mistake. "Um . . . answer him?"

Sam tugged shyly at her sleeve. "Jamie wants to help chase the bad men," he offered in a tone that said he didn't think this was a good idea.

"Chase the . . ." Leonie dragged her gaze from those incredible eyes, gave herself a mental shake, and glared at her brother. "Jameson Kendrik William Fairchild Aulaire, you are going nowhere *near* those men!"

This elicited a groan from Jamie, and Rand smothered a chuckle. As he got up and surveyed the area for danger, he found himself thinking how fond he'd grown of the young scamp. Jamie Kendrik William Fairchild Aulaire was all boy, but he had courage and heart and would make a fine ruler one day. *If I can keep him out of trouble long enough to survive.*

"Leonie, you sounded just like your mama," he heard Sam murmur as he left them to fetch the gypsy mare before she wandered off.

"I expect I did." Leonie smoothed a lock of hair from Sam's brow, which was damp with sweat. He didn't look well, which worried her, but she managed to keep her tone light. "That's because Mama only used all of Jamie's names when he was meant to know she was not amused."

Hiding a smile, Rand urged them to sit on a fallen log and rest. As he went to help Jamie secure the horses, he mused on that princely string of names. *Kendrik* was their grandsire's name, Leona's maiden name explained the *Fairchild,* and *Aulaire* was the present royal house of Mirandeau's surname. But *William* . . . Had Roderik known that one of the names bestowed on his heir belonged to his wife's former—

A moan arose from the shadows near his feet and drew him up short. "What the devil?"

A long, lank figure writhed amid the bracken beside the path. As Rand trained the musket rifle on it, it shifted, rolled to its side, and moaned again.

"On your feet," he ordered brusquely. A patch of moonlight had fallen on the man's face, and he tried to remember if any of the outlaws had red hair. "And I should move very carefully, if I were you."

"Sir, I beg of you, d-don't sh-shoot!"

"I say!" exclaimed Jamie, coming to have a look. "It's the Scare—er, Mr. Petrie. I was wondering where you'd gone to."

"Y-your Highness, please tell this person not to shoot

me!" Petrie groped his way to a sitting position, yelped, and clutched his arm. "I've taken a hit! I'm wounded!"

"You know this man?" Rand asked the prince.

"He's our tutor . . . or he used to be. Er, that is, we *thought* he was, but he really wasn't, 'cause he was just pretending to be a tutor, but—"

"Hold a moment!" Putting up a hand to halt the tumble of words, Rand watched in fascination as Petrie unfolded himself and, whimpering, staggered to his feet. *The missing adult, and a right sorry specimen. That wound he's bemoaning looks as serious as a pimple. Difficult to imagine this odd lean shanks as a useful escort.* "He's traveling with you, I collect." he said to Jamie.

"Well, of course I am!" Petrie huffed, somewhat bolder now that Rand had lowered his weapon. "What did you take me for, one of those dastardly—"

"Someone help me with Sam!" Leonie's alarmed voice cut across the clearing. "He's fainted, and his shirt's wet with blood!"

"In truth, I suspected Sam shouldn't be traveling this soon after . . . after the beating he took, Mr. Randall," Leonie admitted, gazing worriedly at her cousin. Sam had awakened in pain while his wounds were redressed, then immediately fallen into an exhausted slumber. He looked so thin and pale lying there in his blanket, she couldn't help wondering if this entire enterprise hadn't been a ghastly mistake.

Yet when she thought of Roderik—no, she mustn't think of that monster now. Tired as she was, she might say too much. Bad enough Jamie had rattled on to Randall about escaping to England and divulged the regent's hand in the beating, too, before she'd stopped him. Jamie had formed a hero worship for Hawk Randall and was blindly trusting, but she had to be more prudent. As she'd once pointed out, Randall was hired by the regent. Even if he had rescued them from those outlaws, who was to say he wouldn't return them to the palace in the morning? Who was to say he hadn't been sent to fetch them back?

"Unfortunately," she continued as Rand added wood to the fire, "Sam wouldn't hear of waiting, and Lady Emilie felt there was no better time." She paused, biting her lip, for she'd been about to tell him more than she intended.

"Your aunt planned this for tonight *knowing* her son was in no condition to—"

"No! That is, we kept Sam's condition from her . . . not wanting to worry her, you see. But she knew that Sam . . . I mean, we all feared for . . . for his safety."

Rand nodded grimly, noting her reluctance to mention her uncle. He suspected he'd still be under the impression it was again a lackey who'd beaten Sam—horrendous enough, but not quite as incriminating of the regent—if Jamie hadn't let the cat out of the bag. *Poor child . . . she doesn't trust me, not that I blame her. When the cousin you adore has been beaten bloody by your uncle, your trust in the adult world has a way of becoming very fragile.*

"And now," Leonie said with a distraught sigh, "I—I don't know what to think. We can't go back." She cast Rand a swift glance before returning her gaze to Sam. "Yet what good will going forward do if"—she managed to contain a sob—"if it endangers my cousin's life?"

No, you can't go back. Now that he had the grim facts, Rand knew there was no question of their returning. He still found it difficult to control his rage at what Roderik had done. But he'd deal with their need to escape him in the morning. His job now was to keep this child—had he really thought her less courageous than her brother?—from falling apart. Shaken by all they'd endured, she'd held up remarkably, but this new fear for Sam threatened to undo her.

"It isn't as bad as it looks," he said, his voice calm and reassuring. "The lad isn't feverish, and his wounds didn't appear infected. I'm no physician, but I've seen men wounded in battle. I believe he fainted from sheer exhaustion, nothing more."

"My fault," she said tightly. "I should have stopped to let him rest and—"

"You mustn't blame yourself. Perhaps you pushed a little harder than was wise, but I suspect the lad didn't let on he was in difficulty. How were you to judge? It's possible a good night's sleep will restore him."

While she mulled this over, he glanced at Jamie and his erstwhile tutor, another puzzle to be sorted out in the morning, both fast asleep on the other side of the fire. The outlaw's shot had grazed the redhead's arm. As he'd suspected, Petrie sustained a mere flesh wound, despite the carrying on. *He'll survive, more's the pity!*

Leonie stifled a yawn, and Rand noted the tired droop of her shoulders, the bruises of exhaustion under her eyes. She'd pushed herself as hard as anyone. "Princess, hadn't you better get some sleep?"

"Oh, but I—"

"Please don't worry," he said, seeing her eyes dart to Sam. "I'll be on watch." He patted the musket rifle at his side. "I promise to wake you if his lordship requires tending."

Leonie hesitated, then nodded and mustered a grateful smile. He was taking care of so much they'd never thought of, much less be able to accomplish on their own. From disposing of the outlaw's body to foraging for the horses and building a fire, Hawk Randall had proved a godsend. Or so she hoped. Heaven help them if he'd been sent not by God, but by Roderik!

Just then Sam stirred, thrusting his blanket aside and murmuring something in his sleep. Before Leonie could move, Rand reached over and felt his brow. "His lordship remains comfortably cool," he assured her.

Leonie watched him tuck the blanket carefully back around the child. It was a tender, caring gesture, and she felt a twinge of guilt for doubting him. Telling herself she couldn't afford such feelings, she thrust the guilt aside. She knew very little about Hawk Randall, and while his kindness to Sam appeared genuine, he could still be Roderik's man.

Still, that kindness was a mark in his favor. She gave him a tired smile. "In private, those of us who care about my cousin call him Sam, Mr. Randall. I suspect he'd like it if you called him that, too."

"I'd be honored, Princess. And, please, His Highness's, ah, tactics aside, perhaps it's time—that is, I should be doubly honored if you'd all address me as Hawk."

Their eyes met, and held. Each was remembering the last time he'd suggested this. In the darkness beyond the fire, an owl hooted. A chunk of burning wood collapsed, sending up a shower of sparks. Caught in the memory, neither moved, though Leonie's mind couldn't rest. There was too much to consider. And Hawk Randall had suddenly become a major figure in those considerations.

Only yesterday, she mused, she'd stood conversing with him, miffed at nothing worse than Jamie's shenanigans. So much had changed, that seemed to belong to another lifetime. She was not the same green girl she'd been then. If Sam truly was on the mend, she thought as an idea jelled in her mind, then England was still possible.

No, not the same girl at all, though it remains to be seen how Hawk Randall will react.

"Very well . . . Hawk," she said around a yawn, reaching for her sleeping blanket. "But as the boys and I have agreed to take assumed names with our disguises," she added with a faint smile, "in future you must call me Leon."

Leonie was not having a good morning. True, it had begun well, for Sam had come through the night much improved. He'd awakened hungry, an encouraging sign, and ate a modest breakfast. He rejected Petrie's offer of the last of the laudanum, too, saying he didn't need it, and she'd sighed in relief. She'd even laughed when the actor downed the dose himself, and Jamie comically mimed the Scarecrow bleating over his injured arm. Sam actually giggled.

After that, it was all downhill. First, with his incessant complaining over his wretched arm, Petrie had begun to give her the headache. With an eye to escaping him, she'd limped to the stream Hawk had discovered, bent over it to wash up—and slipped. The result was a soaking of her shirt. It was now drying on a bush while she made do with one of Jamie's.

Then she'd had to deal with her brother. When she instructed him not to give Hawk any more information, Jamie had been difficult. "Hawk's our friend!" he'd protested, so loudly she could only thank her stars Randall had been out scouting the area for trouble and couldn't hear. It was only when she revealed her plan that Jamie had been mollified.

Now she had to muster the courage to go through with that plan. Her stomach was in knots as she waited for Hawk's return. What if he said no?

Heaving a sigh as she busied herself finger-combing Raven's mane, she told herself to be sensible. No sense borrowing trouble before it came. If Hawk refused, she'd have her answer soon enough. She'd cross that bridge if she came to it. Meanwhile, she wondered if binding and gagging would be too harsh for someone with a bandaged arm.

Satisfied the outlaws were long gone, Rand made a final reconnaissance of the area and headed back to camp. He'd detected no signs of pursuit from the palace, but that could quickly change. Lady Emilie might contrive to delay the discovery of her son's disappearance, but the absence of the prince and princess was another matter. The regent would soon learn they'd gone missing and instigate a search. It was imperative he fail in that search, and that meant getting the children out of Mirandeau.

It was fortuitous they were already set on going to England. Even more fortuitous that the Foreign Office had a ship cruising off the coast, a ship that was at the marquis of Hawksrest's disposal. He was reasonably certain, providing he accepted full responsibility, that the naval officer in charge could be persuaded to carry them all to England. A perfect solution in many ways.

But there were problems with such an arrangement as well. Beginning with his own interests in the royal children. Divulging his ties to the Foreign Office could frighten them, even if he were at liberty to reveal the nature of his mission, which at this point he was not. His promise to William had best remain hidden, too, for now. The uncertainty in Princess Leonie's eyes was hard to ignore. She still wasn't sure she could trust him.

Jamie, of course, was a different matter, even if poor Sam was not. With what had been done to Sam by his own sire, it could be a long time before the lad trusted as easily as his cousin, if indeed he ever did. It was crucial to gain the trust of all three children before he divulged more.

In truth, trust was the critical factor all around. There was the odd presence of the even odder Mr. Petrie. The Scarecrow, as Jamie had aptly dubbed him. What was he doing here? Until it was firmly established that Petrie was trustworthy, Rand would be on his guard. And until he established his own credibility, the princess and Sam would be on theirs.

Then there was Whitehall and its agenda. He hoped to glean something useful for the Foreign Office, but with or without such intelligence, he was resolved to see Leona's children safely to England. What was to be done with them then, he'd no idea. Perhaps William would have some suggestions. Including how to deal with Whitehall, once they learned he'd as good as kidnapped the prince of a sovereign power.

Rand returned to find Jamie and Sam saddling their ponies. The other mounts still awaited their tack, which lay on the ground. Nearby, the tutor gingerly circled his gelding, saddle blanket held limply in one hand. He eyed the placid animal with such obvious trepidation Rand almost felt sorry for him.

"Hawk, may I speak with you?"

It was the feminine voice that saved her. He'd been looking for Leonie near the horses. Had the voice at his back been male, he'd have acted with the hair-trigger reflex that had saved his life on many a mission. As it was, he released his breath in a *whoosh,* carefully released the musket rifle, and dismounted.

"A word of caution, Leon," he said tightly as he turned to face her. He found himself glad she'd given him leave to use that name; it somehow made admonishment easier. "Never—and I mean *never*—steal upon an armed man from behind. I might have shot you!"

"I—I didn't know . . . I mean I . . ." Her cheeks flaming, Leonie dropped her gaze. "I'm dreadfully s-sorry. It—it won't happen again," she stammered, staring intently at her feet.

She looked so miserable, Rand immediately regretted his tone. He reminded himself she was a sheltered princess, a fragile hothouse blossom quite unused to such rough disapprobation.

Yet he still felt nettled, though it had nothing to do with his blunt speech. The princess he'd thought a child was no such thing.

Before him, seen in bright sunlight for the first time since she'd donned boy's attire, was a woman. Slender and petite, to be sure, but undeniably female and ripe, with high, round, pertly thrust breasts and sweetly curving hips. Curves all too evident in that snug shirt and breeches that fit like a second skin. Not to mention a pair of long, lithe legs that—*Christ!*

Dragging his eyes from the all too distracting sight—where the devil had she come by clothing that tight, anyway?—he focused on her face. Or tried to, for she was still staring unhappily at her toes.

" 'Tis I who should apologize," he said, gently raising her chin with a touch of his knuckles. "My tone was ill chosen. Although my fear for you caused it, that is no excuse for harsh words. Can you forgive me?"

" 'Twas nothing. A-a fleabite," she murmured, meeting his gaze with difficulty. It was more than that, of course, but she'd die before letting him know it. Her gaffe had brought the acute return of all the old discomfort. They were no longer runaway princess and friendly guard. He was back to being an impossibly handsome stranger, while she was just an ugly cripple with no social graces.

"You wished to speak with me," he reminded her with a smile. He gestured in the direction of the stream just visible through the trees. "Join me while I water my horse?"

Managing a nod, she followed him mutely to the stream, never more conscious of her limp. With the return of her awkwardness, she found her courage slipping. What she had to propose seemed entirely possible last night. Yet now that the time had come, uncertainty loomed, with not a shred of confidence to bolster her resolve.

Sensing her diffidence, Rand silently cursed his insensitivity. How could he have forgotten his earliest impressions of the princess? Of that frightened child.

Was that it, then? Had learning she was not a child somehow led him to assume she was therefore not as fragile, not as frightened? He supposed it had, and he cursed himself again. She'd lived for months under Roderik's thumb. That alone was enough to cow any creature, child, or woman. Just look at poor Sam and Lady Emilie.

"Do sit," he said gently, "while I take care of the lass, here." He patted the mare and led her to drink while Leonie obediently lowered herself to the mossy bank beside the stream. Rand saw she was still nervous. Skittish as a newborn foal, judging by the way she started when he left the mare and dropped down beside her.

He gave her a grin meant to ease her apprehension. "While I've been known to run headlong into people on occasion," he said with a playful wink, "I give you my word, I don't bite."

His wink reminded her of one occasion in particular, and Leonie had to smile. "As I recall, 'twas I did the headlong thing last time."

"Ah, but you had that tower of books to excuse you," he replied with a grin that threatened to melt her insides. "While I'd but my own clumsy feet to blame."

There was a pregnant silence as Leonie's gaze dropped to her crippled foot. *Trust me, Hawk Randall, you know nothing of clumsy feet.*

It was as if he'd heard her. "For the second time in minutes," he told her as his gaze followed hers, "I find myself in need of your forgiveness. It seems I am clumsy of tongue, if nothing else. I sincerely beg your pardon and—"

"It is I should beg yours," she cut in hastily, wishing she could recall her unseemly thoughts, hating herself for them, as well as for stupidly calling attention to the last thing she wanted him to notice. She recalled something her mother had once said: *The art of getting on in the Polite World is to conduct oneself with the aim of putting others at their ease.* "I—I made you feel uncomfortable . . . and I am sorry for it."

"A fleabite," he countered with a disarming smile, reaching for her hand and lifting it gently to his lips. "Now," he added, hoping the pulse fluttering at her throat didn't indicate displeasure with the courtly gesture, "I've but one thing to add, and then perhaps we may put this behind us, yes?"

Leonie could only nod. The hand his lips had touched felt their imprint like a brand. And her heart was beating, beating! So hard she feared he could hear it. *Silly girl, do be sensible. Stop mooning over nothing, and pay attention to what he's saying.*

"I was unwise in my choice of words," Rand told her, "because I grew careless. You see, I long ago stopped noticing your lame foot. It simply didn't—"

"Stopped noticing!" Was he making game of her? "How could you possibly?"

Rand stopped to ponder this, for he really hadn't thought about it. "I suppose," he said after a moment, "it's because I live with someone who lost his leg in the war. My father. The fact that he now wears a wooden one and goes about with the aid of a cane . . . well, it has simply ceased to matter. It is merely a part of who he is, and as normal as—as rain in England."

She sat there dumbfounded for a moment, digesting this. "Your father," she said at last, "must be a very special man." *More to the point,* you *are, to afford him that normalcy in your eyes.*

"He is."

Though he let the words stand unadorned, she heard a wealth of meaning behind them. Hawk Randall loved his father, of that she had no doubt. She longed to ask him more. What had his childhood been like to bring about that bond? Had it been loving and happy, like hers? Was his father like him, or different? What kind of life did they lead? Was his mother alive? Did he love her? Was he . . . *married?*

Feeling her heart accelerate with that final query, she chastised herself severely. *Do be sensible. What business of yours is any of it?*

Suddenly it was easier to approach him about more practical matters. "Hawk, I've something to ask you."

He'd been studying her face, wondering at the fleeting emotions that crossed it. An expressive face, as he'd noted before. Now his awareness of her as an adult led him to see a deal more. Her green eyes complemented the coppery hair, which had a delightful tendency to form charming tendrils around the heart-shaped face. Wider than fashion dictated, her mouth hinted at a hidden sensuality she wasn't yet aware of. And some would abjure the freckles across her nose, but he saw how they drew attention to its fine-boned perfection. Indeed, drew attention to a face he found . . . ethereal and delicate. In fact, Leonie of Mirandeau had an elfin beauty that would tempt many a man. But not him, of course. Never him.

"Hawk?" Leonie prompted, wondering at his sudden frown.

"Uh, sorry . . . woolgathering, I confess. Do ask your question."

"Well, as you may know, we were hoping to reach England, where my mother had family we thought to visit."

He smiled. "Come, Leon, say what you mean. You are in need of a safe haven . . . for Sam."

So he was offering plain speech. Well, perhaps that was best all round. "Yes," she said, "and I wish to hire you to get us there."

Nine

"You wish to *hire* me?" With a surreptitious glance at her boy's breeches, Rand wondered how many more surprises Leonie had in store. He'd been pondering how to go about offering escort, for it had to be done without arousing her suspicion. In the end, he'd hoped she might broach it herself, and now she had. He just hadn't expected her to do it on a work-for-hire basis. Yet it made perfect sense: If she paid him, then his motive for coming was simple, and under her control. It was neither of those things, of course, but for now he had to let her think so.

Leonie sighed. "I realize it's a great deal to ask. I mean . . . well, you *are* in the—the palace's employ. . . ."

Aware of her measuring gaze, Rand kept his face bland. "I swore an oath to protect the royal family, but I signed no written terms of employment. I was told either party could end the arrangement if it didn't suit . . . without penalty."

"And without notice?" she asked skeptically.

"I own, it would be . . . untoward done that way." He affected an insouciant shrug. "I expect the result would be no worse than being turned off without a character." *Until the regent puts two and two together. How good are you at sums, lass?* He gave another shrug. "I've survived worse."

"Hawk, do be sensible. When it's discovered you've gone missing along with us, there could be a great deal worse."

"I take your point," he said, biting back a smile. *Awake upon all suits, and no mistake.*

"Escorting us out of the country," she continued, as if explaining to a difficult child, "would mean putting yourself at considerable risk." She dug into a pocket and withdrew a small packet, which she handed to him. "I'm hoping this will . . . will make that risk worthwhile."

While he unwrapped it, Leonie held her breath. Absent the emerald ring, she'd been forced to rely on the few pieces of jewelry she herself owned, hoping they'd be sufficient to pay their way. Unfortunate that she'd given Petrie Grandmama's earbobs before she realized how hopeless he was. This was all she had left to barter. *Please, God, let it be enough!*

When he finally uncovered the strand of pearls her parents gave her when she turned eighteen, she swallowed around the lump in her throat. Unlike the earbobs, left to her by a grandmother she barely remembered, the pearls held memories dear to her.

"Handsome," he murmured, holding them up to catch the dappled sunlight filtering through the trees.

Encouraged, she said, "Mr. Petrie has of me a pair of ruby earbobs, only one of which he was to retain for his services. He felt the other should be sufficient to barter for our passage, and I shall hold him to that. I'll tell him he may keep the one for his trouble. That is, if you replace him . . . not that I expect him to complain. We'll say it's because of his, 'er, wound."

Rand snorted. "No doubt he'll believe it, too."

She smiled. "He is a bit of a put-on, isn't he?"

"A *bit* of one—*hah!* If he'd moaned one more time, I'd have strangled him with that blasted bandage!"

She smothered a giggle. "Simon Petrie was an actor at the Drury Lane before he was engaged to—that is, before he became a tutor."

"An actor," he said, storing away that bit of information for later. He gave an exasperated shake of the head. "Whatever possessed you to take him on?"

She heaved a sigh. "Desperation, I suppose. But he *is* English, and presumed to know the best means of reaching our destination. Beyond that, well, he was privy to what—

what had happened to Sam, and seemed genuinely sympathetic."

Rand nodded absently. A shaft of sunlight had fallen across her face, and he was caught by the porcelain-fine quality of her skin. It was as smooth and lustrous as the pearls he held in his hand. He wondered who'd bought them for her. Wondered, too, how much it was costing her emotionally to part with them. He'd see she got them back, of course. For now, unfortunately, he must play the mercenary. *Devil take it, why does she make me feel uncomfortable in that role?*

"If the earbob isn't adequate to cover expenses," he told her, "these pearls will make up the difference, as well as recompense an escort."

"Does that mean you accept?" she asked, seizing on what his words implied. She hated sounding so desperate, but, as she'd already told him, she *was* desperate. If Randall refused, she'd no idea how to go on. At least he hadn't tried to drive up his price. Was he aware she'd have been unable to meet it if he had?

Watching the play of conflicting emotions cross her elfin face, Rand wanted to warn her, *Never game at cards, lass. You'll give your hand away before it's played.* "My dear Leon," he said with a smile designed to ease her concerns, "you've got yourself an escort."

Within minutes of Leonie's announcing she'd engaged him, Rand had everyone in the saddle. Before leading them out, he paused, meeting the gaze of each with a no-nonsense look. "For safety's sake," he told them, "I wish to establish some basic rules. First, there is to be no unnecessary chatter as we ride. You must be alert for instructions from me. When they come, I expect you to obey them at once, without question. Your safety may depend upon it.

"Finally," he added, with a look at Sam, "anyone in difficulty is to say so. Martyrs are all very well in their place, but that place is not among this company." Then he led them out.

While there were raised eyebrows at his tone, Jamie's were not among them. Well pleased with his sister's success, he wore an ear-to-ear grin. He followed directly behind his hero—down the fork's left prong, as it turned out—with Sam, quiet and subdued, next in line. Then came Petrie, whose sharply raised brows had been telling, with Leonie bringing up the rear.

It didn't sit well with Rand that she rode last, but he had no choice. The risky vanguard must be his, and he couldn't leave the vulnerable rear to a child or a melodramatic rattle-pate like Petrie. She was an excellent equestrienne and was mounted on a superior horse, but speed and horsemanship would go only so far in protecting her if they were attacked from behind. Since the threat he most feared would come from the palace, he had to bank on the fact that the regent's men would know her stallion and desist from endangering its royal rider. Brigands were always a possibility, of course, but they'd be more likely to attack at night, when he'd be better able to guard everyone.

He kept them moving throughout the morning, and they made good time. Still, though he'd on several occasions ridden to the coast and back within a day, Rand had no illusions that such was the case now. He'd traveled alone then, by a far more direct route, using major thoroughfares when it suited him, often cutting across pastures and fields to save time.

Riding through heavy forest, he estimated, would require at least three days to reach the coast, perhaps more. The advantage was the cover provided by the trees; the disadvantage, that it gave Roderik that much more time to organize a hunt and pursue them.

Leonie was pensive as the morning wore on without incident. The tone of Randall's address had at first taken her aback. She wasn't certain what she'd expected, but it hadn't been the blunt speech of a military professional. Yet the more she thought on it, the better she felt. He *was* a professional, and that meant knowing what he was about. For the first time since having this responsibility thrust upon her, she had someone competent to share the enormous weight of it. Hawk Randall, blunt speech and all, made her feel . . . safe.

Shortly after midday, Rand spied sunlight glinting on water and led them through the trees to another stream. Here they paused to rest and water the horses and have a bite themselves. A quick inspection told Rand they'd only enough food for this meal and perhaps one other. Time to do something about that.

"Ever catch a fish?" he asked the boys as Leonie set out bread and chunks of cheese.

"No," said Jamie, an avid gleam in his eye, though Sam merely shook his head and went to sit beside Leonie.

Chewing on a slice of bread, Jamie watched Hawk take a long, flat stone from his pocket. He wanted to ask what it was for, but while his princely education had omitted instruction in fishing, it had taught him not to talk with his mouth full. At least he recognized what Hawk now extracted from his boot.

"Do we stun the fish with the stone," he asked, trying to figure how it was done—and once he'd swallowed, of course—"then finish it off with that knife?"

"Certainly not," said Rand with a chuckle, and began to sharpen the blade. "This is called a whetstone." He held it up. "If we catch a fish, we'll require a means of scaling and cleaning it, and that calls for a well-honed blade. Here," he said, passing both items to Jamie. "You try it."

After a word on the knife's safe handling, Jamie set to, with a grin. After a few awkward passes, he soon found the proper rhythm. Moments later, when Rand tested the blade and pronounced it well honed, the prince laughed. "That was fun!"

Rand's laughter joined his. The lad was a quick study, apparently, at whatever he set his hand to. "Come," he said with a comfortable hand on the prince's shoulder. "I spotted something moving under that ledge"—he pointed downstream—"when we watered the horses. See where it juts out over that pool, where the water's still?"

"Won't we need bait or something?"

Rand cast a glance over his shoulder, hoping Sam had changed his mind. The child was still scrunched up beside the princess, who had an arm around him while she advised Petrie of the best way to secure his horse. With a regretful shake of his head, Rand turned back to Jamie. "If you think you can be very still and quiet, I'll show you how it's done with nothing but your hands. Of course, it wants patience."

With mixed emotions, Leonie watched them go companionably downstream. They were on their way to being fast friends, and she had to be glad of it. While Jamie hadn't pined openly for Papa all these months, she suspected he felt the absence of a father more than he let on. Hawk Randall was filling that absence admirably. She only hoped, when the day came that they must part, as it surely would, losing Hawk wouldn't hurt Jamie overly. Of course, Jamie was made of sterner stuff than most children his age.

Her glance fell at once on Sam, who was quietly nibbling on his cheese. "Shouldn't you like to join the fishing expedition?" she asked with a smile. "I know you were invited."

Mutely, Sam shook his head. A shock of dark hair fell over his face as he focused even more intently on the cheese in his lap.

"Sam?" Using her hand to brush the hair from his face, Leonie gently urged him to look at her. "You nearly always do fun things with Jamie. Will you tell me why you aren't with them?"

He lowered his eyes without speaking, and she thought he wasn't going to answer. At length, he swallowed, and replied in a small, halting voice. "Hawk . . . he was angry. Because I didn't tell . . . about being in difficulty . . . last night. He was right . . . to be angry with me, Leonie, but . . ." The small voice faded, and there was another swallow.

"Oh, sweetheart, I'm sure Hawk wasn't angry with you.

In fact, I don't think he was angry at all. He was just being stern, in the way guards and soldiers are often stern. You see, he was frightened for you—we all were, when you fainted. That stern speech was Hawk's way of asking not just you, but everyone, not to frighten us that way again."

Sam was having none of it. "He was looking at me when he said it."

She sighed. Sam had always been sensitive, but it wasn't like him to be unreasonably touchy. Then again, this was not the Sam she'd always known. This was a nine-year-old child who'd been beaten bloody by his own father. Was he damaged in other ways as well? *Roderik, you monster, you've much to answer for.*

A while later, Hawk and Jamie returned empty-handed. Yet each sported an ear-to-ear grin.

"What, no fish?" Leonie asked.

"Uh . . . no," said Hawk, making her wonder at the conspiratorial glance he shared with Jamie.

"I was too much the rattle-pate," her brother announced, rather as if he were proud of it. "I collect I frightened the fish away."

"We'll try again, this evening." Hawk gestured at the stream. "This appears to be the same tributary we camped about last night. And if I'm not mistaken, it winds in the very direction we're headed. We'll endeavor to camp beside it for our supper. Then we shall see." He threw Jamie a stern look.

"I fear I'm not given to long silences," the prince said with an ostentatious sigh.

Leonie saw him glance at Sam, who sat very still beside her . . . and was definitely listening.

"But I know how it's done," Jamie said to his sister. "You must dangle your hands in the water, like this"—he demonstrated—"but be very still, until the fish grows curious. Soon, it's moving about your fingers"—with one hand, he mimed a swimming fish—"and then you . . . *tickle* it. Fish love to be tickled, and they grow very careless, you see, until"—his hand shot out and grabbed the invisible fish—"got it!"

"Oh, well done!" cried his sister, half-believing she'd seen a live fish in water. Beside her, she felt Sam stir with interest.

"Indeed!" Petrie had been watching, too, and began clapping approvingly. "His High—er, I mean James," he corrected, remembering to use the name Jamie had assumed, "is an excellent mimic."

Grinning, Jamie made an elaborate leg, then sobered at a glance from Hawk. "I'd rather be an excellent fisherman," he said with another sigh.

"Be patient," said Hawk, "and we shall see what develops this evening." He began untethering his mare, a signal they were to be on their way. "Patience is what's wanted," he added—Leonie saw him eyeing Sam—"and a lad who knows how to be quiet and still."

That evening, they did indeed pause beside the meandering stream. And when Hawk asked if there was still a lad about who fancied fish for supper, it wasn't the prince who replied.

"I can show Jamie how to be quiet and still," Sam offered in a small, soft voice.

Leonie held her breath as Hawk Randall hunkered down beside her small cousin until his tall frame no longer loomed above the child. "You're exactly the right person to show him how it's done," he said with a warm smile. "We need you, Sam. Will you join us?"

His answer was a slow, careful nod.

"Good lad." Hawk gently ruffled his hair, then turned to Jamie, who'd been watching with interest. "James," he said with a grin, "I believe we shall have our fish, after all."

The last thing Leonie remembered as she drifted off to sleep that night was the shining joy in her young cousin's eyes as he proudly showed her the two fish he'd caught. And his words, still softly spoken, but the voice no longer small, "You have to know *how* to be quiet."

Setting out cold fish and bread for breakfast the next morning, Leonie found herself alone with Jamie, whom Hawk had asked to help her. Petrie was struggling to saddle the horses, a task he too had been set by their escort, who said he needed the practice. Of course, she'd saddle Raven herself. The stallion had quickly discovered Simon's ineptitude, and took great pleasure in planting his nose at the small of the actor's back and pushing him pell-mell round the campsite.

Sam had also been set a task. He was down at the stream with Hawk, learning how to wrap leftover fish in wet leaves to preserve for later. Watching the small dark head nod as Hawk said something, she noted, with pleasure and relief, the companionable way they worked together.

Hawk had worked magic with Sam, aided in no small way by Jamie. Not every child would have pretended to be a careless chatterbox who'd scared off the fish, when he almost certainly hadn't. Jamie might be charmingly glib at times, but he was no rattle-pate.

"That was a splendid thing you did for Sam last night," she told her brother. "I'm proud of you, Jamie."

"It's *James* . . . Leon," he muttered, flushing pink beneath his tan. He all at once became engrossed in cutting up the bread she'd already sliced.

"James, then," she said, "and you needn't pretend I've said something I shouldn't. I know what you did for Sam"—she gave him a fond smile—"and I'm proud of you."

"It was Hawk's idea," he murmured, still uncomfortable.

"Yes, but it wanted your performance to work." She eyed him carefully for a moment. "What is it, sweetheart? I've seen you accept any number of tributes with flawless grace. It's not like you to be embarrassed by one, especially from me."

He sighed, but didn't say anything. She saw his eyes stray

to his cousin and Hawk, working quietly, side by side, and his mouth tightened. With a shake of his head, he went back to cutting up bread . . . with Hawk's knife.

"You're wondering why Hawk asked Sam to help him, aren't you?" she said softly. "While you were asked to stay here and help me?"

When he shrugged, saying nothing, she all at once suspected what was amiss. Jamie—quite uncharacteristically—was *jealous* of Sam. And finding himself so, he more than likely felt he didn't deserve her praise.

"Sweetheart," she said, placing a hand on his shoulder, "look at me, please?"

He complied, and the hurt in his eyes confirmed her suspicions.

"I think I know what you're feeling," she said gently, "and there's nothing to be embarrassed about." And, when he still didn't reply, "You think Hawk Randall's rather special, don't you?"

He nodded. "He treats me like . . . like a real person. Not merely like a prince, Leonie, but a real *person.* Do you . . . do you take my meaning?"

Oh, Jamie, if you only knew. He treats me like a real person, too. Not like a freak who just happens, by a prank of fate, to be a princess, but a real human being. "Yes . . . I do," she said quietly. She waited patiently, watching his face as he appeared to collect his thoughts.

"With Mama and Papa gone," he said at length, "the only ones . . . the only ones l-left who treated me like that were you and Sam. Then Hawk arrived, and he did, too. I've never had a grown-up friend like Hawk before, Leonie. I can talk to him, just . . . just like I talk to Sam!"

And watching both of them together now, you're afraid there won't be room for you. "Hawk's still your friend," she said with a tender smile, "even if he has chosen to be Sam's friend, too. It doesn't signify that you're to be excluded. I make no doubt the three of you will grow even closer because that bond is shared. That's the way it works."

He threw her a skeptical look.

"Jamie, do you remember Papa saying once that love's the only thing that increases when it's given away?"

With a small smile, he nodded.

"Shall I tell you when it was I first heard him say it? It was right after you were born, Jamie." She gave him an apologetic smile. "You see, I was *not* very pleased at your arrival."

"You *weren't?"*

"Not at all." The smile was wry now. "I was eleven years old, and for all of those eleven years—think of it, more years than you've been alive—I was their only child, the apple of Mama and Papa's collective eye. Why should I suddenly wish to share that?"

His eyes went wide. "You didn't want me?"

"Want you? I told them to send you back!"

"Leonie!"

"Yes, well that's the very reaction Mama and Papa had. Shock, plain and simple. They couldn't imagine I wouldn't at once adore you, just as they did."

"What happened?" he asked, more intrigued than aghast now.

"Oh, a number of things. All of them very wise, on the part of our parents, now I think on it. First, I was given the responsibility of being the *only* one who might lead visitors to see the new little prince. Then, for every gift you received, I was given one, too. I was allowed, as well, to select your infant wardrobe, your little toys, that sort of thing. But do you know what sticks uppermost in my mind, even now?"

Fascinated, he shook his head.

"It was a little talk they had with me about love. Loving you, they said, only increased their love for both of us. And while they didn't expect me to love you straightaway, Mama said, they imagined I might, when I came to know you. Then Papa added, seeing how I loved you, they could only love me, all the more. 'Love's the only thing,' he told me—"

" 'That increases when you give it away,' " Jamie finished with a smile.

"Yes, and do you know what happened after that?"

"You tried to give me away, and found you were stuck with me!" he replied with an impish twinkle.

"Dry boots, you found me out!" She was laughing.

"Found out what?" asked Hawk, coming up and reaching over Jamie's shoulder to snatch a crust of bread.

"Oh," said Leonie, "we were having a *very* philosophical discourse." She smiled at her brother. "About the nature of friendship and how it compares to . . . other things."

"Like love," Jamie chimed in.

"Same thing," said Hawk without hesitation. "Now," he added, clapping Jamie on the back, "I require *this* friend to help us wrap those deuced fish." He caught Jamie's eye and winked. "I made Sam promise to let you talk."

"Then we'd best get to it," said the prince, grinning like the boy his sister recognized, "before I forget what to say!"

It was fortunate, Leonie mused on the trail that afternoon, that she wasn't given to the sort of jealousy she'd helped Jamie conquer, because Hawk hardly spoke to her at all. True, he spoke as little to Petrie, but Simon tried everyone's patience; small wonder Hawk gave him short shrift. Did *she* try his patience, as well? She didn't think so, yet the plain fact was, he spent all his free time with the boys. She was grateful for this, but there were moments when she found herself wishing he'd at least pay her more regard than he did the Scarecrow.

Face facts, my girl. You're inordinately drawn to Hawk Randall. Who wouldn't be? He's kind and courageous and interesting and . . . enormously attractive. But there's no reason on God's green earth why Hawk Randall should be attracted to you. *Be glad your crippled foot doesn't put him off, and stop wishing for more. He's been kind to you, that's all. If you think someone like you merits more than that from a man like him, then you are a fool.*

Having finished this discourse with her sensible self, she felt a great deal better. It was perfectly normal to feel an attraction for such a man. She mustn't chide herself for it.

But it was folly to think it could be taken further. She must keep her head, and that meant maintaining the distance he seemed to prefer. She could do that. She'd been keeping her distance for years.

On the whole, Rand thought as he led his little band of refugees that same afternoon, they were making good progress. They'd traveled more efficiently, now he'd got things organized, and still no signs of pursuit. Knowing that could change, he made listening for it a top priority. Fortunately, his years with the 95th Rifles stood him in good stead; he had no problem keeping an ear to the ground, even while he slept.

Sam's particular progress had also become a priority. Rand had no doubt Roderik's brutality had left scars that went a deal deeper than those stripes on the poor child's back. Sam was slow to trust, and who could blame him? Thanks largely to Jamie, they'd made some headway, but Sam was still given to long periods of unnatural silence. Because he was a light sleeper, Rand often heard the boy cry out at night, even if the others didn't. Sam also jumped at the slightest sound, and he never laughed . . . though Jamie, bless him, occasionally evoked a shy smile.

Jamie, of course, was a pure delight. He amazed Rand with his readiness to lend a hand or perform a task, no matter how menial. There was not a jot of the toplofty royal in him. Someone had done a fine job rearing this prince, and no mistake. One need only consider some of Europe's other royal scions—England's Prinny came to mind—to know how odious this journey could have been.

Princess Leonie, too, gave no evidence of being pampered or spoiled. Still rather shy and withdrawn, though. Perhaps he should try to draw her out. With a reminiscent smile, he recalled those encounters at the palace, when he'd done exactly that. But then he'd been laboring under the impression she was a child. Now, time—and a revealing pair of breeches—had disabused him of that notion, and he felt curiously less inclined to approach her on a personal level.

Best to leave well enough alone. A royal princess of marriageable age ought not to appear too coming. An air of reticence hung about every blue-blooded virgin he'd ever met—as the several boring evenings he'd spent at Almack's could attest. Most of these chits were shy, while others, he'd suspected, were being deliberately standoffish. Presumably they were working their way up to the toplofty hauteur that was a mark of their class.

For all he knew, Mirandeau's princess was already among the latter, though in embryonic form. This "Leon" business was all very well, but given the right setting, wasn't it likely she'd set herself above the common lot?

Surprisingly, it pained him to think so. There was an innocent sweetness about her he'd hate to see corrupted. Still, he'd seen it happen, hadn't he? She wouldn't be the first highborn female of his better acquaintance to grow proud and aloof. When Cynthia had come to him that day and—*no!*

Don't think of Cynthia. Beautiful, perfect Cynthia. Don't think about what she said that day, either. She was wrong, and that's the end of it. The past is dead, damn it!

Ten

Nearing dusk on the third day, they were still deep within the forest. The stream meandered more than Rand liked, yet he'd no choice but to keep to it. The wood had grown thick and wild with brambles. To try for a more direct route through this tangle was folly. Moreover, the stream was a source of food that could be caught on the quiet. He had shot for bringing down game, but couldn't risk having the noise give them away.

Hiding his frustration, he gave word to make camp. They had at least another day of riding ahead. He could only hope as much lay between them and the men he felt certain were in pursuit. He'd yet to hear anything, but huntsmen knew how to move with stealth, including those after human prey. Unfortunately, the advantages of hugging the stream were offset by one enormous disadvantage: the unmistakable tracks they left in the soft earth along its banks.

As they drew rein and dismounted, Rand took stock of his charges. He'd pushed them hard today in hopes of reaching a cove that was still too far away. From the weary slump of their shoulders, he suspected they were feeling it. All but Jamie, of course. The scamp always had energy to burn, and tonight was no exception. He'd already divested his pony of its saddle, and was about to lead it to drink.

"James." Rand laid a hand on Jamie's arm, drawing him aside. "The others look past tired. Would you set up camp while I forage for the horses and see to catching our supper?"

"Happy to," the prince replied. He glanced at his sister,

who'd removed Raven's tack and was wearily leading him to drink. Sam fought a yawn as he struggled with Puck's saddle, while the Scarecrow slumped, unmoving, still on his mount. "Leon and Coz look nearly done in," he said, "and there's no *nearly* about it for the Scare—"

"Coz?" Rand asked.

"Oh, we finally found a name for Sam, now he's feeling better. Leon calls it his soo—soodo—"

"Pseudonym?"

"That's it! And *coz* is an old-fashioned word that's short for—"

"Cousin. Yes, I know," said Rand with a smile.

"Remembered it from the Shakespeare Mama—our mother used to read to us," Jamie told him. "Shakespeare used lots of break-teeth words, y'know. Made 'em easier to understand, hearing the parts read aloud," he added over his shoulder as he went to help Sam with his pony.

Are all children this interesting? Rand wondered as he headed downstream in search of forage. *Was I? Or is it just the fortunate few? The happy ones, who've been raised without fear . . . and with love?*

"Thanks, love," Leonie said, stifling a yawn. Jamie had just fixed her a comfortable bed, using branches and leaves to cushion the ground beneath the blanket, as Hawk had shown them. Across from her, on the other side of the fire pit he'd dug, Sam and Petrie were similarly accommodated. All that needed doing was to build the fire itself. For that, they awaited Hawk, who knew how to construct one that wouldn't be seen from afar. "I don't know what we'd have done without your help tonight," she added with a tired smile.

"No trouble," Jamie replied cheerfully. Attending to his own bed now, he paused, blanket in hand. "I say, it's gone frightfully dark! Wonder what's keeping Hawk."

"Fishing in the dark, I should imagine," his sister said wryly, "and without his two excellent assistants. But as long as he's not here, there's something I've been meaning to—is Petrie awake?"

"Hardly," said Jamie, peering at the longish gray lump revealed by a quarter moon that had just cleared the trees. As if to prove him right, a rumbling snore erupted from the blanket, then subsided. "Fell asleep the moment he lay down."

"Excellent," said Leonie. "We'll wake him later, for supper. And Sam?"

"Coz, are you awake?"

The smaller lump beside Petrie stirred. "Uh-huh. Though I am awfully tired . . . but I'm also a bit sharp set."

"Even for another round of fish?" Jamie asked, grinning.

"Oh, I don't mind." Sam sat up and rubbed his eyes.

"That's the spirit," said Leonie. "Now listen carefully, both of you. You heard Hawk say he hopes to reach the coast tomorrow?"

"Yes," said Jamie, "where there should be a vessel—a fishing boat, maybe—we can engage. But a merchant packet would be best, of course."

"That's been the plan, yes," said Leonie, hoping she was right to assume they'd find someone willing to take them on. "Now do listen, because this is important. I know I've mentioned it before, but I want to remind you: Once we're among strangers, the importance of maintaining secrecy is paramount."

"Well, we know that," Jamie huffed indignantly. *"I'm* not the one who forgets to use the soodo—the new names!"

"You've both done very well—and, yes, better than I—using the pseudonyms," she said. "But the secret of who we are is only one small part of it. There are other things, James, as you well know, which are even more . . . which are too dangerous to mention to *anyone."*

She still wondered if it had been wise to tell him about Lady Emilie's terrible suspicions. Jamie was only a child, after all. A child's innocence could be his best protection. But as this particular child was destined to rule a country, in the end she'd told him. The only thing he wasn't privy to was the regent's treasonous link to the French, a thing so dangerous she didn't want to think about it herself.

"With some things," she told him now, "it's safer for people not to know . . . for their own good."

"But Hawk must be kept in the dark because you don't trust him," Jamie said, his tone faintly accusing. "And the Scarecrow, of course. Honestly," he grumbled, "sometimes I wonder you even wanted Coz informed."

She glanced at Sam, who'd been quietly following their discussion. Because of her difficulty in obtaining a private moment with Sam, she'd been forced to ask Jamie to judge when he was feeling up to it and fill him in. "Have you told him?" she asked her brother.

"Didn't have to," he said with a shrug. "Knew all about it."

Her eyes flew to the small face across from her. "Sam, how?"

"Mama told me," he replied in that small, frightened voice she'd learned to dread. "She—she didn't want to, but when . . . when he . . ." He dropped his gaze, suddenly studying his fingers, which were worrying the edge of his blanket. "You tell it, Jam—James," he mumbled into his lap.

"It's all right," Jamie said gently. He patted Sam on the shoulder, then found his sister's eyes. "That first time, when the blackguard had him beaten," he said with barely restrained anger, "Sam didn't understand why."

Hearing him use Sam's real name, Leonie knew just how angry he was. Jamie never forgot to use their pseudonyms. He also seldom lost his temper, but he could be ferocious when it came to protecting Sam. *Dear God, Sam . . . frightened and bewildered by a beating he'd neither earned nor understood.*

"That," Jamie continued, his voice still taut with fury, "was when he asked Aunt Emilie why it was so important to learn those lessons. Lessons that made no sense!"

Leonie heaved a sigh. "So Aunt felt it necessary to explain to him what she knew . . . what lay behind Uncle's orders.

I see." Emilie hadn't mentioned this, but there'd been so much else on her mind that night. Perhaps there hadn't been time. But it was necessary now to know what Sam knew and perhaps explain certain things. It would be unconscionable if he were frightened by something that slipped out later. Something he hadn't been prepared for.

"Can you tell me exactly what she told you?" she asked Sam gently. "You needn't, if it's too difficult, sweetheart. But I think it would be a good thing if we were, um, all on the same page, so to speak."

Sam seemed to consider this for a moment. At length, he gave a soft sigh and met her gaze. "She said that h-he was . . . he was bent on . . . on setting me in m-my cousin's place, in order to—to have complete p-power. She said it w-wasn't right, but . . . but I must try v-very hard to do as he said . . . until she could find a way to s-stop him."

"She told about Mama and Papa, too," said Jamie, "only not any details. I was the one told him how Uncle made Papa break his neck on that horse, and then had Mama—"

"Jamie!"

"Well, I had to! I know you told me not to frighten him, but I didn't, honest. He already knew Aunt Emilie believed Uncle killed them. He *asked* me how—didn't you, Coz? And it *didn't* overset him. Not even the part about Uncle having Mama poisoned!"

"Poisoned!" The word was a screech from the bundled figure on the ground beside Sam—Petrie, awake and hysterical, by the sound of him.

"I knew it!" he cried, staggering to his feet in a tangle of blanket. The red hair stuck up from his head in tufts, reminding Leonie of an overwrought rooster. "I knew there was skullduggery afoot!" His eyes were wild as they went to the prince. "Your own uncle! My God, it's just like *Hamlet.* We'll all be murdered in our beds by that madm—*mmph!"*

The abrupt silence was startling. As was the well-muscled arm that had seemed to come from nowhere. Or the speed with which it snaked around the actor, immobilizing him, while a strong hand clamped his mouth shut.

"I shall give you a moment to collect yourself, sir." Hawk's voice was unnervingly soft in the sudden quiet, yet Leonie caught a hint of steel in it as he addressed the actor. "Then I expect to have heard the last of such caterwauling. A noise fit to wake the dead, sir . . . or worse, for it could well alert those we must elude. You might have endangered us all, Mr. Petrie, and that is unacceptable. Do I make myself clear?"

The actor's eyes, which had rolled in alarm when he was first captured, closed briefly now, as if in resignation . . . or prayer. When he managed a nod, Hawk released him.

"I apologize if I gave you a fright, Petrie"—his tone said Hawk wasn't a bit sorry—"but the group's safety is my responsibility, and I don't take that lightly." He looked around, absorbing the apprehensive faces about the fire. "Now, would someone please tell me what this was all about?"

"Well, I just heard . . ." the actor began, then caught Randall's frown. "Er, may I explain?"

"If you think you can do it quietly."

"Yes . . . yes, of course. It's just that it was such a shock, Mr. Randall. To learn that madman had murdered his brother!" While not yet loud, his voice began to rise. "And poisoned his brother's wife! I'd no idea, you see, and these poor children—"

"That will be all, Mr. Petrie." Hawk gripped the actor's arm and turned him toward his rumpled blankets. "I can see you're overwrought, sir, as no doubt you've reason to be. Perhaps we'd best have our supper before I hear more."

Leonie swallowed as his eyes found hers. Making it perfectly clear just who was expected to enlighten him.

She had to give the man credit. From an efficiently built fire to a hilarious account of fishing in the dark—a recital that had her brother giggling and won a rare smile from Sam—Hawk gave no indication anything untoward had occurred. Throughout the meal, he conducted himself as he always had: listening attentively to the boys, answering questions, sharing an amusing anecdote or some interesting fact. For Hawk, Leonie could almost believe, it was business as usual.

She knew otherwise.

He'd heard enough from Petrie to try a saint, and Hawk Randall scarcely conjured images of canonization. The man she'd glimpsed in that moment with Petrie was a hard-edged soldier, no matter how soft-spoken. She'd caught the angry glitter in his eyes. Not that Petrie didn't deserve it. But because she'd been careless in discussing secrets where she shouldn't, *she* would soon be the one under his scrutiny. Would he be equally angry with her? She'd hired him for this dangerous task without divulging the full extent of what he was up against. She rather thought he might be.

The bite of fish in her mouth tasted suddenly like sawdust. The tiredness that had earned her Jamie's help was gone, along with her appetite. Replaced by a tension that made her bones ache. Sleep was the furthest thing from her mind now. When Hawk confronted her over the facts she'd withheld, he'd have a wide-awake—and frightened—princess on his hands.

Rand did his best to remain calm as he saw them through the meal. Yet his head spun with the things Petrie had said. Allegations of murder were serious enough, but the murder of a reigning prince and his consort was high treason. Was it true? He rather thought the regent capable of it. Still, that didn't mean it had actually happened.

His eyes slid to the faces around the fire. The boys, fortunately, appeared for the moment to have forgotten the actor's tirade. Contentedly eating the berries he'd found along the stream, they paused frequently to yawn. Petrie was past yawning. He nodded over the last of his fish, already half asleep. Of the four, only the princess gave indication she'd not forgotten. Watchful, apprehensive, she reminded him of a wild doe, ready to bolt at a moment's notice.

He regretted that. He'd no wish to be perceived as a threat.

Yet he must have some answers, and there was no one else to ask. He was loath to question a pair of children on such weighty matters, no matter how much they knew. Especially Sam, who still lived on the edge of terror after what he'd been through. Jamie might have some answers, but he was still a child. And Petrie, though an adult, had apparently been kept largely in the dark himself.

He'd wait until those three fell asleep. Which, from the look of things, would be soon. Then find a means of eliciting answers from Leonie without making her feel threatened. It came to him, then, that he had the means. It would establish him as more than a hired escort. As someone committed to them, who could offer compassion as well as aid. It was not a thing he'd normally do; he'd never been given to bandying his private history about. But he had to gain her trust. It all came down to trust.

It was quiet when Leonie finished tucking the boys in and resumed her seat by the fire. All that disturbed the silence were night sounds that had become familiar by now: the steady chirp of crickets, a furtive rustling of some small creature in the underbrush, the fire's soft hiss and crackle as it burned low.

Hawk was still down at the stream. He'd gone to wash up the few utensils the kitchen had sent with their food, leaving her to hear the boys' prayers and see them abed. *Giving me time to compose myself before the inquisition begins,* she thought with an uncharacteristic lack of charity.

She was, unfortunately, no further along in deciding how much to tell him. He'd overheard Petrie ranting about murder, yes. But there was more, and Hawk wasn't stupid. What she was forced to reveal depended not so much upon what he'd heard as what he guessed.

"Seems I've stolen a page from your book." Not wishing to alarm her, Rand had kept his voice low, yet Leonie started. "Forgive me. I thought you heard me coming."

Leonie realized she would have if she hadn't been so deep

in thought. On the other hand, Hawk had a way of moving too quietly sometimes.

"What—what happened?" she asked, with a sharp glance at the shirt in his hand. He stood just outside the light thrown by the fire, so she wasn't certain, but it appeared to be dripping wet.

"Slipped on a rock, and my shirt took a soaking," he said with a rueful smile. "Fortunately, I carry another in my saddle pack."

As he moved closer, her gaze shifted, and all at once it was impossible to speak. His bare torso, revealed now by the firelight, was . . . beautiful. Clean, sculpted lines . . . curve of muscle and stretch of sinew . . . sun-bronzed male flesh turned copper by the orange glow of the fire . . . it was nearly too much to absorb. She'd never seen an adult male thus unclothed, but the library at home was filled with prints of ancient Greek and Roman statues. Statues of gods . . . who looked like this.

Yet not like this, either. Those sculptures were formed of marble, cold and classical in their perfection, but failing to approach the image of Hawk Randall lit by flame. No, this was like some pagan god of old, wrought from the flames themselves . . . earthy . . . primordial . . . *male*.

"Give me time to change," she thought she heard him say. The words competed with the thunderous tumult beating inside her brain . . . and elsewhere. "I shan't be a moment."

He turned, reached for his pack, which lay on the ground near his blanket—and Leonie gasped. Scars marred his back. The godlike muscle that rippled with strength as he moved, all that primitive male beauty—disfigured by *scars*. Dozens of them, criss-crossing his back!

He must have heard her sharp intake of breath, for he turned and met her eyes with a look of . . . was it apology? The flickering fire cast shadows across his face, and she couldn't be sure.

"Sorry," Rand murmured, pulling the fresh shirt from his pack. "You weren't meant to see that." A lie, but he followed it with the truth. "I'd no wish to frighten you."

"I—I wasn't frightened." They weren't new, the scars. There was none of the newly healed, puckered flesh that signaled recent healing, like Sam's stripes, the lesser of which had begun to shed their scabs, revealing pink, healthy skin. "I just wasn't prepared for—Hawk, what in God's name happened to—"

She bit her lip, ashamed. She, of all people, knew how rude it was to ask such a thing. "I do beg your pardon," she murmured, ducking her head.

"Not at all," he said, pulling on the fresh shirt and reaching for what had dropped to the ground with the one he'd discarded. "I was the inconsiderate one. Careless of me to let you see that. I owe *you* the apology . . . and may I offer these to soften the shock?"

She felt him draw near, and lifted her gaze. "Ohh," she breathed, her eyes on the flowers he held out as he hunkered down beside her. The white petals of the tiny, star-shaped blossoms were wet with dew. "Queen's Grace. It's been years since I saw one in bloom."

"Oddest thing," he said, watching her as she took the bouquet. Was that wonder he saw on her face? For a handful of wildflowers? "I passed the exact spot where they were earlier, when I foraged. Yet I never saw them. They appeared as if by magic."

"Queen's Grace," she said, pushing her nose into the fragile blossoms, inhaling their delicate scent, "is a shy flower that blooms only at night. Even then it's rare to find one, let alone an entire bouquet. They're native to Mirandeau's forests, and may be found nowhere else in the world."

Flowers . . . from Hawk Randall! The hand holding the flowers suddenly felt unsteady. Hoping he wouldn't notice, she laid them beside her on the blanket, managing a smile. It was a wobbly smile, and she hoped he didn't notice that, either—or if he did, that he wouldn't guess the cause. *No one's ever given me flowers.* "They're lovely, and I"—she had to clear her throat—"thank you, Hawk."

He gave her a rueful smile. "They hardly make up for shocking you with something you needn't have seen."

"I wasn't . . ." The protest died on her lips, and she dropped her gaze. "Yes, I suppose I was," she admitted, "but it wasn't shock alone that . . ." *It* hurt *me to see those scars, just as it hurts every time I see Sam's. Who did that to you, Hawk? Who?* "I mean, I just wondered how . . ."

Again, she'd said more than she ought. "I—I'm sorry," she murmured, biting her lip. "I didn't mean to rattle on about . . . such a thing."

"Not at all," he said, keeping his voice light. "It's natural to wonder. But there's no great mystery involved. It happened a long time ago, when I was a lad. You see, I was whipped . . . for not learning my lessons."

Her eyes widened, and she went very still. "Like Sam," she said at last. It was barely a whisper.

"Like Sam," he agreed, doing his best to sound matter-of-fact. "With one important distinction: My father had no hand in it. He was away at war when it happened."

"I see," she said, yet this wasn't entirely true. She tried to piece it out. Had the elder Randall entrusted his son's education to some sadistic pedant while never knowing the man's true nature? It made sense. She'd no experience of common schoolrooms, but she'd heard of these heartless pedagogues. On the other hand, it might have been someone else entirely. Perhaps a brutal relative, she mused, thinking at once of her uncle. "But who—"

"It doesn't matter who," he said curtly. The look in her eyes was disturbing. He'd no need of her pity. The scars were merely designed to deepen the rapport between them. Like the wildflowers, they were meant to break down barriers. He had some hard questions to ask. He stood a chance of getting answers if she saw him in a more human light. Trusted him because they shared common ground.

"The person is no longer alive," he added dismissively. To soften his words, he smiled and took a seat on the end of her blanket, the wildflowers between them. It was time to redirect the conversation.

Eleven

Leonie saw the change in his eyes, and knew the time had come for serious speech. Curiously, she no longer thought of it as an inquisition. Still, she was not free of apprehension. "I collect you have questions for me," she said. She was proud of herself for meeting the steady regard of those indigo eyes without blinking. "And while I owe you answers, I must warn you. Hawk, this concerns matters that cannot be treated lightly."

"Murder can never be treated lightly," he said gravely.

She swallowed to clear a suddenly constricted throat, reminded of whose murders they were about to discuss. "Of—of course not. But what I meant to say was, what you wish me to discuss is dangerous. It can only be told in—in the strictest confidence."

"You can trust me, Leonie," he said softly. "I'd never do anything to harm you or the boys."

The murmur of her given name was not without effect. Nor was the scent of flowers drifting up to tease her senses, their elusive fragrance released by the fire's warmth. She had a sense of being sweetly lulled, cocooned with him, in the softness of the summer night. Serenaded by crickets, bathed in the glow of the fire as he held her gaze, she felt the tension inside her slowly unwind. It was as if they were all alone. Just the two of them, removed from a world that was far away, if it existed at all. . . .

Still, it did exist, in all its terrible aspects. But something had changed. She could speak of it now, freed of that debilitating constriction in her throat. Of the urge to weep and weep, for all that was gone—for Mama and Papa, for her lost childhood innocence—until she was wrung dry. Oh, it would still be hard. Yet somehow, under Hawk Randall's caring gaze, she could do it.

"Not a fortnight ago," she began in a calm, steady voice, "Lady Emilie asked to meet with me in private. . . ."

She told him then, beginning with those first terrible moments when Sam's mother had voiced her shocking suspicions. She took him through the long days of her own doubts and fears, then through the gathering evidence that had erased those doubts, one by one. The boys' description of their peculiar lessons. The regent's brutal treatment of Sam, for not learning what he so heinously, so callously demanded. Then Petrie's description of the illicit coronation rehearsals. And, finally, the chilling conclusion that the tutor had been hired for one evil purpose, and no other.

Hawk listened in silence, only nodding from time to time when she touched on things he already knew. She'd no doubt he believed her, and she found enormous relief in this. Relief, too, in knowing she was no longer alone, for, while the boys shared the knowledge, she'd had to make the decisions. A burden of responsibility she'd lived with for so long . . . so very long.

With a leap of faith, she decided to lighten the burden even further. She described the regent's clandestine meetings in the wood. It was then he finally interrupted.

"You *followed* him?" he asked, incredulous. "Into the forest at midnight?"

"Oh, I know it appears foolhardy," she hastened to say, "but it wasn't . . . not really. I mean, I knew I could rely on Raven. We'd ridden to the river so often it wasn't difficult, even in the dark. And . . . and I was dreadfully curious."

"Curious," he repeated in a choked voice. "Didn't it occur to you that what you were doing was fraught with *danger?* Danger that had nothing to do with finding your way in the dark?"

"You mean, wasn't I sensible enough to fear being

caught?" she asked with a self-deprecating smile. "In truth, I was terrified, but not straightaway. That is, I suppose my curiosity got the best of me at first. It was only when I heard them speak that the real fear struck. Not to mention the terror later, when Jamie and I were in the stable loft, and I realized it was those same . . ." She hesitated, for she'd blundered into territory she wasn't certain she ought to reveal.

"Go on," he urged.

Was it her imagination, or had she just glimpsed an unduly alert look in his eyes? Uncertain, she searched his face. Yet Hawk merely smiled at her now, his aspect gently encouraging. Deciding it had been a trick of the light, she concentrated on how much to tell. A plot to restore Boney to power was no trifling matter. Revealing the regent's hand in a thing of such enormous consequence was a huge step to take.

Still, it was all of a piece, wasn't it? The things she'd already told him pointed to high treason. What difference if she revealed what was, after all, Roderik's ultimate betrayal?

With another leap of faith, she explained that the meetings in the forest had been conducted in French. That it was those same Frenchmen she and Jamie had overheard—but she alone had understood—that night in the loft. Napoleon's sympathizers were plotting to overthrow the Peace, and Roderik was one of them.

Hawk said nothing when she finally finished. Knees raised, forearms resting on them, he stared pensively into the fire. In the lengthening silence, she began to grow uneasy. What was he thinking? She wanted to ask, but felt suddenly tongue-tied. What if he held it against her for failing to act on what she'd learned? Would he understand why she couldn't? Her priority had been the escape. Surely he understood that.

All at once, that unique sense of being alone with him, removed from the world, no longer seemed pleasant. It was discomfiting. She examined his chiseled profile, acutely aware of its masculine perfection. Uncomfortably aware. She was merely Mirandeau's pathetic little crippled princess. What was she doing here, sharing secrets with such a man?

State secrets. Only an addlepate would think the moment personal and special. To look at him, she no longer existed.

Then her sensible self intervened. He had weighty matters to ponder. It might be hours, perhaps not till dawn, before he could respond. Best to curl up in her blanket, then, leaving him the privacy to digest all he'd heard.

She turned with a tug at her blanket to draw it around her. But the blanket was caught on something. Turning back to free it, she saw Hawk was sitting on it. In her dismay, she nearly missed his softly spoken words.

"Tell me, Your Highness, how does one small female come by so much courage?"

She couldn't have heard him right. "Did . . . did you say *courage?"* she managed. "Me?" she added, her voice a squeak.

He nodded, his eyes solemn as they studied her in silence.

"Really, Hawk," she said, a thread of laughter in her words, "you've picked a precious poor time for jests!"

"I wasn't jesting," he said quietly.

"But . . . but I thought I heard you say . . ." She couldn't finish. It was all too absurd. Yet the way he was looking at her . . . he was *serious.* "Courage and I have rarely kept company," she told him, sobering. "In truth, I am the world's greatest coward. Afraid of my own shadow. Not that I'm proud of it. It's just a fact, and I hope I'm sensible enough to recognize it."

"Princess, if I believed you weren't ever afraid, I'd never have called you courageous."

"I . . . don't understand."

"It isn't the absence of fear that makes a person courageous, Leonie. As you so rightly said, it's only sensible to recognize that you are afraid. To do otherwise is foolish, and in no way courageous."

"But—"

"Courage isn't the absence of fear, Leonie, but the *mastery* of it. Consider what made you spy on the regent. If you truly set out with only your curiosity to prompt you, there was no courage in the act, because there was no fear. The courage was all in what came after, because it was done *in spite of* your fear. You were afraid of your own shadow, as you put it. Yet you did everything from plotting your escape to putting it into effect. All the while caring admirably for the boys, I might add, not to mention . . ." He stopped, but not before she caught the direction of his glance.

"Not to mention doing it with a crippled foot?" she supplied with a wry smile. "It's all right to say it, you know. I won't have the vapors upon hearing a fact I've lived with all my life."

In silence, he searched her face. Apparently satisfied at what he saw, he gave her a half smile. "And that, Your Highness, takes a kind of courage all its own."

"Fustian!" she muttered, unconvinced. It was a term her mother had used with courtiers given to bombastic speech.

He was shaking his head. "I would never insult you with insincere flattery, Leonie. You've more courage in your little finger than many a man I've known. When I consider all you did—"

"But . . . but I really had very little choice. I did those things because there wasn't anyone else who could."

"Did anyone threaten you to make you do them? Blackmail you? Hold a pistol to your head?"

"No, of course not."

"Then it was your own choice. A choice made in the face of what you've already described as being terrified." He smiled at her. "That, sweetheart, takes courage."

Her breath hitched with the endearment. It was one she often used, but seldom heard. No one had called her sweetheart since Mama and Papa died. And his smile. It was potent, that smile, bracketed by those devastating slashes that were male dimples, making crinkles at the corners of his eyes in a way she hadn't noticed before. It had the power to stop the protest she'd been prepared to utter, the power to make her heart thud madly in her chest.

To make the moment special, all over again.

Rand saw her go very still, then duck her head, clearly uncomfortable. Had no one ever told her how brave she was—not with regard to the present situation, but long before, when she'd taken her handicap in stride and summoned the will to deal with it? He could still picture the first time he'd seen her, competent and at ease upon that great beast of a stallion, yet totally flustered when he'd apologized for nearly knocking her over.

How had he ever imagined her proud and aloof? If she could be flummoxed by praise that was, after all, nothing but the truth, then she was the very opposite. Devil take it, the lass needed to believe more in herself!

His gaze fell on the wildflowers lying on the blanket.

"Princess . . . please look at me," Rand murmured a few moments later.

Thankful she'd had time to collect herself, Leonie complied. "This isn't to be more of your courage nonsense, is it?" she managed with a twinkle. The idea still made her uncomfortable. Perhaps if she treated it with levity, he'd leave it alone.

"Nonsense? Hardly," he said, his smile mysterious, and came fluidly to his feet.

She never grew tired of watching him move. There was grace and elegance inherent in every gesture. Like now, when he rose to his feet seemingly without effort. But what was that he held behind his back? And his face . . . it had gone so *solemn.*

"I meant what I said, Leonie," he told her softly.

Before she could draw breath, he bowed—elegantly, how else?—and drew from behind his back something she couldn't immediately make out . . . and then she did. A crown, fashioned from his bouquet!

"If words will not suffice," he said, still speaking softly, "then perhaps this will convince you." He set the crown of wildflowers gently on her head. "Leonie of Mirandeau, henceforth be also known by another name. For with this crown, I dub thee Queen of Courage."

Speechless, she stared at him. There was not a hint of levity on his face.

"Good night, sweet queen," he whispered, lifting her limp

hand and raising it to his lips. Without another word, he retrieved the rifle he always took on patrols of their camp and left, his footsteps noiseless on the forest floor.

Wordlessly, Leonie watched him melt into the night. Then she curled up in her blanket, the crown of flowers still on her head, and slept. And while she slept, she dreamed of being whole. Of dancing . . . with Hawk.

Dawn was breaking when Rand heard the first sounds of pursuit. A gray, cheerless dawn, with dense fog curling about the camp, obscuring all but the nearest trees. The bleak weather was enough to sour his mood, yet *sour* didn't begin to describe what he felt on hearing a faint baying in the distance: Dogs. The bastard was hunting them with dogs. His face grim, Rand went to awaken Leonie.

"What—what is it?" Sam rubbed sleep from his eyes, the apprehension in his tone telling Leonie he'd already sensed something amiss as she roused him and Jamie. Hawk had just left. In a voice that held no alarm but was clearly urgent, he'd alerted Leonie, telling her to break camp quickly. He and Petrie were already saddling the horses, leaving her to deal with the boys.

"It's just the hunt with its noisy hounds," she said, keeping her voice light, gathering up blankets as she spoke. She hoped Sam wouldn't see through the lie. She didn't know how long she could keep the truth from him, but she'd do whatever it took. Every moment the child was spared was a moment he'd be free of panic. She was well aware no hunters in their right minds would ride to hounds in weather like this, but perhaps Sam wouldn't know that.

A glance at Jamie's face told her *he* knew these were Roderik's hounds. Roderik was hunting them like animals. Fortunately, the baying sounded distant. Then again, that could be deceiving. When she asked, Hawk had explained the hounds could be closer than they seemed. Fog had a way of distorting sound and making it difficult to gauge its direction and distance.

"I'll wager it's old Lord Moreau hosting that hunt," she told her cousin. Schooling her voice to a careless insouciance, over Sam's head she sent Jamie an arch look.

"Of course it's Moreau," said Jamie, taking his cue as he hurriedly shoved his feet into boots. Everyone knew the aging earl was a zealous sportsman with an unreasonable passion for the hunt. "The old fool all but sleeps in his pinks."

"James!"

"Uh, sorry, Leon. But even Papa called him an old f—"

"That doesn't mean *you* may do so. It's disrespectful and—"

"Don't!" cried Sam. "I know what you're b-both trying to d-do, but it w-won't answer. Even Lord M-Moreau wouldn't be m-mad enough to ride out in th-this," he added with a convulsive swallow. "It's *him,* isn't it? H-he's set the d-dogs on us."

"Now, Coz," said Leonie. Placing her hands on his thin shoulders, she met his frightened gaze and gave him a comforting squeeze. "You can't know that for sure. And even if it's so, Hawk says we're not far from the coast. We'll be safely on a boat before you know it."

"As good as there already," said Jamie, passing Sam his cap and boots. "And I heard Hawk say we'll keep the horses midstream as we ride. Hounds can't pick up a scent in water, y'know."

And so it went, all of them taking turns to reassure poor Sam as they finished gathering their things and mounted up. Even Petrie, whose credit rose several notches in Leonie's esteem when he affected a jovial air. Meant for Sam alone, it half convinced her as well. He might indeed have had a fine success at the Drury Lane (as he'd claimed) she mused, grateful for his effort.

Then all talk ceased as Hawk led them out, somehow managing to keep within a streambed totally enshrouded by fog. A light drizzle had begun to fall. As they passed, branches of unseen trees occasionally emerged from the gray mist, their leaves dripping and slick. And all the while, from behind them in the gloom, came the eerie ululating baying of hounds.

Leonie was glad of the solid comfort of Raven beneath her. Soon even Petrie, a barely seen presence on the horse ahead, succumbed to the oppressive atmosphere. He'd ridden out smiling, chin set at a jaunty angle. Now her occasional glimpses took in the actor's sagging shoulders and hunched posture. She wondered how the boys were faring, Sam in particular. Wondered, too, how Hawk was able to find his way through this dismal miasma. She knew they trod in water only from the splashing of the horses' hooves.

Long minutes passed, then hours, or so it seemed. She wasn't sure. The lack of visible landmarks skewed her sense of time. Her empty stomach told her some had elapsed since they left, but even that was unreliable. She'd passed out breakfast as they mounted up, but saw only Jamie and Petrie finish theirs. Her leaf-wrapped hunk of fish lay in her pack where she'd stashed it, too overwrought to eat.

It was devilish slow going. As the minutes crawled by, she feared they weren't moving fast enough, would never move far enough, to elude capture. Was she imagining it, or had the ever present baying drawn closer? If only the fog would lift!

Minutes later, the order to halt came as a whisper, relayed down the line. She forced herself to take heart. Surely they wouldn't stop unless Hawk deemed it safe? Had they finally reached the coast? She sniffed the air, hoping to sense the familiar salty tang that would tell her they were near the sea. But all she detected was the dank, fetid smell of wet earth and rotting vegetation.

Then she learned why they'd stopped, and her heart plummeted. Sam, in his terror, had wet himself. Several hours back, as it turned out. He'd been too ashamed to say. If his choked sobs hadn't alerted Jamie, no one would have known. Hawk came walking back to explain, holding the sobbing child in his arms.

"The poor darling," she murmured, reaching for her cousin.

Hawk's eyes were grave, his mouth taut as he gave a slight shake of the head. "If it's all right with you, I'd like to keep him with me," he murmured, his big hand stroking Sam's shuddering back. "Raven could easily take the extra weight, but I don't think you yourself—"

"Yes, of course . . . that is, if Sam agrees. Sweetheart . . ."

Again, Hawk shook his head. In the barest whisper, he explained that Sam had begun to stutter and stammer so severely his speech was unintelligible. Hawk had already put the question to him. After trying to reply, the child had clung to him fiercely and managed to nod his assent.

"But if you could locate his spare clothes . . . dry breeches . . ." Hawk told her. He hugged the child tightly as Sam gave a smothered cry, whispering something undiscernible in his ear as he buried his face in Hawk's shoulder.

"Yes . . . yes, of course." Sam's embarrassed sobs were fit to break her heart as she scrambled off Raven's back to do as Hawk asked.

In Hawk's efficient hands, Sam was into the fresh clothes before they knew it. In unspoken agreement, Leonie and the others had turned their backs, giving him what privacy the fog might fail to provide, and they were soon ready to ride. Atop the gypsy mare, wrapped in Hawk's arms, Sam looked somber but was no longer in tears.

As they resumed riding, Leonie thanked God for having the wits to hire Hawk Randall. He'd somehow known just what to do, striking exactly the right note between tenderness and competent male support for the delicacy of Sam's plight. Being female, she certainly couldn't have managed it. And Jamie, she suspected, though male, couldn't have, either. Oddly enough, because he and Sam were too close; and, of course, both were children, when the situation had called for an adult. An adult with wisdom and compassion, she mused thoughtfully, picturing Hawk's face as he'd cradled her cousin in his arms.

On they slogged, their clothing by now thoroughly soaked, except where rump and thigh met saddle and equine flank. After a while, Leonie began to notice two things. A breeze had sprung up, thinning the fog—bane or blessing, she didn't know, for while fog slowed their progress, it also hid them. The other thing she noticed was cause for alarm: The hounds were definitely closer.

Coincident with her thoughts, Hawk began to pick up the pace. He could afford to now, with more visibility, but he'd undoubtedly noted the proximity of the dogs as well. Worse, Leonie realized, the breeze had shifted, and carried on it she heard, mingled with the hounds, the eager voices of men.

Her heart pounded, and a cold sweat beaded her brow as Hawk urged them into a trot, and then a canter—dangerous, because while the stream was shallow, it was deep enough to hide rocks that could cause a horse to stumble and break a leg. The surefooted ponies might be at lesser risk, but probably not at this pace, she thought as Sam's Puck, tethered by a length of rope to Raven's saddle, stretched his stubby legs to keep up.

The baying sounded very near now. Leonie wondered how their pursuers had managed to close the gap. They were meant to be stymied by losing the scent. Then all at once she knew. The ploy of riding through water had failed, for one painfully evident reason. The dogs had followed their scent as far as the stream. Then it was all too simple for their handlers to deduce the truth. With the wood so dense, there wasn't any option for the prey but to flee downstream.

Hawk's voice, up ahead, snared her attention. Then Sam's—poor baby, he was stammering incoherently. But Hawk was reassuring him. "It's going to be all right, lad. See that rise? That's a sand dune!"

"It's the sea, Sam!" shouted her brother, galloping after them on Jumper. "We've made it!"

Thank God! Thank God! Leonie felt the hot sting of tears as she and Petrie raced after, the cries of gulls reaching her over the pounding of hooves, the mad drumming of blood in her ears.

As they rounded the crest, the rise gave way to a rocky slope studded with marram grass. Bits of driftwood lay scattered here and there. Below lay the shingle, strewn with seashells and strands of seaweed drying in the sun. A fresh salt breeze swept away the last remnants of fog.

And—*there!* The turquoise-blue of the sea, shimmering like a splendid jewel in the sun. She squinted against the glare, saw a paler blue that was the sky meet it on the horizon. Tiny specks she knew were fishing boats bobbed on swells in the distance. And closer by, a larger vessel, anchored in the cove, whose shape she could just discern, where the shoreline curved—

"Halt, and drop all weapons—*now,*" demanded a harsh voice at their backs.

No! Leonie whirled Raven about and stifled a scream. Beside her, Petrie made a bleating sound.

"Identify yourselves," said a dangerous looking man, his uniform crisp and bright in the sun. He stood just yards away. Several others, similarly dressed, stood behind him. All held rifles trained on the refugees. "At once!"

Twelve

"The name's Hawksrest," Leonie heard Hawk reply.

Hawksrest? She frowned, her gaze frozen on the shiny barrels of the rifles, her mind a sudden jumble of confusion. Was Hawk a short name? But why use the long form only now? And what had become of the hounds? Moreover, why was Hawk so composed? Beside her, Petrie had fainted, while her own fear was a live thing that clawed at her—the man was *lowering his rifle!*

"Marine Lieutenant Cooper, sir, at your service," he announced. She watched, stunned, as he gave Hawk a smart salute and gestured for his men to lower their weapons!

"If you don't mind, Lieutenant," Hawk said quickly, "we're in a bit of a hurry." He drew his mare abreast of Raven and indicated the direction from which they'd come. "Trouble in our wake—can't say how far behind, but too damned close for comfort. Armed, I make no doubt. I'd be obliged if you could have us aboard the *Fleetwind* before it catches up with us."

Leonie felt lightheaded. What was going on? And next came an unexpected turn of events that left her speechless. These men had nothing to do with Roderik, she learned with giddy relief. They were Royal Marines attached to the large vessel anchored in the cove: HMS *Fleetwind,* a British naval frigate!

Cooper immediately set marines atop the dune to guard their rear. In short order, he had all of them in a longboat she hadn't noticed before. It sat at the water's edge, manned by seamen in charge of an officer from the frigate. The men rowed them to the vessel while a lad the officer assured them was good with horses remained with their mounts. They later brought Raven and the others safely aboard. In the dizzying swirl of events, Leonie never learned how.

She retained only the vaguest images from her own trip to the frigate: Jamie's voice, eager and bright, asking questions; Sam, sitting quietly in Hawk's lap, his upturned face no longer pinched as he listened to reassuring words.

Yet a greater shock came soon after they arrived on the frigate. Another officer addressed Hawk most oddly—if she heard him right—and said the captain wished to see him at once.

She *couldn't* have heard right! She stared at their retreating backs, then turned to the officer from the boat, who'd introduced himself as Lieutenant Briggs. "Lieutenant," she asked in a diffident voice, "did . . . did that gentleman just address, er, Hawksrest as *m'lord?*"

"He did, lad," said Briggs, who clearly had no inkling she was female. "He's the marquis of Hawksrest, you understand. Capital fellow, I'm told."

"Is he?" she murmured faintly.

Briggs nodded. "Father's a duke. Hawksrest's his only son, which makes him the heir, of course."

"Coz, did you hear that?" cried Jamie. He'd been standing a few yards behind her with Sam, whom Hawk, with a brief word, had placed in his care. He rushed forward now, pulling Sam in his wake. "Isn't that famous, Leon?" He grinned up at his sister's stunned face. "Our Hawk's a marquis—with a dukedom in the offing!"

It was growing dark when Rand finally left Captain Lambert's cabin. Swaying lanterns cast flickering shadows on the deck as he passed. A stiff breeze filled the *Fleetwind*'s sails, for they were well out to sea. Though he was bone weary, Rand couldn't help feeling deeply gratified. He'd done it—brought them safely aboard a royal man-of-war bound for England. He'd the added satisfaction of knowing they'd sailed without being spotted. Lieutenant Cooper's marines were the last to board, and Cooper had informed him the hounds had sounded devilish close, but their pursuers had not yet made the cove when HMS *Fleetwind* put out to sea.

The efficiency and speed with which it had been accomplished was impressive, and he'd told Lambert as much. But all the rest had taken hours to sort out. Rand first delivered a briefing on what had brought them to the cove, beginning with the identities of his charges, then answered countless questions. Most of these came from Richard Helmsley, his contact from the Foreign Office, who'd joined them in the captain's cabin. What exactly had Rand seen? Had he witnessed the archduke's treason firsthand? No? But how reliable was the princess's account? Would it bear questioning without her falling to pieces "like your typical female"? How soon . . .

On and on it had gone. They sent for Leonie in the end, after she and the others had eaten and been settled in their quarters, despite Rand's plea that her interrogation be left for later. But Helmsley was a persistent bastard, and in the end Rand had been forced to relent. Yet it irked him no end. He'd intended to divulge his identity, not to mention the other secrets he'd been forced to keep, in a more sensitive, careful manner. But the rush of events—and Helmsley—had put paid to that.

Now that it was over, he wanted only to reach the cramped cabin he shared with a senior officer—apologies from the captain; space was tight aboard ship—and sleep. But there was something he had to do first. The look in Leonie's eyes, just before she'd quit Lambert's cabin, nagged at him. It hadn't been directed at Helmsley, though he'd done most of the questioning. Nor at Lambert, whose rough but kindly courtesy had helped put her at ease. Helmsley, the sod, had been steely-eyed and abrupt. Her look was fleeting, but he made no doubt it had been there—and that it was aimed at him.

* * *

Jamie and Sam emerged from the first officer's cabin, which was theirs for the duration of the voyage. Lieutenant Briggs had kindly vacated it and even offered to show them about in the morning. With a meal and a nap behind him, however, Jamie had grown restless. He itched to go exploring and had persuaded Sam to join him. They were just setting off when they spied Rand coming down the passageway.

"Look, Coz—it's Haw—er, shall we address you as Hawksrest now, m'lord?" the prince asked. A message had come from the captain's cabin earlier. They were to remain incognito. But Jamie didn't know if this applied to Hawk. Some of the officers knew Hawk had a title, but perhaps there were others aboard who weren't meant to know.

"Address me however it suits, my dear James," Rand replied. "Bear in mind, however," he added, winking at Sam, "if you insist on m'lording me, in private, at least, I shall return the favor by addressing *you* as Your High—"

"Never say I mentioned it!" Jamie cried. He produced a mock shudder that would have done Petrie proud, provoking a grin from Sam.

Chuckling, Rand ruffled the prince's hair affectionately. Count on Jamie to be unfazed by the day's surprises, including his escort's metamorphosis into a marquis. He noted Sam appeared equally at ease with this. But how was he faring otherwise? The child's terrified stuttering would haunt them all for a long time to come, Rand suspected.

"How are the bravest lads I know?" he asked, ruffling Sam's hair now.

"James was the brave one," Sam replied with unabashed honesty. Then he paused, thoughtful. "And Leon. Leon was brave, too."

"Indeed," Rand said, remembering a night in the forest when he'd fashioned a crown of wildflowers. "But I want you to know something. We'd never have made it if each of you, in his own way, hadn't done his very best. I'm proud of you . . . all of you."

"Even me?" Sam asked.

"Never doubt it, lad. Sometime soon, I'll tell you both about courage and the way it works," Rand replied, thinking again of wildflowers gracing an elfin face. "Now I should like to speak with Leon. Do you know where he is?"

"Went to check on the horses," said Jamie, "but he's sharing quarters with us." He gestured at their cabin. "No wasted space in a man-o'-war, y'know."

"Lieutenant Briggs told us," Sam put in eagerly. "And James and I are to sleep in *hammocks!* But not Leon. He's to have the—oh, look! Here comes Leon now."

Turning, Rand saw Leonie limping toward them. All at once, she slowed her pace—because she'd seen him, he realized with a frown. Her eyes met his briefly, then skittered away.

"I thought you were sound asleep," she said to the boys as she drew near. Avoiding Rand's eyes, she scowled at Jamie. "What are you two about, if may I ask?"

"We're off to explore the ship," he replied. "Er . . . may we?"

"I'm not certain that's a good idea," she told him, feeling like an ogre when she saw his face drop. "I'm sorry, truly, but it's gone dark, do you see, and without an escort . . ." She gave him an apologetic shrug.

"I collect someone escorted you to the horses," Rand put in, knowing she'd not have found her way to the hold alone. He hoped to resolve this, and not just to relieve Jamie's disappointment. He needed a word with her without the boys hovering. "One of the midshipmen, perhaps?"

Leonie gave him a stiff nod.

"He no doubt employed a lantern," Rand said. "Perhaps he's still available to assist the lads."

Leonie felt caught between the hope on the boys' faces and her burgeoning anger at Hawk. *Make that Hawksrest,* she thought angrily. *What right does he have, to stick his deceitful nose into our lives?* In the end she allowed herself to be persuaded they might go in search of the young man who'd escorted her. Promising to be polite if the officer agreed, off they went.

Leaving her alone with Hawksrest.

Make that the marquis *of Hawksrest!* she thought with another spurt of anger. Wishing she'd paid more attention to what her mother had once termed the Cut Direct, she moved past him, intent on reaching the privacy of her quarters.

A quiet hand on her arm stopped her. "Princess, may I speak with you for a moment?" Rand asked. And when she stared straight ahead, saying nothing: "Please?"

The gentleness of his plea was her undoing. She averted her face, blinking back tears.

Puzzled—the passageway was dimly lit, making it hard to see—Rand cupped her chin and gently tilted her face toward him "Leonie, what's—you're *crying.*"

"I'm not! I—I've simply caught something in m-my eye," she insisted, mortified.

"Come, let me see," he said calmly, capturing her face between his hands before she could demur. Holding her gently, he made a careful show of searching for the offending particle.

Leonie met this scrutiny through a blur of tears. She despised herself for giving in to such weakness, and in front of him. If only she could snap her fingers and vanish, like the characters in old nursery tales.

"Princess," Rand chided softly, shaking his head, "you are not a very good liar."

She bridled, tearing away from his grasp. "Then perhaps I should take lessons from you—*m'lord, the marquis.*"

"Ah." Rand sighed heavily, knowing he'd just had a lesson of his own in the difference between males and females. Jamie and Sam had barely turned a hair upon learning his identity.

"Leonie," he said softly, "I don't blame you for—look, can't we find some privacy"—he indicated the cabin door—"and discuss this calmly and sensibly?"

"As you wish," she said tightly. Never let it be said she wasn't sensible.

Once inside, Rand located a tinderbox and lighted the gimbaled lantern suspended above a brassbound sea chest. Having stanched the flow of tears, Leonie perched stiffly on edge of the cabin's narrow cot. She watched his brisk, efficient movements in stony silence, already regretting having agreed to this. Hadn't she answered enough of their wretched questions? Oh, why hadn't she told him to leave her in peace?

His presence seemed to fill the small cubicle, making her feel even smaller than she was, smaller and insignificant. She wished he weren't half so graceful or so tall or so blazingly handsome. While beautiful people had always intimidated her, Hawk had been the singular exception. Now that distinction was gone, for he possessed not only this blinding male beauty, but a great title—a title he hadn't seen fit to mention, yet she'd trusted him with all manner of secrets. And there was her own title, at best a cruel joke, not to mention her ugly, misshapen—

"Leonie, please look at me." His voice was gently coaxing, yet it startled her. She'd been eyeing her twisted foot. Jerking her head up now, she saw him uncomfortably near, hunkered down beside her, their faces only inches apart. He smelled faintly of the sandalwood soap she'd once seen in his pack. Of leather, too, and horses . . . and an ineluctable essence that was male to the bone.

"I know it came as a shock," he went on, "that I'm not what you believed me to be. But Leonie, there were good reasons for what I did. Just as there were reasons for hiding your own iden—"

"We didn't hide them from *you,* Hawk—or whatever your name is!"

"Actually," he said with an apologetic smile, "it's Randall. My first name, that is. Surname's Darnley. Make free to call me Rand, if you wish. It's what most of my family and close friends call—"

"You only pretended to be our friend!" she cut in, unwilling to be drawn by his charm. She was feeling hurt and deceived, and nothing he could say would change what he'd done. "You *used* us. Pretended friendship while spying for your odious Mr. Helmsley."

"He is not my Mr. Helmsley, and I did not pretend to be—"

"Didn't you?" she snapped. She'd begun to recall certain private moments that had passed between them. Moments she'd cherished, idiot that she was! She couldn't bear it, that she'd been so naive. So stupidly trusting, when all the while he was using her to gain his own ends.

"What a fool you must have thought me," she said bitterly, "wearing that silly crown, and believing it meant something!"

"It did," he said quietly, and reached for her hands, which she'd balled into fists in her lap. "Ah, Leonie, it *did.* It still does."

A fat tear slid down her cheek, then another. She tried to pull her hands from his grasp to dash them away, but he wouldn't release her.

"Sweetheart, you *are* courageous," he insisted with quiet certitude, holding her gaze, "whether it's Hawk or *Lord* Randall who had the sense to see it . . . and tell you. But I'm not the only one. Not ten minutes ago, Sam acknowledged your courage. Said you were brave."

Swallowing back tears, she searched his face. "Truly?" she whispered uncertainly.

"Truly." Smiling tenderly, he delved into his waistcoat pocket for a handkerchief. "Jamie was there. You can ask him, if I've so ruined your trust that you can't believe me."

"I . . . I *want* to trust you, Hawk—I mean Rand," she corrected with a sniffle.

"Rand, Hawk, it is all one," he said, gently blotting her tears with the linen. "None but my intimates call me Rand, but only you shall have leave to call me either from this day forward.

"I *am* your friend, Leonie," he went on, coaxing her to blow her nose. "And I cannot tell you how deeply I regret giving you reason to doubt it. Can you forgive me?"

Again, she searched his face for the truth—and found it.

There, in the violet depths of his eyes, unmistakable regret and a cautious hope that she trust again. And how could she not? she asked herself. With his beautiful eyes reaching deeply into hers, how could she not?

All at once, joy surged up inside her like a thing with wings, and she gave him a watery grin. "Yes—but only if Jamie and Sam may also have that choice of names."

"Done!" he cried, laughing and squeezing her hands.

The ring of his laughter sounded boyish. It reminded her of Jamie, and she couldn't help but join in. "Oh, I am so glad we are past that!" she exclaimed when she'd caught her breath. "I couldn't bear what I was thinking, especially after Mr. Helmsley—Hawk, are you really a spy?"

"I was," he said, suddenly sober, "which is a secret, you understand. My turn, for I am trusting *you* now. Jamie already suspects, and Sam most likely, for he is reticent but far from thick. I must ask you all to keep this confidence. Lives may depend on it."

"Yes, yes, of course. But . . . you just said *I was* . . . a spy, that is. Did you mean that you've done with spying?"

"My official role as an intelligence officer ended when I left my regiment. I sold out after Boney surrendered, do you see. Expected nothing more than to settle down and enjoy the Peace in domestic tranquillity. Unfortunately, the Foreign Office had other plans for me."

"Does that mean you're a civilian spy now?" she asked, fascinated. There was so much about him she didn't know—and she wanted to know everything.

"Yes, but I assure you the position's only temporary. Once the Foreign Office is fully aware of your uncle's treachery, it can take measures to stop him. My role is essentially over, and I intend to keep it that way."

"I see." She was thinking of what he'd said about domestic tranquillity. *Dear God, I really know next to nothing of him. He could be* married, *for all I know.* "Do you . . . do you mean to set up your nursery, then?" she ventured cautiously. "Or have you already done—"

"As I've no wife, it's not in the offing . . . not in the foreseeable future, at any rate."

"I see," she repeated, releasing the breath she hadn't realized she'd been holding. She told herself she'd no reason to feel relieved, but there it was. The mere thought of a marchioness of Hawksrest at home waiting for him was nearly as disagreeable as believing his friendship a sham.

Deep in thought, Rand was oblivious to the emotions passing over her face. *Set up my nursery? Will I ever even contemplate such a thing again? I know William longs for grandchil*—William! *I haven't even begun to tell her about William and Leona!*

But he'd left the emerald ring in his pack, and it really wanted the ring to tell it right. Tomorrow, then, after they'd all had a good night's sleep. He'd tell her then, and Jamie. In the morning, as soon as breakfast was over.

Watching him, Leonie puzzled over the subtle alterations she glimpsed on his face. She was no expert at reading him, of course. As a spy, he'd no doubt learned to play his cards close to the chest. But she'd seen something . . . something deeply unsettling.

Rand, she realized, might well have deeper secrets than Hawk. Not the state secret kind, like Mirandeau and England. But there *were* secrets, private things he wasn't telling her. That had been pain in his eyes just after he told her he'd no nursery.

"Past time I was leaving," Rand said abruptly, rising. He gave her a tired smile. "Thank you for hearing me out."

"I'm glad I did," she said softly.

Promising to send after the boys, he bade her good night and let himself out.

A host of thoughts crowded Leonie's mind. What was behind that shadow in his eyes? She was no stranger to hurts carried deep inside. The more she thought on it, the more certain she grew that Rand suffered from some unseen wound. Perhaps not unlike herself, she mused, recalling the pain of believing herself a hopeless coward. A belief he'd helped shatter. *I dub thee Queen of Courage.*

Not that she suddenly fancied herself a heroic figure. Still, she'd conquered all manner of fears in recent days. And, thanks to him, she knew that took courage!

Very well, then. If he could help heal her wounds, why couldn't she return the favor? Of course, she must first find out what troubled him, and she suspected that would not be easy. Rand, she sensed, was a private person. He'd not welcome prying, no matter how well meant. Still, they had weeks at sea to look forward to with very little to occupy their time.

She'd set about it in the morning, right after breakfast.

Thirteen

In the morning, Leonie found her plans for Rand must wait. A storm had arisen in the night, requiring all the energies of the watch on duty. And when the watch changed, the weather had not improved. Captain Lambert remained on deck, sending his regrets: He must, alas, postpone yesterday's invitation for the passengers to join him for breakfast.

Not that the passengers all had an appetite. Petrie, who shared space with two junior officers, sent word to the first officer's cabin that he was dying. Alarmed, Leonie felt they ought to fetch the surgeon. But the boy who brought the message said they needn't bother. 'Twas only the mal de mer, a common affliction of landlubbers. This greatly intrigued Jamie and Sam, whose stomachs were unaffected, and Jamie volunteered to look in on the actor. Reporting back, he informed Leonie and Sam that Petrie was probably still alive, but oddly green about the face.

Mildly queasy herself, Leonie nibbled on some hardtack, and this soon set her to rights. The boys presented a bigger problem, for Jamie longed to see the "prodigious great waves" the ship's boy had described; nothing would do but for him and Sam to climb on deck to view them. His sister insisted an open deck was no place for children in a storm. Ignoring their grumbles, she rummaged in her pack for writing supplies and set them briskly to work doing sums.

This occupied them for a while, but when the storm began to worsen, Sam found it hard to concentrate. The frigate had started to pitch and roll wildly, the wind outside shrieking like something alive. In no time at all, he was terrified. She and Jamie tried to soothe him, but it was no use. He began to stutter again, and Leonie grew deeply concerned. When they heard him cry out for Hawk, she made a decision. Jamie must stay to comfort him while she fetched Rand from his cabin.

She'd the name of the officer with whom Rand shared, but no idea where his cabin was. Moving uncertainly along the slanting deck in the dim passageway, she nearly collided with a young midshipman who came racing down a ladder. Dripping seawater, he pointed her in the right direction. Wind drove icy rain through the hatch he'd used, and she shivered. Glad she'd thrown a coat over her smallclothes, she limped unsteadily in the direction he'd indicated.

She nearly lost her footing several times. The undulating deck presented no small challenge to someone with her awkward gait. Finally, she located the cabin. Bracing herself against a severe tilt of the deck, she straightened, rapped urgently on the door. "Hawksrest, are you there?"

No answer.

"Is anyone there?" she asked, rapping louder this time. "Hawk?"

Still no answer. Without thinking, she tried the door, and found it unlocked. She began to open it cautiously. Perhaps he was still asleep. After all, he'd looked exhausted when he left her last night. At that moment the ship rolled and pitched sharply forward, the combined effect thrusting her through the door like a shot.

"Oh!" she cried, stumbling into something. A desk, she thought. She felt papers, stacked in odd little mounted baskets. Whatever it was, it held firm. Like most of the furniture on board, it was likely bolted to the deck. She grabbed and held on, glancing about the dim cabin, trying to get her bearings. A sudden lurch of the vessel tilted her backward. The door behind her slammed shut, thrusting the cabin into total darkness.

"Is anyone here?" she asked, mostly for form's sake. She was, after all, in a stranger's cabin. It would never do to find she'd missed the officer in his cot, exhausted from his watch on deck. Rand, she knew, was absent. Impossible to be unaware of him in a space this small. She was already that attuned to him, she realized with a curious sense of wonder. "Anyone?" she called a final time.

Her only answer was a creaking of wood overhead and the muted howling of the wind. The deck had righted itself, but it was still black as pitch. Had she glimpsed a tinderbox secured to the gallery at the top of the desk? She groped, found it. Trying to think what else she'd seen before the door shut, she recalled a lantern similar to the one in her own cabin.

After several minutes of fumbling about in the dark, she had light. The ship had cooperated, for it was pitching less violently now. Was it her imagination, or had the storm begun to subside?

In the next instant, she forgot about the storm. Rand wasn't here, but his things were. There, on the cot to the right of that locker, lay his saddle pack. A few items had spilled out, including a handsome silver-backed hairbrush and a few coins. A shirt she recognized was lying beside them.

She ran her eyes avidly over each item, as if it might tell her something of its owner. Slowly, guilt nibbling at the edges of her mind, she moved closer. When she reached the cot, she perused everything in sight, examining each with infinite care, then touching when at last she dared. She was hungry for anything to do with him.

She froze, not believing her eyes. Out of the pack, quite hidden from view until a sudden lurch of the ship sent it clinking against the hairbrush, tumbled a ring. An emerald ring, its facets winking in the shifting light. And she knew there couldn't be two exactly alike. Not a ring like this . . . no, never. Slowly, like someone caught in a bad dream, she picked it up. *Mama's ring. Rand has Mama's ring . . . has had it all along!*

At once disbelieving, yet knowing she'd no choice, she clenched her fist around it, as if the sharp edges biting into her hand could dispel the pain of betrayal that threatened to bring her to her knees. *I am your friend, Leonie.* His words, so recently uttered as truth, mocked her as she stood there, trembling.

But how? How did he come by it? And why? she asked herself, trying desperately to make sense of it all. Yet all she saw were lies. And now the biggest lie of all—that she could *trust* him—exposed by this ring cutting into her flesh. This ring he hadn't dared to mention, that he could never hope to explain away.

With a convulsive shudder, she flung it on the cot. A sickening thought had wormed its way into her brain. *He's admitted he's a spy, but what if . . . dear God, could he possibly be Roderik's spy?* Fighting nausea, she stumbled blindly from the cabin.

The storm diminished throughout the morning. By afternoon, the sea was slightly choppy, the wind nothing near what it had been. The watch changed, then changed again. The hands were piped to dinner and life after the blow, as the seamen called it, slowly returned to normal. By the day after, it was as if the storm had never been. With no clouds in sight, sunlight streamed through the slanted windows of the captain's handsome cabin.

"More claret, m'lord?" Lambert asked. "Not as fine as the Madeira we had last night, but I fear that was the last of it. Don't come by vintage Madeiras every day. Had the good fortune to liberate that lot—before the Peace, of course—from a prize we took as she tried to slip past our blockade off Toulon."

"Thank you, captain," Rand replied with an absent nod. He sipped the claret, not really attending as Lambert directed remarks to the others at the table. These were all senior officers he'd invited to dine, well pleased they'd brought *Fleetwind* through without losing a single spar. Rand had been invited as a courtesy—and, he suspected, to grace Lambert's table with his lordly elegance. Too bad he couldn't oblige him with sparkling discourse. His thoughts, his disturbing thoughts, lay elsewhere.

It was Leonie again. She was pointedly avoiding him, damn it, and he'd yet to learn why. He'd been deuced busy, of course—spent hours, during the storm and after, closeted with Helmsley, discussing the ramifications of what Mirandeau's princess had overheard in a stable loft. And then there'd been that heated exchange over what would happen to her and the boys once they reached England.

They must be granted political asylum, of course. Rand had made it clear he'd accept nothing less. Helmsley had said he could promise nothing. And Rand had just enough dislike of the man to make a promise of his own: If Whitehall failed to summon all the power of the Crown to protect the royal refugees, Helmsley would answer to *him.*

A ghost of a smile hovered as Rand sipped his claret. The bastard's face had gone white on hearing that, as well it ought. Hawksrest's history as an agent, a ruthless agent when he had to be, was well known to Whitehall's inner circle, and Helmsley was no fool.

A final toast to the king, and the dinner was over. Rand took his leave and went in search of Jamie. With Leona's ring in mind, he'd made two brief attempts, earlier in the day, to see the children. To arrange a time for that all-important talk, perhaps before supper, when he'd finally be free.

Both times, Jamie had answered the door. Both times, he'd looked uncomfortable, informing Rand his sister was indisposed and not receiving. Not receiving? Since when was she given to such tonnish claptrap? Then, when he'd asked if the prince might himself spare a moment, Jamie had looked even more uncomfortable—damned uncomfortable. Said he couldn't, for he and Sam must attend to their sums. Leon had said so.

She was not only avoiding him, just when he thought they were on good footing again; she'd clearly told the boys to avoid him as well. But why? He could make no sense of it.

Indeed, if Jamie weren't so poor at dissembling, he might never have realized how serious the situation was.

What the devil was plaguing her now? Well, she couldn't put him off forever. He doubted the boys, Jamie in particular, would stay on her leash for long. He just needed to find the prince when he was alone—and then he'd have some answers, by God!

As it happened, it wasn't Jamie who gave him answers, but Sam. Rand was approaching the passageway that led to their cabin when he spied him. Sam was hunkered down beside an orange tabby cat, speaking quietly to it as he fed it a tidbit.

"Found a friend, have you, lad?" Rand called out softly, not to startle him.

Sam's head jerked up, but not in alarm. "Hawk, come and see!" he exclaimed. "Isn't he splendid? He ran from the boy who brought our dinner, but not from me. He lets me stroke him, and I can feel him purring under my hand!"

Rand hunkered down beside him. "That's because he trusts you. You're kind to him, and animals are no different from us in that way." He stroked the cat's head gently with his finger.

"Oh, listen to him!" Sam was grinning as Rand had never seen him grin before. "He trusts *you,* too." He added his own stroking to Rand's, eyeing him thoughtfully. "It's because you're kind as well, Hawk. James and I were trying to tell Leon that, when . . ."

When Leon didn't agree, I collect. "When Leon said you mustn't speak to me?" Rand prompted softly.

Sam hung his head, saying nothing.

"It's all right, Sam," he murmured, gently smoothing his hair. "She no doubt has her reasons. And I wouldn't, for the world, have you overset because of this. The difficulty is, I don't know what those reasons are."

"She won't tell us, either!" Sam blurted out, so fiercely the cat bristled. "Oh, I do beg your pardon, Cat." He fished a piece of ham from his pocket, which the tabby accepted after a brief hesitation—and with a slightly injured air, Rand thought.

"We're not to see you, but she won't discuss it," Sam went on. "She only told us because we saw she'd been *crying.*"

"Crying . . . when?"

"When she came back from trying to find you."

"She went looking for me?"

Sam nodded. "Yesterday, during the blow. I—I was frightened, you see, and wishing awfully that you were there, and . . ." He dropped his eyes, suddenly embarrassed.

"Never concern yourself, Sam. I wish I *had* been there. 'Twas a frightening blow, and we might have taken comfort in each other. Now, do go on. Did you learn where she went looking?" He recalled Helmsley answering the door while they were closeted in his cabin yesterday. He'd dismissed the caller with a curt, "We're not to be disturbed." *If that was Leonie he sent away—and without so much as a by-your-leave to me—I'll have his bloody head.*

But Helmsley was safe. *For now, at least,* Rand told himself as he watched Sam leave, the orange cat at his heels. The tabby meowed as they neared the cabin, and Sam bent to pick him up. "You will try to mend things, won't you, Hawk?" he called, hugging the cat close. He'd hugged Rand that way not a moment before, and Rand swallowed thickly before replying.

"I'm certainly going to try, Sam."

"Please do, because we miss you, Hawk. All of us, I think. Even if we don't all know it," he added, glancing at the door. Still hugging the cat, he disappeared inside.

Rand stood there, sifting what he'd learned. Leonie had set off to find his cabin yesterday. Sam remembered hearing her say so. And, of course, Rand hadn't been there. Neither had his cabin mate. If he'd had a visitor, the lieutenant would have said. Yet Leonie might have had a look inside. The lieutenant had returned at one point to shift his clothes, and the poor devil had been so exhausted fighting wind and wave, he'd neglected to lock the door when he left.

Rand recalled being irritated when he found it unlocked, with any Tom, Dick, or Harry at liberty to walk in and pinch what he pleased. Not that there was much to attract a thief, but that damned emerald ring had somehow tumbled out of his—*the ring! Is it possible she saw her mother's ring? Recognized it? And concluded there was no earthly reason—no* honest *reason—it should be among my things?*

"Bloody hell," he growled. "If that's the case, she has every reason to mistrust me—and worse!" He cast a doubtful glance at the door Sam had just closed. She'd be indisposed and not receiving again, of course. Yet, damn it, as an agent, he'd gained entrance to scores of places where he wasn't welcome. If he couldn't use all that experience to get past one little female's door, he bloody well deserved to be put out to pasture.

Unfortunately, Rand's determination was frustrated at every turn. Despite all his attempts, Leonie refused to see him. She remained shut up inside, taking all her meals on a tray, never once leaving the confines of the cabin. What was worse, what was inexcusable in his opinion, she kept the boys inside as well. The *Fleetwind* enjoyed days of clear sailing after the storm. The air on deck was fresh and invigorating, the sun benevolent. Being shut up in a small, stuffy cabin had to be agony itself for a pair of growing boys. Criminal, he decided one day as he fingered the emerald ring in his pocket. Absolutely criminal to lock them up.

He was standing at the taffrail, thinking these black thoughts, when he saw Petrie coming toward him. They'd seen little of the actor since embarking, owing to the poor fellow's bout of seasickness. Rand had looked in on him a few times, offering what sympathy and encouragement he could. Simon had appeared barely human, his already thin frame so wasted he'd the look of a cadaver. Not that he seemed much improved now, but at least he was upright.

"Good day to you, Petrie. How are you feeling?"

Simon gave him a pale smile. "The worst is over, and I no longer look forward to becoming worms' meat"—he eyed the frothy wake stretching out behind them—"or fish bait, perhaps."

Rand noted the clothes hanging loosely on the scarecrow's emaciated body. "We must fatten you up, sir. Have you taken any nourishment?"

A wry grin. "If the thin gruel, which the ship's surgeon had the audacity to name as such, may be called nourishment, m'lord. But I have a hope of better. I've an invitation to dine with Captain Lambert today. I understand you are to be there as well, along with a Mr. Helmsley?"

Rand nodded. Helmsley wanted Petrie's version of the regent's illicit coronation rehearsals. He'd been spared interrogation till now only because he'd been indisposed. *Truly indisposed. Not like another I know!*

"If I may be so bold, m'lord," said the actor, "your face grew, er, rather severe just now. Have I said something amiss?"

"Not at all, sir. I was merely . . ." Rand was silent for a moment, then asked rhetorically, not really expecting an answer, "Do you have any idea how vexing it is to be denied admission to someone's door?"

Simon chuckled. "Indeed, I do m'lord. Directors and stage managers are not always willing to receive an actor who is, er, between engagements. One in my line of work must develop a thick skin, as it were—and a clever means of circumventing these gentlemen's unwillingness to be in the way, of course."

"A clever means?" Rand asked, suddenly alert.

"Why, certainly. When Kemble was manager at Covent Garden and casting for *Twelfth Night,* he refused to see me, despite my splendid success as Feste at the Drury Lane two years before. To remind him, I sent him the very fool's cap I'd worn in the play, and fastened to the cap's bells were copies of the excellent notices I'd received." He smiled triumphantly. "I soon found myself not only admitted, but cast in the part!"

"Did you, by God? Did you, indeed?"

* * *

Moments later, Rand was striding briskly toward Leonie's cabin. Reaching the door, he gave it two short raps.

Sounds of movement inside, and the door opened. Then Jamie's face, alight with pleasure for an instant before it fell. "Er, Hawk, I don't think—"

"You needn't think at all, James, but do listen. As I seem to have come away without my calling cards, be so kind as to inform Leon I'm here, and deliver *this*"—he made an elaborate leg and proffered the ring—"in lieu of my card."

"Jamie," said a cross female voice from inside, "I asked you not to—"

"It's Hawk," said Jamie, not missing a beat as he turned to face his sister, "and he's sent you something extraordinary—see?"

Leonie gazed in open astonishment at the ring he held aloft, then slowly held out her hand. Jamie obliged her, dropping it neatly into her palm. From Sam's lap, as her cousin sat cross-legged at her feet, the orange cat gave a soft meow, but no one moved. All eyes, including Rand's, were on the emerald ring.

At last, Leonie lifted her gaze, and Rand sucked in his breath. The eyes that met his were bleak and hard at the same time . . . harder than he'd ever have thought possible. "If you can tell me whose ring this was," she said tightly, "then you'll know why I've every reason to believe you could not have come by it honestly."

"Leonie!" cried Jamie, aghast.

"Oh, please," Sam's words were softer, yet his involuntary start sent the cat bolting from his lap.

"It's all right, lads," Rand told them, but his eyes remained on Leonie. "The ring belonged to your mother," he answered, "yet before that, it was my father's ring. He gave it to her long ago, before any of us were born."

A look of confusion entered the green eyes, and she frowned. "Your *father?*"

"William, duke of Hartswood. And the reason I have it now—"

"Just a moment," she said, frowning. An image floated into her mind . . . a crumpled piece of paper, yellowed with age and wrapped around the ring. The writing on it, in Mama's hand. *Hartswood! The name on that paper, of the man in England that we were meant to go to, was William, duke of Hartswood.*

"Hawksrest," she said through a shaky expulsion of air, "I think you had better come in."

". . . and that is why I waited to tell you all this," Rand said many long minutes later. He and Leonie were alone in the cabin. The boys had gleefully run off to explore, once they had the bare bones of the ring's history. They'd only needed to hear what they always believed in the first place: Hawk was incapable of being anything but their friend.

"A foolish mistake, I own," Rand went on, "for I should have mentioned the ring when we spoke that first evening. Instead, I waited until I should have the ring on my person, to show you . . . and, of course, the storm intervened. Once again, I must beg your forgiveness for causing you so much difficulty."

"No. No, it is I who must apologize," she said, shaking her head. She could barely take it all in: her mother and Hawk's father, in love so long ago, sadly parted, yet linked by this ring.

"You?" Rand smiled ruefully. Were they forever doomed to be apologizing to each other? "You've nothing to apolo—"

"I hope I may know how remiss I was," she said with some asperity, "to have entered a gentleman's quarters without his leave! I—I don't know what came over me, but it was wrong in the extreme. Can you ever—"

"Forgive you?" he asked with a quick grin. This at once melted into a tender smile. "With all my heart," he said softly, "if you will do the same."

She'd ducked her head, hoping to hide her reaction to that

heart-stopping grin. Now she raised it, peering shyly at him from beneath her lashes. He was so very beautiful, his white teeth flashing against the tan of his face, which lately bore a ruddy gold cast from the sun on deck. Then those devastating grooves bracketing the grin and the jet-black curls tousled by the wind, both giving him a boyish look at odds with his square jaw and carved cheekbones. And always, always, those incredible eyes! Violet deepening to indigo and thickly lashed, sometimes keen and penetrating, which she couldn't always like; sometimes the way she liked them best: lazy with contentment or sparkling with good humor.

Catching the drift of her thoughts, she dropped her gaze to her lap. *You must stop this, my girl. Anyone privy to your thoughts would think you'd developed a* tendre *for him, and it won't answer. He's as far above you as cream to whey, as—as Raven to a carthorse! And a lame carthorse, at that!*

"Uh-oh," Rand murmured as the silence stretched out. "If it requires such pondering, I collect I am deeply in the suds."

"Not at all!" she cried, recovering. "I beg you will forgive my inattentive—what are you laughing at?"

"Both of us," he replied, chuckling. "Only hear the pleas for forgiveness racketing about our heads like tennis balls. Are we not coming it a bit *outré* in the courtesy department?"

She grinned, savoring the mirth in his eyes. They crinkled at the corners, the way she liked them best of all, she decided—then caught herself. "Perhaps we are," she said, sobering, "but there is one thing I must set right." She held out the ring. "This is yours . . . or your father's, I should say, for my mother returned it to him."

"Oh, no, sweetheart." He closed her fingers around the ring, covering her small fist with his hand. "It was only returned to give weight to her message. His Grace would tell you that in a trice, and you must keep it until he can do so. His deepest regret, beyond what he felt on reading your mother's letter, was that he was unable to come himself."

Releasing her, he rose gracefully to his feet. "Keep the

ring, Leonie," he said softly, "and soon perhaps I'll see you wear it. When we're free of all this tiresome disguise business—yes, you must wear it. It goes with your eyes."

"B-but—"

"Shh," he said, stilling her lips gently with his thumb. "Call it a tribute, if you will," he added. "A very fitting tribute"—he bent and kissed her brow—"to my Queen of Courage."

Her heart hammered in her chest. Unable to utter a word in reply, she watched him take his leave. He may have mentioned he hoped to see her at supper; she wasn't sure. The thrumming of blood in her ears had made hearing impossible. *Get hold of yourself,* an inner voice commanded as she collapsed on her cot in dismay. *Be sensible.*

Too late, too late, another voice cried, and she knew it as a voice from the heart. She *loved him,* she realized with startling clarity. Loved him beyond all hope, because she knew it was a love not in the least reciprocated. Opening her fist, she gazed at the ring through a blur of tears.

An hour later, when the boys returned, the tears were gone without a trace. Leonie listened with apparent eagerness as they chattered about meeting Hawk on deck. And smiled as they told her how they were all to be guests at his home, how they'd meet the duke who'd pledged his love with such a "thumping fine ring."

Another hopeless love, she mused, hiding her sadness as she thought of the man her mother had loved. Of his undying devotion to her all these years. Had Mama known? But she must have, to send for him that way in the end.

Perhaps that's what life is meant to teach us . . . that we are not to waste it longing for what is hopeless. Perhaps it's something Mama herself hoped I'd learn.

With one last pang of regret, she reminded herself she must be sensible.

Part II

Fourteen

England

The Hartswood coach, its ducal crest emblazoned on its doors and John Coachman on the box, crossed the downs into Kent. High time, too, Rand thought as he contemplated the lush green of high summer outside the window. After a fortnight at sea, followed by three hectic days in London, he was at long last taking his young charges to Hartswood. At long last fulfilling his promise to his father . . . and William's promise to his beloved Leona.

Across from him, the boys were speculating energetically on the distance traveled and the merits of this conveyance compared with Rand's high-perch phaeton. They'd begged him to take the phaeton, but it wouldn't answer. It could never accommodate four people, not to mention the orange cat that had followed Sam off the ship. Rand had appeased them by spinning them about Hyde Park in the stylish rig, however, and Jamie had even had a go at the ribbons. But for Kent, it was the coach and six that the family kept in the mews behind the London town house.

Rand had piled everyone into it this morning, and he could scarcely wait to arrive. He made no doubt his father and grandmother were anxious, too. He'd sent a message ahead, informing them what to expect, but that had been three days ago.

His gaze fell on Leonie, who sat beside him, peering out

the window. She was trying to appear calm and sedate, but wasn't quite successful in pulling it off. True, she was less obvious than the boys. They were crowding the window on their side, pointing and chattering with great excitement. As usual, Leonie's face gave her away. The sparkle in her eyes, the heightened color along her delicate cheekbones, the animation in her features all spoke of a lively interest and curiosity in everything she saw.

And gave him an odd sense of pleasure that was hard to explain.

What was it about her that drew him? That made him want to smile as he realized he was smiling even now? She was lovely to look at, of course, even in that absurd little bonnet bought in such a hurry. He hoped the traveling gown, stitched by his grandmother's own mantua maker in London, gave her pleasure. Despite the short notice, the modiste hadn't dared to turn down his request to rig up a few things for Her Grace's cousin, whose trunks were lost at sea.

Yes, she was lovely in the way a woman in the first flush of youth cannot help being lovely. Yet he'd met scores of pretty young chits at the tonnish gatherings his position obliged him to attend. None had held his interest above two minutes. But Leonie had, from the very start, with that curious combination of wide-eyed uncertainty and enormous courage that intrigued him still. She'd demonstrated a fortitude unequaled by any female of his acquaintance, save one. Grinning, he wondered what his grandmother would make of her. Would she recognize such an unlikely kindred spirit straightaway?

"Oh, look!" cried Jamie. "There's Jumper—and Raven, too. No, Leonie—over there, in that pasture. And, Sam, that's your Puck near the fence!"

"He's looking a sight better," said Puck's owner, "now he's on dry land. I'm awfully glad Hawk's grooms took the horses to the country straightaway. Hawk, does this mean we're on your family's lands at last?"

"Indeed, we are, Sam. Have been, for the past half hour, give or take." With a grin, Rand noticed Leonie had shed the last of her reserve. At the mention of her stallion, she'd pressed her nose against the window like an eager child.

And that, too, pleased him, though he couldn't for the life of him say why.

"Grand-mère," Rand said with grave courtesy, "allow me to name Her Highness, Princess Leonie of Mirandeau. Her brother and Lord Samuel, of course, you've, er, already met."

The dowager's arched brow said that while she may have met them, it had been most irregular, and not the done thing. Hiding a smile, Rand had to agree. At the same moment their coach had pulled up the drive, the duke happened by, astride his favorite hunter. As a result, introductions had resulted then and there. Then an amazing thing occurred. William and the boys took to each other like roast beef and Yorkshire pudding. Before Rand knew it, all three were haring off in search of food, Jamie having mentioned he was sharp-set. Rand had led Leonie into the house at a more sedate pace, just in time to see his grandmother all but bowled over by two hungry boys and their ducal escort. Pausing to perform the fastest introduction in memory, William had pecked his mother on the cheek, begged her pardon, and whisked the boys out of sight.

"Your Highness"—Rand turned to Leonie, still taking particular care with proper form after that havey-cavey introduction—"Her Grace, my grandmother, dowager duchess of Hartswood."

Despite her own rank, Leonie sank into a deep curtsey, for this was not only her hostess, but a noblewoman of great age and distinction. She'd suspend judgment on the rest, which amounted to mere servants' gossip anyway. It didn't necessarily follow that the dowager was a "right proper Tartar," no matter how often the London servants had mumbled it.

She'd difficulty with the curtsey, however, a problem in any case owing to her crippled foot. Now the added complication of floors rising unexpectedly to discommode her, a phenomenon that had beset her since stepping on dry land, made it a graceless affair indeed. She managed to murmur "Your Grace," and met the *grande dame's* eyes as she rose.

"Welcome to Hartswood, Your Highness," the dowager intoned with staid formality. They were in the rose drawing room, where she stood by her favorite wing chair, hands clamped over the chased gold handle of her cane. A quizzing glass hung from a ribbon on her bosom, but she didn't use it; yet her black eyes missed not a detail of the young woman standing before her.

Delicate, like her mother, though perhaps more petite. Cut of the gown's not bad, but the color—positively ghastly! Green's more the thing, given those remarkable eyes. Excellent skin, but the freckles speak of a careless disregard for the sun. Wonderful hair, though, copper more than ginger, and lots of it. Pity she's scraped it back like that. It wants Polly's clever hands, but all in good time. As for that wobbly curtsey—unfortunate, of course, but the child is lame, and that's that. Yet she endured a daunting journey to get here, from what I understand. A game little creature, then. Hmm. All in all, the child has possibilities.

"How was your trip from town?" she inquired, not pausing for a reply. "The roads are always so dreadfully crowded for the Season, while summer normally does away with all that racketing about. Yet this year, unfortunately, with all those foreigners haring to and fro for the victory celebrations . . . well, I'm sure it cannot have been restful."

Leonie opened her mouth to assure her of the opposite, but never got the chance.

"I expect you'll want a lie-down." The duchess glanced at the drawing room's closed double doors. "Barrows," she called, summoning the ancient butler she'd told to wait outside.

"Your Grace?"

"Conduct the prin—eh?" She eyed her grandson, who'd cleared his throat in warning. *Blast, I almost forgot!*

He was reminding her of the message he'd sent from London. His guests would stay at Hartswood, but Whitehall had insisted none but she and William might be told their true identities. Rand had suggested they be passed off as distant cousins.

"Conduct Lady Leonie to the chamber we discussed," she told Barrows, "and you may as well put the young gentlemen—Hawksrest, what has your father done with the young gentlemen?"

"Ahem," said Rand, pretending to cough, "I believe he escorted them to the kitchens, Grand-mère."

"The *kitchens!*" Her look said it might have been the third circle of Hell.

"Er, to investigate the likelihood of obtaining some of Cook's scones, Grand-mère. It seems His Grace's fondness for them is shared by at least one of the young gentlemen . . . perhaps both."

"Scones," she grumbled, "are all very well in their place. Be so good as to remind your father, when you see him, that place is in the blue drawing room at tea, *not* in the kitchens!"

She rose from her chair and cast a sharp glance at Leonie, who stood poised between Rand and the butler. "What, are you still here, gel? You'll never have your lie-down if you linger, and I apprehend you are in need of one. You appear a bit peaked. Tea is at four o'clock sharp. You'll be prompt, I make no doubt, and the young gentlemen may attend—if they are not so weighed down with *scones* as to render an appearance inadvisable."

She gestured at the butler with her cane. With remarkable agility for his years, he sprang to hold the door for her. Nodding regally, the dowager sailed from the room.

"From what you've told me," William said to Rand later that afternoon, "Archduke Roderik is a monster who must be stopped. Such evil. Is he unbalanced, do you think?"

They were in the library, sharing all that had happened since Rand left. The duke was well connected politically, so he'd clearance from Whitehall to be made privy to some of his son's clandestine work. Rand had been frank, therefore, about what the rescue of Leona's children had entailed.

William had dealt with his private grief for Leona long before Rand returned. But he hadn't known how she died, and Rand's news distressed him greatly. He was now committed to bringing her murderer to justice and helping her children and Sam mend their shattered lives.

"His wife certainly believes he's mad," Rand replied. "But mad or not, he's a very dangerous man."

"Thank God the children are beyond his reach."

"Speaking of which, how did you go on with the lads? I had visions of you lying prostrate on the carpet, sapped of your strength, after your romp with those two."

"On the contrary," William said with a laugh. "After but a few minutes in their company, I felt years younger!"

Rand chuckled. "You're going to need those years, I expect. They've an endless supply of energy . . . especially Jamie."

"Jamie is a law unto himself," said the duke. "Yet I think Sam is capable of holding his own. The child seems to have remarkable recuperative powers. When I consider all he's endured . . ." He shook his head sadly and heaved a sigh. "The durability of youth, I suppose. Still, I'd give anything to have prevented . . . well, they're safe now they're in England. That's what matters. Speaking of which, you've yet to tell me how it went with the Foreign Office."

Rand grimaced.

"As bad as that?"

"You'd not credit the level of incompetence among government officials."

William smiled wryly. "You forget I've dealt with my

share in the Lords. But, come, you knew it wouldn't be easy. You made off with the reigning prince of a sovereign state. And one of our stoutest allies, at that."

"Not for long," Rand said ominously, "if those fools at Whitehall continue to waste time on the nonsense I encountered." He shook his head in disbelief. "They're all atwitter over what's to be done with our royal guests . . . protocol, more than substance. Meanwhile, Roderik may do such damage Mirandeau's allegiance won't signify. God's my life, how I detest the narrowness of minor officialdom! If only Castlereagh weren't abroad."

"Castlereagh may not be in town, but Canning is," William ventured. The former foreign secretary was a close friend, but so was Lord Castlereagh, which spoke for the duke's ability to steer his way through turbulent political waters. The two politicos were bitter enemies, yet William managed to retain the respect of each. "I could put in a quiet word."

"What, and risk a second duel between them?"

"Nonsense. They're both reasonable men, despite their personal differences. But if it will ease your mind, I'll write Castlereagh as well. Will that do?"

Rand gave him a relieved smile. "That just might answer. I'll write him, too. Between us, we may—what the devil's so fascinating?"

The duke had moved to the window, and seemed mesmerized by something in the garden below. "She's the very image of her mother," he said, his voice soft and faintly wistful.

Rand joined him at the window. Leonie had retrieved Sam's cat from the garden, and they watched her carry it inside. She appeared to be in a hurry, which aggravated her limp. "Yet the child is painfully shy, I collect," William added, reflecting on their brief meeting. "Leona was far more coming . . . a feminine version of Jamie, if you will. Is it the lame foot, do you think?"

"It's crossed my mind," said Rand. "But she's shy only when she's not sure she can trust you. I found her good company, actually." *When she wasn't making me live up to that trust.* "Lots of pluck. You'd not credit it, but the black stud in the east pasture is hers, and she handles him with ease."

"Does she, indeed? That wisp of a girl on a brute his size? Remarkable!"

"It wants getting to know her. Remember, you barely had two words with her before the boys had you haring off in search of scones. By the by, I'm to convey a message from Her Grace about scones."

"No doubt," said William with a chuckle. "The advisability of ingesting them in the proper setting, was it?'

"In the blue drawing room, to be precise, which is where we're to repair in"—Rand glanced at the clock—"good God, it's nearly gone four!"

"Then if we value our hides," said his father, grabbing his cane and heading for the door, "we must hurry. Not that I'm inclined to linger," he added, "with your plucky princess waiting downstairs."

What William observed, however, wasn't pluck, but something far more interesting, and it had to do with his son as much as the princess. Rand was . . . different somehow in her company. Curiously attentive to her—attentive in ways he hadn't manifested toward a young woman since Lady Cynthia Shallcross's untimely death. It was all very subtle, but the signs were there.

It began when Leonie entered the drawing room, just moments after them. Rand came instantly alive when he saw her, and the warmth in his gaze was undeniable. Soon William noticed the covert glances when Rand's eyes touched on her again and again, always when she wasn't looking. He noticed other things as well: Rand's smile, the pleasure he took on hearing her laugh, and the way he showed an interest in everything she said, even if it was as mundane as a comment on the weather. Yes, this was an entirely different Rand, but what did it signify?

Perhaps he was seeing nothing more than a bond of friendship forged because of what they'd been through. After all, Rand seemed inordinately fond of the boys as well. Of course, it was hard not to be enchanted by Jamie and Sam. Even the dowager was susceptible. There'd been a twinkle she wasn't able to hide when the lads came to tea but politely passed on Cook's scones.

So perhaps Rand's interest in Leonie was nothing out of the way and he was a fool to think it meant more. He never allowed himself to forget about those lost years, when he'd failed his son in the most basic way and he dreaded making a mistake about Rand now. *Am I reading too much into this?* he asked himself as tea drew to a close. *After all, the grieving could have ended naturally, now enough time has passed. It may have nothing to do with Leona's daughter. Perhaps I ought to hear what Mother thinks.*

"It is nothing more than wishful thinking, William," said the dowager when she and the duke were alone. "Of course he was attentive to her. One is not inattentive to a guest, even an ordinary guest, and a runaway princess, you will agree, is far from ordinary. Moreover, he was also attentive to her brother and cousin."

"He was," the duke agreed, "but not in the same—"

"On the other hand," said Her Grace, "she is head over heels for him."

"What?"

"Really, William, I believe I spoke quite plainly. Could it be you are going the way of Great Uncle Thornton?"

"Great Uncle Thornton," William said irritably, "was deaf as a post. Now, kindly explain what you meant by head over heels."

"It is quite evident. The princess has developed a *tendre* for your son."

"But how can you be so cer—"

"Not that she is to be encouraged, of course."

"But . . . why not?" William was still seeing the warmth

on Rand's face as Leonie had entered the drawing room. He might not be besotted, but he was definitely not immune to her. So if what his mother said was true, why, the possibilities were—

"Come, William, do not top it the muddle-head," his mother replied. "The gel has a life to put back together. Moreover, she has a shocking lack of acquaintance with the Polite World. We cannot possibly allow her to pursue any tender feelings at this stage. Now listen carefully, for this is what we shall do. . . ."

Mirandeau
The Palace

Emilie's hands shook as she picked up the letter that had appeared on her breakfast tray, hidden under a plate of toast. It was sealed and sanded, but scrawled across the surface were the words, *Burn this after you read it.* The imprint in the wax was nondescript, but as soon as she broke the seal, she recognized Leonie's neat, precise hand:

Dear Aunt Emilie,

I pray this letter reaches you and finds you well. I have entrusted it to a gentleman whose business I am not at liberty to discuss, but who may be relied upon. Of course, it is by no means certain he will succeed in transmitting it, given the state of things at home, yet I hope and pray he may do so, for you must be frantic for news. Yet you are not to worry, dear Aunt. Your Sam is safe, and so are Jamie and I! We are guests of an English duke—for safety's sake, I may not mention names—who was Mama's particular friend years ago, before she married Papa. His Grace is ever so nice, and we are extremely fond of him.

But I am getting ahead of myself. You are doubtless wondering how we managed our escape, and in that I have astonishing news. We would never have suc-

ceeded without the help of a palace guard who was not a guard at all, but the English duke's son! He came to our aid because of a letter Mama sent just before she died. So you see, she was of your mind with regard to the danger, and took steps to protect us, even though she was unable to protect herself. The duke's home is currently our sanctuary, and your Sam is positively thriving here. He and Jamie ride their ponies every day, and His Grace is teaching them to play chess and backgammon. As His Grace is a widower, his mother is our hostess, and she has arranged a tutor for the boys, a very kind man who smiles a great deal. And although I am too old for the schoolroom, I am to receive instruction as well. The dowager herself has taken me on, and the lessons are to repair my ignorance of the Polite World. I tried to tell her I was a Lost Cause, but she would have none of it. She is very used to having her way, I collect. She pronounced me a "diamond in the rough" and my lameness "merely a minor inconvenience"! I have no idea how I shall go on, but I dare not give these lessons anything less than my best effort. Her Grace has that kind of effect on people. She is a formidable Presence. For example, because the duke lost a leg in the war, I felt he might understand my doubts about my lameness. I feared it would present an obstacle to Her Grace's plans for me. And while he was every bit as understanding as I had hoped, he assured me it would not hinder the dowager. "Nothing deters Her Grace when she's set on an end," he said. "It wouldn't dare!"

His son laughed when I told him and said he quite agreed. It is all very well, but I sincerely hope Her Grace isn't entertaining notions of dancing lessons. By the by, you may recall who our rescuer is, for he was the guard posted outside your door. He is not in evidence as much as we would like. Sam and Jamie are extremely fond of him. He has much to occupy him, with regard to the family's estates—there are several—after being away for so long.

Now I must close, for our messenger has come, and he is in a tearing hurry. Sam and Jamie send their love, and I am, as ever,

Your loving and devoted niece,
Leonie

Emilie used her serviette to blot the tears that were streaming down her face, then went at once to the fireplace. There was no fire burning, it being summer, but the tinderbox was there. She plucked it from the mantel, quickly struck a spark, and set fire to Leonie's pages. In less than a minute, they were curled and blackened ash. Only then did her breathing return to normal. She never knew when her husband might appear, and he was in a fury these days.

The "kidnapping" had occasioned an all-out hunt, and when he realized his quarry had gotten away, no one escaped his rages. Several servants and retainers bore bruises and blackened eyes. A goodly number, the chambermaid had whispered just last week, had even run off.

Emilie herself had received the back of his hand, but that was nothing new. Roderik never once suspected her hand in the escape, thank God. She was beneath his consideration, far too weak and timid, in his mind, to dare anything of consequence. Still, that didn't stop him from taking out his wrath on her. He enjoyed taunting her, too. "Your milksop son is likely dead, madam. There's been no ransom demand, and who would want him in any event?"

But worse than the blows and taunts was his unpredictability. When weeks passed without a clue to the children's whereabouts, his suspicions grew in tandem with his madness. Despite his contempt for her, he began appearing in her rooms without notice. She knew, too, her personal effects had been searched. Perhaps he thought Sam might have contacted her and given away information that could lead Roderik to him and his cousins.

She had no fear on that score, of course, but she did worry. What if someone recalled seeing her behind the stables with the princess that morning? Roderik was questioning everyone. Even a witness who'd normally have kept quiet might tell if he were sufficiently terrified. Terror could compromise even the best of people, and Roderik was a master at it.

Roderik was terror itself.

Fifteen

England

When Leonie told Emilie that she and the boys saw little of Rand at Hartswood, she wasn't being entirely candid. Jamie and Sam saw him, if only occasionally. They informed her with typical fervor whenever they had: "Hawk let us drive his phaeton today!" or "Hawk looked in on our lessons again!" But *she* hadn't had a glimpse of him in weeks.

And while she'd never dream of telling Emilie how she felt, she was of two minds about this. That sensible voice said she should be thankful he wasn't at hand. Given her unwise attachment, his presence could only cause her pain; without it, she'd soon be her old self again. But even as she tried to heed this voice, there was another, at times no more than a pale whisper. *If only,* it said, *ah, if only you could see him now and then. . . .*

Fortunately, her days were so full she had little time to ponder either voice. Not with the dowager so set on repairing her ignorance of how to go on with the *haut ton.* And as Leonie quickly learned, when Her Grace embarked on an endeavor, she did it with a vengeance. Or, as William put it, "If Wellington had been able to use my mother in the field, we'd have defeated Boney years ago."

Every waking hour was crammed with lessons, and the dowager was her self-appointed tutor. There was instruction on poise: "Hold your head up high, and devil take the limp!" Instruction on suitable subjects for small talk: "Nothing in the personal line, but the witty *bon mot* will serve you admirably." Instruction in responding to invitations: "Accept with grace; reject with finesse."

Indeed, the *ton* had rules for every aspect of a woman's life. But the first rule, the dowager told her, the one that governed all, was paramount: "A woman's character is her most precious possession and, once tarnished, can never be restored. Yet it is not so much what she is as what she *appears* to be that matters. With the *ton,* appearance is all, gel, and never forget it!"

Physical appearance mattered, too, and must be addressed positively. "Great beauty is given to very few," said the dowager, "but even a plain Jane can contrive to make herself agreeable to the eye—and *you* are far from plain." This said, she set about making her royal pupil agreeable with an enthusiasm and energy that left Leonie gasping.

The Frenchwoman in London, as it turned out, was Her Grace's *former* mantua maker. The dowager had shifted her patronage *"the moment I apprehended Madame had developed a fondness for spirits."* The raspberry traveling gown that clashed with the princess's hair was sent to the vicar's charity bin, and Madame's replacement summoned. Leonie soon found herself draped, pinned, basted, and stitched. Within a fortnight, she possessed a wardrobe the duchess pronounced complete to a shade.

Then came sessions with Her Grace's ladies' maid, a plump, apple-cheeked girl named Polly. Polly was good-natured—*"always a virtue in personal servants"*—but her chief asset was an absolute genius for producing glorious coiffures. "You may say what you like about those mincing hairdressers who arrive with their curling papers and frizzing irons," the dowager sniffed, "but they don't hold a candle to my Polly!"

And so it went. From the instant she awoke until the time she retired, Leonie rarely had a moment free. Fortunately, she saw the boys and William at table, so she wasn't totally bereft of their company. On the other hand, she sorely missed those simple pleasures that had formed such a bulwark against loneliness at home. Raven remained in the east pasture, unridden, and when she attempted to read, she usually fell asleep on the first page.

But perhaps this was just as well. There was the occasional night when she didn't fall asleep straightaway, when the soft voice whispered and echoed in dreams that made her toss and turn. *If only you could see him now and then. . . .*

Rand left his phaeton and team at the stables, choosing to walk to the house. The day was fair, the air fresh and clean. London, in vivid contrast, had been dirty, hot, and crowded—not that he'd spent much time out of doors. But at least his latest round at Whitehall had clarified some things. They were still not happy with his decision to bring the royal refugees to England, but a letter from Castlereagh had smoothed the waters. Leonie, Jamie, and Sam were now Rand's *official* responsibility, to be kept under wraps while Whitehall investigated the situation in Mirandeau.

He'd also learned his agent friend had successfully passed Leonie's letter to her aunt. He'd seen little of the princess and the boys since installing them at Hartswood—partly owing to his crowded schedule, partly because he wished to give them time to adjust to their new circumstances. He was particularly gratified by the relationship that had developed between his father and the lads. William showered them with the same warmth and affection Rand himself had received at a time in his childhood when he'd been starved for both. Sam, especially, had need of the healing William's kindness afforded, while Jamie, so recently orphaned, must also benefit.

Pausing on the path, Rand frowned. Leonie, too, had lost her parents, yet he'd hardly given her losses the consideration he'd done the boys'. Of course, she was an adult, so perhaps she'd no need of . . .

Even as he tried to rationalize, he knew he was lying to himself. Fact was, she was every bit as subject to grief and loss, as vulnerable and in need of healing as the children.

Perhaps more so in some ways. How could he forget the night he'd realized she needed to believe more in herself? Yes, Leonie was vulnerable in ways that Jamie and perhaps even Sam were not.

Yet the plain truth was, that very vulnerability scared him. The longer he was in her presence, the more he was drawn to her, and who was he to play the healer? And that, if he were honest with himself, was the real reason he'd been keeping his distance from Leonie of Mirandeau. If she had need of shoring up, the dowager would see to it. Indeed, his grandmother had more to offer her than he ever could.

Problem was, he'd been finding it deuced difficult to maintain that distance. He missed her, he realized, more than he could have imagined. Well, he didn't need to be totally invisible, did he? At present, he'd a perfectly valid reason to see her: the news about her letter to Lady Emilie.

A smile tugged at the corners of his mouth. How her face would light with pleasure at the news. The gamine's smile would appear. Her lovely eyes would sparkle and look twice as green.

A loud whinny had him looking up to see a black streak tearing across the pasture: Leonie's stallion, racing to greet the petite figure limping toward him. Rand found himself grinning as they greeted each other through the fence, a high one meant to keep randy stallions contained. They were touching noses, nuzzling each other with great affection.

Rand watched her take a carrot from a bunch she carried and feed it through the rails. He chuckled. The fence was taller than she was. The stallion made short work of the carrot, then looked for more, and Leonie—

His grin vanished as she set foot on a rail. She was climbing the bloody fence! A precarious task in any case, given her handicap, but now made doubly dangerous. The carrots she toted left only one hand free, and she was wearing skirts.

He was about to call a warning when she became entangled, missed her footing, and tumbled backward. He was in motion before she hit the ground. She was over fifty yards away, but what had his heart in his throat wasn't the distance he must cover to reach her. It was the way she lay so still and unmoving when he did.

"Leonie?" He was only dimly aware of Raven's distress as he knelt beside her. His own escalated as he ran his eyes over her. She lay motionless on her back, eyes closed, arms outflung. One hand still loosely clutched the carrots. "Sweetheart, can your hear me?"

She didn't respond, and he began running his hands carefully over her limbs, checking for injuries. The stallion was working himself into frenzy, neighing shrilly, charging back and forth and butting the rails.

"Leonie, can you hear me?" Rand shouted over the black's frantic calls. He saw her eyelids flicker. *Alive, thank God.* Sweeping away the tangle of curls that had come loose from a narrow yellow ribbon, he put his mouth to her ear. "Leonie!" he called, desperate to make himself heard over Raven's piercing whinny.

Noise and shouting, coming from far away. It took her a moment to sort out what she heard. *Raven . . . greatly overset . . . must calm him . . . and . . . is that Rand? No, silly girl, Rand is away in London. Stop imagining . . .*

She struggled to open her eyes, vaguely aware she ached in several places, including her head. Finally succeeding, she found herself gazing into a pair of violet eyes. *Rand!* Her heart gave a joyous leap, instantly quelled when she realized he was scowling. "Rand?" she asked with a thread of uncertainty. "Is something amiss?"

"Amiss!" He nearly choked on the understatement. "Leonie, you took a tumble and blacked out. Can you tell me where it hurts?" This was all shouted, for Raven continued to fret noisily.

"Just my head . . . a little," she murmured, struggling to rise.

"Don't move!" His words were nearly obliterated by the sound of smashing fence rails.

She paid him no heed and pushed up on an elbow, straining to see the stallion. "Raven!" she called to the frantic animal. "Raven, *look.* I'm all right."

The black stopped battering the fence, but the *whuffle* he gave as he stretched his head over the rails sounded far from satisfied.

"Would you perhaps feed him one of these?" she asked Rand. "Carrots are his favorite—"

"Devil take the carrots!" he growled. "You could have been killed in that fall, and—oh, give me the wretched things!"

Ordering her not to move, he took the carrots and passed them gingerly through the rails.

Raven ignored them entirely, eyeing Rand with deep suspicion. Fortunately, this lasted only until his mistress urged him to take them, in a soft, reassuring voice.

"I'm dreadfully sorry," she said when Raven at last settled and began munching his carrots.

"As well you should be, endangering yourself like that," Rand replied testily. "Now, where are you hurt?"

"I meant I'm sorry for the broken fence," she said contritely.

"Stuff the deuced fence," he muttered, "and tell me where it hurts." He was clearly not as mollified as the stallion.

Leonie wriggled her toes and was about to test other parts when—"Oh, no!"

"What is it—*where?*" he shouted.

"Just look at my new frock!" she wailed, indicating the torn muslin. "Oh, Her Grace will be in such a taking!"

"Don't be a goose," said Rand, greatly relieved. He eyed the high-waisted yellow gown, now torn and marred by grass stains. "Frocks are replaceable." He scooped her up and rose with her in his arms as if she weighed no more than a feather. "While you"—he kissed her nose—"most definitely are not!"

Leonie's pulse accelerated dangerously for someone determined to be sensible. *A brotherly kiss, my girl, nothing more.* To cover her reaction as he carried her up the path, she focused on the ruined gown. "Yes, but Her Grace said this particular frock—"

"Her Grace," he said as patiently as he could—he was

having difficulty eradicating that image of her lying still as death on the ground—"will be relieved to know you haven't killed yourself. She takes a dim view of such things."

"What . . . death?" she asked, startled.

He frowned. *I cannot abide young persons who lack the fortitude to refrain from sticking their spoons in the wall prematurely.* His grandmother's words, uttered on two separate occasions, years apart, each indelibly fixed in his mind. *Stop it. The past is dead, damn it!*

Leonie saw his face cloud over, his eyes grown dark and troubled. It was an echo of that moment on the *Fleetwind* when he'd dismissed setting up his nursery in the foreseeable future. "Rand," she said, searching his face, "what's wrong?"

He glanced down at her and blinked, almost as if he'd forgotten she was there. "Nothing's wrong. That is, I sincerely hope so, which is why I'm sending for MacTavish. I'll feel a deal better once he's had a look at you."

"MacTavish?" They were nearing the house now, and a wide-eyed footman sprang from inside and held the door for them.

"Jenks," said Rand, "go and fetch MacTavish. Take the gig, and don't let that ogre of a housekeeper put you off."

The footman hurried away, and Rand proceeded into the house with Leonie. "MacTavish," he told her, "is the physician in the village."

"Oh, but I feel perfectly fine!"

"I am glad to hear it, but until MacTavish assures me—Barrows," he said as the butler came rushing toward them, a pair of anxious housemaids in his wake, "where's my grandmother?"

"Gone to the village, m'lord. His Grace drove her in the barouche, and the young gentlemen went with them. May I be of service, m'lord?"

"The lady has taken a fall," said Rand, proceeding up the stairs. "I've sent for MacTavish, but"—he looked at Leonie—"have you your own abigail?"

She shook her head no. "Her Grace's present errand is to

fetch one for me, actually . . . Polly's sister from the village," she said, feeling a stab of guilt. The minute the barouche disappeared down the drive, she'd stolen out to see Raven when she was meant to be practicing her lessons.

"Send Polly up to Lady Leonie's chamber, then," Rand told the butler, "and MacTavish when he arrives." Then, to Leonie, "You're in the east wing, as I recall. The corner room?"

She nodded absently, absorbed in where he was taking her. He cut through a room that looked like an office. It had doors at both ends, each of which he shouldered ajar. Now they advanced along a gallery of some sort. What made it remarkable was that she'd not seen this part of the house before, and she'd been here nearly a month. "Where are we?" she asked, gazing down a long row of framed portraits, all in elaborate gilt frames.

"This is the quickest means to the east wing," he replied, "and those are my illustrious forebears, of course. Don't look so surprised. I saw yours displayed at the palace."

"Yes, but these aren't really on display," she mused, gazing at a likeness that reminded her a little of William, except for the long curled wig and Cavalier's garb.

He noted her interest and paused before it. "The first duke, elevated to the rank by Charles II for defending his king against the Roundheads. The Darnleys began as mere knights in the days of the Conqueror, eventually rising to marquises, but it was this fellow who earned the dukedom."

"And that's his duchess, I collect," she said, nodding at a haughty looking beauty in the next frame. "But why are they all hidden away in here?"

He took a moment to respond. "The dowager regards the ostentatious display of ancestors, for any but a royal household, as a vulgar showing away. 'Twas she had the gallery enclosed when I was a lad." *Why the devil did you add that last bit? The less said, the better.*

"Then she didn't always feel it was vulgar?" she asked when he resumed walking. At a slower pace, she was pleased to note, for this allowed her to better peruse the portraits.

"No," he replied after another hesitation, "there was a . . . an incident changed her mind."

They were nearing the end of the gallery, and he suddenly picked up his pace.

"Rand, stop—please!"

With a reluctant sigh, he complied, pausing before the portrait of William. A much younger William, painted when he first came into the title. He wore the dress uniform of his regiment and stood holding the reins of a magnificent chestnut horse.

But it wasn't the duke's likeness that claimed Leonie's attention. It was that of the stunningly beautiful woman in the frame beside his. Clad in a gown of deep violet, she wore her shiny black curls unpowdered, and her ghost of a smile displayed a pair of coy dimples. Dimples that looked familiar, as did all her other perfect features. Her face was a mirror image of Rand's.

But terribly wrong, somehow. And then Leonie saw it was the eyes. They were identical in shape, the same incredible hue, yet nothing like Rand's. They were violet shards of ice. "Your mother?" she whispered, suppressing a shiver.

"My mother," he said flatly.

"She was . . . very beautiful."

"Yes . . . wasn't she?" His mouth was tightly drawn, his tone grim with irony. "The reigning beauty of her day. So perfect, so beautiful, that when the smallpox marred that perfect face, she couldn't bear it—and killed herself."

She gasped. "Oh, Rand, I'm so—"

"Save your pity," he said tightly. "I count that the most fortunate day of my life, save one."

She was at a loss what to say, reeling from the implications of what he'd revealed. *Deeper secrets than Hawk . . . terrible secrets!* "Save one?" she murmured feebly.

"The happiest was the day my father came home from the war." For the first time, his eyes left his mother's image, warming perceptibly as they moved to William's. "I never knew him, do you see. Unfortunately, he had to lose a leg to reclaim a son, as he puts it, but I truly believe he made the exchange gladly. God knows what I'd have done if he hadn't."

"How long ago?" she whispered, still trying to take it all in. This was more of Rand than she'd learned in all the months before. More than she wanted to know? No! She couldn't make him love her, but she could be his friend. And a friend didn't shrink from the disturbing events of a person's past. "That His Grace came home, I mean," she clarified, for she'd no wish to pry for details of his mother's death.

"Ironically, it was the day after she died. I was eleven years old."

And counting yourself fortunate—fortunate!—*that your mother was dead!* "Dear God," she murmured shakily.

It was as if he hadn't heard her. "The dowager didn't live here while my mother was alive," he went on in a taut voice. His face became an emotionless blank as he returned his gaze to the figure in violet. "She knew Regina for the selfish, bloodless creature she was. Yet rather than interfere in her son's marriage, she chose to live in town. The town house where we stayed was part of the dowry she brought to her own marriage. But with my father wounded and sent home to find himself widowed and with a small child to raise, she returned to live at Hartswood.

"Then, after the mourning interval," he continued with a heavy sigh, "she began to entertain, for the duke's position demanded it. During one of her lavish balls she noticed an inordinate number of guests milling about the gallery . . . clustered about this portrait, actually."

"Oh, no." Leonie could picture them all too well: avid, drawn by a ghoulish fascination with the suicide. They wore the faces of those countless dozens who'd stared at her crippled foot over the years, vultures feeding on the carrion of human misery and pain.

"The very next day, the dowager gave orders to enclose the gallery," Rand finished.

Leonie nodded, unable to speak.

Again he sighed and looked at her—for the first time since beginning his tale, she realized. Mostly, he'd just stared woodenly at the portrait. "Forgive me for boring you with all this," he said. "I'm not in the habit of—"

"Not at all!" she cried. "That is, I'm honored that you would share it . . . trust me with it."

He tried for a smile, but didn't quite succeed. "Then perhaps you'll forgive me for trying to fob you off with that showing away business. It's always been the explanation the dowager gives out, do you see. And it's true, in a way. She has a horror of vulgar ostentation."

Leonie nodded, pensive for a moment. She glanced reluctantly at the portrait. "I . . . I couldn't like her, you know, even from a painting. That is, I felt there was something . . . *wrong* about her."

He nodded grimly. "You know something of monsters now." His eyes raked the figure in the violet gown a final time before he turned away. "And she could have given Roderik lessons."

Mirandeau
The Palace

"I'll see him now," Roderik told the nervous aide who stood at the door to his office chamber.

"Yes, Your Grace. At once, Your Grace."

As the aide went to fetch the man he'd deliberately kept waiting, the regent lowered himself into the chair behind his desk. He never received a guard while standing. They all towered over him, and he'd not put himself at such a disadvantage. *Make them wait. Then make them stand while you sit. And if they sweat, so much the better.*

The captain of the Palace Guard entered, saluted with rigid formality, and stood at attention.

Roderik eyed him in silence for several long seconds. "Well?" he said at last.

"I believe we may have a legitimate response, Your Grace."

"It had better be, Captain. The reward has been posted

for more than a fortnight, and what have you brought me? Dozens of false leads! I won't tolerate another, sir, I warn you."

"Yes, Your Grace."

The regent was pleased to see sweat beading the man's brow. Fearful sweat. It was summer, but the season's heat rarely penetrated the palace's thick stone walls. It wasn't from the temperature of the room. This was the sweat of a nervous man.

First, he and his men had failed in tracking down the kidnappers and their hostages, even when they'd had scent hounds at their disposal. They'd come back empty-handed, claiming the scent must have been old. The dogs had led them to the coast, where the only evidence in the sand was, in all probability, the tracks of smugglers who'd been known to ply their trade in that particular cove for ages.

Then, after posting a handsome reward for information leading to the kidnapping, he'd placed the guards in charge of sifting through the responses. Yet all they'd done was waste his time. Charlatans and fools, that's what they'd brought him! Old women with imagined sightings, greedy farmers who thought they'd enrich their pockets by reporting a trampled cornfield, a gypsy who'd sold a horse to a stranger fitting the renegade guard's description, but who couldn't even say in what direction he'd ridden the nag. Well, he'd had enough. Which was why he'd added a little incentive for the captain last week—a hundred gold pieces for a true lead; a hundred lashes for a false one.

"Very well, then, Captain," he said, amused. "Get on with it."

The captain licked his lips nervously. "A man came forward last night—a fisherman, Your Grace. He saw something about a month ago, when his boat was offshore. In the waters off—off the same cove the dogs led us to. We're near certain it was the very day we came to our dead end. It was the fog made us so certain. He mentioned a heavy fog reaching far inland, just like what we ran into when—"

"Yes, yes, I collect what you're saying! And what was this *something* he saw?"

"A foreign ship, Your Grace, possibly a British naval frigate. He swears he saw it pick up four or five passengers from the shore. Passengers and their *mounts,* Your Grace—in broad daylight!"

"Did he sound believable?" Roderik forced himself to remain calm, but he knew the man wouldn't risk his hide unless he believed he had a reliable witness.

"He did, Your Grace."

"And where is he now?"

"Waiting below, Your Grace."

"Fetch him," said Roderik.

Sixteen

England

Dr. MacTavish pronounced the marquis's "cousin" slightly bruised but otherwise uninjured, cautioned her against climbing fences, politely declined a cup of tea, and left. " 'Tis a shame aboot her puir foot," he told his housekeeper when he returned. "An' her sic a bonnie wee lassie, too. Th' young laird fairly dotes on her, ye can tell. He was that worrit aboot the lass. I told him tae see she rested a spell, an' she'd be right as rain."

Reassured by MacTavish's words, Rand left Leonie in Polly's care. Just before he took his leave, however, he remembered to give her the news about Emilie's letter. This cheered her immeasurably after that disturbing exchange in the gallery. Rand, on the other hand, seemed oddly quiet, almost brooding, and his cheerless farewell sent her spirits plummeting once more.

He was going away again—off to see the estate manager of his property in Hampshire, she later learned from William. The duke, as well as the dowager and the boys, came to see her the moment they arrived. Embarrassed, Leonie explained how she'd come by her tumble. She began to stammer an apology for the ruined gown, but the duchess waved it away.

"I'd no idea you were so enamored of riding," she said. "Why on earth didn't you say so?"

"I . . . I feared there might not be time for it, Your Grace."

"Piffle! If something is important, you simply *make* time for it. You must learn to be more assertive, gel. Now, would a ride each morning suffice, do you think? Once you are recovered, of course."

"Oh, Your Grace, that would be splendid!"

Her Grace nodded. "Taking the air is good for the complexion, providing you wear a proper bonnet. Which reminds me, I've your new abigail waiting downstairs, and Polly assures me Sally is up to snuff on which apparel suits what occasion. I shall send her up directly with a tray, for it is nearly tea time. Come along, Master Jamie. And you, Master Sam. Cook has made a fresh batch of scones, and the princess needs her rest."

This said, she swept them out of the room. But the duke, assuring his mother he'd not be long, remained behind. "Is there anything I can do for you while you're confined?" he asked Leonie.

"How very kind of you to ask," she replied, smiling. She liked this tall, unassuming man with his cap of white hair and gentle eyes. Except for his height, he'd imparted no outward physical characteristics to his son, yet she saw a resemblance in the way they carried themselves, with a grace and elegance that seemed as natural as breathing. "And as I dearly love books," she went on, "perhaps you would do me the honor of sharing some from Your Grace's library?"

"Make a list of what interests you, and I'll send some up. I well remember how tedious bed rest can be." Grinning, he tapped his wooden leg. "Even though mine occurred years ago."

"I daresay you do." She admired the way he spoke of his loss so openly, and replied in kind, though not without sympathy. "It cannot have been easy to bear."

He smiled. "Oddly enough, I don't recall those first moments in the field hospital at all. Yet every dragging hour of bed rest in the months following is fixed in my memory like one of those boring refrains from a song with too many verses. And the day I took my first steps with this"—he patted the leg affectionately—"what joy!"

She nodded. "For me, it was the day I received a pair of riding boots—oh, and a custom-made stirrup—designed to accommodate my deformity." She smiled, realizing how easy it was to discuss this with him. "I did nothing more than guide my pony round the ring at a sedate walk, you understand—but the sense of freedom!"

He chuckled. "Freedom of movement is so often taken for granted, but for those of us who've been denied it—why, it is everything!

"Now, tell me, my dear," he went on in a different vein, "how are you going on? I've been meaning to ask you, but the time seems to have slipped by without my realizing it. I fear I've neglected—"

"Not at all, Your Grace! I can't tell you how I value your generosity in receiving us. Your kindness toward the boys has been especially gratifying. I do hope they haven't been a bother."

"A bother? My dear, they have positively rejuvenated me! But I am straying from my purpose. What of you? I adore my mother, yet I know she can be rather daunting at times—no, do not deny it. It occurred to me these lessons she's embarked upon . . . well, I was wondering how you feel about them. That is, if you find them off-putting, I beg you might tell me. Her Grace may seem indifferent to appeal, but I've been known to sway her on occasion."

"Off-putting?" She smiled ruefully. "Not that exactly, but I do wish I had Her Grace's confidence in the outcome. She seems to feel I've but to will it and I'll be transformed into a social butterfly."

He nodded. "You have doubts about succeeding, which I understand entirely." He indicated his leg again. "I had my share of doubts, especially in the beginning. But as I lay there, I had time to contemplate the alternative. To wit, it soon dawned upon me that if I didn't regain my freedom of movement, I could look forward to a lifetime of the tedium I found so oppressive." He grinned at her. "I persevered."

Leonie nodded pensively. He was telling her she had a choice. She could persevere, and perhaps gain more freedom of movement than she'd ever known in the sense of moving freely in society. Or she could give up trying and be no worse off. To wit, she could look forward to a lifetime of what she already had.

"You're saying if I persevere," she replied, wondering why she hadn't realized this herself, "I've nothing to lose."

"Indeed," he told her, tipping her a wink that reminded her of Rand, "and everything to gain!"

And so, as the summer days passed, Leonie persevered. Buoyed by her morning gallops on Raven, she set about attaining the dowager's goals with renewed energy and a determination to succeed. The dowager's goals became her goals, and she soon found herself enjoying the challenge of meeting them. Moreover, her new abigail proved an asset in this regard. Sally may not have been as deft as Polly at coiffures, but she was a font of invaluable information.

She'd been trained by none less than one of the great patronesses of Almack's, Lady Jersey. "Seein' as 'ow my name was same as 'ers, she took a kindly interest in me, milady," she told Leonie. "Raised me up from chambermaid, she did. Oh, Lady Jersey's a rum 'un!"

Still, when Sally Jersey had hared off to Paris recently, her abigail gave notice: "I takes sick somethin' cruel—beggin' yer pardon, milady—in a movin' boat. Ain't no love nor money could make me cross 'at bleedin' Channel!"

Yet Lady Jersey's loss was Leonie's gain. Servants, as Leonie already knew from at home, were notoriously well informed about everything that went on in the lofty world of their betters. And while the dowager condemned gossip as vulgar, Sally was cheerfully unencumbered by such principles. Out of loyalty to the duchess, Leonie tried to curtail it, but trying to stanch Sally's chatter was like trying to stop a runaway horse with the bit in its teeth. After a while Leonie gave up trying—and was glad she did.

The abigail's unvarnished accounts of the *haute monde* gave new meaning to the dowager's dry precepts. Helping

Leonie with her toilette, she'd rattle on about all manner of eye-opening *tonnish* doings. The duchess's warning about ruined reputations was merely an abstract in Leonie's mind until she heard Sally's tale of an earl's daughter brought low by a mésalliance initiated in Gretna Green. So was her advice that if one couldn't be clever, it was best not to speak at all. Lady Jersey had remarked of one young bore, "Whitley's lack of wit is exceeded only by his lack of matter. Not a day ago, I was subjected to an hour's discourse on his riding gloves!" And the duchess's admonition against high-stakes gaming was never so real as when Sally spoke of Lord Carlisle's loss of two hundred thousand pounds at Brooks's one night. Sally had it from Lady Jersey's groom that his lordship had paid a visit to Howard and Gibbs next morning. Who were Howard and Gibbs? "Why, they be cent per cent blokes, milady. They lends the blunt t' toffs what loses their shirts at the tables."

As July became August, the dowager's instruction, fleshed out by Sally's concrete tidbits, began to bear fruit. It was decided that by September Leonie would be ready for her first foray into society. Nothing on a grand scale, however. They'd begin with an introduction to the area's minor gentry. Of course, a ball, even a small affair with simple country dances, was out of the question. But an at-home musicale would be just the thing. Europe's preeminent musicians were in London for the celebrations, and Her Grace had no doubt she could engage a few to entertain at her country estate. Afterward, refreshments would be served while the guests mingled.

She and Leonie had their only disagreement at this time, however, and it was over the matter of dancing—or, to be more precise, dancing masters. "I no less expect you to perform a minuet than I expect you to take up that vulgar import, the waltz," Her Grace said. "What I am saying, however, is that your physical comportment will benefit from Monsieur LeBeau's instruction. Dancing masters teach more than the steps. They teach balance and grace and elegance of form."

And when Leonie still demurred, "What, afraid, gel?" the

dowager snapped, which made her pupil concede she probably was. "All the more reason to do it, then!" came the sharp reply. "All it wants is courage." Remembering a crown of wildflowers, Leonie stopped arguing.

Of Rand she saw nothing, except for a chance encounter one morning at the stables. Out of breath from an exhilarating gallop, she rode into the yard just as he was leaving. Seated on a magnificent gray she'd not seen before, he nodded a greeting, then, "Quicksilver's fresh from Tatt's, and I cannot as yet answer for his manners near another stallion," he informed her. "I'd be greatly obliged, m'lady, if you'd rein in the black till we've passed." Polite words, of course, but so coolly delivered, Leonie felt a chill to the marrow of her bones.

He was back to being distant again toward her—though not toward others that she could tell. He was so vastly different from the man she'd known in Mirandeau and aboard the *Fleetwind* and then again, briefly, the day she'd fallen. As if he were two different men in the same skin.

And while those moments in the gallery offered some insight into his darker side, she'd no idea what it had to do with her. Perhaps he regretted confiding in her. Yet that didn't explain the weeks of aloofness before. And the day of her fall, why had he allowed her to see the other Rand, the one she cherished in her dreams? It was all so puzzling.

In the end she told herself it didn't matter. She must be sensible. And so she threw herself with even greater determination into preparing for her country debut. The dancing master, as it happened, was the soul of kindness, and he had a sense of humor. One day Leonie told him she'd never seen the waltz, and longed to see it done, but feared she never would: Her Grace felt it unseemly for ladies. *"Vraiment?"* replied Monsieur LeBeau with a twinkle. After which he set Leonie at the pianoforte, had her bang out something in three-quarter time, then grabbed a broom and—*voilà!* the waltz!

September came, and the dowager pronounced Leonie ready. Invitations went out to the crème de la crème of the country set: Sir Wilfred Mumfrey, his wife, and two daughters; the vicar and Mrs. Sedley; Squire Braddock and his son—"Handsome and home from the war in one piece," the duchess informed Leonie; Admiral Lindsey, R.N., his wife, and twin sons, one a post-captain, the other a commander; the Misses Wriothesley and Mr. Wriothesley—"The sisters sadly on the shelf, but their brother another matter entirely," said Her Grace, "Thirty, charming, and ninety thousand a year"; and Dr. MacTavish: "Always helpful to include someone you've met."

Thanks to the servants' grapevine, curiosity about the duke's cousins ran high. The invitations stated that the musicale was in honor of Lady Leonie Darnley. There wasn't a single refusal. Ushered in by perfect weather, the evening of the musicale arrived, with everything in a state of absolute readiness, including the guest of honor.

"Oh, milady," Sally sighed as Leonie moved before the cheval glass in her dressing room, "ye looks jest like a princess. Don't she, Polly?"

"Now, ye've made 'er blush," Polly reproved as she secured Leonie's coiffure with a final tortoiseshell comb. "There, I think that does it, milady." She stepped back to regard the effect of several hours' preparation. From bathing in scented water to being dressed and groomed with exquisite care, milady had been pampered and polished to a fare-thee-well.

Leonie had kept her eyes closed, waiting until everything was in place. Now she opened them, and blinked: *Am I . . . am I that woman in the glass?* Gazing back at her was a vision that didn't seem real. *Surely not. Surely, it is merely the gown.*

Fashioned from layers of the sheerest ivory silk, the gown was breathtaking. At its high waist was a sash of the palest coral-pink satin, and Polly had threaded narrow satin ribbons of the same shade through her abundant curls. These cascaded from a topknot at the crown of her head, a style known as *à la grecque.* The satin slippers that peeked out from her hemline matched as well, and Hoby's had been prevailed upon to redesign the left slipper, sewing in a special arch and padding it with soft cotton wool to give her poor foot more balance.

No, it wasn't just the gown, she realized as Sally handed her an elegant walking stick, its ivory head carved in the shape of a rosebud. It wasn't any one thing, but the whole. And the whole was greater than the sum of its parts. Again, she blinked. *Why . . . I look like Mama!*

"I'll get it," said Sally as someone scratched at the outer door. Polly and Leonie followed her into the bedchamber in time to see Sally accept a small parcel from a footman. "Milady," she said, bobbing and handing it to Leonie.

The sisters returned to the dressing room to clean up, leaving Leonie the privacy to open her parcel. This was wrapped in several layers of tissue paper, nothing more. Unwrapping it, Leonie gasped, for there were her pearls and ruby earbob!

A folded note lay beneath, and she opened it with trembling hands.

Dear Leonie,

I meant to return these weeks ago, and beg you will forgive the delay. Petrie has happily agreed to a recompense for his earbob, and I have taken the liberty of inviting him to Hartswood, for nothing would do but that he return it to you in person. Until then, you have your pearls. Perhaps you will do me the honor of wearing them tonight.

Hawksrest

He's going to be here! It hadn't occurred to her that Rand would attend, perhaps because he was rarely home, perhaps because Jamie and Sam were to be absent. But this, she remembered, was for reasons of security, as the duke had put it. If a pair of boys matching the description of the children missing from Mirandeau were to appear publicly, along with a young lady whose description matched that of the missing princess, there was a possibility—remote, perhaps, but nonetheless real—that word would reach the wrong ears, and

Whitehall was taking no chances. Sam and Jamie were happily on a fishing trip with the head groom and his ten-year-old son. But Rand posed no threat to security. As the duke's heir, perhaps it would be *de trop* should he fail to put in an appearance. The realization sent her pulse into double-time.

As she'd told William, Leonie had had her doubts about the dowager's plans, not to mention moments of vexation with the woman herself. Yet she was never so grateful for Her Grace as she was that evening. Standing beside her as the duke and duchess greeted their guests and presented the guest of honor, Leonie felt the dowager's presence like an enormous bulwark against defeat. William helped, of course, with his kindness and gentle charm. But it was Her Grace who made the difference. Regally serene, radiating unquestionable confidence in the authority of her position, she made it impossible for Leonie to doubt herself.

Even though Rand was nowhere in sight.

If the dowager noticed her grandson's absence, she never let on. But in a whispered aside as they led the guests into the music room, the duke explained to Leonie, "I'm to tell you Rand's been unavoidably detained. Something about a sick horse. Sent a note from the stables, begging to be excused a tardy arrival . . . hopes you'll forgive—"

"But of course," Leonie murmured as they took their seats on little gilded chairs.

He patted her arm. "Knew you'd understand, but Her Grace is another matter. You wouldn't know it to look at her, but she's in high dudgeon over this." His chuckle was muffled as the musicians entered to gentle applause. Leonie caught only the tail end of the words that followed. ". . . glad I'm not in his shoes right now."

"He appears on the mend," Rand told the stable master as they left Quicksilver's stall. "Some warm mash with treacle in an hour, Luke, and keep an eye on him. Don't hesitate to send to the house if there's any reversal."

"Aye, yer lordship," said Luke, but his lordship was already out of sight.

Rand grimaced at the state of his clothing as he hurried down the path. He'd just finished dressing for the evening when Luke's urgent message arrived: The big gray was down in his stall. Fortunately, the stallion's stomach gripes had responded to their treatment, and a serious case of colic had been avoided.

But his master now looked and smelled like the stables. He must bathe and shift his clothes, which would make him very late indeed. William would be sympathetic, but he made no doubt he was in the dowager's black book. Regrettable, but even worse, he feared his absence might have hurt Leonie. She was so damned vulnerable, and he'd done quite enough of running roughshod over her feelings in the past. Was he forever to be relating to her in terms of damage control?

He pondered this as he entered the rear of the house at a run. The distant strains of a Mozart *adagio* told him the musicians were still at it, thank heaven. He'd learned from the boys that Leonie had spent countless hours every day over all these many weeks preparing for this come-out. And while he'd initially thought it best to be engaged elsewhere tonight, his grandmother hadn't given him the option. *I desire you to attend without fail. Her Highness has worked diligently toward this end. She deserves our unfailing support, and she shall have it.*

Oddly enough, as the date drew near, he found himself looking forward to it, after all. A smile hovered as he neared the back staircase, a forgotten image teasing his mind of Leonie the day he'd carried her up these very stairs. He'd been too worried at the time to pay much regard to how she looked, but now it came to him, clear as day. Her curls had come a-tumble after escaping their ribbon, bits of grass tucked charmingly among the auburn strands. Her face was flushed with a healthy outdoors glow, accentuated by the smattering of freckles he found delightful. And her lovely eyes had been enormous in that delicate, heart-shaped face. The chips of gold in their mossy depths were never more apparent. She'd looked for all the world like a wood sprite, light as down in his arms, and twice as delicate. A creature out of faerie . . .

God's my life, I'm beginning to think like someone besotted. If I didn't know better—

"There you are, m'lord." Harley, his valet, hurried toward him. "I've taken the liberty of laying out the blue superfine and—" He wrinkled his nose and sniffed. "Never you fear, m'lord. There's fresh bath water heated. Won't a lady in the room know you've been anywhere near the stables."

With two notable exceptions, Rand thought as they hurried toward his chambers. *And I find the opinions of both matter to me. No surprise in the one, but . . . yes, face it, her good opinion matters.* She *matters. And what the devil am I going to do about it?*

Rand hadn't found any answers by the time he reached the music room. What he did find as the violoncello and the violin completed the final movement of a duet by Handel was that he couldn't take his eyes off Leonie.

What had become of the wood sprite? The creature sitting next to his father was as far from the image recently invading his mind as chalk from cheese. And yet she was exquisite—every inch a princess. A fairy-tale princess whose gossamer beauty rendered everything in the room drab and mundane by comparison.

He frowned. The dowager and her army of maids and dressmakers had done their job well, transformed his wood sprite into a civilized beauty the *ton* would approve wholeheartedly. And that was the objective, wasn't it? Why, then, did he find the prospect so disturbing?

Could it be that you fear the Leonie within may also be altered? jeered a voice inside his head. *And, coward that you are, you've lost what you've only begun to realize was worth keeping?*

"Bloody hell," he growled, stalking to the vacant seat

beside his grandmother and dropping into it. Fortunately, his oath went unnoticed. The music ended at that moment, and the guests broke into applause. Fortunately, too, the dowager took one look at his face, and the blistering set-down she'd been about to deliver died in her throat.

The dowager looked up from her perusal of the *Post* as Barrows entered the morning room bearing a familiar silver salver.

"The mail, Your Grace," he announced quite unnecessarily. He'd performed this ritual for decades. Mornings only if there were local mail delivered by servants, afternoons for the post conveyed by the Royal Mail. But the butler was as much a high stickler as the duchess. Neither would dream of forgoing proper form. "As Lady Leonie has yet to return from her ride," he asked now, "shall I leave her missives with Your Grace?"

"Do so, Barrows," said Her Grace, not in the least surprised to see so many addressed to her guest. She had no doubt all, like her own, were invitations. The child's unofficial debut was an unqualified success. She'd known as much halfway through the evening, of course, but it always helped to have confirmation. She wondered what Leonie would make of it. As they'd all been tired at the end of the evening, they'd discussed the affair only briefly.

"Good morning, Your Grace." The object of her thoughts entered the room with a smile.

"Ah, there you are, gel. Shifted your clothes, I see." The dowager nodded approval. "I find little so off-putting as an odor of the stables with one's dish of morning tea. Enjoy your gallop?"

"Extremely," said Leonie, taking the seat the dowager waved her into. "Raven was frisky as a colt." A gurgle of laughter. "Trying to impress the mares in the south pasture, no doubt."

The dowager smiled to herself. That lilting laughter was as much responsible for the child's success as the surprising wit she'd displayed. Beauty was all very well, but in the end it was the total package that counted. "Here you are, my dear," she said, handing over Leonie's mail. "All tributes to your success."

"Good heavens—so many?" Leonie opened and read while the duchess poured her some tea. There were invitations from all the women she'd met: to tea, to dine, to attend a hunt. And, under separate cover, Mr. Wriothesley and the younger Mr. Braddock invited her to go riding. Each of the seafaring twins wrote as well, asking if he might call. It seemed they were shore-bound with the cessation of hostilities. And Squire Braddock—the *widower* Braddock—had invited her for a ride in his new carriage—with Her Grace as chaperone, of course.

"It appears I shall be frightfully busy in the coming fortnight," she told the dowager.

"Get used to it, gel. You've made a brilliant beginning, and every bit of it earned." She sent Leonie one of her rare smiles. "By the by, you are to be congratulated on your sang-froid with our guests. I can yet recall the wretched state of my nerves at my own come-out, years ago. I own that was during the Season, yet it is all one for nerves. The London *ton* is no different. It merely thinks it is. Tell me, how did you manage it?"

Leonie smiled to herself. *By taking Sally's advice: "Jest imagine they all be standin' there wearin' nothin' but their inexpressibles, milady. Won't even them stuck-up baronet's daughters come it the toplofty then."* It had answered beautifully. Moreover, as the evening wore on and she saw how silly, vain, and insipid the baronet's haughty daughters were—indeed, how empty-headed they all were—her confidence had soared. *Oh, Mama, I wish you could have seen! The vaunted* ton *is nothing more than a pack of stiff-rumped idlers full of boring tittle-tattle.*

Yet prudence demanded she now voice a different reply. "Realizing I'd nothing to lose, Your Grace—and everything to gain, as the duke once put it—I simply decided to be myself, but a self shaped by Your Grace's advice. You've no idea how freeing it was to consign my limp to the devil." She paused, thoughtful. "But then again, I expect you do. That's why you said it."

"Good morning, ladies," said William, coming through the door. "Said what, if I may ask?"

Returning the greeting, Leonie explained.

"Excellent advice," His Grace remarked as he kissed the dowager's cheek.

"What nonetheless amazed me," said Leonie, "is that they all behaved as if getting about with a cane were the most normal thing in the . . ." She bit her lip, eyeing the duke's cane as he rested it against his chair. "I do beg your pardon, Your Grace. No doubt I've you to thank for—"

"Nonsense, my dear," said William. "My title and the fact that I was injured fighting Boney purchased me instant acceptance. With you it was that splendid positive attitude." He chuckled as his mother poured him some tea. "Remarkable, isn't it? *You* made no evident exception for your limp, therefore *they* made none."

"Do you really think so?"

"I do," he replied with a smile. "You were the soul of self-possessed insouciance, my dear."

"I might even venture to say," the dowager added thoughtfully, "the positive face you put on it lent you a certain cachet. I distinctly heard Lady Mumfrey remark to Sir Wilfred that it had been ages since she'd met an Original."

"Is that good?" Leonie asked uncertainly.

"Good?" said the duke. "My dear, it is better than good! Originals don't come along every day. And from Violet Mumfrey, one of the *ton's* prime matrons for gossip—"

"Now, William . . ."

"Come, Mother, you know she is. Drinks scandal broth for breakfast." He winked at Leonie. "But in your case, the word will be positive. An Original! Once she carries it to town for the Little Season, your advance reputation is assured!"

"Advance reputation?" Leonie asked. "Does . . . does that mean I shall be going to London?"

"Not anytime soon," said a voice from the doorway.

"Rand!" exclaimed his father.

"Whatever are you doing at Hartswood?" the dowager demanded. "I distinctly heard you say you'd be in town the week."

"And good morning to you, too, Grand-mère," said Rand with amused irony. He kissed the cheek she offered, nodded greetings to his father, and bowed to Leonie. "M'lady."

"Good morning, m'lord," she murmured, dismayed to feel her face heat. He'd the power to do that to her simply by entering a room. Hadn't she blushed unforgivably when he all at once materialized last night? After she'd given up on him, resolving not to feel hurt, to be sensible? Then, suddenly there he was, looking dashing and elegant in his formal clothes. Yet utterly male: tan, lean, and muscular . . . heart-stopping. And all her resolve had shattered like breaking glass.

The only thing that saved her was the immediate crush of guests as the music ended. They'd positively surrounded her. By the time Rand reached her side—with profound apologies for arriving late, of course—she'd been well into Her Grace's devil-take-the-limp mode, thank heaven. She'd actually managed a smile and consigned her injured feelings to the devil as well.

"What's this about not going to London?" asked the duke.

"A courier arrived early this morning," Rand replied, glancing at his grandmother, "with a message that changed my plans. I'm to remain here for the foreseeable future."

"Are you at liberty to say why?" William inquired.

"The Ministry's had some . . . disquieting news."

Leonie had gone very still, and he immediately damned his rash reply. *Devil take it, I should have told William in private. This is meant to be a carefree time for her, with nothing more worrisome than which gown to choose.* He exchanged a look with the duke, who seemed to be thinking the same thing. "Er . . . perhaps now is not the time or place to—"

"Has it to do with me and the boys?" Leonie cut in abruptly, then wanted to bite her tongue.

The dowager made a reproving sound. Both Rand and the duke blinked.

Scarlet flags rose to her cheeks. She hadn't intended to be rude, but she'd caught that silent exchange: She was meant to be spared this disquieting news perhaps until it could be watered down—if it reached her at all! Well, learning the social graces did not mean she'd become one of those milk-and-water misses she'd met last night.

"I beg your pardon," she said, collecting herself, "but if this concerns me and mine, m'lord, I am entitled to know."

Rand's brows lifted. How utterly self-assured and assertive she sounded. Neither a glimmer of the waif from the palace, nor of the sprite he'd carried from the pasture.

Yet he said nothing, and neither did the duchess. It was William who spoke, after a thoughtful silence. "She's right, of course. I own, my first inclination was to spare you any distress in the offing," he told Leonie, "but I see I was mistaken. You're made of sterner stuff than that."

"Quite right," said the dowager. "Hawksrest, I deem it advisable for you to take our cousin for a private stroll about the gardens."

The ducal gardens were a vast, formal affair covering countless acres. There was a deer park with a lake, a hedged maze leading to a central reflecting pool where topiary beasts stood watch, and a classical folly resembling a Roman temple on a hill above acres of perfectly clipped lawn.

Yet it wasn't to any of these Rand took her. Tucked behind an ancient stone wall near the house was another sort of garden. Half hidden, small, and informal, it was essentially a deeply wooded glade, with riots of summer flowers blooming here and there in patches of full sun. The rest was all shade-dappled paths winding beneath the trees, with myrtle, ivy, fern, and moss-covered rock adding to an impression of lush green wherever the eye chanced to rest.

Each immersed in thought, they walked in silence along a tiny silver stream, barely visible amidst the ground cover. It formed a small natural pool at one end of the garden, and here a small bench, its stone surface worn with age, rested beneath an ancient elm. Eyeing her morning gown of peach muslin, Rand took a handkerchief from his pocket, spread it on the seat and gestured for Leonie to sit.

Murmuring her thanks, she lowered herself to the bench with a grace she'd once thought beyond her. Monsieur LeBeau's efforts and hours of practice with her walking stick had made the difference. With a secret smile, she rested the slender stick against the bole of the elm.

"You go on very well with that," said Rand, dipping his chin at it. He'd chosen to stand, but leaned forward, right leg bent, the boot propped on a rock, his forearm resting across his thigh. "I wonder that you never used one at home."

She smiled wryly. "As a child I chose not to, largely because what was on offer was the sort of ugly, clumsy looking affair I'd seen old men use. Elegant walking sticks somehow never made it across our borders, I suppose. At least, I'd never seen one." She shrugged. "I eventually grew so accustomed to doing without, I never gave it much thought."

And now? Do you give it, and everything else that has transformed you into this elegant figure, much thought? Is it all artifice now, planned and deliberate, with the old Leonie nowhere to be found? "I collect your debut with the locals has been a triumph," he said.

Another shrug. "The dowager is content, but it is merely a beginning. I'm not at all sanguine about going on in town. The essence of which, it seems to me, is that young ladies are required to attend balls and assemblies no end. In short, to dance, which will not answer, of course.

"Speaking of London," she went on quickly when she saw him frown—a frown being perhaps one step away from pity, and she'd rather die than have that from him—"I believe you've some disquieting news for me."

Whatever his misgivings about the changes, he had to

admire this new assertiveness. *If this concerns me and mine, m'lord, I am entitled to know.* Then again, perhaps the quality had always been there, in embryonic form. Whatever she may have believed, she never lacked for courage.

"Whitehall's contacts," he told her, "recently informed us that the regent posted an attractive reward for information about your . . . kidnapping, he calls it. At first, he had no success, but that has now changed."

"Go on," she said. *Steady . . . remain calm.*

He sighed heavily. "Someone identified the *Fleetwind* as a Royal Navy frigate and saw it take us up in that cove. It's possible he knows you're in Britain, Leonie."

"I see," she said, swallowing. *Does this mean we flee once more? And what if he tracks us down again? Are we meant to spend our lives running from that madman?*

Rand saw the trapped look in her eyes, and wanted to gather her close and promise she needn't worry. But he made promises only if he knew with absolute certainty he could keep them, and he had no absolutes to offer. Still, she wasn't alone in this, and she needed comforting, as well as reassurance that all wasn't lost.

"Leonie, listen to me," he said, reaching for her hands—so cold—and cradling them between his. "This is unwelcome news, but it needn't herald disaster. Knowing you and the boys are somewhere in the British Isles is one thing. Knowing where, precisely, is quite another. And Whitehall believes that as long as you maintain a shallow profile—"

"Stay hidden in the country, you mean," she said, savoring the comfort of his hands. They were firm-textured and well shaped, long-fingered, but not overly large for a man, yet large enough to swallow both of hers. She could feel the calluses he'd gained from swordplay and riding and the like, and these she also savored, for they said things about the sort of man he was. But most of all, she savored the warmth and comfort they gave her. "And away from London."

"Exactly. As long as you go on as you are, you're not likely to be discovered."

"But there is always the possibility, isn't there?" she said tightly. *I cannot let him find Sam. I won't. If it means traveling to the ends of the earth, he shan't have him. I swear it!*

"I own, nothing of this nature is without risk," said Rand, stroking the soft flesh between his palms, gently massaging her knuckles with his thumbs. *Her hands are so small and delicate. And smooth . . . soft as a babe's.* "But we're taking measures to counter it. You and the boys are to have a highly trained, experienced guard with you at all times now."

"Those Bow Street Runners I've been hearing about?"

"One will be, yes, for the boys, who are always together, and at Hartswood, in any event. But we cannot very well send a common stranger to all the places you're likely to be. Here, yes, but not inside the drawing rooms of the gentry, where he must be if he's to protect you. It won't answer."

"What will, then?"

With a wry smile, Rand rose and made her an elegant leg. "Behold your experienced guard, m'lady."

Seventeen

Sally bent a critical eye on the green sarcenet pelisse that matched the trim on Leonie's ivory dinner gown. "Per'aps the Kashmir shawl'd serve better, it bein' warmer, milady," she suggested as Leonie considered the pelisse. "There be a nip in the air t'night."

"Perhaps it would . . . yes, thank you, Sally." Leonie drew on her gloves as the abigail fetched the shawl. "I fear autumn's truly—good heavens, it *can't* be half eight already!" she exclaimed as the clock chimed the half hour. "Oh, Sally, do help me with these endless buttons!"

"Now, don't ye fret, milady." Sally laid the shawl on a chair and began buttoning the long gloves with brisk efficiency. " 'Is Grace only jest went down, an' 'er Grace ain't left 'er rooms yet. 'Course, 'is lordship's been ready this quarter hour, but 'e's always early *these* days. There ye be, milady, all done up proper."

Leonie smiled to herself as Sally fetched her reticule and fan. Since he began escorting her everywhere, his lordship had scrupulously avoided being late. Whether this owed to a desire to make up for the night of her debut or to his professionalism as a guard, she'd no idea. She only knew he was ready well in advance of every outing. He rarely left her side once they arrived, her trips to the necessary or a room set aside for ladies to repair their persons being the exception, and he attended without complaint, no matter how dull the affair.

She saw Rand so frequently now, she ought to be pleased.

Yet to be honest, she wasn't certain how she felt. While he was often in her company, and always the soul of courtesy, it was strictly the public man she saw. He might be cast in the role of guard again, but there was nothing of Hawk in him now. The Hawk she knew had a private face he'd shared with her from time to time. The marquis of Hawksrest had secrets he'd shared with her, but the face he wore might be a stranger's.

Moreover, within the public persona she sensed that private brooding creature contained, but never far from the surface. His behavior at the Wriothesley's garden party was a prime example. She'd been strolling with some of her fellow guests when, suddenly, her walking stick slipped on the damp grass. "Really, Sir Hobble," she'd quipped, "do stop being such a stick!" This had produced a chuckle from His Grace and guffaws from the Lindsey twins; Squire Braddock had simply roared out loud. All at once she'd felt Rand's eyes on her. She'd glanced up, and saw him standing across the terrace, looking straight at her, not a smile on his face, not a mote of humor, not even approval.

The duke had later related her quip to the dowager, and both had voiced their approval. They always did when she was clever enough to inject some wit into her discourse. But not Rand. If anything, she felt he *dis*approved somehow.

But of what did he disapprove?

Sighing, she told herself a sensible person would stop such fruitless inquiry and get on with her life. Thanking Sally and telling her not to wait up if they were very late, she made her way downstairs. Tonight they were dining at Lady Mumfrey's. The senior Mumfreys were pleasant enough, but she couldn't like their haughty daughters very well. Eugenia was a sharp-tongued shrew, Caroline a Friday-faced glumster—and a bigger gossip than her mother. According to Sally, Lady Mumfrey was desperate to find them suitable husbands. They'd each had a Season, two in Eugenia's case, without an offer, despite generous dowries.

Leonie smiled ruefully. Sally had also learned Lady Mumfrey entertained a faint hope that Hawksrest might be brought to offer for one of them. Faint, because a duke's heir was an overly ambitious aim for a baronet's daughter.

The source of Sally's information was Jenny, Lady Mumfrey's abigail, whom she'd met in the village on market day. Jenny had added something about Lady Mumfrey being encouraged now his lordship was out and about again. After all, it was over two years since the tragedy, whatever that meant. Sally never found out; Jenny had been called away at the critical moment, and hurried off without saying.

Of course, Sally was like a hound on the scent when it came to a juicy *on-dit.* She at once applied to her sister for an explanation, but the dowager had Polly and the rest of the staff so thoroughly terrified of repeating family gossip this had proved useless. Nonetheless, Leonie made no doubt Sally would have an answer by next market day.

As it happened, Leonie learned about the mysterious tragedy a deal sooner than market day. The talebearer was Lady Mumfrey herself at her dinner party that evening.

The dinner was rather grand for a country affair, with twenty guests. The Mumfreys made an even two dozen at table. At one point Leonie counted twenty-five dishes comprising a single course, and there were no less than seven removes. As the Mumfreys kept town hours, they sat down to dine at nine. Leonie thought the meal would never end.

Finally, just past midnight, their hostess led the ladies into the drawing room, leaving the gentlemen to their port. The drawing room was so arranged that there were several conversation areas, with tables set up for those who enjoyed gaming. Most of the ladies chose conversation over cards tonight. To be precise, they chose gossip over gaming. Unfortunately, Leonie didn't realize this until she found herself in a group that included her hostess.

"Tell me, Lady Leonie," Lady Mumfrey inquired after Mrs. Lindsey had related the latest *on-dit* about the Prince Regent and his set, "how does Hawksrest go on these days? Has he finally put it behind him, poor man?"

Poor man? Leonie groped for a response. As she was ostensibly a Darnley cousin, it would never do to appear ignorant, but what on earth could the term signify? "I believe he goes on very well, Lady Mumfrey," she said. A safe reply, if not terribly illuminating.

"So happy to hear it," Lady Mumfrey replied. "Lady Cynthia's family have been out of black gloves this age. And while his devotion to her memory is admirable, surely his lordship's loss cannot be said to have been greater than theirs."

"Yet consider, Mama. The Shallcrosses do have other daughters," Caroline put in, "while poor Hawksrest had but the one fiancée. And losing her only days before the wedding—too tragic!"

Fiancée! Rand . . . engaged to be married? Leonie felt stupefied. Why had no one mentioned it? As the gossip went on around her, she sought desperately to collect herself. Her glance fell on a table across the room, where the dowager played whist with the Wriothesley sisters and a colonel's wife whose name she couldn't recall. Something the dowager had once said saved her from making a fool of herself. *Nothing in the personal line, but the witty* bon mot *will serve you admirably.*

"No doubt," she replied when Caro presumed to ask what Hawksrest's plans were now he'd finally come to terms with poor Cynthia Shallcross's death, "my cousin *shall cross* to a future that treats him more kindly."

On the way home, William and Rand discussed politics, a leftover discourse from the dinner table. The duchess said nothing, having nodded off.

Leonie, too, was silent, but not because she was tired. Lady Cynthia Shallcross's name kept going round and round in her head, as well as the many relevant details Caro Mumfrey had been only too eager to repeat. The daughter of the earl and countess of Rantry, Lady Cynthia had been the Season's foremost debutante, so stunning a beauty poor Eugenia hadn't had a chance to shine.

She'd brought Hawksrest up to scratch before the Season was half over, as she'd boasted to all her friends she would. She died in a freakish sailing accident days before what was being hailed as the wedding of the year. And Hawksrest was so grief stricken, many feared he'd never get over her.

In the days that followed, Leonie said nothing of what she'd learned at Lady Mumfrey's, but she couldn't help thinking about it. Was Rand still grieving for the beautiful Cynthia Shallcross? It would account for his brooding aspect. True, he'd exhibited none of this in Mirandeau, but perhaps the return home had renewed his sense of loss. She could well imagine how painful it might be going to the places they'd been together, seeing mutual friends and acquaintances, being reminded of her constantly.

And if this were so, it had nothing to do with herself. Indeed, if he were still torn by grief, she'd be a fool to suppose he even thought of her. Of course, his loss was more than two years old. With the formal period of mourning over, the *ton* would naturally deem it time he put it behind him. Yet did that really signify? Grief had an odd way of ignoring the rules. She'd often go days without consciously thinking of her own losses. Then she'd see Jamie's smile, and it would look so like Papa's! Or she'd hear a piece of music, recall it was one of Mama's favorites—and a piercing sense of loss would send a stab of grief to the heart.

These thoughts occupied her one afternoon as she sat on the stone bench in the informal garden. Crickets chirped the end of summer, and the September sun felt warm on her shoulders. This had become one of her favorite places in the estate. Because it was a walled enclosure, she could come here without her "guard," when she had time to herself. It was a good place to read, or simply to think.

The air was redolent with the scent of late blooming flowers, and she was just trying to identify a particular scent when she heard someone coming. "Your Grace!" she exclaimed, smiling when she saw who it was.

"Hoped I'd find you here, my dear," he said, smiling back. "Mind if an old man joins you?"

"Never say so, Your Grace," she replied as she made room for him on the seat. "I hardly think of you as old."

"That's kind of you," he said, "and sometimes I don't, either. Still," he added with a chuckle, "when one reaches my age, his physical person tends to remind him of it. But I didn't come here to talk about my old bones, my dear. I'm hoping you'll not think it rude if I inquire about your young ones. What's this I hear about your taking a tumble on the ballroom floor?"

"Oh, that," she said with a shrug. With her lessons a thing of the past, she'd more free time. In good weather she rode, but they'd had a rainy spell recently. Feeling in need of exercise, she'd spied a maid using a broom, and it gave her an idea. She'd teach herself the waltz! And while it could never amount to anything creditable, it did distract her from constantly thinking of Rand.

She'd told no one, of course. LeBeau was long gone, and she'd no wish to be seen making a cake of herself. Unfortunately, the maid had come looking for her broom yesterday just as Leonie was picking herself up off the floor after one of her many spills. "A mere slip as I practiced my curtsey," she added reassuringly. "I took no hurt, Your Grace. Please don't concern yourself."

He studied her in silence for a moment. "As you wish, my dear," he told her, "but I do beg you will take care. We've all grown deeply fond of you and should be devastated if you came to any harm." He smiled warmly. "Fact is, I've come to think of you . . . forgive me, but it's almost as if you were the daughter I never had. I don't suppose it's necessary to explain why?"

Swallowing past a constriction in her throat, she looked away until she'd mastered the stab of grief. Then she withdrew a ribbon from about her neck. Suspended from it was the emerald ring. "I've been remiss," she said, "in not returning this sooner, for it belongs to you." She held it out to him. "And I thank you with all my heart for heeding my mother's plea when she sent it."

William smiled tenderly at her and shook his head. "Please do me the honor of keeping it, my dear. There's no one else I'd rather had it. You are very much like her, you know."

She flushed, embarrassed and pleased at the same time. "Perhaps I favor her side of the family."

William was shaking his head again. He closed her hand around the ring. "I don't mean just in appearance," he said, "though there's a true resemblance. No, what I meant was that you remind me of her in many ways."

"Will you . . . can you tell me about her?" she asked. "What she was like when you knew her?"

"Nothing would give me greater pleasure." Smiling fondly, he spoke at length then, painting a picture of a Leona who was younger than Leonie was now, a woman vibrant with life, given to easy laughter, and deeply in the throes of first love. Soon they were sharing memories, exchanging stories. Leonie described the mother she knew and, most importantly for William, a life that saw her mother content. "I cannot say she and my father ever gave me reason to doubt they'd a good marriage," she told him. "Yet as I think back, it seems to have been more a union of mutual respect and liking than—than . . ."

"Heartfelt passion?" he suggested gently, seeing her blush.

She nodded shyly. "What stands out in my mind, mostly," she offered after a moment, "was their devotion to us children. We knew we were loved. Children have an unerring sense of it, you know." *Yet I wonder if adults do. Has Rand guessed? Surely not, and I pray he never does. Oh, Mama, how wonderful it must have been to know you were loved in return!*

Of this last there was no doubt. William had loved her mother deeply and completely, with a love that transcended time, decades of separation, and now death itself.

"I can't tell you how much it means to me to hear she was happy," said William. "I hoped and prayed she'd find fulfillment in her new life."

That's the real test, Mama. Nothing less than true love could be that unselfish. "And what of your own happiness, Your Grace?" she asked without thinking. "Oh—I beg you will forgive me!" she cried. "I've no right to—"

"Never mind it, my dear. It's common knowledge my own marriage was less than happy. But, do you see, there could never be room for another woman in my heart. It is . . . it always has been Leona and no other."

She saw a flicker of some nameless emotion in his eyes then. It reminded her of Rand that day in the gallery. But she'd be prudent this time and not ask about it. As it happened, she didn't have to.

"You're wondering about my choice to wed as I did," he said with a rueful smile, "and it's only natural you should. I'll be frank with you, my dear. The union was a disaster, and much of what went wrong was my fault. I wed, as many of our class do, out of duty. And as a sop to my conscience, I told Regina the truth . . . about loving another, I mean. Problem was, I assumed that would suffice, that we'd go on and make the best of it, but I was wrong. She never forgave me."

"Did she love you so much, Your Grace?" she asked, trying to feel some sense of sympathy for that cold woman in the portrait.

"Regina?" He smiled bitterly. "Regina loved no one but herself. No, it was her pride I wounded, and this enraged her. When I learned how she felt, I acknowledged my fault, took full blame, and proceeded to absent myself from her life. I told her she was free to . . . er, go her own way, as long as she used discretion."

He heaved a sigh, shook his head sadly. "What I never dreamed she'd do, to my complete shame and regret, was take out her rage on an innocent child. You see, she used Rand as a weapon . . . to punish me."

And as Leonie sat, horrified, he explained what he'd learned, when it was nearly too late, of his son's fate at the hands of his wife. Not only the beatings and tongue-lashings, but the years of emotional neglect, the complete lack of nurturing maternal care. "She'd some kind of twisted idea of shaping Rand into a total reflection of herself," he explained. "An image of perfection, as I understand it. She regarded herself as perfect, and as Rand was her mirror image physically, she sought to make him completely like her—in some warped notion she could thereby rob me of my son as she felt I'd robbed her of myself. Or of the life she'd envisioned for us."

"Dear God," Leonie whispered, hearing Rand's voice. *She could have given Roderik lessons.*

"It was completely irrational, of course," William added. "Fortunately, Rand had a strong enough sense of himself to withstand such abuse. That is, by the time I arrived to try to make it up to him, he wasn't beyond saving. Many a child would have been, but Rand responded beautifully to the love and affection his grandmother and I lavished on him. Became a happy, healthy child—thank God."

He paused, for the first time noting the look of pain in Leonie's eyes—pain she felt for Rand. *Mother thinks she's developed a simple* tendre *for him, but she's mistaken. She loves him. Best to warn the child, then. Hope it's not too late.* "The sole inkling I've had," he told her, "that Rand may suffer some ill effects from what he'd been deprived of in those early years is this unnatural lingering grief he carries. Er . . . you've heard something of the matter, no doubt?"

Flushing, she swallowed and managed to answer, "That he lost his fiancée, yes."

"Then perhaps you can understand what I mean. When Lady Cynthia died, Rand's withdrawal from society was total. Wouldn't weep, wouldn't even speak of it. Threw himself into his work for the crown, but even that didn't answer. I began to hear reports of his taking unusually high risks—asking for assignments so dangerous no one else wanted them."

Seeing her look of alarm, he patted her hand. "Don't overset yourself, my dear. With the Peace, we needn't fear for him on that score. But you do see what I mean . . . about the grief? I collect you've noticed he appears silent and brooding at times?"

"Yes," she said softly, "I've noticed."

He nodded. "And now you know its cause. Rand seems unable—or unwilling—to put his grief by, but you mustn't let it concern you." *And now, dearest Leonie, perhaps you'll summon the strength to free yourself of him. Like my Leona, you deserve a chance to get on with your life. To be happy.*

When William had gone, Leonie thought about all he'd said. She'd been deeply touched by his noble, unchanging love for her mother. She only wondered he didn't recognize himself in his son. Rand's lingering grief wasn't hard to explain, and it had nothing to do with his wretched mother. It was simple, really. Like his father, he'd love but one woman—for the rest of his life.

Rand smiled as he left the boys in the schoolroom that had once been his. How much happier a place it was now. Their tutor was every bit as learned as Snopes, but he was encouraged to give his natural kindness free rein. Poor Snopes had been turned off for his. As for Snopes's sadistic successor, William had sent him packing the moment he learned what sort of man Regina had—

"Sorry I took so long, yer lordship," said a large, burly man who hurried toward him.

"Never mind, Stebbins. Did you find her?" Stebbins was the Bow Street Runner hired to protect the boys, but this morning Rand had asked him to see if he could locate Leonie. She'd said she'd be in the garden, but shortly thereafter it began to rain, and Rand had gone looking for her. He was her guard, after all. When her abigail said she didn't know where Leonie was, he'd grown concerned. His own search had led him to the schoolroom, where the boys told him they hadn't seen her since breakfast. Not wishing to alarm them, he'd quietly sent Stebbins on a hunt while he stayed to hear their lessons. "Did you speak to her?" he asked Stebbins now.

"Er . . . not exactly, yer lordship, but I think I know where she went. There be a maid swears she's not seen the lady, but a guinea to a copper says she's lyin'. I been around enough t' know, an'—beggin' yer pardon, yer lordship, but I think the lady bribed the wench."

"Bribed! What the devil do you mean?"

"This maid kept dartin' looks at a door down the hallway from where she parked herself, an' she had this smug look when she told me the lady weren't there. Then, when I went to look, she got kinda nervous. Said I hadn't oughta go in there. Said they was washin' the ballroom floor."

"The ballroom floor?" Why did that ring a bell?

Then he had it. His father had mentioned something about Leonie falling down there—on another occasion when she was supposed to be in the garden, come to think of it. As a precaution, William had ordered the floor sanded. But why the devil was she even in there? And why wash a sanded floor? "Stebbins, are you sure she said they were washing the floor?"

"That's right, yer lordship. She—" Stebbins shrugged as his lordship ran off. *Queer lot, the gentry.*

* * *

"No mat-ter how hard—just try, just try!" Leonie grinned as she sang, swirling the broom she'd dubbed Sir Broomstick around the floor. Her made-up words to the three-quarter-time tune wouldn't steal any laurels from Lord Byron, but they made waltzing seem easier. "And soon we shall fly," she sang on, "shall fly, shall fl—oh, *no!"*

She hit the floor with a thud, the broom clattering beside her. The racket brought the sound of running feet. "Oh, milady!" cried the little maid she'd paid to keep watch. "Are ye hurt?"

"Not at all, Abbie, thank you," she said, rubbing her posterior.

"Could be we oughtn't-a swept the floor, milady," said Abbie, eyeing the pile of fine sand they'd swept into a corner.

"Nonsense," said Leonie. "It spoiled my glides. Now, do stand back, dear."

Wringing her hands, the maid watched her struggle to her feet. She'd been paid handsomely to stand guard when she wasn't wanted in the kitchens, but the lady always insisted on picking herself up. *She might have a game leg, but she's a rum sport, she is!*

Just then, the clock on the stairs chimed the hour. "Best run along, dear," Leonie said as the girl gave a start, "or you'll be in the suds. Go on, I'll be fine. Thank you again for watching—and not telling!"

"Thank *you,* milady!" Holding up the coin she'd earned, the maid grinned, bobbed a curtsey and scampered off.

"Now, sir,"—Leonie held the broom at arm's length—"where were we? Ah, yes. And soon we shall fly, shall fly. . . ."

The ballroom was at the other end of the house, and though he hurried, Rand knew it could take him twenty minutes to reach it. He made use of that time, however, by pondering Leonie's behavior of late. If she was in the deuced ballroom, why hadn't she told him? It was almost as if she were avoiding him. Did she chafe under their current arrangement, view it as too great a restriction of her freedom? He did need to know where she was at all times, of course; but when escorting her to various functions, he'd tried to be as unobtrusive as possible. And if she found the arrangement disagreeable, why the devil hadn't she said so?

Did she think *he* enjoyed it? Seeing her transformed into a self-possessed young woman who had every eligible male within miles smitten? Bloody hell, if William hadn't put it about that the family would entertain no suggestion of a match until she was presented at court, she'd already have had several offers! This pleased William and the dowager, no doubt, but he'd be damned if *he* could like it.

Fact was, at every affair to which he'd escorted Leonie, he'd been deuced miserable. The dowager's doing, and he couldn't refute her reasons. The princess was to have every opportunity to come into her own amidst the blasted *ton,* and Rand was not to interfere, whatever that meant. Even when it became necessary for him to act as her escort, his grandmother had been quite clear. "Keep an eye on her, Hawksrest, but keep out of the way. The child must develop the social skills needed to go on. She can scarcely do that with you hovering. It requires practice with new people in new situations. You are a known entity. I fear she's already too accustomed to depending upon you, and it won't answer."

And so he'd stood back, never suspecting how hard it would be. To stand by and watch while other men, young and old, danced attendance on her. To hear her laugh and know it was not for him. To hear that old fool Braddock roar at her wit; listen to that dandy Wriothesley praising her new gown, or see those damned naval twins falling over each other to fetch her a glass of ratafia. By heaven, he'd rather face the French again!

It was a damned uncomfortable thing, feeling that way. At first he hadn't known what to make of it. This had never happened to him before. But after some thought, he'd finally been forced to face facts. He was *jealous,* damn it! Jealous of the attention paid a woman he'd no business imagining he might—

He was only too glad to put aside his discomfiting thoughts as he rounded a corner and spied the ballroom straight ahead. Slowing his pace, he was just pondering what he'd say to her when he heard something quite unexpected. Leonie's voice, he was sure of it, and she was . . . *singing.*

The quarter hour since Abbie left was proving disastrous, Leonie thought glumly. She'd fallen down countless times, and the pleasure was gone from the morning's endeavor. She'd thought of quitting, but that didn't sit very well with her conscience. *What, are you giving up after a few piddling little spills?* That nagging voice inside her head was beginning to irritate. Still, she mustered on, though her spirits had begun to take as much of a battering as her person.

Too dispirited to invent more lyrics, she gave up and began to hum the waltz melody now, doggedly circling the floor with the broom. There, that was better. Much better. Yes, she actually seemed to be making progress. She'd completed an entire—*nooo!*

Her cry of protest was silent, but the sudden tears that arose unbidden were not. Crumpled in a heap on the floor, the broom tangled in her skirts, she gave vent to helpless frustration and began to sob.

Rand heard. He sprinted across the last few yards to the half-open door and thrust it wide. "Leonie!" he cried, rushing to her side. "Sweetheart—oh, God, what's happened?"

Rand! Horrified that he, of all persons, should come upon her like this, she buried her face in the crook of her arm. "Go away!" she sobbed. "Oh, please, just *go away.*"

"Don't be foolish!" he snapped, not meaning to, but desperate to know what the matter was. "Are you hurt? Leonie, tell me where it hurts."

This demand was shouted, and the alarm in it must have penetrated. She raised her head and swiped at her tears with the heel of her hand. "I am n-not hurt," she replied, meeting his anxious gaze, "except—"

"Not hurt! I've found you lying on the floor *crying.*"

"Except in my p-pride," she finished, and when he just stared at her: "I was trying to do the impossible, you see," she added, the last remnants of that pride leaking out of her, "and only n-now realized it."

"Leonie," he said with barely controlled exasperation, "stop talking in riddles and—"

"If you must know," she cried, her own exasperation boiling over, "I was trying to waltz. And this"—she grabbed the broom and flung it across the floor—"was my erstwhile dancing partner. Is that plain enough for you? The little lame *Original* was actually fool enough to think she could dance—with a *crippled foot!*" The outburst behind her, she hung her head, bowing to the twin miseries of shame and defeat. She couldn't look at him, couldn't bear to see the pity that was certain to be in his eyes.

Rand sighed and reached out to stroke the shining curls that had come loose of their pins. So that was why she'd come here without telling him, he thought, aching for her. *Except in my pride.* He knew something about pride, knew what it was to be keenly aware of a failing and dread having it exposed. Her hair was like burnished silk. The long skeins had parted behind to fall forward over her shoulders as she bowed her head. He was struck by how slender and fragile the nape of her neck appeared. "Are you certain you've taken no physical hurt?" he asked softly.

Mutely, she shook her head.

He was silent for a moment as an idea took shape. "Come," he said, rising and helping her to her feet. When they were both standing, she with her head lowered, still not looking at him, he raised her chin with gentle fingers until she was forced to meet his eyes.

"Put your hands on my shoulders," he instructed, holding her tearful gaze.

"But . . . why?"

"Because, my lovely Original," he said placing her hands where he'd said and his own firmly at her waist, "I make a better partner than a broom." And with that, he began to hum the melody he'd heard her singing, lifted her effortlessly off the floor, just enough for her feet to skim the surface—and began to lead her in a waltz.

It was at first more than she was willing to believe or accept. Rand dancing . . . with *her?* It wasn't real. She'd somehow fallen asleep on that wretched floor and was dreaming, just as she had once in a forest late at night. An impossible dream, no more. She gazed doubtfully at the floor, wondering if the sight of her twisted foot would jar her awake. All she saw were her skirts swirling gracefully about their legs as Rand's voice, a melodic baritone, kept three-quarter time. It sounded so real.

She dared to raise her eyes. Some nameless emotion resided in the violet depths of his gaze. A tenderness as well, that was echoed by his smile, but something more. And it wasn't really nameless, just so vastly impossible she feared to give it a name that would prove false. As if he'd read her mind, his hands tightened about her waist, giving it a squeeze, and he nodded. The tender smile became the dazzling grin she loved. He winked at her, and she felt something shift and settle in affirmation. The dream faded, and reality hit home. They were gliding gracefully over the ballroom floor. They were! She and Rand . . . were *waltzing.*

Rand saw her eyes widen with surprise and then delight as he skimmed her across the floor. A gurgle of laughter followed, and he laughed, too. He knew a heady sense of joy just watching her. A lovely wash of color had spread across her delicate cheekbones, and her eyes shone green as jade, chips of amber sparkling in their depths. She was once again his winsome sprite, an elfin creature out of faerie, and the Leonie he loved.

The Leonie he loved?

Leonie saw it again, the emotion she wouldn't name for fear it was nothing more than a reflection of her own longing, of an untrustworthy imagination gone wild. But now it came with something she could identify: surprise. Something had surprised him, yet she'd no idea what.

"Rand?" she questioned as he abruptly brought them to a halt. He was looking at her so solemnly. "Is something wro—"

Her breath caught as he threaded his fingers through her hair and captured her face. His eyes were so intense, so filled with that emotion as they reached deeply into hers, she couldn't think.

"Leonie," he murmured into the breathless instant that followed. Before her world tilted on its axis and spun madly out of control. Before his head lowered, and he claimed her lips in a kiss that left her reeling.

Eighteen

Head spinning, unable to form a coherent thought, Leonie felt the impossible happen: First kiss. For her, as improbable and remote as a dream. And that it was *Rand's* mouth on hers went beyond anything her poor brain could conjure. Unimaginable but moments ago, yet now as real as the rapid thudding of her heart and Rand's solid, muscular shoulders beneath her hands. She felt the lazy warmth of his lips stealing over her senses, was acutely aware of his mouth taking tender possession of hers; beyond that, she could not go: no room for sensible thought here; only the magic of the impossible come true. And the sheer sense of wonder, and awe . . . that a miracle could happen—to her.

Rand, too, felt stunned by what had somehow . . . happened. What began as a simple attempt to support her courageous efforts to dance—God above, to *dance*—had suddenly become something else entirely. Something so compelling he could no longer gainsay it or deny its right to exist. *Ah, Leonie . . . sweet sprite, I can't run from you anymore!*

And she *was* sweet, sweet beyond telling. Her mouth—ah, God, her mouth!—was moist and soft as petals washed by summer rain. Shy and uncertain at first, then warming by degree as he sipped and tasted, never breaking contact, letting her untutored lips learn the contours of his own.

He took his time with her, holding her still for his gentle possession, while his mouth coaxed and guided, shaped and instructed the sweet uncertainty of hers. And when he felt her relax and lean into him, he widened his stance and pulled her firmly into his arms.

Leonie's heart gave a wild leap as he drew her against him. She stood on eager tiptoe, wound her arms about his neck, and, with a surge of unbearable joy, felt him tighten the embrace. *Ah, Rand—my love! My love!*

And still they kissed. Lightly tracing the seam between her lips with his tongue, Rand felt them part shyly at first, under his careful persuasion, then with growing confidence. Tongue still gently questing, he began to explore the soft inner recesses of her lips. He felt a tremor run through her, and then her tongue as it ventured forth to meet his.

So eager, so quick to respond! Blood began to pound in his ears, and Rand realized with dismay he was reacting in ways he hadn't forseen. Not to a simple kiss! Yet not so simple, apparently.

The inescapable evidence was impossible to ignore. He was growing hard. She was a total innocent, yet with this single kiss, he knew he'd tapped a deeply sensual vein in her, as ripe and ready as it was unexpected. Gasping, fighting for control, he released her, and stepped quickly back from the conflagration he knew was imminent if he did not.

"R-Rand?" she questioned, half dazed, slow to acknowledge the separation. Her pulse was still racing, every nerve exquisitely alive to the flood of sensation coursing through her body.

Rand was having his own problems with the effects of that kiss. That single, extraordinary kiss! Hot blood surged through his veins—as well as other parts. Hands on his hips, he bowed his head and shut his eyes; took a deep, shuddering breath, and released it slowly. He only hoped her innocence would keep her from realizing what his breeches couldn't hide as he sought to bring it under control.

But it was deuced difficult with the feel of her willing lips still imprinted on his. Raising his head, he sought those wide green eyes and barely stifled a groan. Her pupils were so widely dilated they were nearly black. He'd enough experience in bedding women to know this was as sure a sign of passion as his, if not as obvious.

Clenching his teeth, focusing on Leonie's needs, not his own, he reached for control—and found it. Now, with a tender half smile, he stroked her cheek with the backs of his fingers and tucked an errant tendril of auburn hair behind her ear. "I seem to have rearranged your coiffure," he offered lamely.

He couldn't think what else to say. His mind had suddenly shifted to another plane, stunning him with the truth of what had just come clear. He . . . *loved* her. *Ah, lass, how long have I been watching you with eyes too blind to see? Denying what my heart knew all along?*

And with that truth, there came another, a soaring realization that rocked him to the very depths of his soul: He was . . . *free.* Sweet God in heaven, free! *She* and all her ugly words no longer had a hold on him.

"It doesn't matter," Leonie murmured. And seeing Rand's bemused look as her words pulled him back to the moment: "My coiffure, that is." She was coming down to earth now, but still unable to move. She'd been watching the play of shifting emotions on his face. Not the closed stranger's face of recent weeks, but a far more open one. Her heart gave a lurch of recognition. The naked look in his eyes, the look she'd only glimpsed while they were dancing, was still there.

"Good," he agreed, fingering a silken strand of her hair, "for I'm rather fond of it just as it is." He searched her face for a long moment, wondering if he should tell her now or wait until she'd some warning. Perhaps until he'd courted her? The dowager was always going on about how she deserved that sort of thing, the rituals he supposed most young women delighted in. But, damn it, he was full to bursting with how he felt. Why the devil wait?

But he knew the answer to that. She could always reject—no! He wouldn't think of rejection. *Stop being such a bloody coward.*

"Leonie," he said, making up his mind, "what I'm hoping does matter . . ." He caught her hand and brought it to his lips, then turned it over and placed a second kiss in the sensitive center of her palm. Still holding her hand, he met her gaze with solemn eyes. "What I'm hoping does matter is that I—"

"Leonie!" Jamie's excited call rang from the hallway.

Rand smothered a groan. Leonie gave a start, her hand still in his, every nerve in her body aware of that sensual kiss to her palm.

"She's here—and so's Hawk!" Sam's excitement echoed his cousin's as the two burst into the ballroom. Panting and out of breath, Stebbins brought up the rear.

"You'll never guess who's come to pay a call!" cried Jamie.

"They won't," Sam agreed, observing the peculiar looks on their faces and taking this for confirmation, though why Leonie was blushing, he couldn't imagine. "Not in a million years—unless we give them a hint," he added, grinning at Jamie.

"Right." Jamie paused a moment to reflect—on several things, as it happened: He, too, had seen his sister's blush, as well as a queer sort of look on Hawk's face. He'd also noted him holding her hand, though he'd quickly released it when they came in. Something interesting going on there. He'd have to think about it, but later. For now, he must summon the right sort of hint. "Who's the worst horseman we know?" he asked, miming a bumbling equestrian.

Rand chuckled, giving Leonie's arm a surreptitious squeeze to let her know they'd unfinished business. "A lean shanks?" he asked, joining the game by imitating his grandmother using her quizzing glass. "Ginger-pated fellow, not at all the thing?"

Grinning, Jamie nodded. Sam started to giggle.

"Doesn't surprise me," sniffed Leonie, in imitation of Lady Mumfrey and her set. "In autumn, we're fairly overrun by *scarecrows.*"

* * *

Mirandeau
The Palace

Roderik paced the length of the balcony off his bedchamber, then pivoted and paced again. In the moonlit courtyard below, a pair of Guards stood sentry. The city of Rienna, spread out beyond the palace walls, lay dark and silent. It was well past midnight, and he'd just received a coded message from a most reliable spy. It confirmed what they'd already suspected. His quarry was in England. All it wanted was for his man to track them down to the exact locale, which he was already in the process of doing, and then tighten the noose.

Of course, his man wasn't really his at all, and spying wasn't his only skill; known only as The Serpent, he was an expensive and highly trained assassin. The best, belonging to a secret society that had operated in Mirandeau for centuries. Poor Frederik had been under the delusion they were all long gone, the last remnant caught and hanged in their grandfather's time.

Roderik knew better. The only surprise had been that there were women among them. The Serpent would employ one as an accomplice on this very mission. Their specialty was poison. *My dear Leona, you were not only far too clever, but far too trusting of humble serving maids.*

Prince Jamie was the next victim, of course, always had been. But Sam must now join him. Unfortunate, but the earlier plan had proved unworkable. The brat was a milksop, too like his mother. More to the point, he was incapable of acting the part the scheme had required. No matter. With the prince dead, dear Uncle Roderik was next in line for the throne in any event, unless . . .

Roderik halted his pacing. *Unless the little cripple weds and produces an heir . . . unlikely, but not beyond the realm of possibility.*

Best dispatch them all, then. Blame the kidnappers. Then it only wanted getting rid of his whey-faced wife—after a plausible interval, of course—and finding a suitable breeder of sons among the current crop of peers' daughters. Yes, that should answer very well.

The sentries down below glanced at each other as they heard the regent's laughter. Neither would voice what he was thinking, but they were of one mind. It had the ring of madness.

England

Rand decided to court Leonie after all, which, of course, meant informing his father and his grandmother. Nothing went on at Hartswood that escaped the notice of either, so it only made sense. Though William wouldn't say so, he'd be hurt to learn of it secondhand, Rand suspected; and while the dowager might not feel injured, she'd doubtless deem it disobliging and bad *ton* for him not to inform her beforehand.

Yet beyond this, Rand found he truly *wanted* their input . . . and, if he were honest with himself, their approval. Of course, courtship was a prelude to marriage. Was he really contemplating such a step again? he asked himself at one point. He'd only to think of Leonie's smile to reply with a heartfelt yes. And for the marriage of a duke's heir, the legal and financial consequences alone demanded family involvement.

Yet these were the least of his concerns. Foremost, this was a matter of the heart . . . his and Leonie's, he hoped. He knew all too well he'd been down this road before. And before he committed himself again, he wanted the assessment of older and wiser heads, he realized. Whether he was merely being careful or didn't trust his own judgment, he really didn't know. What he did know was that he could trust the judgment of the dowager and of his father. They not only loved him, but had come to care for Leonie as well.

He spoke with them that same night, after everyone else had retired, including Petrie, who'd been invited to stay on a few days. Their reactions were encouraging, but as different from each other as day from night.

William's first response was astonishment. *"Court* Leonie? But I thought . . . that is—well, never mind what I thought. Do you *love* her?"

And when Rand said he did, there was open delight: "Then court her, by all means—and with my blessing!"

The dowager, on the other hand, approved, but with a caveat: "You are free to court her affections, of course, but at present, any public suit is out of the question. Your courtship must remain private, conducted within the confines of Hartswood. Until the business in Mirandeau is sorted out, you can pursue no official future with its princess.

"And to be fair to her," she added, "you must somehow contrive to make her understand this, even as you seek to win her. Not an easy task, but if you love her, surely you can see the need to be honest with her."

Not an easy task, but if you love her . . . Unfortunately, Rand knew exactly what the dowager meant by those words. What man who was in love, who desired an honest courtship ending in marriage, wished to couch his romantic intentions in uncertainty? What to say? *Darling, I desire you for my wife, but I dare not as yet propose marriage? I adore you, but I cannot offer for you until who knows when? I love you, but, for now, we must forget about exchanging vows?*

No, not an easy task, but somehow he'd find a way through it. Fortunately, what he'd to look forward to, in the immediate offing, promised to be far more enjoyable. At present, all he need do was make Leonie aware of his feelings. To let her know, in subtle ways, of the sea change in his mind and heart. He couldn't wait.

While Rand conferred with the duke and duchess, Leonie lay wide awake in her bed. Tired from a full day that included sweeping a ballroom floor and waltzing on it, she was unwilling to surrender to sleep. She wanted to sift through all that had happened, to savor every impossible moment, to hold in her heart the delicious feelings careening about inside her.

Her one regret was that there wasn't someone, a confidante, with whom she could share them tonight. If only her mother were alive to see that miracles could happen to the daughter she loved. *Ah, Mama, if you're there, can you see what's in my heart?*

Since she'd mostly only heard them secondhand, Leonie used to wonder about things said at court: "Rouchard's eldest chit has a developed a *tendre* for d'Arnoult's heir," she recalled Mama once saying. "If he's brought up to scratch, she'll be in transports." *In transports.* She distinctly remembered pondering what it meant.

Now she knew.

Mama, I am in transport. Overjoyed, ecstatic, and deliriously happy! So acutely happy just to be alive, she had to pinch herself to be sure she wasn't dreaming. Had she actually *danced*—with Rand? Had he truly—but he had, he had! Poor Sally had been so puzzled when she refused to let the maid draw her a bath before bed. But how to explain that if she closed her eyes, she could smell the faint scent of sandalwood on her skin? *It happened, Mama!*

She could remember going through the motions of normal behavior afterward: hearing the boys' chatter as they all went to welcome Petrie; receiving Simon and introducing him to the duke and dowager; making small talk while they took tea. But all the while, she'd the sensation of floating, of being absurdly suspended inches off the ground. Responding not to Mr. Newton's law of gravity, but to an irrefutable truth repeated with each giddy beat of her heart: *Rand kissed me, Rand kissed me, Rand kissed me!*

Hugging her pillow, she grinned into the darkness, remembering the feel of his body aligned with hers. A yawn interposed, and she felt her eyelids growing heavy. Her last thought before sleep claimed her was of Rand's whispered words as he'd bidden her good night: "Dance with me tonight . . . in our dreams."

* * *

"Good morning, m'lady." Rand's dimples were deep grooves bracketing his mouth, his smile a flash of white against bronze skin as he greeted Leonie. They met at the stables, having agreed to ride before breakfast, weather permitting. It was a perfect morning for riding, crisp and cool, the air redolent of wood smoke and the scent of fallen leaves. Nearby, a pair of grooms held Raven and Rand's mare—Quicksilver and Raven did not get on—and the horses pranced with eagerness. "I trust you slept well last night?" Rand asked as he drew nearer.

"Good morning, m'lord," she murmured, helpless against the look he sent her. There was a teasing light in his eyes that had her blushing furiously. "Quite well, I thank you."

Rand's lips curved in a lazy smile. He was well aware of the reasons for that charming blush. Closing the remaining distance between them, he bent over her ear, then murmured, too softly for the grooms to hear, "Did m'lady . . . dance?"

His warm breath feathered the tendrils of hair at her ear, and Leonie's pulse raced. She felt herself go hot all over, but managed to nod. She'd done more than dance with him in her dreams. She'd relived that kiss over and over, and she felt certain he somehow knew it.

"So did I," he whispered. His eyes danced as they locked with hers. "Ah, m'lady . . . so did I."

Her knees went weak, and she wondered if the grooms noticed. Rand, she suspected, knew exactly how he made her feel—deliciously aware of him, and unable to hide it.

"Come," he said. Catching her gloved hand, he led her to the stallion. He dismissed the groom and set his hands about her waist. She swallowed hard, remembering his touch as they'd waltzed. Lifting her as if she weighed nothing at all, he set her atop the sidesaddle. About to adjust the stirrup, he paused.

The fashionable riding boot Hoby's had customized to accommodate her foot was made of soft, supple leather. As if he were seeing it for the first time, he cupped it in one hand and ran the other slowly over it. Leonie's breath hitched as she felt his touch through the soft leather. The leisurely stroke could only be called a caress.

Tucking the boot into place, he raised his head and gave her a tender smile. "Queen of Courage," he murmured for her ears alone, "beside you, the rest of us are piddling cowards."

Before she could comment, Rand handed her the reins and turned to his mare, dismissing the second groom. Seated, he eyed with appreciation the lovely figure she made in her velvet riding habit. The matching bonnet framed her heart-shaped face, the forest green a perfect complement to her auburn curls.

He gestured beyond the stable yard. "About the park, then south across the downs—the ruins of an old monastery, from King Henry's time. The locals say they're haunted. Care to see if they're right?" he asked with a grin.

With the familiar feel of Raven beneath her, Leonie felt her sense of equilibrium return. She laughed. "Why not? After all, what are a few ghosts to a queen of my, um, ilk? I've a reputation to uphold."

With a bark of laughter, Rand nudged the mare's flanks, and they were off.

They held to a canter while skirting the park, unwilling to disturb the deer they saw grazing. On reaching the downs, however, they gave the horses their heads, and raced over the gently rolling hills. Breathless when they reached the ruins, they dismounted and cooled their mounts. The wind tugged at Leonie's bonnet, and she pulled it loose, let it hang down her back by its ribbons. She ran her fingers through her hair as well, welcoming the cooling breeze on her overheated skin.

When she bared her head, Rand's breath caught in his throat. Sunlight turned the auburn curls a fiery copper. He made a mental note. Their marriage bed must stand by an east-facing window. He wanted to awaken to such loveliness each morning of their lives. He wanted to hold her in his arms and tell her how she made him ache just to look at her.

Dragging his thoughts to the present, he cast an eye at the

sun, then gave her bonnet a playful tug. "The dowager will no doubt disapprove," he said, grinning at her.

"No doubt," she agreed cheerfully. "I fear it's to be buttermilk and lemon juice on my poor freckles tonight. And just when she'd believed them bleached to perdition, too!"

He laughed. "As I'm quite fond of your freckles, I shall protest."

"Hah! As if that would make a dent in her determination."

"You've come to know her well, I see," he said, chuckling. "Perhaps now you can appreciate why the London staff called her a Tartar."

"You *know* about that?"

"My darling Leonie, I encouraged it."

"What!"

"Sweetheart, I had to give you some warning, didn't I?"

My darling Leonie . . . sweetheart . . . Warmed by his endearments, she didn't reply. Then his response sank in, and she giggled.

Chuckling, he took Raven's reins from her and tethered both horses to a clump of gorse. He caught her by the hand and led her toward the ruins.

The monastery lay nestled in the lee of a grassy slope. Spread over half an acre were the remains of several buildings. A few were reduced to rubble, but most retained their stone walls. All were open to the sky, their roofs long gone.

"Whose ghosts are supposed to haunt this place?" she asked. Shading her eyes from the sun with her free hand, and very much aware Rand still held the other, she scanned the ruins.

"The monks. Henry's soldiers slew the poor devils when they resisted his new laws."

"Resisted?"

"He ordered them disbanded, the monasteries closed when he broke with Rome."

"Oh," she said, nodding, *"that* Henry."

He led her inside the largest structure. Its walls were high and steeper yet at the eastern end, where they may have supported a clerestoried sanctuary. This was likely the chapel. Once inside, Leonie noticed the walls sheltered them from the wind, which could be heard outside.

"I wonder how often the moaning of the wind has been taken for ghostly voices," she mused.

Rand arched a brow at her. "You're certain it's just the wind, are you?"

"Absolutely. Any sensible person would be."

"Ah." They were standing beside one wall, Leonie's back to it. Rand released her hand and braced both of his against the rough stone on either side of her shoulders, caging her with his arms. "And so you're sensible, are you?" he asked, looking down at her with that roguish grin she loved.

"I most certainly . . . am," she replied, her breath catching in her throat. That teasing light was in his eyes, and she was beginning to love that, too.

"At all times, of course," he said with mock seriousness as his gaze dropped to her mouth.

"Of—of course." The words escaped on a hesitant breath as his head descended. Then his mouth claimed hers, and there were no words at all.

If Leonie had a sensible bone in her body, at that moment she was unaware of it. A sensible girl would have questioned why her world—not always a safe place, but one she'd managed to navigate with a modicum of good sense—had, since yesterday, been turned upside down. A sensible girl would have questioned how a hopeless love could suddenly soar on the wings of possibility. A sensible girl, yes, but the one whose lips returned Rand's kiss that morning was another creature entirely. Like a fragile butterfly emerging out of the long night of her cocoon, this one questioned nothing. She simply flew.

The kiss was a joining of their mouths alone, but an exquisitely sensual joining. Rand kept his arms braced, hands flat on the wall, letting just his lips savor the taste of her. Nor did Leonie move. Her entire being centered on that narrow world where mouth met mouth. On the lazy, unhurried movement of his lips and tongue. Gently questing at first, then sweetly lingering, now moving with delicious slowness, now even playful. He caught her lower lip with his teeth, lightly grazing the sensitive flesh. The act was sensual beyond telling, and she gasped. When her lips parted, his tongue delved between, then slid across and dipped into the sensitive corner of her mouth.

Attuned to every nuance, Rand felt her shudder. Her response sent an instant message to his groin. With a groan, he pulled her into his arms and deepened the kiss. Her mouth opened to him at once. And when her tongue tangled with his and she arched against him, his already fragile control slipped another notch. Without thought, he curled his hand about the nape of her neck. His splayed fingers drove through bonnet strings and auburn silk, capturing her head and holding her still. Now his other hand moved to the soft mound of her breast. And when, even through all the layers of fabric, he felt her nipple spring erect, Rand heard a roaring in his ears.

With a nameless longing she didn't understand, Leonie pressed her body closer. Then she felt Rand's hand close over her breast, and something began to unravel deep inside her belly. When he found the sensitive crest and began to pluck and lightly pinch, a jolt of exquisite pleasure shot from the place he fondled to her woman's core. She went hot and cold all over. Wanting him became an elemental need she neither understood nor paused to consider. Rand was all that mattered. Rand and the sweet, soaring beauty of his touch!

Later, Rand would damn his loss of control and be grateful for the intrusion, but when the first heavy drops of rain drove them apart, a frustrated groan tore from his throat. "What the devil—"

"Oh!" Caught in the maelstrom of her spinning senses, Leonie blinked as Rand released her. Then reality penetrated: It was as if the heavens had suddenly opened. A torrent of rain was—

"Come!" Rand shouted over a crack of thunder. He grabbed her hand, began to run with her. The horses were neighing and pulling at their tethers when they reached them. Raven settled as soon as he saw Leonie, but the mare was wild-eyed and frantic. About to set her on the stallion, Rand saw her heavy velvet skirt was a sodden mass twined about her legs. He paused, doubting she could ride effectively, so encumbered.

"Will the black carry double?" he shouted as thunder rumbled and a jagged fork of lightning split the sky overhead.

"What?"

"You can't ride this way!" he shouted, indicating the soaked train of the riding habit she was trying to pluck away from her legs. "I want to turn the mare loose and take you back on Raven. Will he accept both of us?"

"Yes!" she yelled over another peal of thunder.

A minute later, Leonie found herself on Raven's back, seated in front of Rand as he took them home. She was sitting sideways, caged within the shelter of his arms: a different kind of caging than she'd experienced against that monastery wall, yet it reminded her of what had passed between them.

Despite the thunder and driving rain, a delicious smile hovered about her lips all the way home.

Nineteen

Jamie eyed his sister and Hawk as they strolled along the garden path. Holding hands . . . *again.* They didn't know he was watching, which didn't surprise him. Far too occupied looking at each other, he made no doubt. What was going on?

He'd come here looking for Sam's cat. And as he'd rounded the bend, there were Leonie and Hawk looking just like those lovey-dovey couples in Mama's illustrated Shakespeare—Rosalind and Orlando, Miranda and Ferdinand, Romeo and Juliet—before their heartless stars crossed them up so cruelly, of course.

"Jamie, did you find him?"

Jamie whirled at the sound of Sam's voice. "Sh-h-h!" he said, putting a finger to his lips. He pointed to the pair just then vanishing around another bend in the path.

"Was that Leonie with Hawk?" Sam mouthed.

Jamie nodded, and motioned him closer.

Sam came and whispered in his ear: "Then why the secrecy? We could ask them if they've seen Cat." *Cat* was the name Sam had given his orange tabby. He knew his cousin felt it wasn't very original, but if Sam liked it, Jamie had said, that was all that mattered.

"Because," Jamie replied, "I don't think they fancy being seen at the moment. Sam, they're *holding hands* . . . like lovebirds! And it's not the first time, either. I saw them doing it last week. When we found them in the ballroom, remember?"

"Really?" Sam asked, fascinated. "D'you suppose he means to offer for her?"

"I don't know," said Jamie, considering. "But if he does, who's he to make an offer *to?* It's always the parents of the girl, but Leonie doesn't have any—we're orphans, don't forget."

"You know I could never forget, Jamie," Sam said softly.

"I know, silly. 'Twas just one of those figures of speech the Scarecrow was always rattling on about."

Sam smiled and nodded.

"But I'm right about Hawk's difficulty," Jamie said. "With everything at sixes and sevens, there's not even a proper guardian for him to—"

"I have it!" cried Sam, grinning. "You're meant to assume your father's responsibilities now, aren't you? Hawk could make his offer to *you.*"

"It was pleasant seeing Simon again," Leonie remarked as she and Rand strolled along the garden path. "Coming downstairs this morning, I forgot for a moment that he left yesterday. I found I actually missed him."

Rand chuckled. "You're just impressed by that pretty speech he made when he returned this." He brushed his fingertips lightly along her ear, where the ruby earbob dangled.

Leonie's breath hitched. She couldn't help it when Rand touched her like that. Which was often now, even if he hadn't kissed her again—not in that delicious way that made her toes curl—since the monastery. He seemed oddly disinclined to repeat what had happened between them then. Still, he was always inventing reasons to touch her in more subtle ways, as now. He'd used the earbob as an excuse to give her a . . . caress.

Well aware of her reaction, Rand congratulated himself. He'd made the right decision. Since losing control at the ruins, he'd imposed limits on how and when he might touch her. Leonie's unsuspecting, deeply sensual nature had nearly cost her her virginity that day. If the storm hadn't intervened, he'd have taken her right there on the ground, like a common trollop—with her innocent complicity, he made no doubt. He accounted himself an honorable man, but he wasn't made of wood.

He smiled wryly to himself. *Unless it's wood about to ignite.* Innocent though they were, her responses had been like a torch touched to dry tinder. He'd not risk her innocence that way again.

"Perhaps Simon should write plays instead of acting in them," Leonie said. The breathless moment had passed, and she could speak again. Though with her hand in his, she suspected her voice was always a little unsteady, but at least she could function. "Not only did he make a lovely speech about the ruby gracing my earlobe—"

"A very lovely earlobe," Rand couldn't help observing. He resisted the urge to kiss it—just barely. If he did that, he suspected that faint floral scent of her skin, the scent he'd no trouble remembering, would have him nuzzling it, and that simply wouldn't answer. *Ah, but someday, love.*

"Yes, well"—the look in his eyes made Leonie's throat constrict; she paused to clear it—"it wasn't till later, when Simon sent me a written copy, I realized his speech was in blank verse."

"A fellow of hidden talents, our Scarecrow."

"Hawk!" she chided. "I thought we agreed to be kind to him."

"Now, don't fly into the boughs over it! 'Twas said in private, after all." He paused and grinned at her. "So I'm Hawk when you're vexed with me, am I?

"Well, I hadn't really thought about it . . . but I suppose you must be." She grinned back at him. "If I've flown into the boughs, it makes sense that a hawk would have sent me there."

"Touché!" he replied, laughing. Her wit never ceased to delight him. What a long way she'd come from those days when she'd reminded him of a frightened deer. Like a lovely butterfly emerging from a chrysalis, his shy, timid princess

had become what she was always meant to be: a complex woman with hidden depths and infinite possibilities.

"In any case," said Leonie, "I'm glad His Grace offered to use his influence to help Simon's career. I believe the man has talent, even if I haven't actually seen him on stage."

"So does my father," said Rand, "or he'd never have offered to use his interest on Petrie's behalf." They'd reached the stone bench, and he withdrew a handkerchief to protect her gown. "Ah," he said as a fold of paper fluttered to the ground.

"This note"—he retrieved it—"is from our estate manager. He needs me to inspect some drainage ditches on the southern boundary. Half a day's ride from here, and muddy work once we arrive. Tomorrow, and I must go. Leonie, I regret it, but I cannot take you on such a trek."

"It's all right," she said. He was telling her he was obligated to do this, though it meant he'd not be here to protect her. "I'm sure Mr. Stebbins won't mind guarding me for a day."

He nodded. "Stebbins is a good man, and I've already spoken to him. Yet I cannot help feeling . . . concerned, shall we say?" He sent her a questioning look as he smiled at her. "I was hoping you'd agree to do something for me."

"Anything." *I'd find a way to fly to the moon, if you asked it.*

"I'd like you to wear male attire again, just for the day. And especially when you're out of doors, to borrow the crutches my father will lend you, to disguise—"

"The reason for my limp?" she supplied, smiling. She didn't think he felt uncomfortable alluding to it, but she wanted him to know she took no discomfort from it, either.

He nodded. " 'Twill ease my mind to know you're less recognizable to anyone wishing you ill while I'm not here to protect you. Will you mind?"

"Mind?" She sent him a dazzling smile. "I rather miss our old masquerade. I intend to enjoy it!"

Rand released a breath he'd not been aware he was holding. For some reason, he felt deeply uneasy about leaving her, even for one day. Her positive attitude was reassuring. "You've no idea how relieved—" He caught her hand and pressed a fervent kiss to it. "Thank you."

She was both surprised and touched by his fervor. "However," she warned with a twinkle meant to lighten the mood, "Her Grace may not approve."

"As Her Grace will nonetheless comply, her approval isn't necessary," he said, meeting her twinkle with solemn eyes. "But *you* are . . . to me."

"I cannot like your going about in masculine garments, in any event," sniffed Her Grace as she and Leonie met in the morning room after breakfast. "But *these . . .*" She eyed with distaste the stable boy's cast offs Leonie had brought with her from London. "I own you had good cause to wear such rude attire once, but such is not the case now. This is Hartswood! I insist we find you something more suitable."

Leonie eyed the boys, who sat off to one side of the large, airy chamber. Jamie and Sam were showing Stebbins how to tie sailors' knots they'd learned aboard ship. On a temporary reprieve from their lessons because the Bow Street Runner had her, as well as them, to protect today, they were in high spirits. They quite liked their tutor, but they said Stebbins told such thumping good stories of bully ruffians and the like—and he carried *two* barking irons!

"But the boys are wearing, er, informal attire," she countered. She'd a fond attachment to her former disguise, and the clothes were marvelously comfortable as well.

"The young gentlemen are to have a boxing lesson," the dowager replied, "which Hawksrest has prevailed upon Mr. Stebbins to conduct after nuncheon. Moreover, their rustic garments are to serve as *their* disguise. And while I cannot like them any more than I like yours, your brother and Lord Samuel are but lads, after all. *You,* gel, are a young lady. Now, come and see what Barrows has fetched from the attics.

* * *

Late that afternoon Leonie found herself in the mews behind the stables, watching Stebbins teach the gentlemanly art of self-defense to a pair of eager boys. The lesson was to have taken place in the ballroom, but because the stables were nearly deserted today—the hands were in Tunbridge Wells for a horse fair—and it was a warm day for October, they'd moved it here.

Indeed, the day was so warm, Leonie felt perspiration trickle from beneath the old-fashioned tricorne the dowager had urged upon her. Not that Leonie had needed much urging. Her entire outfit—but for the Hessians customized by Hoby's—had once been Rand's. Styled after the cut and colors of William's regiment, it had been his favorite, the dowager recalled. Outgrown when Rand was twelve, it was the first apparel his father had had a hand in selecting. She said all Rand's clothing from before, even if it fit him perfectly, had been burned—at the child's insistence. Leonie didn't need to guess why.

Plucking the starched stock away from her throat in a vain attempt to loosen it, she heartily wished they'd remained indoors. She recalled Jamie wearing such a costume once in a parade under a blazing sun and wondered how he'd stood it. There was no shade in the mews. They'd been here an age, and the sun was hotter than ever. The boys themselves looked hot and scruffy, but wouldn't hear of quitting. She'd asked.

She sighed. Even removing the tricorne wouldn't answer, for it at least shaded her face. Furthermore, she'd promised Rand she'd keep her head covered, her hair hidden. But, drat, she was so beastly hot.

"Mr. Stebbins," she called, "might I fetch another drink from the well?" The well near the front of the yard served just the stables. Since it was out of sight, Stebbins had accompanied her earlier, always taking the boys. The three of them, however, made do with a bucket and dipper. Not that Leonie was too fastidious to use these—after all, she'd drunk from streams in the forest—but the well, located under a stone overhang that jutted off the side of the stable, was always in the shade. "You really needn't come, Mr. Stebbins. Please?"

Stebbins glanced at her and frowned. He was crouched low, trying to manage what looked to her like a cross between a pas de deux and a mill between the boys. "I don't know, lad," he said, addressing her as Rand had instructed. " 'Is lordship said—"

"I'll have *this,"* she said, thinking fast. She brandished a crutch, hoping it looked like a weapon she might use to defend herself if the need arose. *Not that it will. I'll only be about twenty yards away, for heaven's sake.*

Stebbins still looked doubtful. "I'd prefer—'ere now, lads!" he cried, for Jamie and Sam were suddenly rolling on the ground not like boxers, but wrestlers—very enthusiastic wrestlers. Poor Stebbins had his hands full separating them.

"Oh, bother!" Leonie muttered, knowing he'd forgotten all about her now. Suddenly she brightened, recalling an old adage: *Silence gives consent.* Wiping her damp brow, she gathered both crutches under her. She checked the bandage wrapped about her knee—the ostensible reason for her crutches—to be sure it hadn't slipped, and hurried off before Stebbins could notice. *Huh, from the looks of that tangle, I'll be back before then.*

The shade beneath the overhang looked cool and inviting as she approached, her eyes trained on the well. So thoroughly trained on it, she failed to notice a dark figure slip noiselessly into the shadowed doorway opposite.

When the east pasture came in sight, Rand knew he'd made excellent time. He grinned as Raven began running along the fence, trumpeting a challenge to Quicksilver. The black knew this wasn't the mare he'd ridden out this morning. By having the gray taken to a farm on the boundary last night, and leaving before dawn on the mare, he was returning far earlier than he'd originally surmised. Not only had he finished the inspection before noon, but by returning on a fresh mount—his fastest—and leaving the estate manager t bring the mare, he'd be back to protect Leonie himself well before dark. He couldn't wait to see her.

The assassin known as The Serpent eyed the boy on crutches. He'd been angling for a clear chance at his primary victim all day. *Dispatch the prince first,* the regent had said, *then worry about the others. If it raises an alarm, we'll at least have the critical target out of the way. You can always attend to the others later. Of course, if you can eliminate all three at once, so much the better. Do that, and I'll pay another thousand—as a bonus.*

But was this the prince? He'd been shown portraits of him, but that stupid hat hid so much of this boy's face, there was no telling. The burly cove with *bodyguard* written all over him had been watching over the brat and the other two like a mother hen. He was guarding some of their quarry, for sure. Not the girl—no sign of her. But a cripple likely stayed indoors.

Might have to send Marta in to do her, he mused, thinking of the accomplice he'd left waiting in the woods. He normally worked alone, but the stakes were too high here. Roderik paid well, but fail him, and you were as good as dead. Poison might be the only sure way to kill the cripple.

Yet of these, which was which? And who was the third brat? A servant? Not that any of them looked like the fancy toff in those paintings. The smaller pair were too scruffy. Could be they were *both* servants, which left only . . .

The assassin's eyes narrowed on the slender figure dipping water from the well. He was remembering a parade he'd seen once, with Prince Jameson riding the same fat pony now munching hay in the stable. *Couldn't see his face in that parade, what with him wearing a hat that hid . . . well, I'm damned! The little snot was wearing a hat just like this one with the crutches! Obliging of you to have a hurt knee, Your Highness. Makes my job even easier.*

Now, to lure his quarry into the stable. . . .

* * *

Starting back to the mews, Leonie drew to a halt, nearly dropping her crutches. A distressed whinny came from inside the stable. It sounded like Jamie's pony! The boys had ridden rather hard before breakfast, and it was decided the ponies should rest in their stalls for the remainder of the day. Now the sound came again, louder and a bit frantic.

Jamie's Jumper, for certain—and something's wrong. As she debated fetching the others, she heard Sam's Puck add his distinct whinny to Jumper's. And the next from Jumper was more like a cry of pain. "Hold on, Jumper," she called, "I'm coming!"

Stebbins helped the boys dust themselves off, and scowled at them. "Just look at the two-a ye! Scrapes an' scratches from head t' toe. An' rollin' in the dirt like a pair-a beggar lads! I tell ye, common brawlin' ain't in it! What'd 'is lordship say if he'd-a seen, huh?"

Glancing at each other, Jamie and Sam grinned sheepishly.

"Well, that's enough fer one day," said Stebbins. "Best get ye back and cleaned up before the duchess sees . . ." He glanced around the mews, frowning. "Where's the prin—I mean, Leon?"

"Don't know." Sam gazed about in bewilderment.

"He was here a minute ago," said Jamie, "I think."

Stebbins muttered something unintelligible under his breath and started running. "C'mon!" he shouted over his shoulder.

When they reached the well and saw no sign of Leonie, Stebbins forced himself not to panic. The poor lass had looked damned hot and uncomfortable in that rig the old gal stuffed her into. What in hell got into the gentry? he wondered. Not this young lot, though. He'd seen that right off. Even the little princess, who seemed as sensible a mort as he'd ever—that was it! Being sensible, she likely went b to the house to rest, even if it *wasn't* sensible to do it without her guard. "C'mon, lads!" he said, urging them toward the house at a run.

Leonie knew something was terribly wrong when she saw the old stableman lying on the floor of an empty stall, his head twisted at an odd angle. Jed was his name, and he'd been left to keep an eye on things while the others went to the horse fair. He was too old to—

Jumper's squeal of pain jerked her eyes toward the end of the aisle. The long row of stalls to either side was quiet, their usual occupants in the pastures. But the door to one of the twin stalls at the end was ajar. Jumper's stall. As she moved toward it, she slowed her pace, then halted. One of the high windows at that end admitted a shaft of sunlight that threw a shadow onto the scrubbed stone floor in front of the stall. Someone was in there with Jumper—and a pitchfork!

With a silent cry of rage, she clapped both crutches together, raised them like a double-sided club, and advanced.

Quicksilver had begun fighting the bit, so determined to answer Raven's challenging calls he was barely manageable. "No, you don't, my lad," Rand muttered, and reined him smartly into the stable yard. He was about to dismount when he heard a frantic squeal coming from inside the stable. A horse in trouble—no, a pony! What the devil?

Acting on pure instinct, he rode the stallion straight through the wide double doors—left open on a sunny day—and into the stable. What followed all seemed to happen at once. He saw a small, oddly clad figure moving toward the stalls at the end of the aisle—*limping* toward them. Leonie, with her crutches raised like a weapon. Through the open door of one stall, he saw Jamie's pony lash out with his hind [illegible]et at a shadowy figure. A pitchfork clattered to the floor. [illegible] figure—a man dressed all in black—cursed, turned toward Leonie. Sunlight gleamed along a blade in his hand as he—

"Leonie—move!" The screamed warning hadn't left Rand's lips before the testy stallion was plunging forward. Leonie swung to look at him, dropped the crutches, and jumped aside, just in time to avoid Quicksilver's hooves. Already riled by the black in the pasture, the gray was out for blood. As he barreled down on the threat, Rand tried to check his stride before they collided. The stallion twisted his great head, fighting the restraint—just as the assassin threw the knife: a scream of pain, and the stallion stumbled. With a snarl, Rand threw himself off and lunged for the assassin, who'd drawn another knife. He never got to use it.

And Rand never recalled stopping him. He only knew, when the red haze of his rage lifted, he was standing over the body. Breathing hard, and watching crimson ooze from the pitchfork impaled in the assassin's chest.

Leonie crooned to the gray stallion, holding its head steady as Rand dressed the wound in its neck. Not a mortal wound, thank heaven. Because Quicksilver had twisted at the critical moment, the blade missed his jugular. Still shaking inside, she hoped her shattered nerves didn't compound the distress of the wounded horse. In their stalls, Jumper and Puck fretted nervously, though poor Jumper had calmed somewhat after they'd applied salve to the pitchfork gouges in his rump.

"That should answer," said Rand, setting down his bag of medicinals. He fed Quicksilver a lump of sugar from his pocket, spoke softly to him, and nodded for Leonie to turn him loose in the large box stall. "Come," he said, picking up the bag and curling his free arm about her shoulders, "we'll—you're trembling!"

"I—I'm all right," she lied, stumbling against him as he led her out of the stall. She leaned into his strength as he caught her about the waist. "Though my knees feel—"

"Leon! Are you in here?" Stebbins came rushing through

the open doors, Jamie and Sam at his heels. They stopped and gaped as Rand moved toward them, carrying Leonie in his arms.

"She's fainted," Rand said tightly, "and I'm taking her to the house. Stebbins, you'll oblige me by escorting the boys while I explain why. And then, sir, you'll further oblige me with *your* explanation of why the devil she went into that stable alone."

Rand watched Leonie frown in her sleep. The branch of candles burning low beside the bed threw shadows over her small form moving restlessly on the mattress. She gave a muffled cry and murmured something he couldn't make out. She'd been tossing and turning half the night, and small wonder. *Frightened out of her wits . . . though not when it counted, by God! Functioned when I needed her, helped with the pony, the stallion, never once betraying a hint of what must have been screaming inside to get out. Fell to pieces only when it was all over. Damn it, I never should have left her!*

He still felt terror when he thought about it . . . and gnawing guilt. His fury at Stebbins had abated halfway through the runner's recital of events. Leonie's departure while he'd been legitimately attending to the boys had been contrary to orders. Rand smiled grimly. *Orders* . . . a military term. She was no soldier, yet he'd expected her to behave as one. He made no doubt her departure had been innocently heedless of the danger in which it placed her. He blamed himself for failing to make her aware of it, and for expecting Stebbins to do the work of two men.

Poor Stebbins had been so overwrought, he'd offered to resign without a character. Jamie and Sam would have resigned with him if they could. All three blamed themselves. He and William had taken great pains to soothe the lads and convince them they weren't at fault. He wished he could have concealed the entire business from them, but it was important that they understood the danger. He only regretted that his initial anger at Stebbins had thrust the details upon them so baldly. He should have waited and told them more gently, after Leonie was cared for.

MacTavish had seen Leonie and given her a sleeping draught, having been told, as had the servants, only that she'd been in the way of a runaway horse. And Rand had refused to let Stebbins quit. Instead, he'd asked him to go over every inch of that stable *and* the body, for what might be learned of the assassin's purpose.

Not that they couldn't easily guess. Stebbins's discovery that the assassin's boot heels were hollow, with Mirandeauvian gold coins hidden within, merely confirmed it. Stebbins surmised unhappily that Leonie alone had been attacked because she'd been unguarded. He also speculated that her brother was the real target, and she'd been taken for Jamie because she wore that fancy suit of clothes. Rand tended to agree, but he wouldn't put it past Roderik to want both royal children out of the way.

In any event, William was by now in London, handing all the evidence over to the Foreign Office. The local magistrate would not be told anything as yet, and the servants believed poor Jed had surprised a horse thief and killed him, but had taken a mortal wound in the process. It was up to the Ministry to decide how much of the truth got out, if any.

"Hawk?" Leonie's voice was groggy with sleep. "Hawk, *where are you?"*

"Here, love," he said, moving from the bedside chair where he'd been keeping watch. "I'm right here." He stretched out on the bed and reached for her.

"Rand." She came eagerly, curling into him like a kitten. "I—I'd the most horrid nightmare. I was running, and I . . . but it *wasn't* just a nightmare! It was—*Quicksilver.* Rand, how is—"

"Shh," he soothed, pressing a kiss to her brow. "He's going to be fine. You're safe in your own bed, and I've been here with you since MacTavish left."

"MacTavish? But I'm not ill . . . or hurt."

"No, thank God," he murmured into her hair, trying not

to think of what she might have suffered. "But you fainted, sweetheart, which gave us quite a turn." She was all warm and muzzy from sleep, and as he gathered her close, he wondered if this was wise. Yet he could do nothing less. When he let himself think about what nearly happened, he wanted to keep her in his arms and never let her go.

But the satiny warmth of her skin, the silk of her unbound hair gliding beneath his chin, were stealing over his senses. Going to his head like wine. Breathing in that faintly floral scent that was hers alone, too aware of the yielding softness of her pliant body, he gritted his teeth against a quickening in his loins.

"Fainted?" Leonie lifted her head to look at him. A tiny frown puckered her brow. "But why would I . . ." Her eyes darkened, and she shuddered. "That man! Rand, he *hurt* Jumper. And he was going to—to kill me! He was w-waiting for me in the stable—"

"Shh," he said, stroking her hair, trying to calm her. She'd begun to shake, and now words tumbled out as she recounted what she remembered. But as she recalled each detail, she seemed to relive it. Watching her fear build, Rand knew he had to head off the dark thoughts that fed it. Drawing her small body beneath him, he stopped the torrent with a mind-numbing kiss.

A deep, drugging kiss that didn't end until he felt the tremors subside.

But in the time between, something new was born. Where terror receded, passion came on stealthy wing and interposed. And now it raked them both with talons of need. Life-affirming need to counter the nightmare shadow clothed in black.

"Rand," she breathed, moving against him.

With a groan that was her name, Rand buried his face in her hair. Leonie twisted restlessly beneath him. Her hands found the front of his shirt, locked in the fine linen, and pulled. With an intake of breath he understood her need and helped her. Buttons flew as he tore his shirt free and drew her hard against him. With only the thin cotton of her nightshift between them, the aroused peaks of her nipples pushed against the fabric, burning his bared chest like twin points of fire.

With another helpless groan, he rolled, bringing her with him, one arm wrapped about her tiny waist to hold her close. His free hand swept the twisted nightshift upward, baring her thighs, and then the smooth swell of her buttocks. She moaned as his hand closed over her naked flesh and pressed her into the heat of his loins.

Now their mouths met again. Opened. Sought. Found. Tongue mated greedily with tongue. She lay stretched on top of him, her fingers tangling in his hair, then gripping the sheets as he dragged his mouth to her ear and murmured her name in a voice thick with desire. When he tested her velvety lobe with his teeth, he felt her shiver. He pressed hot, fevered kisses to her brow, her temples, and all the tiny pulse points where her blood leaped to his touch. He nuzzled and kissed while she murmured his name over and over, a litany that was prayer and passion, comfort and desire, solace and hunger.

He trailed his lips to the delicate flesh beneath her ear, and along the slender column of her throat. Downward, still, while she wriggled and pressed the cradle of her hips against his turgid strength, her nails digging into his shoulders as she tried to bring him closer. When his mouth met the modest neckline of her shift, it was an obstacle he could not bear. Shifting her weight until they lay side by side, he kept one hand firmly about her naked buttocks. With the other, he grasped the thin fabric of her shift and tore it asunder.

"Oh!" she cried as her breasts spilled free. Her startled eyes flew to Rand's, and he saw the rapid pulse beating at her throat. Her pupils were dilated, the green of her irises darkened with desire. Moaning again, low in her throat, she swayed toward him. "Rand." Her lips were cherry red and swollen from his kisses, trembling. "P-please," she murmured on a shaky expulsion of air.

Rand held himself very still. Her breasts were generous for her size and perfectly formed, their creamy swells crowned with coral crests that tightened further under his devouring gaze. But it wasn't that lush perfection that nailed him in place, that urged a return to sanity even as the erection pressing against his breeches grew painful. It was what he felt below, where the hand cupping her buttocks had urged her thighs apart.

At first there'd been the moisture gathered at the juncture of those thighs, a heady spur to his desire. Then his fingers found the entrance to her slippery heat and dipped inside, and her creamy flood of welcome had urged him on. But now . . . now he felt the fragile membrane of her virgin barrier. The barrier he must not breach, no matter how his body screamed for him to bury himself in the sweet heat of her willing flesh.

"Leonie, *no,*" he murmured, shaking his head, though it cost him every ounce of his self-control to do so.

She blinked, then again, and gazed at him with bewildered eyes. At long last, with a sigh so sad it twisted his heart, she lowered her gaze. Her small fist flew to her mouth to stifle a sob, but she wasn't quick enough. It erupted with a shudder. "I—I'm s-sorry," she murmured, turning her head swiftly aside. "You couldn't p-possibly w-want me."

"God—no!" He gathered her trembling body close, and stroked her hair as frustrated need shuddered through him like a drum. "Couldn't *want* you? My sweet innocent, I cannot think straight for wanting you. Do you understand, goose? I want you like the very devil! But you're an innocent, my darling, and I'm trying"—he gave a shaky laugh—"trying like the very devil, to behave honorably. I've never yet deflowered a virgin, and I don't intend to start now. Not with you. Especially not you."

She froze, pulled back from his embrace, and searched his face in the guttering candlelight. "You mustn't . . . you mustn't think to pacify me with a—a clanker, no matter how kindly m-meant," she whispered uncertainly.

"Leonie," he said with more patience than he felt. His blood had hardly had time to cool, and she was only inches from him, naked to his starving gaze. "Do I look like a man who beats innocent children? Tortures helpless animals? Pulls wings off flies, perhaps? No? Then why the devil would I fib about something—some*one* so precious to me?"

"Precious?" She said it with a note of wonder, as if it were a word so alien she couldn't place its strangeness in the lexicon of her mother tongue.

Now . . . now is the perfect time to tell her I love *her.* He ached to tell her. Yet if he did, he knew he'd take her in his arms, and that would lead to the very thing he was trying to avoid. *And deuced close to doing.*

"Precious," he repeated, his solemn gaze reaching deep into hers. He cupped her cheek and ran his thumb along her lower lip, still passion-stung and trembling. "And someday, love, I shall tell you how precious.

"But not tonight," he added with a wry, tender smile. Urging her back on the pillows, he was about to tuck the sheet about her, when he glanced ruefully at the torn night-shift. "Uh . . . you'd best tell your abigail—"

"I'll tell her I did it," she said as he tucked her in. "That it was the nightmare," she added with a sleepy smile. "A true clanker, that. For 'twas done by my lord Hawk . . . who took the nightmare away."

Twenty

William returned the next morning and handed Rand a sealed letter from the Foreign Office. The Ministry was in a tear about the assassination attempt. Its spies had informed Whitehall that Roderik's madness was the source of open speculation in Mirandeau. A series of public hangings for trivial offenses had sent many Mirandeauvians scurrying for the borders. Rand was ordered to bring his charges to London, where Whitehall felt it could offer them better protection.

As he read the damning words, Rand swore viciously under his breath. What rankled wasn't the implication that his protection had been inadequate, but that it was true. His mission had been to protect his charges, and his failure to do so had nearly cost Leonie her life. With another oath, he set servants to packing and gave instructions that the ducal coach be made ready for a trip to London.

By mid afternoon, he was armed and riding beside the coach as it rumbled along the post road. Stebbins rode inside with the royal refugees, his pair of pistols primed and ready. Two days later an entourage including several exhausted servants—and the mountain of baggage they'd packed with inordinate haste—followed at a brisk pace. The duke and dowager duchess rode with them.

* * *

Mirandeau
The Palace

Roderik stared at the woman named Marta, his face livid. "You dare—*dare* confront me with this?" he questioned, his voice quivering with rage. "To confess your failure—"

"Not *my* failure, Archduke," she cut in acerbically. "The Serpent's."

"Who is dead!" he screamed. It was the high-pitched voice that had lately warned many an underling to make himself invisible if he valued his life.

"Dead," she agreed coldly, "and the gold coin taken before I could complete the task. Do you expect me to do your killing without reward? I am fully prepared to return to England, to succeed where he failed. They are in London now, as it happens, where this duke of Hartswood keeps a town house. I followed them there: preparatory work on your behalf—without pay. More than that requires compensation in advance. I am a professional, and I am not a fool."

Saying nothing, Roderik began to pace. His mood had not abated, and he needed to defuse the rage boiling inside. She'd come to him in his chambers, slipping in through the window undetected, despite the sentries below. They'd deadly stealth, these assassins. He'd give them that. Yet their vaunted leader, the deadly Serpent himself, had bungled.

He slanted a glance at the woman. Of average size and nondescript appearance, she'd pass through a crowd without notice. She appeared fit . . . fairly young. The Serpent's trollop, no doubt, yet she stood there without a glimmer of regret he was dead. A cool one, sneaking into these rooms without a by-your-leave. Daring to confront him—*him*—bold as brass, demanding more gold! *More,* despite the king's ransom he'd already paid. The greedy bitch! She must think *him* the fool, to present such a demand. Was he to wait here like some lackey, wondering if she'd the wits to succeed? He'd be better off doing the thing him—

He stopped pacing, his eyes narrowing as an idea took

shape. *Yes . . . yes, it makes excellent sense. I know where they are now.*

"Very well," he snarled, heading for the coffer where he always kept a tidy sum. Opening it, he hefted a leather bag. The weight of the coins shifted, clinking dully as he tossed it at her. "If you dispatch all three"—he watched with a secret smile as she caught the bag, tested its weight—"you'll have an equal sum upon your return. Now, leave me."

The woman grunted and headed for the window. She never saw the pointed blade he took from the coffer. Whirling as she heard his sleeve rustle when it left his hand, she was a fraction of a second too late. Roderik's dagger flew with unerring accuracy, embedding itself in her back. With a strangled cry, she dropped to the floor, the bag of coin inches from her twitching hand.

"Squeeze me for more, would you, bitch?" Roderik hissed as he prodded her lifeless body with his toe. Retrieving the coins, he returned them to the coffer. "I've better things to do with my gold. I'll no longer squander it on inept assassins. Not when I can do the thing myself!"

In the hallway outside, Emilie tried to shut out her husband's mad laughter and hurried back to her rooms. He never noticed her these days, even when she eavesdropped, but it paid to take care she wasn't seen. He talked to himself a great deal lately as the madness deepened. She'd found it rather easy to listen in without being discovered. But not until tonight had she overheard anything so significant . . . or dire.

Dear God, he means to kill the children with his own hand. All three, he told that wretched woman—all three! Shaking inside, she forced herself to calm, and sat quickly at her escritoire. She dipped her quill in ink, then began to pen her warning. She must somehow contrive to send it to London, to the home of this English duke.

* * *

Hartswood House
London

With Stebbins close behind, Jamie and Sam ran into the library, where Leonie was reading Rand's personally autographed copy of Lord Byron's *The Giaour.* In a chair nearby, Stebbins's cohort Higgins perused Southey's *Life of Nelson.* "Boys, you know better than to run indoors," Leonie chided as they skidded to a halt near her chair. Her smile took the edge off the reprimand. "What's afoot?"

"More flowers," Sam announced with a groan.

"Drawing room's choked with 'em," said Jamie. "Minnow says if this keeps up, we shall all have to move out to make room." Minnow was Hartswood House's major domo; his wry sense of humor had made him a favorite with the boys. The bouquets that had begun pouring in since Leonie's foray into London society were the chief source of that humor at the moment.

"Do you know who sent them?" she asked, trying to sound insouciant. There was only one man from whom she wished flowers—or *some* form of communication—and she hadn't seen or heard from him in nearly a fortnight. With the arrival of the duke and dowager at the town house, Rand had suddenly vanished. A brief note, delivered by a footman, had given her only a terse explanation.

> *Pressing business in Town. Rely on Higgins while I am away. Go* nowhere *without him.*

Higgins was her new bodyguard. He and Stebbins, along with several other men Whitehall had sent over, formed a wall of protection around the royal refugees. Only her bed and privy chambers were exempt from Higgins's watchful eye.

"No," Jamie replied, "but Minnow said he'll send up the gentlemen's cards, just as soon as he finds a crane to lift 'em."

Everyone chuckled, and Stebbins settled into a chair

across the room with a copy of the *Times*. Sam nudged Jamie in the ribs. "Go on, ask her," he murmured.

"Ask me what?" Leonie threw Higgins a smile of thanks as he switched to a chair farther away. Whenever they could, the runners removed to a discreet distance from where their charges conversed with family members. She suspected the dowager had had something to do with this, though neither Higgins nor Stebbins seemed to mind.

Jamie hesitated, cleared his throat. "Leonie, do you think I'm the, er, head of the family now, with Papa gone? I mean, I know I'm just a lad, but . . . well, I am his heir, even if I've not yet been crowned. . . ."

As his words trailed off, she could see his discomfort. For Jamie, this was so unusual she at once gave him a reassuring smile. "In my estimation, you are."

"Told you," Sam muttered smugly.

"What's this all about?" she asked, her eyes going from one to the other.

Jamie took a deep breath and plunged in. "We were wondering if you'd think it proper form for me to be the one Hawk addresses when he offers for you."

"What?"

"We thought he might have come up to scratch by now, do you see," said Jamie.

"Only he hasn't," Sam put in, "and he hasn't been at home, either."

"And we think it might be that he's at sixes and sevens over how to go about it," her brother explained. " 'Cause he certainly looked as though he might make an offer before we left Kent."

"Only then we all hared off to London," Sam said.

"And Hawk's been devilish scarce ever since," Jamie pointed out.

"Perhaps 'cause he doesn't know what to do about the whole muddle." Sam added. "But if we could let him know Jamie's the proper one to approach—"

"Then he'd return straightaway and come up to scratch," Jamie finished, beaming at her.

Leonie knew she was blushing furiously. "What makes you think . . . that is, have you mentioned this to—to anyone?" *I'll die if they said anything to him. It could even be the reason he's kept away without—*

"Oh, no," said Jamie.

"We wouldn't," said Sam.

"Not without checking," Jamie added, then brightened. "But now we know it's proper form for me to—"

"Jamie Aulaire," she said sternly, "don't you say a single word, d'you hear?"

"But why not?" He looked vastly disappointed, and so did Sam.

Leonie wondered if her dashing water on their scheme was what had disheartened them. Or was it something else—the same something that had been nibbling at her own happiness for the better part of a fortnight: Rand's disappearance from their daily lives?

Looking at their crestfallen faces, she heaved a sigh. "Because I promised Hawk," she lied. "He's some very important duties to attend to now we're in London, and must give them his complete attention. All personal affairs must wait. You wouldn't want him to neglect his duty, would you?"

Gravely, they shook their heads.

But Leonie thought she saw relief in their eyes as well. *Drat it, Rand! If you won't consider my feelings with regard to your strange behavior, you might at least give a thought to the boys!* "Then I want you to promise me you won't say anything to him, even if you should see him. Not until I say it's the right time. Will you do that?"

As they both promised, Leonie dropped her gaze to hide her thoughts. *If ever there can be a right time. If I haven't somehow been dreadfully mistaken about us. Oh, Rand, what's wrong?*

"You wished to see me?" Rand addressed the dowager in clipped syllables as he entered her private sitting room.

"As I am not in the habit of sending an army of footmen

to comb the city for you without cause," she replied tartly, "that would seem a valid conclusion. Where the devil have you been?"

"At my club," he snapped. "And variously with friends, in Jackson's Rooms, at Whitehall, even Carlton House, heaven help me. In short, I've been in any and all of the numerous places you desired me to be, so long as I remained apart from Leonie. If that is not to your liking, madam, I suggest you say so."

"Do not be impertinent! I—oh, do stop pacing like a caged tiger, Hawksrest. Sit down!"

Rand ground his teeth. He loved and respected his grandmother, he really did, but the strictures she'd placed on him since arriving in London were fast approaching the outside of enough. Determined to contrive an air of mystery about Lady Leonie Darnley, as she and the duke set about introducing Leonie to the *ton,* the dowager had told him, bluntly, he must take himself out of the way.

"The gel deserves a Season," she'd said. "The Little Season now, the greater in the spring, with all the trimmings: presentation at Court, adoring young men dancing attendance, parties, assemblies at Almack's, the lot. We shall polish what was begun in Kent and establish her as a true Original. To succeed, she needs room in which to blossom, and how is she to do so with you hovering?"

She'd huffed with exasperation. "Bad enough you've developed a *tendre* for her. Anyone with eyes will see it, and then where shall we be? At the first sign *you* are in the picture, any gentlemen desiring to pay her court will vanish. You will therefore oblige me by making yourself absent from Hartswood House for the duration."

And so he had—not willingly and not at all happily. Deny himself Leonie's smile? The sound of her laughter? They brightened his day. And the devil of it was, he was not to say anything to her about why he was suddenly not in evidence. For that, too, the dowager had given reasons: "The gel is sensitive to others . . . courteous almost to a fault. If she knew why you weren't dwelling under this roof, she'd be reluctant to discommode you, and cry off before we've even begun."

"But I intend to marry her!" he'd countered in hot disbelief. "Why the devil should I leave her to the fawning attentions of every young buck in town?"

"If you've faith in whatever feelings may have developed between you, then you won't mind putting them to a test," she'd returned shrewdly. And that, blast her, was what had finally made him consent to this cork-brained scheme.

"What do you wish to discuss?" he said resignedly, taking the seat she waved him into.

She hesitated, then waved her hand in what was meant to appear a careless gesture, but Rand wasn't deceived. Something had got into her craw. "It's possible," she began reluctantly, "I may have . . . underestimated the gel. She's a bit off her stride. Passed an entire evening at Almack's last Wednesday without uttering a single witticism. Kept glancing at the entryway so often I finally asked if she were expecting someone. Turned that unfortunate shade of red that doesn't agree with her hair and admitted she was hoping *you* might put in an appearance."

Rand chuckled. "Did she? *Did* she, by God!"

"Do not gloat, Hawksrest! It doesn't become you."

He chortled wickedly. "What else has she said? Come, I know there's more. You'd hardly send a pack of footmen haring all over London for me on the basis of a single incident."

The dowager sighed. "She's begun to question the reasons for your absence, and not only of me. She's even asked the servants. Thank heaven they know nothing about it, though her abigail remarked that the lady seems to be . . . pining. Unfortunately, your father overheard that remark, and you know how he adores the gel."

Rand was grinning. "And how he hates to lie."

"It's in a good cause!" she snapped irritably.

"Is it?" he asked. "I wonder. . . ."

He gave her a probing look. "Why, I wonder, are you going through all these machinations? Simply to launch a young woman who may or may not even care much for it? Or is it that you've some larger purpose? Ah! Struck a nerve, have I?"

"You always were too perceptive for your own good," she grumbled. "Very well, then. Long ago, I sat by, resolving not to interfere when perhaps I should have. We both know how that lack of involvement, on my part *and* your father's, cost you. It was only because of . . . events that we did arrive on the scene, and you at last found the happiness every child deserves."

"Thank God you did," Rand said softly. "Go on."

"There came a second interval in your life," she continued, "an interval in which I refrained from involving myself once again, though I longed to do so. I am speaking of your engagement to Cynthia Shallcross. An unfortunate liaison from the outset, and well you know it! What, in God's name, ever possessed you to—"

"I don't care to discuss it," he said tightly, his expression closed and shuttered.

"Very well," she said with another sigh. "But you asked about a larger purpose in separating you from Leonie, and that is why I brought up the painful past. Looking back, I realized I may have done you a disservice by *not* interfering. Certainly that was the case in your childhood. As to the other . . . well, I can only surmise, of course. Yet I confess to you now, I could not like the Shallcross chit. I kept thinking if I'd said why, perhaps it wouldn't have fallen on deaf ears."

He gave her an unreadable look. "As I said, I won't discuss it."

"Be that as it may, we now come to a third significant interval in your life, and what we have discussed has direct bearing on—"

"Just a moment," he cut in. "Are you saying what I think you are? That your larger design is to separate me from Leonie *permanently* to spare me some sort of . . . pain?"

Another sigh. "To spare you both, actually, for it can be no secret I've grown deeply fond of the child. And, no, I shouldn't say permanently. But you must own the gel has no future as it stands. If things go badly, she may well be a woman without a country, without any legal standing. You say you wish to wed her, but what if she's unable to wed? Is it too much to ask that you allow an old woman her fears? That two persons for whom she cares deeply may not run headlong into hurt?"

"Grand-mére, I *love* Leonie. I wouldn't see her hurt for the world! And as for myself—"

"Then prove it to me. Give yourselves this time."

"And if she's . . . pining?" he said archly.

"Ah, now that is what I wished to address. It occurs to me I may have been too severe in asking you to sever all contact. It has seemed unnatural, given the time you spent together until now. The *ton* is already speculating you and your "cousin" have had a falling out. I therefore suggest you occasionally appear in public with her . . . while keeping the appropriate distance, of course. Stanhope's rout on the tenth will do for a start."

Rand smothered a groan. She wanted him to stand idly by, tantalized by what he craved but couldn't have. To watch, while others had free access to his forbidden fruit! It would be torture, pure and simple. *Then prove it to me. Give yourselves this time.*

"Very well, you old Tarter," he said, standing and making her an ironic leg, "you've won. I shall appear at Stanhope's around nine."

"Make it half ten," she said, offering her cheek for a peck. "And the accurate phrase is, as I collect, *a right proper old Tarter!*"

Chesterfield House in Great Stanhope Street was the perfect setting for a formal gathering of the *ton.* Built by a forebear of the present earl, it was currently occupied by Chesterfield's distant cousin and adopted heir, Philip Stanhope. The Palladian mansion boasted many elegant rooms, each decorated in a different style. Particularly admired, however, was its magnificent grand staircase made entirely of white marble.

At the base of this staircase Leonie paused and gave William a wry grin. "If you're game, Your Grace, then so am I."

"Appears there's no help for it," he replied pleasantly. He eyed the ramrod-stiff posture of the dowager ascending ahead of them. Using her cane with practiced efficiency, she barely leaned on the arm of her escort, Simon Petrie. "If Mother can manage at her age, we should appear a pair of proper cowards if we desist. Moreover, Skeffington's gone upstairs, and I promised Petrie an introduction."

Leonie smiled at him as they made their way gamely up the long flight, using their walking sticks for balance. "Thank you for arranging it, Your Grace. Simon's in transports simply at being invited."

"Thank the duchess for contriving his invitation." Chuckling, he added, "Not that Stanhope had any choice in the matter. My part consists merely of putting Petrie in the way of Skeffington. I make no doubt they'll go on famously. Skeffington was in Prinny's box last night at the Drury Lane, laughing himself silly. Petrie's Bottom was brilliant!"

Leonie nodded. Lumley Skeffington was not only an influential member of the regent's Carlton House set, he was also an avid theater *aficionado.* If he enjoyed Simon's performance, he could prove an invaluable contact. Skeffington didn't merely patronize the theater; he wrote plays himself. "I wish I'd seen it," she told William wistfully as they reached the top of the stairs. *"A Midsummer Night's Dream* is my favorite comedy, and I've yet to see Simon on stage."

William patted her arm as they stepped out of the way to catch their breath. The staircase, like the rest of the house, was thick with guests. "You shall, I promise, soon as Whitehall arranges more protection. The openness of a public theater presents enormous security problems." He winked at a footman who approached, gingerly balancing a tray bearing glasses of bubbling champagne. "Isn't that so, Higgins?"

Leonie smothered a giggle. The burly runner looked comical stuffed into the fancy livery of Chesterfield House. But she was glad of his presence, and that of several other Bow Street Runners she knew were nearby. Disguised as footmen and grooms, postilions and linkboys, they'd been secretly in attendance wherever she went in London.

Their presence helps, yes, but I never feel as safe as I felt with Rand. A frown puckered her brow. She'd promised herself she wouldn't fret anymore over his absence. No doubt he'd good reasons, including the official duties she'd cited to the boys. Hadn't the dowager explained that he frequently stayed at his club when in town? So as not to put a strain on the staff of Hartswood House with his inconvenient hours, she'd said. *But I miss him so! Why hasn't he at least written? Surely he can't be* that *busy.*

She was saved from these disturbing thoughts by the approach of several laughing guests. "There you are, Hartswood!" cried a large, florid man at the fore. "And this must be the charming cousin we've heard so much about. Come, make us known, lest I expire of curiosity!"

Curious herself, Leonie considered this portly gentleman who addressed His Grace so boldly. He seemed oddly familiar . . . reminded her of a jovial, overweight elf. Suddenly she realized she was looking at none other than the Prince Regent!

"Your Highness," said William, bowing, "allow me to present Lady Leonie Darnley. My dear, His Royal Highness, the Prince of Wales."

Leonie sank into a deep curtsey, grateful for the hours of practice that had schooled her to do it flawlessly. As the prince extended a hand and raised her graciously, she heard William give the speech they'd prepared. This was strictly for the benefit of the onlookers, who'd be shocked by a green girl of her presumed social standing mixing with royalty without first having had a formal Presentation. One was in the offing, but in the meantime the Prince Regent, who'd been apprised by Whitehall of her identity and circumstances, had agreed to this necessary charade.

"I confess," said William, "my cousin has not yet had

the honor of being presented at Court. We beg Your Highness will forgive the irregularity. She has, however, been presented at another court. That of Your Highness's late cousin, Prince Frederik of Mirandeau, where she spent a deal of her youth."

"Not too irregular, then," said Prinny, playing his part with obvious enjoyment. "For just as our knights enjoyed mutual recognition in ages past, so do we recognize each other's peers today. And when the subject is such a lovely lady," he added with a smile for Leonie, "with great pleasure, I must say."

"Your Highness is too kind," she murmured, dipping a brief curtsey.

"Not at all," he replied. "But come, you must meet everyone." He gestured at his cohorts. "Alvanley, Cholmondeley, Skeff—now where the deuce is Skeffington?"

"Believe I see him by the punch bowl," said William. "Need to have a word with him, myself, as it happens. I'll fetch him, shall I, while Your Highness does the honors here?"

Prinny waved him on. With a word to Leonie, William pushed through the crowd. The regent performed introductions to Lords Alvanley and Cholmondeley, then asked if she'd met Lumley Skeffington. "I'm told his father's ailing, poor man," he remarked. "Skeffy may be *Sir* Lumley presently."

"I've not had the pleasure, Your Highness," she replied, "but His Grace and I have a mutual acquaintance we wish him to meet this evening. Perhaps Your Highness recalls the actor who portrayed Bottom at the Drury Lane last night?"

"Oho—I do, indeed, m'lady. Capital clown, I must say! Shall be happy to meet him myself."

Simon will be over the moon, she thought with a secret smile. As the gentlemen exchanged observations on the theater, she glanced about for Petrie and the dowager. She hoped they weren't so lost in the crush Simon would miss his chance. Then all at once she froze. *Rand!*

Entering the room from the far end, he was impossible to

miss. Easily a head taller than those around him, he carried himself with that unconscious grace that had drawn her eye from the first. *Like a hero or a god out of ancient myth,* she thought, her heart leaping wildly. *At once so male, yet so very beautiful.* He looked impossibly, heartbreakingly handsome in his formal attire. His immaculate stock accented a complexion even more deeply bronzed than she remembered, and his blue-black curls shone with health. *Rand, Rand, I shall disgrace myself mooning over you like a lovesick schoolgirl. Why didn't they tell me you'd be here? Why didn't* you?

Leonie wasn't the only one who'd spotted him. "I say," cried Prinny, "there's Hawksrest!"

"Don't remind me," Alvanley groaned. "Won a tidy sum from me at White's last night, the lucky dog! 'Course, Yarmouth and Norfolk lost even more."

"That," said Cholmondeley, "is because he wasn't imbibing with you. Hawksrest is infamous for his sobriety at whist."

Leonie frowned. *Rand was at White's last night playing at cards? Gaming for money, while I assumed—*

"M'lady, are you ill?" Alvanley's arm shot out to steady her elbow.

"No . . . no, I thank you," she murmured. "It's merely . . . it's a bit close in here."

"Looks rather pale," said the regent, peering into her face solicitously. "Cholmondeley, be so good as to fetch—ah, here's a fellow with some water!"

The fellow with the water was Higgins. He murmured, too low for anyone but Leonie to hear, "You all right?"

She nodded, then drank, grateful for the chance to regroup. *Silly of me. There could be any number of explanations. He might have been doing some of that . . . what was it? Undercover work, I think he called it . . . for the Ministry.*

Two more footmen materialized, and offered to find her a chair. She started to refuse, but suddenly the crowd around her became unusually dense. People were milling about. Was it her imagination, or did they seem excited? The buzz of conversation rose, became a din that hurt her ears. Impeccably dressed ladies and gentlemen alike pressed in close. She lost sight of the regent and his friends in the crush. Nodding at Higgins, she allowed him to steer her toward the relative safety of a small alcove.

"What is it?" She had to shout over the noise. "What has everyone so stirred up?"

"I'm not sure, milady," said Higgins, craning his neck to see over the heads of the milling crowd. "Looks like somebody important's arrived. Gordon," he said to one of the other runners posing as footmen, "see if ye can find out what the fuss is."

But it wasn't Gordon who gave her the news. Seconds later Leonie found herself sharing the alcove with a pair of bejeweled matrons who also sought shelter from the press. "My God," said one, "I still can't believe it!"

"I couldn't either," said the other, "if I hadn't seen her with my own eyes. Imagine, after all this time!"

"Walking in here bold as life," said the other with a nod. "Headed straight for Hawksrest, too!"

Leonie's head swung toward them. "I . . . I do beg your pardon," she said to the one who'd spoken last, "but it's difficult to hear anything in this din. Did . . . did you just mention something about the marquis of Hawksrest? I . . . he's a cousin of mine, do you see, and—"

"Why, it's the little Original!" exclaimed the woman. "So happy, my dear. Name's Beckley . . . Lady Anne Beckley. Met you at Sally Jersey's—oh, but you must be in shock, then."

"Indeed," said her companion, "the entire family must be in shock over this."

"I—I don't understand," said Leonie. "Which family?"

"Why, Hawksrest's—and yours, of course! It isn't every day a grieving man's fiancée returns from the dead, as it were."

The buzzing around Leonie grew louder. "Fiancée?" she questioned faintly.

"Lady Cynthia Shallcross. Didn't you see her? Came up that staircase not a moment ago—made straight for Hawksrest's arms!"

Twenty-one

The body is a curious thing, Leonie would tell herself later. *It can function without direction from the mind when it must. When pain is so acute, all is rendered meaningless and void.* These were the things she'd reflect upon, but later. When she could pull herself back from the abyss. From the gaping maw that beckoned . . . uncaring . . . pitiless.

She would remember how she stood in that alcove, numb, when the crowd suddenly parted. When her unwilling gaze fell upon Cynthia Shallcross. A creature so exquisite, she gave new meaning to the word. Peerless, stunning, the cynosure of every eye in the room. A tall and willowy goddess, graceful and slender as a sylph. Flaxen curls, artfully arranged in short tendrils, spoke of sophistication, as did the *chic* elegance of her gentian gown with its daring décolletage.

Later, too, Leonie would recall the china-blue eyes and alabaster skin and reflect: Countless poets must have felt the inadequacy of language when gazing on such a paragon. Words lacked the power to describe a thing so beautiful it didn't seem real. Couldn't possibly be real . . . and yet she was.

Finally Leonie would remember how she'd turned and stumbled blindly from that alcove, seeking only a place to hide. How Higgins had somehow contrived to spirit her out of there. How a carriage had materialized and she found herself inside. How at last she came to be in her own chamber, where Sally clucked and fussed, undressed her as if she were a helpless child and put her to bed.

It was still dark when she awoke and the pain began. Startled out of sleep by a dream she couldn't recall, she sat up in bed, breathing hard. And memory came flooding back, in a cruel, relentless tide. Images . . . words . . . announcing the end of hope. Pointing to one irrevocable truth: Rand was lost to her now, and she must somehow find the strength to go on.

She didn't realize she'd uttered a sound until the door swung ajar, and Sally rushed in. "Milady?" The abigail's night braid flew behind her as she hurried to the bed. Setting her chamberstick beside the bed, she hovered uncertainly, a frown on her plain round face. "I heard ye cry out. Are ye hurt?"

Hurt? What a small little word to contain this mountain of despair! Hurt? Only to the depths of my soul. "I . . . I'm fine," Leonie lied. "What time is it?"

"Nearly four, milady. Their Graces finally went t' bed 'round three. Said I must stay with ye in case ye needed . . . well, jest in case. I been sleepin' on a cot in the dressin' room. Can I fetch ye somethin', milady?"

Leonie started to say no. Then all at once it came clear to her what she must do. "My brown carriage dress. Please fetch it from the armoire," she said, climbing off the bed.

"Carriage dress! But—"

"And the pelisse with the fur," she added, her tone brooking no argument. "Is Higgins outside?"

"I-in the 'allway outside yer door, same's 'e 'as been," the abigail replied diffidently.

Leonie nodded. *He won't like it, but he'll be obliged to go along—once I explain his choices are to escort me or take the chance I'll slip away on my own.* "After you've helped me dress, tell him I want a word—please, Sally. Don't stand there gaping."

"Aye, milady, but . . . please, won't ye take me with ye?"

"You don't even know where I'm going."

"It don't matter, milady. I'm yer abigail, ain't I? Er . . . where *are* ye goin'?"

"Hartswood." *Where, please God, no one's yet heard of the miraculous return of Cynthia Shallcross. Where I can ride Raven or lose myself in a book for hours, until sense and sanity return. Where I can lick my wounds . . . where I can hide.*

Sally was gazing at her anxiously.

"Very well," she told her with a sigh, "but do hurry."

Once Sally understood she might come, she became a willing accomplice. The only thing Leonie wished absent from her able assistance was her endless stream of chatter. The abigail had garnered from the grooms who'd ridden with the coach the gist of what had happened, both before and during the rout. Leonie listened with listless passivity, too drained by the night's events to stop her.

Word had it a fisherman rescued Lady Cynthia from drowning. She couldn't send word because she'd suffered a head wound that caused a loss of memory. For a long time she didn't know who she was. According to the Shallcross grooms, her family was right anxious to make it known she had excellent chaperones in the fisherman's wife and daughters. "Meanin'," said Sally with a knowing look, " 'er ladyship's reputation is safe."

Word also said her ladyship was on her way to becoming the latest darling of the *ton.* By morning, many an abigail was sure to receive instructions to cut her mistress's locks in imitation of Lady Cynthia's. The head wound had required hers to be shorn, but her clever arrangement of what had grown back was sure to be all the go. London would be atwitter with the romance of her return from the dead and reunion with her handsome fiancé. Hadn't gentry in the dozens rushed to their gentlemen's clubs to wager on the date for their wedding of the year?

This last finally made Leonie put a stop to the abigail's careless chatter. "We shall have no talk of weddings, Sally," she said in unconscious imitation of the dowager. "Now go and tell Higgins I wish to see him."

But Higgins was having no part of her scheme. "If the duke didn't 'ave my 'ead, Stebbins would," he told her. "I ain't unwillin' t' take ye, milady, but only with 'Is Grace's blessin' . . . er, make that *both* Their Graces. I'd include 'is lordship, but the marquis ain't been much in the way lately."

No, the marquis has definitely not been in the way lately. Did he know, then, in advance of the rout? Did her family contact him first, discreetly reconciling him with his lost love, before she made that dramatic appearance? Rand, Rand—you might have warned me!

In the end, Leonie was forced to wait until the duke and duchess came down for breakfast. Both had had difficulty sleeping after the shock and were worried about Leonie in the extreme. Her removal from Chesterfield House had been explained by one of the runners Higgins left behind, but as she'd been asleep by the time they returned, they'd no notion how badly she'd taken it.

Now, seeing the shadows beneath her eyes, how she held herself glacially still when she made her request to leave, William knew. The fragile composure she'd somehow contrived to wrap around her seemed held together by a thread. He feared the slightest breath would shatter her to pieces.

"I'd rather you were here, where all the Ministry's powers of protection are available to us," he said with a sigh. "Can't we dissuade you?"

"Forgive me, Your Grace, but no," she replied in a pale whisper. "I think . . . surely, you must know why."

Stricken by the raw pain in her eyes, he gave a helpless nod. He wanted desperately to reassure her, to tell her Rand had said he loved her and wished to wed her. But even if he'd leave to divulge that confidence, William couldn't. Not now. His son had left the rout with Cynthia. *My God, Rand, I thought I knew you!*

"Very well," he told her reluctantly. "I'll sanction this, provided you're escorted by Higgins and his men. Stebbins will remain with the lads, of course, and I'll hire additional guards as well. Whitehall will be unhappy, but I trust I may deal with them."

He kissed her brow. "Give yourself time," he said. "It may yet turn out to be less than you assume. And if it isn't, please know how deeply we care. We've come to love you, child . . . and the lads. We'd do anything to see you happy."

Fighting tears, Leonie turned to the dowager. She'd been uncharacteristically silent during their exchange. Running her eyes over that aristocratic face, Leonie noted how old and tired she appeared. For the first time, the duchess looked all her seventy-odd years.

"Your Grace, I am sensible of your great kindness in having me here," Leonie told her. "I beg you will not think unkindly of me for leaving. And that perhaps you will . . . understand." These were words she would have left in a letter, had she been successful with Higgins. Now she was glad she'd the chance to say them face to face.

The dowager nodded and, in a distracted voice, bade her take care for her safety. Then Leonie turned to go. Yet at the door, she turned back. When their gazes met, she performed a flawless curtsey. The old woman's ghost of a smile said she recognized the tribute.

When Leonie went to take her leave of the boys, they were astonished she'd wish to go. London, with its unique sights and sounds, fascinated them. Under the watchful eye of Stebbins, they'd visited the Royal Menagerie, the Tower of London, and various other sights. There was so much to see and do!

Keeping her voice light, Leonie managed to navigate through their attempts to convince her to stay. Then came a question she hadn't counted on. "Is Hawk going with you?" Sam wanted to know. And Jamie, too, by the query in his eyes.

She'd all she could do to maintain the fiction that official duties kept Hawk in the city. "It's just that I've been missing Raven terribly," she told them, which was true, yet a lie all the same. "But I can't expect the lot of you to drop everything and hare off with me simply because I'm being silly over a horse."

They assured her they didn't think her silly, and asked if

she'd look in on Puck and Jumper. Promising to feed the ponies apples every day, she made herself listen to their excited plans for teaching Stebbins backgammon. It was late morning when they finally hugged good-bye. But when Jamie said they'd convey her farewell to Hawk if they saw him, she lost the battle she'd been waging and hurried off before they could see her cry.

Miles away, Rand was fighting a battle of his own—not with tears, but with the seething anger that had threatened to erupt since the moment Cynthia Shallcross walked into Chesterfield House. She'd put him off when he endeavored to escort her home, pleading the late hour. Against his judgment, he'd acceded. Cooling his heels at his club, he'd arrived at her town house this morning at a respectable hour. Only to be informed by the housekeeper that Lady Cynthia and her family had removed to their estate in Surrey!

Furious, Rand had climbed into his phaeton and headed for Surrey at breakneck speed. Hours later, dusty and tired, he'd reached their home. To be told by the butler that the earl and countess were indisposed and Lady Cynthia was not receiving.

Rand gave him five minutes to produce her.

"Really, Hawksrest, it was too bad of you to frighten Perkins that way!" Cynthia said irritably as she entered the drawing room. Rand noted sardonically that for someone who was not receiving, she was groomed to perfection: every hair in place, her flawless silk gown exactly matching the sapphires at her ears.

"He isn't the only one who'd reason to fear, had you not appeared," Rand said tightly. He glanced at the ashen-faced butler. "Leave us, and shut the door, Perkins—*now.*"

The door banged shut, and Rand turned back to his erstwhile fiancée. "Be thankful I was raised a gentleman," he told her in a voice deceptively soft, "or you'd have heard what I'm about to say at Stanhope's. You doubtless relied upon my discretion not to make a scene. Yet I warn you,

Cynthia, I'll have an explanation of this charade, or I'll treat all London to a show you'll never forget!"

She raised her chin in the haughty manner that was all too familiar, but not before he caught a glint of fear in her eyes. "I meant to stay away, Randall, I really did," she said, wetting her lips nervously. "But . . . but I couldn't abide America. My cousin's plantation is all very well, but horribly remote. Endless miles from any city. It—it was too rustic for me!"

"So, spoiled infant that you are," he said through clenched teeth, "you blithely undid all the elaborate arrangements you forced upon both your parents and me. Need I remind you faking your untimely death was *your* idea?"

He remembered every detail of the night before she "died," mere days before their wedding, when she came to him and told him she couldn't go through with it, when she'd accused him of being obsessed with perfection, and said she couldn't live up to his standards. And he'd believed her. Of course he had. At the time, he felt certain he *was* obsessed with it.

So when she told him she'd arranged to disappear rather than wed him, he'd gone along with the hoax—not before offering to let her break with him and let him take the blame, of course. But she'd already set things in motion. She'd a "longing to see America," and while he'd suspected she'd more than one reason for crying off, he'd not questioned her motives.

Now the temptation was too great to resist. "What happened, Cynthia?" he asked in a silky voice. "Couldn't abide the touch of those rustics any more than you could mine?"

Watching her blanch, he knew he'd hit the mark. "My dear, you're as much a fraud as that drowning!" he added with vicious satisfaction. *You had me believing I was hostage to the poisonous legacy of my bitch mother. Believing that terrible lie. That I couldn't abide any form of imperfection, much less love a woman who was less than perfect. Now I know better. It took a loving sprite with an imperfect body to show me my mother's hold on me is gone. I'm free of her, of all the pain of her legacy—and the pain of your cruel rejection as well.* "The next time you reject a man," he told her, "at least be honest with him!"

"That . . . what you just implied," she said after a moment's hesitation, "had nothing to do with it. I . . . merely changed my mind. My family understood. Why can't you?"

Heartily sick of this spoiled, selfish creature and her lies, he decided to prove something to himself, if not to her. Closing the distance between them, he caught her in an intimate embrace. With one arm, he held her still while his opposite hand found her breasts and fondled them through the thin silk of her gown. The revulsion on her face told him all he wished to know.

"There's your real reason for wanting out," he said, flinging her from him in disgust. "You cannot bear the touch of a man. What puzzles me is why you returned and staged that sham last night. Why return to what you left two years ago if you couldn't stand—"

"Mama wrote that you were inconsolable!" she cried. "Said I deserve to be a duchess, and there you were, pining after me. She said I could still have you, and it needn't be so bad. She—she has a potion, a laudanum tincture I might take to—to help me through it. Everyone knows all a wife need do is breed an heir. She'll be left alone once she's done her duty. That's what mistresses are for, isn't it?"

When he said nothing, she licked her lips and hastened on. "You can still have me, Randall. Think of it! My flawless beauty beside you, for the entire world to see! And as many mistresses as you like in bed. You don't need me to satisfy your animal lust!"

"No," he said with quiet disgust, "I don't need you at all, Cynthia. I'll give you one day to break with me publicly, or I'll bring this fraudulent house of cards down upon your head. Use any excuse within reason. I'll take the blame."

Turning smartly on his heel, Rand strode out of the house. He only hoped he wasn't too late to salvage any damage last night's spectacle may have caused at home. After this farce, the dowager's bloody Season could go hang. He was done with waiting—and hungry for Leonie's honest love.

"There, didn't I tell you?" William said to the dowager. He had to pitch his voice above the sound of thundering applause. The audience at the Drury Lane was showing its appreciation of *A Midsummer Night's Dream.* Yet what had it on its feet and cheering was the actor who'd just stepped forward to take his bows. "Petrie's Bottom is a triumph," His Grace added unnecessarily.

His mother nodded. She'd not seen the performance before; but that wasn't why they were here. When she'd time to digest last night's shocking turn of events, she'd told William they must at once appear in public and act as if nothing untoward had happened.

"I refuse to give the scandalmongers an ounce of satisfaction," she'd told him. "They may speculate how that distasteful display affected us, but they shan't see a shred of evidence it affected us at all. We shall attend tonight's performance and behave as the true nobility have always behaved: as if such low behavior were beneath our notice."

"Well, Mother," said the duke as the applause died down, "as half London's observed us in our box, I make no doubt we've established the desired impression. Shall we exit by the rear stairs to avoid—"

"We shall avoid nothing!" she snapped, taking up her cane. "We shall proceed backstage and congratulate that lean shanks on his performance. I confess, I didn't think he had it in him. But Petrie is as brilliant a comic actor as Kean is in the tragic roles, and I shall tell him so."

William allowed himself a smile as he escorted her out of their box. He wondered if Petrie would realize what a rare honor this was. Her Grace patronized the arts, but never went out of her way to bestow accolades in person. Still, any actor worthy of the name had to be a keen observer of the human condition. He was bound to know how disinclined someone of her temperament was to congratulate a performer backstage. Petrie would be in transports.

Yet the man they saw when the theater manager conducted them to Simon's dressing room was far from happy. He was as pale as a ghost, and shaking in his boots.

"Good heavens, man, what is it?" William asked, for Petrie's hand shook as he motioned the manager to close the door behind him.

"Out—out there," Simon stammered. He gestured wildly in the direction of the house seats. "I *s-saw* him! Third r-row, p-plain as day. When I t-took my b-bows."

"Petrie, get ahold of yourself!" William exclaimed. "Saw whom?"

"The r-regent!"

"Nonsense!" snapped the dowager. "Prinny's box was empty this eve—"

"Not the Prince Regent of England, Your Grace!" Simon snatched a handkerchief from his dressing table and mopped his brow. "It was *Mirandeau's* regent I saw. Archduke Roderik!"

"Give them an extra ration of oats, Ned," Rand told the stableman at the town house. He indicated the tired team Ned was unhitching from the phaeton. "With the ground we covered today, they've earned it." He didn't like to work his cattle so hard, but his state of mind when he'd gone after Cynthia hadn't been the best. Fortunately, he'd had Quicksilver brought up to London and could ride him. "They're not to be used again this week."

"Aye, yer lordship," said Ned. "Rest 'em the week it is."

As he approached the house, Rand noted light pouring from every window. Why the devil was the place lit up like a Vauxhall fireworks—

"Stop right there," said a rough voice behind him, "an' state yer—oh, it's you, yer lordship."

"Stebbins, what the devil are you doing here?"

The runner pointed to an upper story window. "Jest

checkin' the lads' room fer access from outside, yer lordship. Left a pair-a blokes with 'em whilst I'm 'ere, so ye needn't fear they ain't covered. I didn't trust no one else t' do this. What with all 'Is Grace's orders fer us t' button things down extra tight, some-a the new men—"

"*Extra* tight?" Rand felt a stab of alarm. "Stebbins, what's going on?"

The runner scratched his ear. "Mayhap ye'd best go inside, sir, an' speak with 'Is Grace about—"

Rand was already gone. The first thing he noticed was a number of men milling about, some of whom he recognized. Agents from the Foreign Office, experts like himself, who did clandestine work that was often dangerous. His alarm grew. When he asked a nervous housemaid where he might find the duke, he was directed to the main drawing room. Servants gaped as he raced toward the front of the house.

Upon entering, Rand halted. William stood at the fireplace in close conversation with Richard Helmsley, Rand's contact aboard the *Fleetwind*. Helmsley was a special agent, called in on the most extreme, politically sensitive cases. *What the devil—*

"Rand, thank God you've come!" His father gestured at Helmsley. "You know each other?"

Rand exchanged perfunctory nods with the agent. "What's happened?" he asked. "I saw Stebbins—" Just then, he spied a familiar figure sitting across the room, staring glumly into a brandy glass. "*Petrie?* What the devil's going on?"

"Rand," William said gravely, "Petrie swears he saw Roderik of Mirandeau in the audience at the Drury Lane tonight."

"What!" Rand eyed Petrie's ashen face. "But . . . is he certain? Sometimes these artistic types let their imaginations—"

"At first I thought the same," said William. "But Helmsley just delivered this"—he withdrew a folded sheet of fine vellum from his waistcoat and handed it to him—"after it arrived from Whitehall's agent in Mirandeau. Came addressed to me personally."

Rand willed his hands steady as he unfolded it.

Your Grace,

We've never met, but through your kindness in sheltering my son and his cousins, you are doubtless aware who I am. I am deeply grateful for all you've done, and hope someday to have the honor of thanking you in person. But for now, please, please take heed. *All three of your young guests are in the gravest danger! Having learned his hired assassin failed, my husband has gone to London. He is perilously mad, and plans to kill all three by his own hand. I beg you will take what measures are necessary to protect them!*

Emilie Aulaire
Archduchess of Mirandeau.

"God in heaven," Rand murmured. He shoved a hand distractedly through his hair. "No wonder you've added all these men. How are Leonie and the boys taking it?"

The look on his father's face sent fear lancing through him. "What? *Tell me.*"

"Leonie's not here, Rand."

"Not here!" He looked wildly about the room. As if he might somehow conjure her out of thin air and prove William wrong.

"My fault, I'm afraid," said William with a deep sigh. "Having witnessed that . . . that scene at Chesterfield House last night, Leonie immediately left the rout. Rand, she was extremely overset. This morning she begged to leave—"

"Where?"

"Hartswood."

"Whitehall was not happy about it," Helmsley put in.

"Whitehall didn't see her face," William said grimly.

Rand winced. *What in hell was the matter with me? Instead of chasing after Cynthia, I should have gone at once to Leonie and explained. Damn me for an insensitive fool! Now she could be—*

"Rand," William added more gently, placing a hand on his arm, "Hartswood could be a deal safer than here. After all, the letter says Roderik's coming to London, not Kent. And Leonie's not alone. Higgins and two other armed men . . ." His words trailed off as Rand raced from the room.

Helmsley ran after him. "Hawksrest, wait! Whitehall's assigned me to fetch her," he called as he raced to catch up. "I'm coming with you!"

Without slackening his pace, Rand thought of the big gray waiting in the stable. Aside from horses meant strictly for the racecourses at Newmarket, he didn't know of a horse with more bottom. "You're welcome to try," was all he said.

Roderik lowered his spyglass and smiled. At last the lights were going out in the windows of the duke of Hartswood's country house. They were all there, no doubt thinking themselves safe and snug in the country. Too bad they were so entirely mistaken. It paid to plan well, and his planning hadn't failed him yet. True, he'd at first been on the wrong track, assuming the brats would remain in London. But now he was definitely on the right one, thanks to his foresight.

While he'd been busy learning the direction of this duke's several residences, as well as the places in the city he was known to frequent, he'd learned His Grace was planning to attend the theater last evening. And when he'd also learned the identity of the actor being celebrated, the temptation to stalk the carrot-topped weasel who helped the brats escape had been too delicious to resist. Perhaps, he'd thought, the brats would even join Hartswood in his box to see the play. Unfortunately, he'd had only that stiff-rumped old crone for company. A disappointment, that.

Yet it didn't signify. The ruffians he'd paid to spy on Hartswood's town house had observed the ducal coach pulling out of its drive this morning. And while they'd not been able to identify everyone who entered the conveyance, they'd assured him one of its passengers was "a ginger-pated mort with a limp." They'd also learned the coach was bound for Hartswood's estate in Kent. It had cost a deal of gold to gain all that information. But what was gold for, if it couldn't smooth the way for life's little . . . necessities?

After that, it had been all too easy to make his way here and to wait in His Grace's wooded deer park until opportunity presented itself. Now all it wanted was to wait. He and Frederik had camped out often as boys. He was well prepared. He'd food and water to last several days, an array of weapons including several poisons, and enough laudanum to fell a horse. He'd spare clothes suitable for any turn of weather, flint and firewood, fodder for the pair of nags he'd hired, even an oilskin to keep out rain. Yes, he was splendidly equipped for any turn.

He was a patient man when he had to be. Sooner or later, the brats had to emerge from the house. It would help, of course, if he found them all conveniently together, but he mustn't be hasty. If need be, he'd pick them off one by one. Then he'd go back after the carrot-top. And before he finished him, he'd use a little "persuasion" to learn the whereabouts of the actor's accomplice, that traitorous palace guard. They'd made a fool out of him, and they'd pay. Oh, yes, they'd pay.

But the brats came first. It didn't signify that they had bodyguards in attendance. There were clever ways to create a diversion, to drug or distract a guard long enough to gain access. The Serpent had once discussed such tactics. It was really too bad the assassin and his doxy were dead. They'd have appreciated his resourcefulness. But one couldn't expect to have everything.

Twenty-two

"Won't ye try the turbot, milady?" Sally shook her head disapprovingly at the untouched supper on Leonie's tray. "Ye ain't ate nothin' all day."

"What? Oh, sorry." Leonie made an effort to shake off the brown study that had set her gazing absently into the fire for the past hour. "What did you say?"

"Ye ought t' take some nourishment. 'Tain't good t' go without, milady."

"I'm not hungry, Sally." She motioned the abigail to take the tray away. A glance at the clock told her it was very late. "Please apologize to Cook, and then I think you should find your bed." She'd dozed, albeit fitfully, on the journey to Kent, but Sally clearly hadn't, judging by the yawns she kept trying to hide.

"Are ye sure?" Sally asked doubtfully.

Leonie nodded, indicating the stable lad's clothes she'd donned soon after they arrived. "As I'm able to shift out of these by myself, I won't require your assistance. Go on, get some sleep."

"Well . . . good night then, milady." Picking up the tray, Sally bobbed a curtsey and withdrew.

When the door closed, Leonie rose from the chair and wandered aimlessly about the chamber. A pile of unread books sat on the stand beside the bed. She'd tried to lose herself in them earlier, but without success. She'd find herself staring at a page while an image of Rand's face swam before her—because her eyes kept filling with useless tears.

No more transports, Mama. No more fairy-tale dreams. Fairy tales, do you see, aren't meant for the likes of me. Your sensible child dared to fly, but she fell down. A bruising fall, Mama. Not one of those childhood tumbles, when I'd dust myself off and try again. But I love him, Mama. It will always be him. So tell me, Mama, what's the point of trying again?

With a heavy sigh, she removed the ribbon holding the emerald ring from around her neck and set it on the dressing table. She'd learned from the dowager it was the Darnley betrothal ring. She felt like a fraud wearing it. She'd speak to Barrows in the morning, see it was returned to His Grace. Cynthia Shallcross would wear it. Not a foolish, lame princess who'd dared to think she could fly.

Catching sight of herself in the dressing table mirror, she paused. The stable lad's clothes reminded her where she might find solace. Going to the armoire, she found the ragged boy's coat she'd once worn and donned it. No sign of the cap, though, the simple cap she'd worn when escaping Mirandeau. *Dear God, was it only a few months ago? When he was still simply Hawk, and he fashioned a crown of wildflowers—*

"Foolish girl!" she cried aloud. "Haven't you shed enough tears thinking about what might have been? Find your sensible self and reclaim her."

If you can, taunted a voice from the darker reaches of her mind. With a shake of her head, she forced herself to ignore it. *Focus on the positive. Go to Raven, whose love you can trust . . . who will never hurt you. Go!*

Unwilling to take the time to braid her hair, she twisted it at her nape and stuffed it underneath the coat as best she could. Crossing to the outer door, she pulled it ajar. "Mr. Higgins, are you awake?"

Higgins cocked an eye at her from his seat outside her door. He stifled a yawn. "Beg pardon, yer ladyship. Been a long day."

She nodded in sympathy. He was to take turns guarding her in six-hour shifts with the other runners, but they were all tired from the long trip. He'd apparently drawn the short straw for the first turn, poor man. Higgins was a deal older than his cohorts and likely more in need of sleep.

"Mr. Higgins," she said gently, "I hate to do this to you, but if I don't leave these chambers, I fear I shall go dotty."

Giving his head a shake, he rubbed a hand vigorously over his iron-gray hair and came to his feet. "Where to, yer ladyship?"

"The stables, please. I . . . wish to check on my stallion. It's true I went to see Raven when we arrived, but I've since grown concerned for him. You'll recall the stable help were going into the village tonight to celebrate Luke Barleycorn's—that is, the stablemaster's—wedding."

"Aye," he said, suppressing another yawn.

"Well, they're not expected back before dawn, and I need to assure myself Raven's all right."

" 'Tain't a problem, yer ladyship." With a tired smile, he gestured her ahead of him. "That wind's playin' Old Harry with the likes-a what ain't tied down out there t'night. Mayhap"—he stifled another yawn—" 'twill wake me up."

From behind the stables, Roderik's eyes followed the rustic pair he'd taken for servants. Huddled against the wind that buffeted them, they were stumbling awkwardly toward the stable block. Suddenly his eyes narrowed. The burly one, who'd paused to check the priming of a brace of pistols when he emerged from the house, was undoubtedly a bodyguard. But the other, the small one dressed like a stable boy, wasn't stumbling against those gusts of wind after all. A slow smile spread across Roderik's face. The "boy" was *limping*.

The smile became a grin as Roderik watched a blast of wind whip a flag of yard-long hair from under the ragged coat. Even by the gibbous moon's faint light, there was no mistaking its coppery color. *As I live and breathe, if it isn't the little cripple!*

He'd rather it was her brother, but this opportunity was just too good to pass by. With the exception of a pimpled bumpkin nodding in the tack room, the stable help were not in the way, and the cripple was. For some reason the entire lot had piled into carts and wagons and made off toward the village. Which could explain the chit's visit to the stables, even at this hour.

She was always coddling that black stud Leona had bought her. He remembered a night he'd returned from a trip and nearly stumbled over the brat when she limped out of the stable. Scared the wits out of her, too, from the way she'd stammered when he asked her business. Said she'd been helping that old groom tend her stud. Working in the straw with the help! Stupid brat.

Stupid, too, indulging a cripple with a prime blood like that black. He'd always assumed she'd break her neck on the brute and save them the trouble of feeding her. She hadn't, but wasn't it deliciously ironic? The stud was still the path by which she'd meet her end!

Roderik's shriek of laughter vied with the cry of the wind as he slipped inside the stables.

Rand swore an oath as he led Quicksilver forward a few paces. The gray was definitely favoring its rear leg. With a growl of disgust, he flung away the stone he'd found wedged under the stallion's shoe. No permanent harm, but Quicksilver had definitely sustained a bruise. He could be ridden no farther.

He wondered where Helmsley was. The agent was trailing far behind him even before he'd reached the outskirts of London. Too bad. Helmsley's horse would have come in handy now. Rand bit back another oath and eyed the lights visible through the trees. The Boar and Hind was doing a brisk business tonight. Not that the inn wasn't always the last in the village to snuff its candles, but at this hour it could only mean a celebration of some sort. Well, wedding or wake, at least he needn't rouse Mr. Tierney from a warm bed. The innkeeper would lend him a mount.

And a mug of Mrs. Tierney's strong Irish tea wouldn't go amiss before he rode on, he thought, wearily leading the gray forward. He was dead tired, and riding hell-bent-for-leather in this bitch of a wind hadn't helped. But he had to reach Hartswood tonight. The thought of Roderik even remotely near Leonie froze his blood. And the thought that she believed he'd betrayed her with Cynthia Shallcross squeezed his heart.

Higgins could hear the princess crooning to her stallion at the end of the aisle as he stood in the tack room, frowning. Something wasn't right. Once again, he sniffed the contents of the jar he'd found lying on its side beside the stable lad who lay senseless on the floor. The dregs at the bottom of the jar smelled like ginger beer, not spirits. But the lad was out cold. *Odd . . .*

Dipping his finger into the sticky liquid he coaxed toward the lip of the jar, Higgins raised it to his mouth. Screwing up his face, he spat the residue from his tongue. There was only one substance with that taste. Prodigiously sweetened with honey, but unmistakable just the same.

Laudanum, and no mistake! Is the lad an addict? He glanced sharply at the pimpled face of the snoring adolescent. *But an addict would know his doses. Why would he ruin his pleasure by taking enough to drop him? Unless . . .*

Turning on his heel, he headed for the box stall where the princess sang to her horse. As he emerged from the tack room, pain exploded through his head. Higgins slid to the floor, as senseless as the lad behind him.

Setting the brush aside, Leonie smoothed her hand over Raven's glistening flank. He was well cared for at Hartswood and hadn't needed grooming. But he enjoyed having her tend him, and the soothing movements had taken the edge off her frayed spirits. "You big pussycat," she teased, feeding him an apple from the bag Barleycorn kept on hand. "You love the attention, don't you? If only they could see you now, those simpletons who think you're such a bruising big—"

The stallion's snort startled her. Catching a movement out of the corner of her eye, she spun about. A chasm of dread yawned, ready to swallow her whole. *Roderik. Sweet merciful God, Roderik . . . not half a continent away, but here at Hartswood!*

"Surprised to see me, my dear?" Roderik's tone was as snidely insinuating as his smile.

Leonie said nothing, her eyes on the long, blunt instrument in his hand. She'd seen the heavy iron used to pry a damaged coach wheel from its hub. Yet it wasn't its utilitarian shape that drew her sickened gaze. It was the patch of iron-gray hairs, matted and sticky with blood, clinging to its blunt end.

Noting the direction of her gaze, Roderik grinned. "That's right, my dear. Your bodyguard is unable to answer your call. Or anyone's ever again, I daresay," he added with a high-pitched giggle.

Recoiling from the crazed sound as if it were a snake, Leonie took a backward step. As she met the solid strength of Raven's shoulder, the tension in her frame communicated her fear to the stallion. The black's ears instantly flattened. Fixing Roderik with a baleful eye, he bared his teeth and lunged.

With a shriek, Roderik leapt aside. "You stinking nag!" he screamed, raising the crow bar high. "I'll show you—"

"No-o-o!" Leonie threw herself in front of the horse, her arm raised to ward off the blow.

Roderik hesitated. While he could dispatch her as easily as he had the bodyguard, that would be too quick, too simple. The cripple had always responded with such delicious terror. Why shouldn't he amuse himself first? There were such interesting things she and her brother might be told before they died.

"Out of there—now!" he snapped, raising the crow bar higher and glaring at the angry stallion. "And shut that devil in the stall. One false move from either of you, and I'll smash his skull in."

Shaking uncontrollably, Leonie managed to murmur a

quiet command to the stallion and did as she was told. Raven clearly didn't like being separated from her. Well trained, he made no move to follow. But his ears remained flattened, and the outstretched neck, flaring nostrils, and infuriated gaze he directed at Roderik left no doubt as to his frame of mind.

"Much better," said Roderik. He lowered the weapon, but kept a wary eye on the stallion. The black was tossing his head, snorting, and angrily pawing the floor of his stall.

"Wh-what do you—what do you intend to do with me?" Leonie stammered. She forced herself to meet Roderik's eyes, then wished she hadn't. They held a strange, peculiar look of excitement, an unnatural glitter that sent a shudder through her. *Can one reason with a madman? Is it worth even trying? But if I keep him talking, I may purchase some time. It's always possible the stablemen will return before he can act.*

Swallowing, she raised her chin a notch and indicated her lame foot. "S-surely, I'm no threat to you, Uncle. What—what possible quarrel could you have with me?"

"Quarrel?" He tilted his head to one side, as if to consider this. "Why, none that I can think of. You simply know too much, my dear. A great deal more than I gave you credit for, actually."

Suddenly he leaned toward her, menace in his gaze, his voice shrill. "Do you take me for a fool? Expect me to believe the three of you left Mirandeau so stealthily for no particular reason? Because you wished to go on holiday, perhaps?"

As there was no possible response, Leonie said nothing. Behind her, Raven showed no such restraint. Tossing his head, the stallion moved fractiously to and fro in the large stall.

"Thought not," Roderik said smugly. "As I said, you know too much. Such a clever little cripple . . . but not clever enough, hmm?"

Suddenly Leonie couldn't bear all the sly innuendo, the torment of this cat and mouse game at which he'd always excelled. "You killed them both, didn't you?" she cried, anxious to have it over. "You murdered our father and mother!"

"As I said, a clever little cripple!" he exclaimed with a mocking grin. "Tell me, when did you guess? Was it after Leona? Before? No, surely not before. Leona herself didn't guess then. Clever creature that she was, she'd have instigated an inquiry into Frederik's sudden demise!"

Mutely, Leonie waited, sensing his need to talk, to boast, about the evil he'd done.

"Frederik was the easy one," he went on. "Never suspected a thing, do you see, until the moment I pushed him off that cliff." He eyed her horrified look and smiled. "Didn't you know? Well, of course, I told them we were coursing after a stag when it happened, but it wasn't a fall from his horse. He wasn't even mounted! Broke his neck all the same, however," he added with a giggle.

"You lured him . . . to a cliff?" she whispered, trying not to envision her poor father's trusting face as his own brother lured him to his death.

Roderik nodded, chortling. " 'By the by, Freddy,' I told him, 'discovered the trail that old buck takes through the woods. If you stand up here and look down, you can make it out. Do come and see!' "

Losing the battle against her too vivid imagination, it was Leonie who saw all too clearly in her mind's eye the image of her father falling to his death. Desperate to blot it out, she bit her lip, drawing blood. In his stall, Raven nickered his distress and paced ever more restlessly.

Intent on relating his successes, Roderik paid neither of them heed. He described Leona's murder now. With relish, he told how he'd located an ancient cult of assassins. How he'd hired one of them—a woman, to masquerade as a servant. How she'd poisoned Leonie's mother with deadly nightshade. ". . . a slow, subtle death, my dear," he concluded with unctuous satisfaction. "Surely you remember that. You were there, weren't you? Watching her die by inch—"

"Monster!" she screamed. Caution thrown to the wind, she lunged at him, intent on raking the evil leer off his face.

Now several things happened at once. Enraged by her distress, Raven bugled a challenge, reared, and began to kick the door of his stall. With a disbelieving shriek, Roderik dodged to the side, the crow bar slipping from his hand as Leonie came at him. "Attack me, will you?" he screamed, shoving her to the floor with a brutal thrust. "Useless cripple!" Spittle flew from his lips as he recovered the crow bar.

Leonie landed half on the floor, half on a bale of hay, the wind knocked out of her. She was only dimly aware of the sound of splintering wood as Raven's iron-shod hooves crashed into the door. Her horrified eyes were fixed on Roderik as he slowly raised his weapon. On the sick gaze that went to her twisted foot. On the inhuman glee signaling the intent she suddenly read in that gaze. A scream tore from her throat as the heavy iron came crashing down on her crippled foot.

Rand released a tired sigh as he spied the ornate gates flanking the entry to Hartswood's oak-lined drive. Tierney's gelding was slow and plodding, but they'd finally arrived, if a deal later than he'd hoped. Bloody hell, it was long past midnight!

He'd been forced, by custom and plain decency, to stay and drink a toast to Luke Barleycorn and his bride. Mrs. Tierney's bracing tea offset the effects of that single glass of ale, but he'd been delayed far longer than he could have wished.

Eyeing the clouds scudding across the moon, he muttered a caustic invective at the unflagging wind, and urged the gelding into a canter. If he knew the lad they'd left in charge of the stables at all, the lazy miscreant would be deep in slumber by now, impossible to rouse. He'd likely have to bed the gelding down himself when all he wanted was to find Leonie and assure himself she was safely asleep in her chamber.

With another curse, he prodded the gelding into a lumbering gallop.

Fighting pain and nausea, Leonie struggled to raise her head. *Hurts so . . . can't seem to gather . . . my thoughts.* Gripping the bale of hay, she tried to pull herself up to a sitting position. Pain lanced through her shattered foot, and she whimpered. Gritting her teeth, she tried not to focus on the throbbing agony radiating from her boot. *Must concentrate on—dear God, Roderik! Where?* Wildly, she looked about, ignoring another wave of nausea that came with the pain. But the monster was . . . *gone, thank God.* Her head spun as she tried to move it again, and she realized she was having trouble thinking clearly. *Must have blacked out.* Noises assaulted her ears from the immediate vicinity, and she covered her ears. *Think . . . concentrate!*

She remembered the vicious blow, the scream torn from her throat as excruciating agony ripped through her, but then nothing. That Roderik was gone and that she didn't recall seeing him leave told her she must have blacked out from the pain. But why had he gone when she'd been certain he meant to kill—

The sound of splintering wood and a frantic whinny broke into her muddled thoughts. Her mind cleared. *Raven. Not just angry—terrified.* She shifted her weight, welcoming the pain now, for it kept her alert. *You've known pain, my girl, dealt with it all your life. You just need to concentrate.*

She finally realized Raven was kicking apart the door of his stall. Up and down the aisle, horses relayed distress. Rand's mare whinnied fretfully, echoed by the ponies. William's hunter neighed shrilly from his stall across the aisle. *What could be oversetting . . .*

She smelled it then, an odor that shouldn't have been there, obliterating the ordinary stable smells of hay and leather and horses. *Smoke.* Glancing down the long center aisle in panic, she saw a tongue of orange flame licking at a bale of hay midway between her and the outer doors. An overturned lantern lay atop the bale. *My God, the fiend's set the stables on fire.*

Roderik shrieked with laughter, the sound torn from his mouth by the wind as he raced toward the house. The little bitch and her black devil would soon be charred meat! Now, if he was quick enough, he just might locate the other two brats and make a clean sweep of it. Now to raise an alarm over the fire, then steal into the house in the confusion and make short work of dear Prince Jamie and—

What's that? A rider? Yes, coming up the drive! With a start, Roderik realized he'd been careless. He was out in the open, on the clipped lawn that flanked the drive, with no place to hide. Cursing, he dug in his coat pockets for his pistols, realizing he'd yet to prime them. Not wanting to call the wrong sort of attention to himself when he instigated the alarm, he'd thrust the weapons out of sight. He'd be just an anonymous figure crying the alarm. No one questioned the identity of a man crying fire, the Serpent had said.

Muttering an obscenity, he pulled one pistol free, then the other. He tucked the second in his boot and went to work on the first. He'd need to prime them in this blasted wind, and bleeding fast, judging by the nearness of those hoofbeats.

Coming abreast of the stables, Rand decided to ride on to the house. He'd press a footman into taking care of the gelding, go straight to Leonie. For some reason, an uneasiness had crept upon him as he neared the stables. Only a vague feeling, but he was suddenly desperate to see her safe. The gelding's sides heaved. He regretted pushing the animal this hard, but—

What the devil? Reining in, Rand narrowed his eyes as he caught movement off to his right, about thirty paces away. With clouds whipping across the moon, the light was poor, but it appeared to be a man in a greatcoat. He was busy with his hands . . . doing what? The wind flapped the coat's capes this way and that, making it difficult to tell.

But anyone standing there in the middle of the night was suspect. Rand reached for his saddle pack, then ground out an oath. The pack—and the pistol he'd stashed inside—was back at the inn with Quicksilver.

That instant the clouds parted. Moonlight etched the saturnine features of a face Rand could never forget, and his blood ran cold. Roderik! In the same instant, he spied what the madman held in his hand: a pistol, which he now raised and leveled—

The sudden thunder of hooves drew the attention of both men to the stretch of drive behind Rand. He recognized the rider, even though he'd also changed horses. "Helmsley!" he shouted to the agent galloping toward him. "Go back—"

"Hawksrest!" Helmsley shouted. "Stable's *on fire.* Saw it from the—"

A shot rang out. Helmsley's horse slowed as it neared Rand's gelding, but the agent wasn't guiding it. He was slumped over its withers, half his head blown off.

Rand moved quickly. In the same instant he dismounted, he saw Roderik fling his spent pistol aside and withdraw another from his boot. Rand ducked behind the gelding and turned. Pulling Helmsley's body from the saddle, he began searching for a weapon. He'd just located the agent's pistol when he heard a crash of splintering wood.

And then an inhuman scream.

Leonie sobbed as she clung to Raven's bare back. Her broken foot dangled against his flank, a white-hot agony. But Raven had broken through the locked doors. They were out of that burning hell! She was so relieved, she didn't realize her enraged stallion had spied his quarry and screamed a challenge. Gulping in air, she tried to focus. *Men and horses in there—get help!* "Raven!" she cried, pulling on fistfuls of mane. "Raven—halt!"

But for once Raven wasn't listening. Raven was racing

for the man in the flapping coat. The man who'd hurt his beloved mistress. The man who now cursed and screamed and flung away his useless pistol. Who tried to run from the great beast bearing down on him with death in its eyes.

"Leonie!" His heart in his throat, Rand watched, never feeling more helpless, as she clung to the enraged stallion's back. A stallion in the grips of a bloodlust was past dangerous. If Leonie remained there while he engaged his prey, she'd be thrown and trampled under those lethal hooves.

He took a step forward, uncertain what he could do, yet unwilling to stand by helplessly and watch. His hands balled into frustrated fists, he took another step, then hesitated, his eyes on the stallion and the tiny figure clinging like a burr to its back. Intent on the man running from him, Raven gave a furious toss of his head, then plowed to a halt, a few yards from the fleeing regent. He was about to rear and issue another challenge, Rand realized, reading the signs. He began to run.

"Leonie—get off before he moves forward again!" he cried, running as he'd never run in his life. "Leonie, for the love of God, jump—now!"

Leonie sobbed, feeling Raven's mane slip from her grasp as he tossed his head and reared. Why hadn't he obeyed? And why was Rand's voice telling her to jump? Foolish girl, imagining Rand. He was in London with his Cynthia. Foolish voice, telling her to jump, when she was falling . . . falling. . . .

Twenty-three

MacTavish shook his head at the unkempt figure slumped in a chair beside his patient's bed. The marquis had been there since the wee hours of yesterday morning. He'd carried the lass up to her chamber himself, then refused to leave her side. Sat and held her hand, even after she'd been dosed with laudanum. Even while MacTavish and his colleagues had labored for hours to save her foot. The laird had to be drained by the tragic events that had left two men dead and the stables burned to the ground. Yet he'd taken interest in naught save the lass, except for a brief nod when someone told him they'd saved the horses.

Now it was nigh on noon of the second day. But had the daft man sought his bed? Of course not! Hovered over the lady's instead. Or, rather, the *princess's,* MacTavish reminded himself. "Great bluidy hell," he grumbled as he made his way out of her chambers. " 'Twas trial enough tendin' the puir lassie's foot. Now I must cudgel m' brain t' remember she's royalty in the bargain!"

"How is she faring, Mr. MacTavish?" William asked as the physician stepped into the hallway. Using his cane, he levered himself from the chair where he'd been sitting since MacTavish had arrived to look in on his patient this morning.

The physician ran a professional gaze over him. Unlike his foolish son, the duke had at least taken time to shave and shift his clothes. Not to sleep, though, judging by the circles under his eyes. "Asleep, Your Grace," he replied, "fra' the sleeping draught I ga'e her. As t' her foot, 'tis too soon t' tell. But ye'll perhaps recall, when he left, that foreigner seemed weel pleased."

William nodded. The foreigner was an Arab-born doctor Prinny had sent to Hartswood, along with his own personal physician. The Austrian war hero, Blücher, had brought the man to London for the victory celebrations. A specialist in broken bones, the Arab had worked wonders on men in the field, Blücher maintained. William could only hope all the cutting and suturing, not to mention the strange looking plaster he'd applied to Leonie's broken foot, would save it. *God knows, I thought she'd lose it. My leg couldn't have been any worse when they took it off.*

"Frankly, Your Grace," said MacTavish, "at present I'm inclined t' be more worrit aboot his lairdship than Her Highness. I canna seem t' make him understand he's sairly in need o' rest himself."

William smiled tiredly at the grouchy Scot. "My son believes he's *more* sorely in need of remaining with the princess. But I shouldn't worry. He grew accustomed to stealing sleep howsoever he could on campaign. As an old soldier, I can assure you there are worst places to sleep than a bedside chair."

"Aye, Your Grace," MacTavish grumbled, "but there are better as weel. Now I beg ye'll excuse me, for I must look in on Mr. Higgins." He shook his head. "Mon's lucky t' be alive."

"Thanks to you, sir, I make no doubt."

"Hmph," MacTavish muttered as he headed for the chamber where they'd put the wounded Bow Street Runner. He hiked a thumb over his shoulder, indicating the door to Leonie's chambers. "See yon laird puts some food in his belly. If ye're able, that is. Hmph, an' they call us Scots stubborn!"

The duke smiled as the doctor trudged off. He was past grateful to MacTavish. He'd not only tended his patients tirelessly; he'd calmly accepted the intrusion of the Prince Regent's fancy physician, not to mention the arcane practices of the "foreigner."

"What, still here, Hartswood?"

William turned to see his mother approaching from the end of the hall. Beside her were Jamie and Sam, who cast worried glances at Leonie's door. The dowager had personally taken them in hand when the news reached London, conveyed by one of the runners Rand had sent. When the boys arrived with her by coach last night, they'd been quiet, but understandably concerned about Leonie.

"I've just seen MacTavish," William said reassuringly, "and he's quite satisfied with Her Highness's progress."

"Is she awake yet?" Jamie asked anxiously.

"Not yet," the duke said with deliberate calm, "because the doctor gave her a sleeping draught. Sleeping will help her mend, do you see."

"May we see her?" Sam asked. The child had shown no emotion when told his father was dead. He'd immediately asked after Leonie, the duchess said, then asked for writing supplies, that he might write his mother. "We know how to be quiet," he added now.

"You may have a brief look-in after nuncheon," the dowager said briskly before William could reply. "A more lengthy visit must wait upon MacTavish's word." She eyed the clock on the landing. "I apprehend it is nearly noon, and Barrows has assured me nuncheon will be served on time. Come along, boys. I'm told Cook has prepared her excellent trifle for the sweet."

As she sailed off with the boys in tow, William couldn't help grinning. Thank God for his mother's unflappable presence. The mangled corpses of *ten* homicidal madmen could be lying in the conservatory at the moment, yet Her Grace would still have nuncheon served on time!

The grin faded as he eyed Leonie's door. MacTavish was right about Rand. Something must be done to pry him away from that bedside. Just before the news reached London, word had come through the servants' grapevine that Cynthia Shallcross had jilted her fiancé, saying they no longer suited. When William reached Hartswood, he'd spoken with his son about it. Rand had smiled a rather nasty smile at the mention of Cynthia's name, and confirmed the fact of his broken engagement, if not the cause.

Clearly, his feelings toward Leonie hadn't changed. William felt a twinge of shame for having doubted him. One need only look at him now to know how deeply he loved her. *Poor Rand! How guilty he must feel, sitting beside that bed, knowing she believes the worst of him.*

But Leonie wouldn't thank him for looking like God's holy wrath when she did awaken. With that two-days growth of beard and his rumpled, bloodstained clothing, Rand looked more like an East End thug than a man in love. Something had to be done to jar him out of that guilt-ridden brown study. Hailing a passing footman, William gave him a message for the dowager, then went to speak to his son.

Rand didn't look up when he heard the outer door open. His eyes remained on the pale features of the slight figure on the bed as they had every moment since he brought her here, except when he'd dozed. Even then, he'd been attuned to her, starting awake when she made the slightest sound. Terrified she was in pain. More terrified he could do nothing for it.

He could still feel his shock and anguish when they'd cut her boot away, when he saw what had been done to her. She'd regained consciousness then, and her first words had been to ask if they'd gotten the horses out. The *horses!* And when told they had, she'd sobbed.

Only then did they learn of the foolish, impossible act of courage that led her to ask. In one of those fleeting thoughts that occur at such moments, he recalled thinking she'd been aptly named. *Leonie, Leonie, you shame us all with your lion's heart of courage.*

She'd actually taken the time, despite what ought to have been forbidding pain, to open each stall and try to coax the horses out as fire threatened them all! But they'd balked, too frightened to leave. And so she'd climbed onto Raven—*climbed onto his back, with that horribly injured foot!*—and urged the black to break out of the burning stable, bent on going for help.

Rand would never forget her tearful smile as they'd explained how Roderik's pistol shot had brought servants and Bow Street Runners pouring from the house. How some had formed a bucket brigade from that convenient well; how they'd held back the flames while others had blindfolded the frightened animals and managed to lead them out; how they'd saved Higgins and a stable boy as well.

"Higgins . . . alive. So glad," she'd whispered. Then, her words slurring as the laudanum began to take effect, she'd described what that madman had done to her. In his rage, Rand had at first felt bitter resentment toward the stallion for killing the bastard, for robbing *him* of the chance to do it. He still thought about it, picturing the many ways a man could die slowly, as those involved in intelligence knew all too well. Being trampled to death by an enraged stallion was too good for—

Leonie uttered a small cry, bringing him out of his chair. When he saw she'd already quieted, he sighed and settled back again to wait. Most of the sounds she made were disjointed murmurs, but occasionally he'd make out a word. More than once she'd called out, "Mama," which needed no interpretation. Less enlightening had been the word "transports," which made no sense. Indeed, it had all been a senseless jumble. *Ah, sprite, I'd give anything to ease—*

"Son, may I have a word?"

Rand dragged his eyes away from the bed, met his father's concerned gaze, and nodded.

"I collect you're loath to leave," said William, gesturing to the bed. "But, Rand, I fear you're needed downstairs. If I stay with her, will you—"

"Needed . . . how?"

"One of those fools from the Ministry is a mite too anxious to avert the diplomatic reverberations that could ensue from this tangle. Says Whitehall's nervous about explaining the manner Roderik died. Suggested, before we inform Mirandeau, the stallion be destroyed, to appease—"

"His name," Rand growled, coming out of his chair. "I want the bastard's name."

The duke bit back a smile. "Smythe, and I last saw him in the . . ."

Rand had disappeared through the door. William settled into the chair he'd vacated, allowing the smile now. *Nothing like giving a man something to act upon to draw him out of a brown study!*

Smythe stammered a "Y-yes, m'lord," and quickly retreated. Rand watched with satisfaction as the fool ran for the hay barn, where they'd temporarily sequestered the horses. He hoped his blistering set-down had been heard as far as Whitehall. Destroy her stallion? On a cold day in hell!

Intent on returning to his vigil, he spun on his heel and went back inside the house.

"Hawksrest!" Heading off his approach to the stairs, the dowager planted herself before him. She ran her disapproving gaze over his disheveled person. "What do you mean by appearing here"—she sniffed, visibly affronted—"in such a shocking state of attire?"

Rand's jaw tightened. He was in no mood to indulge her fastidious concern for the proprieties. "I'm sorry, madam, but you must excuse me. I left Leonie but for a moment, and I must return before she awake—"

"She has already awakened, and you may thank your stars you weren't there to frighten her out of her wits!"

"What!" He began to storm past her.

She detained him with a grip on his arm—a surprisingly strong grip for a woman her age. "Control yourself," she said in that adamant voice he recalled from his childhood. "Leonie has no need of such histrionics. She requires calm and loving support, which at present she is receiving from the young gentlemen."

"D'you mean Jamie and Sam are—"

"Upstairs, regaling her with a very interesting account, as it happens."

Rand's eyes narrowed on her. He'd seen that expression

on his grandmother's face before. The cat that ate the cream wasn't in it. "What are you trying to say, Grand-mère?"

"You'll recall we'd news, before we left London, the Shallcross chit cried off?

"What of it?" he demanded impatiently.

"It seems the young gentlemen were privy to a far more interesting version of it than your father or I. They were in the garden with Stebbins at the time, and chanced to overhear two chambermaids discussing—"

"Gossiping, you mean."

"With great relish," she went on, ignoring this, "a rather shocking scene that by now is undoubtedly making the rounds of every drawing room in London. It appears that after a certain marquis left a particular estate in Surrey, my lady Cynthia Shallcross had a fit of pique. Smashed every breakable object in sight. Then proceeded to blacken her abigail's eye. Tsk, tsk. I really cannot imagine what came over the chit. Can you?"

Rand had been about to comment caustically on idle gossipmongers, to throw her own back at her. Digesting her words, he felt the corners of his lips twitch. "Yet Jamie and Sam had no trouble imagining what came over her. Is that what you're telling me?"

"More to the point, it is what they are telling Leonie. As I said, she requires loving support . . . as well as some answers. The young gentlemen are doubtless providing both."

Suddenly the dowager's forbidding manner evaporated. With a tender smile, she laid her hand on his. "Allow the gel time to absorb all of this. Go to your rooms and attend to your person. Then come to her as befits a man in love . . . a man with marriage on his mind. The way has been paved for you, my dear. Make the most of it."

"Everything's lovely." Leonie smiled at Sally and Polly as they finished tidying her chamber. "That will be all, and thank you."

The sisters curtsied—with a degree of awe, she noticed

with a smile, now they knew her true identity—and left. Stretching like a lazy cat, Leonie gave a long, luxuriant sigh. Propped against a mound of silk pillows on the high tester bed, she was beginning to feel like her old self again. After that wonderful, enlightening chat with Jamie and Sam, how could she not?

And after the boys left, she'd been bathed and groomed to a fare-thee-well, though with great care taken for her injured foot. Polly had braided her hair and fashioned it into a coronet, with soft tendrils gracing her face. The narrow peach ribbons she'd woven through the coiffure matched those trimming a new bed gown the duchess had sent, along with a delicate new scent, just arrived from Paris, with which they'd perfumed her bath. The gown itself was a confection of lace and soft white batiste, its high waist caught with yet another peach ribbon.

She sighed happily, eyeing the mound beneath the covers where her injured foot rested in its plaster. The plaster felt awkward and clumsy, but then so had the crippled foot she'd lived with all her life. Other than that, she was scarcely aware she'd been injured. The pain was gone.

She smiled, tempted to pinch herself, make certain she wasn't dreaming. It wasn't just the physical pain that was behind her. The other, that soul-deep pain that had sent her running for a place to hide, that was gone as well. Hope was hers again. It had flared to life inside her like a lovely flame, thanks to Jamie and—

A sound in outer room scattered her thoughts. The maids had left her inner door partially ajar, and she heard footfalls. Then: "Leonie . . . may I come in?"

She made herself swallow past a sudden constriction of her throat, and still her voice trembled when she answered. "Rand . . . yes, do."

And then he was there. Tall and handsome and wonderfully familiar. For a long moment he stood just inside the door, without words. His violet eyes missed nothing, Leonie suspected. She was glad the abigails had fussed with her appearance. As he studied her, she returned the favor, searching for changes, trying to decide if it was Rand or Hawk she saw.

Her first thought came with a leap of her pulse. This man she loved, had never stopped loving despite everything, wasn't just beautiful, he was utterly, *wickedly* male. Her breath caught as she ran her eyes over him, hungrily, shamelessly, alive to his presence as to nothing else on earth.

An immaculate white stock contrasted with his bronzed, clean-shaven jaw. His midnight hair, evidently damp from a bath, fell over his brow and curled above his collar. A superbly tailored coat of dark blue superfine graced his broad shoulders and lean waist with nary a wrinkle. Dove gray breeches hugged those long, muscular thighs, and his black top boots were buffed to a mirror shine. He was Rand and Hawk both, every inch the polished aristocrat, yet masculine to the bone.

Suddenly she realized what was missing: those grooves bracketing his mouth that could turn her to jelly. Why wasn't he smiling?

"Is something"—she had to pause, clear her throat—"Rand, is something amiss?" *So much has happened. What is he thinking? That I made a cake of myself by running away? That I brought the danger upon myself?* She tried for an insouciant smile. The result was something wobbly and uncertain. "Why . . . why so solemn?"

"I can summon a dozen reasons," he replied, frowning as he came toward the bed. "Beginning with how you looked last I saw you." Still frowning, he glanced at the mound beneath the covers. "How do you feel, sweetheart? Are you . . . are you in much pain?"

Sweetheart. Her smile broke over him like sunshine. "None," she replied, a note of laughter in her voice.

Rand blinked, unable to believe his ears. Closing the remaining distance between them, he examined her more closely. She looked remarkably fit, not to mention incredibly lovely, but . . . how was it possible? With all she'd been through . . .

"Are you dosed with laudanum, then?" he ventured cautiously. He wouldn't blame her for using it to dull pain, but she must be careful. In the war, he'd seen more than one injured soldier grow addicted.

"Not at all," she replied, smiling. "Remarkable, isn't it?" Indicating the mound, she shifted it from side to side with no trouble, and chuckled. "My abigail made the sign against evil when she saw the plaster. Said that foreign doctor must practice the dark arts. Took me a time to convince her there was no magic in it."

Rand relaxed visibly, and for the first time smiled. "The Arab knows his business, I daresay. But . . . the magic is in *you,* Leonie." He speared a hand through his hair and shook his head in wonder. "If you only knew what's been going through my . . ." *So much to say. Where do I begin?* "Are you *certain* there's no pain?"

"Quite certain. I made the servants take away those drops. Had me feeling lightheaded and strange. Took a deal of time to clear my head when I awoke, I can tell you. Jamie and Sam thought it funny, but I most certainly did not. And, do you know, once they began rattling away, my thoughts cleared admirably!"

A troubled frown creased his brow, and he hunkered down beside the bed. "Are you indeed clear about . . . what happened in London, Leonie?"

She couldn't bear the pain in his eyes. Without thinking, she reached out to smooth the knot between his brows. Something very like a current passed between them. Rand gave a start and inhaled sharply. Leonie withdrew her hand, hoped he hadn't felt it tremble, tried to collect her thoughts.

"About London," she said after a moment. "When Her Grace brought the boys to see me this morning, she explained why we saw so little of you there. Said she'd made a grave mistake in assuming I required a Season with all the trimmings. Actually *apologized,* if you can imagine such a—"

"Hang the Season," he growled. "I was referring to that abysmal scene at Stanhope's bloody rout." He heaved a sigh. "Sorry. Didn't mean to take my temper out on you . . . especially not on you."

She swallowed, trying to gauge his mood. "Rand, the boys overheard some . . . some gossip in London. And if what they heard is true—"

"It's true."

"Then I was a fool, jumping to conclus—"

"You were *not* a fool. Half of London believed the lie! That scheming baggage—ah, hell!" He caught her hand and pressed a fervent kiss upon it. Holding it gently sandwiched between both of his, he met her gaze. "I'm the one must apologize. God's my witness, Leonie, I wouldn't have hurt you for the world, and yet I did. And sent you straight into Roderik's snare!"

"And saved me from certain danger when Raven . . ." She closed her eyes, as if to shut out those harrowing moments. "He's dead, Rand," she said quietly, meeting his troubled gaze. "What's more, I cannot find it in my heart to be sorry for it. And if that is wicked—"

"Wicked? You haven't a wicked bone in your lovely body!"

She smiled ruefully. "My *imperfect* body, which is hardly—"

"Which is *lovely,* even as it is less than perfect!" he replied heatedly. "Allow me to tell you something about perfection, Leonie . . ."

She listened solemnly, then, as he told her. About the damaging legacy from his mother and how it had been so far reaching it came close to poisoning his entire life. How his erstwhile fiancée had fit into that legacy, convincing him he was hopelessly tied to an impossible demand for perfection to the exclusion of all else, of things that had real value. Of love itself.

"Yet Cynthia didn't love me at all," he finished with a weary sigh. "She's so bound by her own skewed values, she's unable to love a real human being, a flesh-and-blood man. What mattered to her was the dukedom, of course. After staging her death, she realized what she'd thrown away, and decided to come after it again. Convinced herself I'd find her physical perfection such an asset I'd be willing to suffer a cold, unloving wife. She'd the audacity to suggest I take a mistr—"

"Rand, how dreadful for you! To learn the woman you loved was so shallow—"

"Loved?" He gaped at her. "Leonie, haven't you listened, really listened, to anything I've said? I *never* loved Cynthia Shallcross. I merely settled for her because I thought myself too damaged to love *any* woman. It's the reason it took me so bloody long to realize I'd fallen in love with you!"

It was her turn to gape. After several paralyzed seconds, her mouth began to work, but nothing came out. She'd thought, after the healing talk with Jamie and Sam, she'd been prepared. Now she realized she'd been prepared merely to hope again. She hadn't let herself venture beyond that fragile new beginning. That the greatest hope of her heart had just been realized was more than she could take in. Again, she tried to respond, but tears stung her eyes, and she couldn't speak.

"God, sprite, don't cry!" Rand sprang from the floor and slung his hip on the bed, leaning across the space that separated them. "Didn't you guess?" he asked softly. Cupping her chin, he raised her face to his. With a tender smile he wiped a tear from her cheek with his thumb. "Surely you knew I was courting you?"

Swallowing a sob, she shook her head. "Y-yes . . . no. I mean, I began to . . . but not r-really. I s-started to h-hope, but then—oh, Hawk, I love you so much!"

"Say it again," he whispered huskily. His gaze met the shimmering green of her eyes, his own fiercely tender. "Say the words, Leonie. A man in love—deeply, irrevocably in love—cannot hear them enough."

"I love you, Hawk!" she cried, laughing through her tears. "I love you, Rand," she added, giddy with the freedom of being able to say it. "My beloved Hawksrest . . . Darnley . . . every name and shape you own—I love you, love you, love you!"

He laughed, a boyish sound the boy he'd been had never known, and took her in his arms. "My turn," he said, grinning down at her, kissing her nose. "I love you, sprite." He smiled into her shining eyes. "Kitten with a lion's heart"—he kissed one eye—"queen of immeasurable courage"—and then the other—"first love . . . heart and soul's love . . ."

His gaze dropped to her mouth and grew solemn. "I love you, Leonie," he said, his voice thick with emotion. Then, with infinite tenderness, his lips captured hers.

Twenty-four

Brimming with happiness, with a joy so keen she ached with it, Leonie kissed him back with all the love in her heart. Rand's lips moved on hers with tender care. They were as warm as she remembered, and pliant, yet gently questing, too, as if he would learn her mood and mind. Eager to show him, she wound her arms about his neck to draw him closer. Like a tender bud reaching for the living warmth of the sun, her lips trembled . . . parted, inviting the sweet invasion of his tongue.

Instant heat blazed through Rand, taking him by surprise, and he wanted to laugh. How could he have forgotten Leonie's ready and honest passion? Without another thought, he obliged her, deepening the kiss, relishing her eager response. And then the gentle sweetness of moments before became something new, a more sensual, heady joining. Tongue met tongue . . . engaged and tasted . . . danced and mated. Greedily, they savored each other, starved from the separation they'd both abhorred.

Now Rand's hunger grew apace, feeding on hers. He caressed and molded, shaped with his hands and lips the silken planes and delicate curves of her responsive body: sweep of back . . . arch of neck and roundness of shoulder . . . the sensual place where they joined. "God, how I've missed you," he breathed against her mouth. "How I love you"—he caught her lower lip, sank his teeth gently into the sensitive flesh—"adore you"—he nuzzled her ear, traced its delicate contours with his tongue. "Leonie, Leonie, I cannot get enough of you."

"My Hawk," she whispered giddily against his mouth. Her breath mingling with his, she declared her love softly, then again, humble and triumphant, drunk with the wonder of it. As he'd taught her, she nibbled and kissed, nipped and nuzzled, playful at first, teasing his senses.

But soon this was not enough. Threading her fingers through the dark curls at his nape, she brought his mouth firmly to hers, kissing him deeply, a devouring, scorching kiss that left Rand stunned and reeling.

When at last they came apart for air, desire beat in his veins, thundered through his pounding pulse. "Leonie," he murmured thickly. Without thinking, driven purely by the sweet siren's call of her willing heart and body, he found her breast, cupping its fullness. Her nipple sprang erect at his touch, and he groaned. His sex was hard and throbbing against the taut fabric of his breeches. How had they come to this full-blown heat so quickly? But he knew, he knew! Desire was a feeble thing called lust till borne on the wings of love. Ah, but then, then! Nourished and fed by the heart, it had strength beyond ken.

He tried to think, to master some restraint, but her innocent passion drove rational thought from his brain. Only when she began to move tellingly beneath him, tugging at his clothes, did he feel the prod of sense and sanity intrude.

With a gasp, Rand tore his mouth free. He hadn't acted a moment too soon. Leonie lay sprawled beneath him on the rumpled bedclothes, her lips parted, swollen from his kisses, her eyes dark with passion. The ribbon threaded through the lace beneath her breasts had come undone. The nipple he'd aroused jutted against the thin fabric of her gown. Rand swallowed thickly and shifted his gaze.

"H-Hawk?" Leonie's bewildered voice was low and sensual, throaty with desire. "What . . . is something wrong?"

"Not wrong, love," he assured her, "never wrong, but . . ." He tried not to look at the tempting mounds rising and falling with her quickened breathing, tried not to notice how they threatened to spill over the loosened neckline of her gown. "But if we go on this way," he said, trying to master his own breathing, "I won't be able to stop. Sweetheart, I shouldn't even be in your chambers, let alone your b—"

"Why should you wish to stop?" she asked with a tiny frown.

Rand chuckled ruefully. "Because, my sweet innocent, I want you like temptation itself." He kissed the tip of her nose, nuzzled it with his, then thought better of indulging in even that simple love play, and frowned at her, as if at a willful but charming child. "Which puts your virginity in jeopardy."

"Well, I certainly hope so," she said with a fetching grin, and reached for him.

"Whoa!" he cried, too aware how her movement had shifted the bodice of her gown, bringing one coral bud perilously close to escaping confinement. "Sweetheart," he added shakily, holding her by the arms to keep her at a distance he could live with, "you're not thinking clearly. I love you too much to—"

"Hawk." The dazed look of passion had begun to fade. She met his gaze with a determined look. "I am thinking quite clearly. I *want* to lose my virginity. Now."

"Leonie," he countered with a groan, "you cannot possibly mean—"

"My dear Hawksrest," she said impatiently, reminding him oddly of the dowager, "you did say you were *courting* me, did you not?" With a thoughtful look, she ran her finger along his lower lip. And smiled like a naughty child when he shuddered.

"Minx!" He grabbed her finger to still it. "I'm still endeavoring to court you," he said with exasperation, wondering what she was about, "and you're making it deuced difficult."

"And by courtship, you mean you wish to wed me?" she asked softly.

"Of course," he growled, then hesitated, giving her a penetrating look. "If you'll have me."

"Silly Hawk," she replied with an adoring smile, "how can you doubt it?"

His eyes softened, and he went to give her a gentle kiss. Suddenly he paused, remembering something he'd glimpsed when entering the chamber. "Don't move," he said, tapping the tip of her nose with his finger. With a quick grin, he scrambled off the bed.

Perplexed, Leonie watched him cross to her dressing table. With his back to her, she couldn't see what he did, and her curiosity grew. It was only when he returned that she understood. "The Darnley betrothal ring," she breathed.

Rand nodded solemnly. "With this ring," he murmured, taking her hand and slipping it on her finger, "I pledge to you my troth"—he kissed her hand—"my heart"—he met her shining eyes—"my love"—his voice low and husky, he bent to capture her lips—"and my life." The kiss that sealed his words was exquisitely tender.

It was several moments after they broke apart before Leonie could summon the words crowding her heart. In the end, her eyes glistening, she said simply, "And I, to you, pledge the same." She stroked the ring with her finger, gazing at it in wonder, then raised her eyes and gave him a dazzling smile. "Are we truly betrothed, then, my lord Hawk?"

"It but remains to tell the world," he said with a grin, wondering how he'd lived without that smile for the first thirty-two years of his life. Yet as he considered her question, his grin faded. "Not that it will be simple, sprite. All that confounded officialdom must be inform—"

"Oh, *that,"* she said dismissively. A gleam had entered her eye that had nothing to do with officialdom. "Now, where were we?" she asked, reaching for him in a manner that left no doubt what she'd in mind.

Taken aback, he blinked. "Leonie . . ."

Ignoring the warning in his voice, she slid her hands seductively up his chest and curled her arms about his neck.

"About to put an end to my virginity as I recall," she whispered against his ear.

The sultry whisper of her breath had Rand gritting his teeth. He endeavored to set her away, but she was having none of it.

"Now, my Hawk," she murmured, kissing his ear, then nibbling sweetly on the lobe. "Take it from me as I gladly give it to you . . . now."

"Sweetheart," he groaned. In mere seconds she'd undone the mastery he'd summoned over his body. He was instantly hard, the erection pressing against his breeches painful and yearning for relief. "Betrothal isn't marriage, and—"

"Rand," she said, sounding slightly vexed as she withdrew and sat down, "when do you imagine this wedding will occur?"

Running a hand through his hair, he sighed. "As you're a princess, and I've the dukedom to consider . . ." He sighed again. "I imagine it could take weeks, even months, to sort through—Leonie, what the devil are you driving at?"

"Why not scotch all that sorting out by informing those who'd drive us mad with waiting that we've a need for you to . . . make an honest woman of me? Isn't that the cant expression?"

The smile she gave him had a familiar cat's-got-the-cream look. Again, Rand was reminded of his grandmother. Yet as understanding dawned, his breath caught. Still, he hesitated, glancing at the mound still covered by the bedclothes. "But . . . your foot."

"A minor inconvenience," she said with a shrug. This had the effect of further dislodging her gown, baring that peak Rand had been trying to ignore.

"How . . . minor?" he asked, needing to be sure, even as his pulse began to accelerate.

"Come," she whispered with a smile as old as Eve, "and I'll show you. . . ."

And Rand was lost. With a helpless groan, he closed his eyes as she began to divest him of his clothing. Taut with effort at containing the heat threatening to consume him with every innocent brush of her hands on his body, moving only to help her when he must, he held himself all but motionless while she undressed him.

Not unfamiliar with male apparel, Leonie deftly removed his stock. His coat took longer, for her fingers grew clumsy with anticipation as she undid the buttons. Finally, when his shirt landed on the floor with the rest, she paused and went completely still.

"You are wondrously made, my lord Hawk," she breathed, taking in the taut curves and sinews of his muscular arms and shoulders. She ran her eyes hungrily over the dark hair that curled in thick whorls over the broad expanse of his chest, that narrowed as it approached the flat plane of his abdomen before disappearing into the waistband of his breeches.

Hesitating yet a moment as he allowed her to look her fill, Leonie at last reached out and ran her fingers through the hair on his chest. "So crisp!" she exclaimed. Circling a flat male nipple, she was so fascinated with the shape and textures of him she failed to hear him gasp.

"I've wondered," she whispered, meeting his passion-darkened eyes, "what it would be like to . . ." She drew her thumb across his other nipple, and her eyes widened as she saw it tighten. "Does that . . . does it hurt?"

"What do you think?" he countered huskily. With a sensual grin that revealed the devastating grooves framing his mouth, he reached out to brush her own bared peak. A deft, informing touch he quickly withdrew, but not before he saw it pucker, saw her shiver with pleasure. "Tell me, love . . . does it hurt?"

"N-no," she murmured, suddenly shy, lowering her eyes at the light now dancing in his. But shyness gave way to curiosity as her eyes fell on the narrowing band of hair that pointed toward his breeches. She considered the fastenings that held them closed, began to reach for them, then hesitated.

"Well?" Rand drawled huskily, both amusement and adoration in his eyes. "What are you waiting for, minx? We can't confound those beastly ministers of protocol with the fastenings to my breeches left undone."

Blushing furiously, she swallowed. Only now did she truly discern the great bulge beneath those fastenings. Indeed, it grew larger as she watched. Tentative, fascinated, she reached out and gingerly stroked its length.

With a ragged groan, Rand caught her hand. "That's enough for now, sprite," he murmured thickly, but kissed her hand before releasing it.

"B-but—"

"Shh," he breathed, and pulled her beneath him, burying his lips in the soft skin below her ear. Pressing sensual kisses along the underside of her chin, he moved to the slender column of her throat, murmuring words of praise and love as she moved restlessly beneath him. Soon his lips moved to her breasts, and he heard her breath quicken. When his mouth traveled to a pouting coral bud, drawing it in, grazing it with his teeth, he heard her cry his name.

"Softly, love," Rand murmured, then suckled and nipped while he freed its twin and abraded it with his thumb. "So lovely . . . so eager . . . your body tells me what you want, Leonie, even before your words do. Did you know?"

"I . . . I . . ." What he was doing robbed her of thought. Each sweet abrasion, each grazing by tongue and teeth, called forth an answering response. She felt heat spiraling downward, spreading from her belly to that untouched place between her thighs—and then an embarrassing wetness there that just couldn't *be*. "H-Hawk . . . what's h-happening to me?"

As if he'd read her mind, his hand slid gently downward, and came to rest at the juncture of her thighs. Even through the fabric of her gown, he could feel the dampness gathered there. "Here is another place where your body speaks for you, love," he told her softly. He kissed her then, thoroughly and deeply, while his hand slid to the hem of her gown and drew it slowly upward. Knowing fingers caressed the satin softness of her inner thighs as they moved. By the time they reached the silken nest of auburn curls, she was dewy wet and trembling sweetly against his hand. "Do you understand how?" he asked softly.

"N-no," she replied, her breath fragmenting as she felt his fingers probe that embarrassing wetness. His hand was cupping her, touching her . . . *there,* she realized with a mixture of shock and need. *There,* where no hand had ever been, and yet she wanted it—dear God, she wanted it.

"You're so wet for me, love," Rand murmured against her ear. Gently, he sank his teeth into her lobe, felt her shudder as his fingers stroked the slick, sultry petals below.

"I-I know, a-and I'm sorry," she stammered. "I d-don't know wh-why—"

"Hush," he commanded, stilling his fingers, shifting to see her face. "Look at me, kitten."

She did, blushing to the roots of her hair, and Rand smiled tenderly at her. "Never, never be sorry for it, sweetheart. This lovely wetness"—he caressed her slick opening again, willing his own burgeoning need aside for this all-important instruction—"is completely, sublimely natural. 'Tis your woman's gift to me, Leonie, your body's beautiful way of telling me you want this joining. That you want me here"—he slipped a finger inside her—"where I'm to enter you and make us one. Do you understand now?"

With giddy relief she nodded and saw him smile. Then, before she could think, his hand moved: a curious little pass of his thumb, and then! Pleasure so keen, she cried aloud, arching against his hand.

"So passionate," he murmured, stroking damp tendrils of hair from her face, "so beautifully responsive." Again his thumb worked its magic, and Leonie shattered beneath his hand. Again, she cried out, her body splintering into a million fragments of brilliant, searing pleasure.

"H-Hawk!" she cried a third time, twisting restlessly, urgently beneath him. "Hawk . . . I-I need—"

"I know, love," he whispered, "I know." He drew her close, held her in a reassuring hug until she settled somewhat. Then, before she could summon words to question him, he was in motion. One boot hit the floor with a *thud,* then the other. Breeches and hose followed. Next, he removed her gown, careful not to jar her injured foot. When her trembling body was bared to his gaze, Rand felt his breath unravel.

"You are lovely beyond telling," he told her, meaning every word. Though slightly built, she was beautifully proportioned: full, ripe breasts, a tiny waist he could span with his hands, the generous flare of her hips giving way to long, lithe legs, where the nest of auburn curls at their apex beckoned. All proclaimed her sweetly feminine yet womanly to the core. "Lovely," he repeated softly.

"So . . . so are you, my lord Hawk," she said with an audible swallow. Her eyes had at last traveled to the rampant evidence of his passion. Now they flew to his, and she added uncertainly, "And l-larger than I . . . I mean, how . . . ?"

With soft laughter, he eased beside her, drew her into his arms. "Shall we fit?" he teased. When she nodded, looking concerned, he grew serious and shifted to better meet her eyes. "Of fit I make no doubt, love, but there will be some pain for you the first time, I'm told."

"Told?" A tiny frown, then her eyes widened. "Hawk, never say *you* are virgin too!"

He chuckled wryly, forcing his mind away from the things the touch of this naked woman was doing to his body. "No, my innocent, I'm not." With his penchant for attracting females, he'd had liaisons in the dozens, but he thought it prudent not to mention them. They mattered less than nothing. This was the only woman he'd bed for the rest of his days.

"But," he told her, "I've never had a virgin, do you see, yet I understand how it must be done." Searching her face, he saw another tiny frown.

"Gently, goose," he told her then, and kissed her lightly on the mouth. "It shall only be done gently, I promise . . . and with all love. Trust me?"

She sighed and smiled at him. "With all my heart."

And then speech ceased as Rand made good on his promise.

His kisses were slow and unhurried, reminding Leonie of those first precious moments in the ballroom. Lazily, languorously, as if they'd all the time in the world, he took her through the sweet, delicious foreplay of love. Sometimes he seemed bent on learning the contours of her face alone, with lips and fingers only, his touch a butterfly's caress, his kisses featherlight and soft as swansdown. Other times he paused to study her, smiling that slow, lazy smile that turned her insides to warm honey, his eyes heavy lidded and sensual.

And then there was his voice. Ah, his voice! Now soft and coaxing, now low and teasing, it stole across her senses like a heady brew. At times it crooned paeans of praise to her loveliness; at others, it murmured seductive promises of how he'd give her pleasure. "Do you like that, love?" he'd whisper as his fingers stroked an unsuspected niche that came suddenly alive at his touch. "And if my mouth were to follow my hand . . . here . . . or here? Would you like it?" His low, delighted laughter as she blushed furiously, even as she stammered her assent, both trebled her blush and heated her blood.

"I want to taste every inch of you," he murmured as his mouth closed over the aching crest of her nipple. "I want to feel you quiver with need . . . yes, darling, like that," he told her as his hands cupped her buttocks, raising her while he nuzzled her belly. I want to hear you cry your pleasure—yes, sweetheart, yes!"—he urged as his hand found softer flesh. Flesh already slick with the gift he'd explained to her and trembling with need. And when his thumb found the tiny nub hidden within her silken nest and deftly stroked . . . and stroked again: "Come to me, love," he coaxed with a seductive smile. "Ahh . . . now, again!"

Her sweet cries of pleasure as she climaxed under his hand were both joy and agony for Rand. He'd been pacing himself, clamping down on his own need with an iron will. He'd promised her a gentle initiation, and he'd die before giving her less. But the exertion required to muster such control was taking its toll. Sweat beaded his brow. The heaviness in his loins was a pulsing, clawing need that bordered on pain. Thus it was when Leonie's third cry of rapture had her reaching with mindless abandon for his throbbing shaft, he nearly lost it.

Mouthing a word that was both reverent and profane, he caught her hand and pulled it away. His erection was throbbing, ready to spill its seed like any boy with his first taste of a woman.

"Wh-what?" Leonie murmured, her lovely eyes glazed with passion.

"Not to worry, kitten," he murmured shakily, nuzzling her ear as he drew her gently beneath him. "But it's time, love . . . now . . . open for me," he urged raggedly, gently nudging her thighs apart with his knee.

Leonie needed no urging. Suspended halfway between repletion and a nameless longing for something more, she obeyed without question. When the blunt satin tip of him slid easily along the sultry entrance to her woman's core, she gasped with pleasure. When it slipped teasingly over the nub his thumb had made her exquisitely aware of, she moaned, deep in her throat. When Rand coaxed her, in a voice sounding oddly hoarse and strained, to flex her knees, when the blunt tip of him edged slowly into her liquid heat, even as he drove her mad with pleasure by fondling her nipples, she sobbed his name.

And when at last she heard his whispered, "I'm sorry, kitten," and felt him, huge and swollen, push gently past the fragile barrier, tearing it, she whispered urgently in his ear: "No need, my Hawk, to be sorry. A little pain . . . for so much pleasure . . . so much love . . ."

With joy and relief, Rand knew she meant it. "Queen of infinite courage," he rasped, her heat burning him like a firestorm. Shaking with need, he kissed her with a fierce tenderness, even as he willed himself still, intent on letting her body adjust to him. "Ah, love," he murmured thickly, "you fill my very soul with your generous heart."

She asked, then, her voice shy, tremulous. "And . . . and will you fill my very womb with your seed, my Hawk?"

"Are you certain?" he questioned. He'd been prepared to

disengage first, though she couldn't know that. "Truly certain?" he added, even as his loins ached for completion.

Leonie smiled against his mouth. "A princess who's . . . who's breeding ought to put the spur to confounded officialdom."

With a laugh that emerged half a groan, he began to move on her. Gently and with all love, as he'd promised. Yet when Leonie's muted cries of pleasure urged him to quicken the pace, Rand acceded gratefully.

Soon they found themselves caught in the primal rhythm of the age-old dance. Hearts beating in tandem, bodies so fused neither could have said where one began and the other ended, they tasted ecstasy together—ecstasy and untrammeled joy in a soaring, shattering climax that flung them out of themselves and beyond to the nameless, timeless stars. A union of mind and flesh, soul and heart, that left them sated and replete among the pillows.

And joined an imperfect princess and the wounded hawk she taught to fly in perfect love.

Epilogue

Rand offered Raven an apple, but the stallion ignored him, thrusting his head over the fence and neighing in the direction of the house. "Ungrateful brute," Rand groused, "See if I ever offer another!"

A trill of laughter had him turning to see Leonie coming down the path. "Raven," she chided, "do take that apple, or my lord Hawk will feed it to Quicksilver."

As if on cue, a clarion call came from the far pasture where Rand's stallion grazed. "Your gray's in high spirits," Leonie remarked, smiling at her husband as Rand caught her to him and planted a kiss on her brow. "Do you suppose it's from having got your mare in foal?"

Rand grinned at her. "If he's anything like his master." His wife of six months was beautifully rounded with child. A child MacTavish surmised would arrive nine months after their wedding. Its parents suspected the babe might make its appearance a tad sooner, but they kept that suspicion to themselves.

"Poor Raven," Leonie said as the black neighed shrilly at the gray. "I rather think he's feeling left out of it."

"He'll get no sympathy from me," Rand grumbled. "He may suffer me on his back while you're unable to exercise him, but the ingrate turned up his fancy nose at this"—he handed Leonie the apple—"soon's he saw you."

"Poor Hawk," she said with a chuckle, feeding Raven the apple. "Given the Cut Direct by Prinny's hero!"

"Huh," said Rand, glaring at the black, "with Brummel

beyond the pale, Prinny was simply desperate for something to lionize." Raven wasn't exactly being invited to Carlton House, but he'd received a special medal from the Prince of Wales for heroic service on behalf of His Majesty.

"As for me," Rand added, stroking Leonie's cheek, "I prefer the true lionheart in our midst." His hand moved to the swell of her belly. "How are you feeling, sprite?" The night before, the babe had been restless, keeping them both awake long after midnight. But since this had led to a delightful interlude that left both its parents sated and sleeping like babes themselves, Rand wasn't about to complain. Yet he guarded his wife's health and happiness zealously. Observing them together, the *ton* had taken to calling their marriage the love match of the decade.

"I am feeling cosseted and loved," she assured him with a soft smile.

"Excellent," he said, kissing her nose, "and I intend to see you remain so." Smiling into her eyes, he bent to capture her lips for a soft, lingering kiss. "You're certain you've had enough sleep, love?"

"You know I slept in this morning," she replied, then grinned at him. "The dowager, however, insisted I have a lie-down after nuncheon. Said I looked tired. Unfortunately, I had the bad grace to blush when she said it. Her quizzing glass came up on the instant!"

He chuckled. "You could always blame the blush on your delicate condition."

"Instead of the behavior that caused my condition?" she returned with a saucy grin.

Rand threw back his head and laughed.

"Fortunately," she went on, "I was saved from explaining myself by Barrows, who arrived with the—oh, I nearly forgot!" She fished in her pocket, withdrawing a vellum envelope. "This just arrived with the post."

"From Her Grace, I see," he said, recognizing the archduchess of Mirandeau's stationery. Lady Aulaire would never be addressed by the puerile form of "Lady Emilie" again. Sam's mother was now Mirandeau's well-loved and respected new regent. In the months since assuming the position—shortly after her traitorous husband's death—she'd begun to make a name for herself throughout Europe for her wisdom and intelligence in governing the tiny principality.

"Yes," said Leonie, "but she's enclosed sheets from the boys, and—oh, Jamie added a postscript on the back, and I've only just noticed!" She handed Rand the other sheets, and began eagerly to peruse her brother's postscript.

Rand smiled at her as she devoured every word. Indeed, he couldn't help smiling every time he looked at her. How much had changed in half a year!

The change pregnancy had brought to his wife's small body had been only the first. If not entirely predictable, it had certainly been hoped for. The very *un*predictable, unhoped-for change in Leonie, the change few who'd known her could believe when they saw her now, was that *she no longer limped.* In setting the broken bones in her foot, Blücher's amazing Arab physician had all but totally corrected the malformation she'd been born with. A miracle of modern medicine, as MacTavish called it.

Yet when Leonie's overjoyed husband had tried to reward the modest foreign gentleman, he'd been politely refused. The physician explained he'd done nothing more than what the holy *Qur'an* taught: man must honor *Allah* through good works.

"Darling, listen to this!" Leonie exclaimed, and she read from Jamie's postscript.

> *Parliament agreed to postpone my coronation until the late autumn, when my niece or nephew's arrival is well in hand, so that all of you may attend. Petrie is coming, and will grace the festivities with a special production of* A Midsummer Night's Dream*—playing Bottom, of course. Sam and I are in transports over our new high-perch phaetons! Thank Hawk again, please. By the by, Sam is an absolute* nonesuch *at the ribbons—makes me look* ham-fisted! *The phaetons almost make up for our lessons with a silly dancing*

master Aunt Emilie has engaged, so we won't disgrace ourselves at my coronation ball. Can't wait to see your famous new foot! Insist you dance the first waltz with me. Sam wants you to reserve the second for him. Do you think Hawk and His Grace will mind taking third and fourth? Do write soon."

Rand chuckled as she handed him the sheet. "Your brother's letters always sound just like Jamie talking. I can almost hear him rattling away. Hmm. His spelling's improved."

"If you read the opening," Leonie said wryly, "you'll see why."

"Ah . . . Sam's been helping him. Seems neither knows how to spell 'marchioness,' however."

"More to the point," said Leonie, "what do you think of Jamie's insisting the parliament officially return to me the title of princess?" The principality's time-honored protocol had established that, once wed, a Mirandeauvian princess surrendered her title and assumed that bestowed on her by marriage. "I certainly don't mind being a marchioness," she added with an adoring smile at her husband, "so long as I am *your* marchioness. Why should Jamie?"

"Because," said Rand, wrapping his arms around her and smiling into her upturned face, "I suspect Jamie believes as I do: once a princess, always a princess." He kissed her brow, then moved on to both eyes and her nose. "Of course, that's just the half Jamie knows about," he added, sampling her lips with a thoughtful look Leonie recognized.

"And the . . . other . . . half?" she asked between further samplings, each sending her pulse racing progressively higher.

"Once a princess . . . always a princess," Rand murmured huskily, grazing the plump flesh of her lower lip lightly with his teeth, "but forever . . . queen . . . of my heart."

Leonie's breath hitched as he touched the sensitive corner of her mouth with his tongue. "You spoil me," she began but couldn't finish. Her breath fragmented as his tongue slipped along the rim of her lip.

"I intend to do more than spoil you, madam," he said with a wicked grin. Scooping her up in his arms, he began carrying her toward the house.

"Hawk!" she cried breathlessly. " 'Tis mid afternoon!"

Her husband whispered something in her ear that had Leonie hoping the dowager and her quizzing glass were nowhere in sight.

She had one final thought before thinking in any coherent form became an impossible task. *Still in transports, Mama! Now, what do you think of that?*